A Taste for Murder

A Taste for Murder

MATT BAKER

MICHAEL JOSEPH

PENGUIN MICHAEL JOSEPH

UK | USA | Canada | Ireland | Australia
India | New Zealand | South Africa

Penguin Michael Joseph is part of the Penguin Random House group of companies
whose addresses can be found at global.penguinrandomhouse.com

Penguin Random House UK
One Embassy Gardens, 8 Viaduct Gardens, London SW11 7BW

penguin.co.uk

First published 2026
002

Copyright © The Writers' Room Publishing Limited, 2026

The moral right of the author has been asserted

Penguin Random House values and supports copyright.
Copyright fuels creativity, encourages diverse voices, promotes freedom
of expression and supports a vibrant culture. Thank you for purchasing
an authorized edition of this book and for respecting intellectual property
laws by not reproducing, scanning or distributing any part of it by any
means without permission. You are supporting authors and enabling
Penguin Random House to continue to publish books for everyone.
No part of this book may be used or reproduced in any manner for the
purpose of training artificial intelligence technologies or systems. In accordance
with Article 4(3) of the DSM Directive 2019/790, Penguin Random House
expressly reserves this work from the text and data mining exception

Set in 13.2/16 pt Garamond Premier Pro
Typeset by Six Red Marbles UK, Thetford, Norfolk
Printed and bound in Great Britain by Clays Ltd, Elcograf S.p.A.

The authorized representative in the EEA is Penguin Random House Ireland,
Morrison Chambers, 32 Nassau Street, Dublin D02 YH68

A CIP catalogue record for this book is available from the British Library

HARDBACK ISBN: 978-0-241-79526-2
TRADE PAPERBACK ISBN: 978-0-241-79527-9

Penguin Random House is committed to a sustainable future
for our business, our readers and our planet. This book is made from
Forest Stewardship Council® certified paper

To Jo, who makes dreams come true

Prologue

Left to his own devices, Casey would have spent that Sunday lazing by the pool, and death would never have cast its shadow across his day.

It was the third of their four-day stay in Capri, which was supposed to be the 'rest and recuperate' leg of their Italian tour, with the rigours of Vesuvius and Pompeii behind them, but Rome and Florence and their sites of historical 'interest' to come. Shortly after breakfast, however, Tanya had announced she was bored and demanded a shake-up in their routine . . . something, anything, she *really* didn't care. A walking tour of Roman ruins had been tabled, and, lying on his sun lounger, Casey was still congratulating himself on having suggested they hire a scooter and hit the beaches instead, when the speedboat puttered slowly into the crystalline shallows and the surly-looking Italian at the wheel started trying to engage the assembled tourists in turn. Casey had already begun to raise his hand to make the universal sign for 'Thanks, but no thanks', when Tanya put down her book and called out a query. A five-minute stand-off had ensued, with his fiancée hands on hips in the shallows looking impressively toned in her thong bikini, before a price was agreed, grudgingly on both parts, and the cash handed over without Casey having been consulted.

As they left the comforting certainties of the beach behind,

Casey experienced a vague sense of foreboding. Being on the water made him nauseous. Being in it awakened fears of what might lurk beneath. Yet it wasn't the thought of sharks or jellyfish or even drowning that was stoking his disquiet as the boat motored out to sea, but the suspicion he was moments away from being humiliated. The last time he'd tried – God, how he'd *tried* – to match his fiancée's fearless athleticism had been in Barbados at spring break the previous year. After half a dozen attempts to stand upright had all produced the same result – him face-planting at speed into the sea's unforgiving surface – he'd been forced to add waterskiing to the long list of things that Tanya was better at than him.

The tooth-kiss of disdain with which their dreadlocked instructor had greeted his efforts was still reverberating somewhere in Casey's psyche as the engine was cut and the boat slowed to an unsteady halt some distance offshore. When Tanya announced that she would go first, the two men in the boat glanced instinctively at Casey. In that split second, as he contemplated the self-reproach that would surely follow yet another failure to challenge her, he almost wished he could be rid of his alpha bride-to-be entirely. Afterwards, although he would only admit it to himself, he was relieved it had been her and not him and, for once, he was glad he was a coward.

Unlike her fiancé, Tanya Harper, soon to be Tanya Dean (or possibly Harper-Dean . . . she hadn't yet decided), was unencumbered by doubt as she allowed herself to be strapped into the harness of a parasail at a quarter to one o'clock on that fateful afternoon. She wasn't disconcerted by the fumbling of the glassy-eyed deckhand as he negotiated his way through the clips and buckles intended to keep her moored to the vessel.

Or much bothered by the way the captain's hands brushed her breasts as he checked his subordinate's handiwork with a series of pats and tugs. She wasn't even unduly irritated by Casey's attempts at reassurance . . . *You got this . . . just relax . . . it's gonna be awesome . . .* which were surely meant for himself rather than for her.

Her only hint of concern came in the first moments, as the captain revved the throttle in what was clearly a deliberate attempt to unsettle her. She was jerked into the air unexpectedly and her heart dropped into her stomach, forcing out an involuntary cry of alarm. Flushing, she fixed him with her coolest stare, and ignored both his apology and Casey's suggestion that it was *never too late to change your mind, babe.* 'Just make sure you freaking film this,' she admonished her fiancé, unable to mask her irritation.

Apparently satisfied at having caused a tiny crack in her veneer of self-possession, the captain busied himself at the controls and, with Casey withdrawing sulkily behind his phone camera and the deckhand lost in silent contemplation of who knows what, Tanya felt able to give herself over to sensation. At first, as the boat accelerated over the waves, she was all too aware of the violent forces buffeting the cable that was winching her skywards, and the deafening flapping of the canvas that billowed behind her. As she rose higher, however . . . ten, twenty, fifty, eighty metres into the air . . . such considerations fell away and she felt herself hovering high above the earth, suspended on the wind. She was transported by a jolt of pure exhilaration, as if she might even be having some sort of out-of-body experience, before she reconnected with a sense of self and started to take in the view. Far below, on the deck of the boat, the three men appeared as insignificant as sandflies. To her right, the vast expanse of the Tyrrhenian Sea stretched away into nothingness. And to her left, at perhaps half a kilometre's remove . . . the limestone jewel of Capri, its cliffs jutting jagged and chalky, like shark's teeth, straight from the aquamarine. As the boat sped on, they reached the island's limits, and the mainland came into view some distance beyond. They veered north and then west again in a broad semicircle and Tanya found herself swinging back the other way, with Capri on her right at closer quarters. Close enough, at least, to make out the contours of the rock face and the texture of the trees and bushes that found purchase in its crevices. And close enough to notice a splash of red at the foot of the tallest cliff.

Her first instinct was that it must be a sail cloth, ripped free and deposited overboard in a winter storm and only recently made shore now the gentler tides of summer had come. But the colour was too vibrant, too eye-catching to have suffered a long immersion at sea, and instead she reasoned it must be something dropped from the clifftop, a towel perhaps, or even a coat. In the blink of an eye it had passed out of view, and she might just as quickly have forgotten about it, had the boat not turned for a final pass, bringing the rocky shore closer still. This time, there was no mistaking it. The shapeless thing took form, sprouted arms and legs. A head.

The body of a woman in a red dress lay sprawled at the bottom of the cliff.

Tanya felt herself go cold. Now, for the first time, she was afraid. She imagined herself dropping from the sky, spinning uncontrollably, anticipating the concussive impact of flesh on rock, the split second of insight as she realised this was it . . . this was all there was and ever would be. She tried to shout, to call to the insects below, but she found she had no voice, or none that would carry across what now seemed an impossible distance. Casey was looking at something on his phone, oblivious. She floated on the wind, feeling utterly helpless. And then the captain turned back to check on her and she started to flail her arms and point.

I

Later it would occur to Joe that the body might already have been lying there on the rocky coastline just visible below as his plane circled in a lazy holding pattern above Capri, waiting to turn decisively northwards and start its descent into Naples. That day, however, as he sat in a middle seat towards the back of their crowded flight, craning his neck to see past his daughter's head, which was blocking a large proportion of the tiny window, and trying to catch a glimpse of their destination several thousand feet beneath them, murder was the furthest thing from his mind.

For some reason, the name-board that greeted him and Angelica at the arrival gate some fifty minutes later carried his full title – Detective Chief Inspector (*'Ispettore'*) – as well as a version of his name he hadn't used since primary school: Joseph Mottram. But Joe was not coming to Italy in an official capacity. A 'well-deserved break', his superintendent had euphemistically called it when Joe had come to confront him over the application form he'd found waiting on his desk one morning towards the middle of May, already signed and initialled 'DK'. 'Special Leave' was the technical term for it. But Joe knew it for what it was. An enforced lay-off. An intervention from above. He'd tried to argue the toss. The last thing he wanted was to be sat at home, *brooding*. He still had fourteen days of bereavement leave outstanding. He would book a fortnight somewhere hot. Come back tanned and refreshed, ready to get stuck back in. But Dan Keely was having none of it. Joe had given twenty years of outstanding service, his boss told him, and he had high hopes he'd give many more. In the circumstances, however, there were legitimate concerns about his work–life balance, his *mental health*. Leave *would* be taken.

Six long weeks.

It had been Angelica who proposed they take the opportunity to spend time with Sofia's parents on the island where her mother had lived the majority of her tragically short life. Feeling guilty at the minimal contact he'd had with his in-laws since the funeral, and miscalculating that a fortnight was the longest his daughter could bear to be away from her friends, Joe had agreed, in principle at least. By the time he realised she was expecting them to spend most of the summer in Capri, an excited Angelica had already broached the idea with Elena and Gennaro and received an equally excited and approving response. Even then, despite the risk of causing offence, he'd done his best to back out. Perhaps Angelica could pass the summer with her grandparents, he'd suggested, and he could join her for part of it. Maybe a week. Or two at a push. After all, what would he do on a small island for a month and a half?

'Spend time with me,' had come her reply.

As they made their way to the taxi that his in-laws had booked for them, Joe listened as his daughter gave the Italian she'd learned from Sofia a run-out with their driver. Already she seemed more animated, maybe even more alive than he'd seen her since that day when their lives had changed in an instant. With her darker colouring and her expressive gestures, she seemed instantly at home amongst the Neapolitan throng, in sympathy with the reuniting families, the lovers saying their heartfelt farewells. Sofia had always seemed happy here, Joe reflected, and this might be where Angelica would relearn to be happy too. But for him it invoked only sadness. A feeling of unease.

This feeling only grew on him as the taxi nosed its way through the crowded Saturday evening streets of Naples towards the ferry port, their driver accelerating into every tiny suggestion of space and sounding his horn at the slightest provocation. The city was exactly how he remembered it. Loud. Colourful. Vibrant. Oozing a zest for living in the shadow of the great volcano. But shabby and dirty with it. Almost slatternly in the way it displayed its poverty for everyone to see. The weeds growing out of the broken asphalt. The graffiti covering every surface. The grimy, faded grandeur. Inevitably, the air-conditioning wasn't working and they were forced to ride with the windows down, assailed by the stench of diesel fumes and the sewers ripened by the summer heat. And was there just a whiff of something even more sulphurous... the city's dark underbelly? In Joe's experience, no one exuded a greater contempt for the law – and for those like him who were charged with upholding it – than the inhabitants of Naples. Nowhere better exemplified the sly cynicism lurking in one corner of the otherwise sunny Italian soul.

He hadn't always felt this way about his dead wife's birthplace, Joe reflected, as he stood on the quayside at Molo Beverello, waiting for the approaching ferry and keeping a close eye on their luggage, while Angelica played a game of peek-a-boo with a wide-eyed child in a buggy. When Sofia had first brought him home to meet her parents, he'd been so hopelessly besotted, so mesmerised by her exoticness, he'd expected to fall as madly in love with the people and the culture that had given rise to her. Unfortunately they hadn't proved quite so eager to embrace him back. Her mother, Elena, had been the exception, but she was as English as he was, although she was constantly reminding anyone who cared to listen that she could trace her roots on her mother's side back to Sicily. But Sofia was an only child and there was no chaotically large and loving family to grasp Joe to its bosom. And the one pure Italian in her immediate bloodline – her father, Gennaro – proved persistently cool towards his prospective son-in-law. It wasn't so much disapproval, Sofia explained, as disappointment that she'd chosen London over Capri. It didn't help, of course, that whenever Joe visited, Gennaro was working. It would be the height of summer and the family's restaurant would demand all his energy and attention from first thing in the morning to last thing at night. And yet, outside the kitchen, the old chef was ebullient and gregarious, endlessly warm towards his customers and his employees. It was only towards his daughter's husband that he seemed to maintain a wary reserve. Joe was dreading the prospect of the summer ahead, without Sofia's essential sweetness to mitigate the lingering suspicion of hostility between them.

'We're here.'

Angelica's hand tugged at his arm and pulled Joe from his reverie. Through a window in the passenger cabin, he could see the north side of Capri laid out in front of them. The sun had dropped below the horizon but it still gave off a peachy-purple glow that outlined the contours of the island. The busy waterfront was ablaze with light and colour, which reflected off the blackening surface of the sea as the boat manoeuvred to make its final approach. Behind the port, the dark mass of rising ground was dotted with the lights of villas and hotels, looking, from this distance, like nothing so much as fairy lanterns. Seen reflected through Angelica's eyes, there was something undeniably magical about the island. But Joe had been taught to view it through a different lens.

A gilded prison, Sofia had called it, seeking to reassure him that, however much she loved her parents and looked forward to her visits home, she hadn't the slightest intention of ever going back to live there. Capri was the polar opposite of London, she told him: Catholic, conservative, monocultural, claustrophobic. A place where everyone seemed to know everyone else's business and made it their business to make sure everyone else did as well. A place where questions were better not asked, and explanations were seldom offered. A place where feuds flourished and enmities lingered, but the greatest hatred of all was reserved for the foreigners who flocked to the island from Easter to the Feast of St Francis in early October, and were only to be tolerated as long as they didn't question the price of anything.

And yet, despite all that, there *was* something enchanting about the place, Joe couldn't help reflecting a half-hour later, as the water taxi they'd transferred to rounded the final headland and the terrace of his in-laws' seafront restaurant came into view. Bathed in soft radiance from the lights that were strung above it, Da Vinale's gave off a palpable sense of warmth and welcome. As the driver killed the engine, and they floated the last few metres towards the restaurant's private jetty, Joe could hear a hubbub of conversation calling to him, like siren voices, could detect an aroma of something intoxicatingly delicious in the air.

Perhaps Angelica was right, he told himself, watching the tears flow a few minutes later as Gennaro embraced his granddaughter with such tender emotion in front of his clapping customers, and a smiling Elena gestured to Joe with open arms to invite him into the family's moment of joyful reunion. For all his lingering fears and misgivings, perhaps this might just be where the two of them could start to heal.

2

The moment she saw the body, Lara instantly regretted her comment about lunch.

She and her colleague Gianni Gallo had been sitting in the open-plan office on the fifth floor of the State Police headquarters in Naples, bemoaning their luck at being stuck in the office on a hot Sunday in July, when the call had come through. Listening to the voice on the line as it reported the discovery of a body at the foot of cliffs on the north-east coast of Capri, Lara had sighed inwardly and contemplated leaving the matter, which had all the hallmarks of an unhappy accident, for the late shift to pick up. When she googled Tiberius's Leap, however, she couldn't help noticing it was less than fifteen hundred metres from a restaurant she and Nicky had visited in those first weeks of freedom after the pandemic, and memories of the glorious things they'd eaten at Da Vinale's, and the equally glorious sex that had followed on a darkened beach nearby, came flooding back. Consulting her watch, and then grabbing her vape, badge and gun in that order, Lara had jokingly asked if Gianni fancied taking a boat to Capri for lunch.

Frozen there, with the indignity of her grim and pitiful death for all to see, the young woman looked like tenderised meat. The back of her skull had disintegrated from the impact of the fall, with the flesh of her scalp ruptured like twisted metal, and grey matter lying half in, half out of what remained of her cranial cavity. One leg was twisted backwards, while the other jutted unnaturally to the side. Her exposed flesh was livid with bruises and cuts, so many raw abrasions it almost looked like she was covered in a rash.

Lara breathed in deeply through her nose, was forced to admit to herself she felt queasy. She looked on with admiration as Gianni went about his business, matter-of-fact and cheerful, chewing gum, exchanging banter with the local constables. They were all male and *very* out of shape, and they stood around watching and appraising her in that way so many of the male inhabitants of her native country seemed to specialise in.

Inevitably it was Gianni who found the phone lodged in a crevice between the rocks, almost seven metres from the body, but less than a metre from the water's edge, where the evidence it contained would have sunk without trace. How it came to fall so far from the hand that held it, and how it survived a drop of three hundred metres would later become the subject of her fevered speculation, but for now Lara restricted herself to expressing gratitude as he brought it to her, like a dog returning a ball to its mistress. While Gianni went to continue the search, Lara was left to bag up the phone and try to gather her scattered wits sufficiently to resume the duties expected of her as a recently promoted State Police inspector.

The first thing to go under her mental microscope was the deceased's outfit. Lara knew next to nothing about fashion – she was dressed, as always, in a T-shirt, fatigues and army-issue boots in varying shades of charcoal and black – but even she could tell that the woman's dress had been lovingly cut from expensive cloth. Belted at the waist and sleeveless, it made Lara think of dancing or cocktails on the terrace of a grand hotel. The same could be said of her sandals, which were not at all suited to sightseeing the archaeological remains that lay hidden from view, high on the clifftop above.

Then there was her bag to consider, a leather knapsack of obvious quality. A search of it had turned up nothing so practical as sunscreen or a hat or even a bottle of water, which were surely prerequisites for a climb in this heat. Instead, it contained an unused panty-liner, lipstick, hairbrush, a key card so discreetly branded it was impossible to identify which of the island's many hotels it belonged to, and €186 in assorted notes and coins. Just like the outfit, it seemed a selection one might make in anticipation of a lunch date or a shopping trip. And why was the deceased not wearing the bag? Surely it should either be across her shoulders or safe on the clifftop above.

A distinctive ringtone sounded, and for a split second Lara imagined an acquaintance of the deceased might be calling with the answer to the many questions crowding in on her. But the device in the evidence bag was silent and she realised it was her own phone – newly issued at work and still on its factory settings – that was trilling for her attention. It was her boss, Curti, and she knew instantly why he was phoning . . . urgent, impatient, anxious for information to help him manage those above him in the chain of command. She resolved not to speak to him until she'd something to tell him. The woman's name not least of all.

As she declined the call and switched off her phone, Lara remembered, with a flash of irritation, that she'd made arrangements with friends for later, but there was no way she'd be back in Naples in time. She was about to key in her passcode so she could make a call when it did its new party trick of recognising her facial features and opened unbidden. A thought struck her and, instead of making the call, she put her phone away and turned her attention to the dead woman's device. Donning a pair of latex gloves that were kept handy in the pocket of her trousers, she took it out of the evidence bag and removed its shattered screen protector. She crouched by the dead woman's side, turning the phone to face its erstwhile owner. Flipping the phone back in her own direction, she saw the ruse had worked – the phone's camera app was open, and a live video feed of her immediate surroundings was displayed on the screen ready to be captured in a photograph. Beneath it was an icon representing the last photo taken and, instinctively, she pressed it. As the photo expanded into the centre of the screen, the foremost of Lara's myriad questions – *What happened here?* – appeared to find the beginnings of an answer.

3

If Joe had been informed of this young woman's demise as he'd lain in bed earlier that Sunday, less than a nautical mile from where Lara would find herself studying the contents of her mobile phone, he wouldn't have been disconcerted, or very much surprised. In a decade with the southern command of the Metropolitan Police Service's Murder Squad, he'd learned to accept death whenever and wherever he found it.

What was bothering him as he lay in bed at sun-up, watching the first beams of daylight creep between the shutters, was the absence of Sofia. He'd felt it the night before when all the niceties and formalities that surrounded their arrival were over, and a weary Elena had walked him along the landing to show him the room he'd be sleeping in. Joe had recognised it as the one he'd shared with his soon-to-be wife when they'd arrived for that first visit, freshly engaged and infatuated, almost twenty years previously. Then, Sofia had delighted in giving him the tour of what had been her teenage bedroom, still lined with her favourite books and posters, still marked by her youthful miscalculations, including the time she'd nearly burned herself alive while reading beneath the sheets with a candle. Now, though, in the aftermath of her death, all the old signs and stains had been smoothed out or painted over and her things had been tidied away to who knew where. There'd been no trace of her, as Joe searched the drawers and cupboards late at night, unable to sleep, restless to find proof his memories were not failing him.

When he next awoke, the first thing he saw was the travelling alarm clock he'd placed at his bedside. Cursing, he sat up. Ten fifty-three! He'd only intended to doze a few minutes. Flushing slightly in anticipation of how his in-laws might react to such slothfulness on the first morning of their stay, Joe jumped out of bed and raided his suitcase for fresh clothes.

Stepping out of his bedroom, he glanced along the landing to where he imagined Angelica still lay sleeping. He thought about knocking for her, but the idea of entering her private space, of encountering the aura of wariness – or was it outright hostility? – with which she now seemed to greet him, gave him pause. Deciding she was old enough to negotiate her own house rules, he made his way along the corridor to the front door.

Crossing the courtyard that separated the family's apartment from their place of work, he entered the restaurant by its rear door. The building consisted of a small brick structure that housed the kitchen and toilet block, with a more spacious wooden 'lean-to' attached to the front and overlooking the sea. The overall effect was to make the restaurant's 'front of house' feel light and airy, with every inch of wood whitewashed, and generous windows giving spectacular views out over the shallow cove that Da Vinale's nestled in. The roof was made from a translucent corrugated plastic that let in yet more light, but also added to the impression that the wooden structure had been thrown up in a hurry while plans were made for erecting something more solid and permanent. A set of folding doors opened out onto the terrace, where the majority of the restaurant's covers would typically be seated. To his right, the turquoise waters of the Tyrrhenian Sea sparkled lazily in the late morning sunshine. Ahead he could see Elena out on the terrace and, deciding that she represented his least intimidating option, given the rather alarming noises emanating from the kitchen to his left, he stepped through the open door to join her.

Sofia's mother had her back to him as she busied herself laying tables. Joe took a moment to look around. At the far end of the terrace, a set of metal steps connected the restaurant to the street above. The terrace itself was partially shaded by a wooden pergola, which was wreathed in a startling profusion of purple bougainvillea that was covered in turn by an equally impressive quantity of bees. Beneath it were a dozen or so tables, some of them basking in direct sunshine, some entirely out of it. Their size and shape varied, but each was covered in starchily pristine white table linen, and identically dressed with cutlery and glassware, and napkins of such a pure azure they could only have been cut from Italian cloth. And each was crowned with a bowl of fresh lemons.

Joe cleared his throat, but Elena gave no sign she'd heard him. 'I can't believe I slept so long,' he ventured.

'It's nearly the afternoon,' she agreed, making no attempt to reassure him.

'I'm usually in the gym by six.'

Still she did not look at him. 'You've missed breakfast.'

'Fasting's good for you.'

Only now did she turn and fix him with those intelligent eyes, so warm and brown, so like her daughter's. 'Nonsense.' Her tone said *There's an end to it.*

Joe felt the weight of her gaze, probing and studying, and he considered how he must look through her eyes: greyer and gaunter than the last time he'd been here, no doubt, hollowed out by grief.

As if she could read his thoughts, Elena reached out and cupped his upper arm, communicating with a squeeze right through to the bone. 'At least we've got the whole summer to fatten you both up,' she said, indicating he should take a chair.

'Really, Elena. I'm all right.'

'Sit!'

Joe did as he was told.

At the door to the interior, she turned back. 'Should I take something up to Angelica?' she asked.

Joe grimaced. 'Maybe leave her.'

A look passed between them – of understanding if not quite complicity – before Elena disappeared inside.

Sated by the coffee, bread and cherry jam Elena had brought for him, Joe would happily have sat there all day, listening to the cries of childish excitement from the beach nearby, watching the birds circling and the boats and jet-skis passing by. He'd fallen into a reverie, warmed by the sun, enjoying the feeling of not having to analyse or decide anything, of not having to *think* about very much at all.

His peace was broken by the sound of breaking crockery. It was followed almost immediately by cursing in Italian. Joe looked at his watch, suddenly aware the restaurant must soon be opening and his lingering presence might not be appreciated. Collecting his cup and plate, he steeled himself to enter the lion's den.

As Joe pushed open the doors to the kitchen, Elena was on her knees, picking up shards of shattered ceramic and wiping up a spattering of whatever the broken dish had contained. The lion himself, Gennaro, had stopped roaring, but it was obvious his stress levels were rising. He hovered over the clean-up, brush and pan in hand, his unruly mane of grey hair only half tamed by the band that was supposed to hold it in a ponytail, the white T-shirt straining to contain his belly already speckled with sauce. Behind him, a pan sat forgotten over a low flame. It had started to smoke.

Elena was first to look up and Joe held up the items in his hands by way of explanation. 'In the sink, please,' she instructed him, unflustered as always, as the doors behind Joe swung open and a youngish man hurried into the kitchen, a basket of fish on his shoulder, almost bumping into him in the process. 'No clams today. No scallops,' he barked, removing the basket from its perch and dropping it onto the nearest surface.

'*Madre di Dio!*' Gennaro muttered. 'Do we have bottarga?'

'I'll check,' the younger man volunteered. As he crossed Joe's path, he flashed a cheery smile and raised a hand in greeting, gave his name as Luca. *Ah. So, you must be the cousin*, Joe thought, watching him make his way towards the storeroom, the shelves visible through an open door. Luca had spent time in Bristol studying to be an actor and Sofia had visited him once, although Joe had never been introduced in person before his abrupt and unexplained return to Italy. As Luca reappeared with a block of something reddish-brown, presumably bottarga – which Google would later inform him was the dried and salted egg sac of a tuna or grey mullet – Joe remembered what he was supposed to be doing and crossed to the sink. He started to rinse his plate but was told by Elena to leave it. Aldo, the pot-washer, wouldn't take kindly to being usurped.

Joe looked around. Luca was now busy combining flour, eggs and water into a dough, a pasta-maker standing ready nearby. Elena was counting plates and transferring them to a trolley. Gennaro was focused on cutting the bottarga into wafer-thin slices. Surrounded by so much focus and purpose,

Joe felt himself becoming exactly what he feared when Angelica had first broached the idea of spending the summer with her grandparents . . . a spare part. He contemplated beating a retreat, but to where and to do what? Suddenly the next six weeks yawned almost limitlessly ahead of him. It had been a mistake to come.

'Can I help?' he blurted out, and almost instantly regretted it.

There was no immediate response. Heads remained bent, eyes remained fixed on whatever task was in hand. Joe breathed an inward sigh of relief and shaped to leave.

'Gennaro?'

The old chef lifted his head to find Elena looking at him.

'Joe's offering to help,' she explained, with infinite patience.

The frown deepened. 'Is this a good time, *tesoro*?'

Evidently not, Joe couldn't help thinking.

A look passed between the old couple and Elena seemed to concede the point. 'Why don't you take Angelica to the beach?' she suggested, stopping short of explicitly rejecting Joe's offer, but ushering him towards the door all the same. 'Come back at four when the lunch service will be over. We'll all sit down together to eat.'

Joe was only too happy to make his escape.

For the second time in an hour, Joe found himself hovering outside Angelica's bedroom, but this time he knocked, softly. There was no response and he knocked again, a little louder, but still she didn't reply. Thinking she might already have risen and gone out, he opened the door and looked in.

His daughter was sitting on the bed with her back to him, staring at her phone. She was wrapped in a towel, her hair gathered messily on top of her head in a scrunchie. An earbud was protruding from the ear nearest to him and Joe could detect a ghostly trace of music. He paused, uncertain whether to advance or retreat, glanced around for something to guide him, and that was when he saw it.

A photo of his dead wife on the bedside table.

He recognised it instantly. Taken on their wedding day at her most devastatingly beautiful. The sight of it, framed and brought here by his grieving child, floored him, and it took all his self-control not to cry out. He retreated onto the landing, closing the door as quietly as his shaking hands would allow, resting his head against it, trying to control the flutter of panic as those familiar, unwelcome thoughts came crowding in.

Joe had been working late, later even than usual, when Angelica called.

'Have you heard from Mum?' she asked without preamble.

'Not since this morning. Should I have?'

There was silence at the other end of the line.

'Is something the matter, love?'

'She wasn't here when I got back. I can't get hold of her.'

Joe looked at his watch. 9.43pm. Wednesday. 'She's got yoga.'

'She's usually home by nine.'

'Maybe she stayed for a drink.'

'I've texted Julie. She left an hour ago.'

The first tremor of anxiety was detectable in her voice, but it didn't occur to Joe to worry. Sofia's bus had broken down. Or she'd stopped to buy wine and a takeaway. The explanation was bound to be mundane. He'd agreed to come home all the same.

He took the Overground, allowing him to continue texting and phoning on the way. By the third time of calling, Angelica was semi-hysterical – 'Something's happened, I can tell' – but Joe refused to get carried away. It was only as he left the station, and started the short walk home, that the first inklings of disquiet came calling. Turning the corner into Stratton Avenue, he saw the aura of blue light up ahead and was able to make out the line of police tape across the end of the street. A knot of worried residents had gathered, and he called out to them, asking what they knew. Some kind of accident, an old man told him. A woman had been knocked down. Was in a bad way. *The speed they drive up and down here*, someone else ventured, *it's a miracle it's not happened before . . . we need cameras, speed bumps.* But Joe had stopped listening, was hurrying towards the cordon.

Flashing his warrant card, he ducked beneath the tape. As he saw the ambulance and the squad car parked across the centre of the road, doors open and lights flashing, all the desperate need to *know* suddenly went out of him and he slowed to a halt. He could see a female paramedic kneeling in the road a few metres in front of him, attempting CPR, with the lower part of the injured party's legs visible behind her; the colour and design of the trainers they were wearing were sickeningly familiar. A male paramedic now emerged from the ambulance with a medical bag, and something of his urgency communicated itself to Joe. He started moving again, still hesitant, sensing he was sleepwalking towards the end of his life as he knew it, but unable to stop himself manoeuvring into position so he could see the victim's face.

It was Sofia and he knew instantly she was dead. There was something pathetic about the way she looked, stripped of animation, T-shirt lifted to expose the bruised and paling flesh beneath. The second paramedic knelt to inject something into her prone and lifeless body, while his colleague continued with her chest compressions but, unable to bear witness to their doomed attempts at resuscitation, Joe had already turned away.

It took a long moment for his agitation to subside, for his breathing to become regular and his pulse to normalise. At last, when he was as satisfied as he could be that any trace of the distress Sofia's photo had caused him would no longer be detectable, he knocked again, this time much more loudly, and made a show of re-entering his daughter's bedroom, as if for the first time. Angelica started and whipped round to face the door with a look of surprise, clutching her towel to her chest.

'What the hell, Dad!'

'Sorry, sorry.' Joe raised his hands apologetically, pointing one finger towards his daughter's earbuds as he did so. Perhaps it might help if she took those off?

Barely bothering to hide her indignation, she obliged him. 'What do you want?'

'Fancy going to the beach?'

'With you?'

Joe could only shrug. Who else?

His daughter took her time to consider this proposal. 'All right,' she agreed at last, in a tone that made clear she considered it a mighty concession on her part.

'Downstairs in five?' Joe ventured.

Angelica looked at him like he was an idiot.

'I mean . . . whenever . . . just take your time,' he conceded, knowing he would be waiting at least half an hour.

4

He was never there when she wanted him and too often there when she did not, Angelica reflected as she watched her dad pick his way through the bar towards her.

Half an hour ago she'd needed him. In his absence, a French guy wearing an astonishing pair of fluorescent-orange swimming briefs had latched on to her at the beach and threatened to turn nasty when she'd asked to be left alone. It was Daniele who had rescued her, flopping down on the empty sun lounger beside her and pretending to be her boyfriend. He was just as much a stranger as the other man, but something about his manner had been reassuringly guileless, in a way the Frenchman's was not, and it helped, of course, that he was lithely good-looking, with soulful eyes and cheekbones to die for. She'd agreed to his suggestion that they go to the beach bar until she was sure her tormentor had departed, maybe get themselves a drink to enhance the deception. Now, just as beers had been bought and she was starting to enjoy herself, Joe was back.

She could guess, of course, where he'd been. Despite protestations to the contrary, he'd soon grown bored of the beach, just as she knew he would when the idea of coming had first been mooted. Donning her earbuds and pretending to be absorbed by her phone, Angelica had watched out of the corner of her eye as Joe grew increasingly restless, huffing and rolling his eyes at the crime novel she'd lent him, putting it down and picking it up again at least half a dozen times before abandoning it completely. He'd tried sunbathing, on his front and then his back, before retreating under a beach umbrella, declaring the heat a threat to sanity and safety.

The only thing that seemed to hold his attention was the passage of traffic at sea. A sleek super-yacht – *Calypso* – was anchored off the beach, and Joe had watched with apparent fascination as a party of guests was ferried noisily ashore, no doubt making their way for a booze-fuelled lunch somewhere nearby, possibly even Da Vinale's. A tall man with ginger hair, which clashed unpleasantly with his red Hawaiian shirt, was striking a 'Land ahoy!' pose in the stern, and ostentatiously singing 'Row, row, row your boat' for his companions' amusement. Angelica felt an instant stab of dislike for him.

As time ticked by, she'd noted the presence of police speedboats as they hurried back and forth, had observed Joe observing them in turn. Later, a helicopter could be heard hovering, hidden by the island's mass, and she saw him look away east, calculating distances and timespans. It was soon after that he announced he was going to hire a jet-ski. She watched him start it and perform a few experimental loops before accelerating away around the corner of the bay. He was such a bloodhound, she thought, sniffing out trouble wherever he went.

When Daniele had suggested going to the bar, she'd felt the need to warn him her dad might soon be coming back, that he was prone to act protectively. She figured if the boy's intentions were dishonourable, then this might give him pause.

'How old are you anyway?' he'd asked, returning with two bottles.

'Old enough to drink beer.' She took a swig.

'But seriously. How old?'

'Seventeen,' she confessed, trying to sound casual.

'*Sicuro*?'

'Honestly.'

Daniele had shrugged languidly. 'It's no surprise, your father . . . he's protective.'

'He can't help it,' she retorted, deciding to drop the bomb. 'He's a policeman.'

The boy laughed. Either he was a good actor, or he was genuinely unfazed. Unlike so many of the boys she encountered at home.

'*Salute!*' he announced. 'To fathers . . . and getting away from them.' He raised his bottle in a mock toast, clinking it against hers before drinking.

But there *was* no getting away, because here Joe was.

Sensing a slight stiffening of her demeanour, Daniele turned and rose at the older man's approach. Joe loomed over him, seeming at least twice his size.

'This is Daniele, Dad,' she offered cautiously, unsure how he was going to react.

Daniele put out a hand, but Joe ignored it. He was staring at the bottles instead.

'What's that?'

'What does it look like.'

'Where did you get it?'

'It was me,' Daniele admitted.

Joe turned his gaze on him, seemed to consider him for the first time.

'She's seventeen.'

'She told me.'

'It's just a beer, for fuck's sake,' Angelica interjected.

Joe ignored her, and the profanity. 'It's illegal.'

'In Italy? No. If she's with an adult. And she has the permission of the parent.'

'She doesn't.'

Daniele glanced towards Angelica. She felt herself flushing to her roots, but Joe seemed impervious to the embarrassment he was causing. Taking his wallet from the pocket at the back of his swimming shorts, he opened it and doubled down in the dickhead stakes by showing his warrant card to the younger man.

Daniele grinned. 'She told me this also.'

'Then what are you still doing here?'

There was really no coming back on that. Angelica watched as Daniele downed his beer in a number of slow gulps and put the bottle back on the table. He reached out to pick up his phone, which was resting up against hers, and with a wink, he was gone.

It was a few minutes before Angelica realised that Daniele had been one step ahead of her and that the proximity of their phones had been deliberate . . . he'd used NameDrop on his iPhone to suggest exchanging contact details. As she unlocked her phone and accepted his contact card, sending hers back in response, she smiled, but to herself; she didn't want that *arsehole* to think she was anything other than furious.

5

The last of the lunchtime diners were still on the terrace at Da Vinale's as Lara passed by in the speedboat taking her and Gianni to Marina Piccola, where a police car was waiting to transport them into town.

A call to the Travel and Tourism Federation had yielded a lead to help with her most pressing of challenges: to put a name to the dead woman. The discreetly branded key card had quickly been identified as belonging to the Hotel Americano, so called in honour of Capri's past as one of Hollywood's favourite playgrounds. It was a connection Lara was quick to work out for herself as she walked into the lobby twenty minutes later to be confronted by a wall of headshots of the glamorous and famous. Even the manager, Signor Carlotti, looked like a tribute to the golden age of movies, with his pencil moustache and slicked-back hair, his slim-cut suit and narrow lapels.

Up in the room, a search of the safe, accessed with a key supplied by the eager-to-please Carlotti, turned up a passport that confirmed the details from the hotel register: Shannon Elizabeth Headley, a British national, born 7 June 1990. Slipping this first piece of proof into an evidence bag, Lara turned her attention to the rest of the suite.

There was little of interest in the bathroom, save for a half-empty blister pack of birth-control pills in the bottom of a washbag. In the wardrobe were a couple of low-cut cocktail dresses and a collection of the sort of lingerie that, when considered in harness with the contraceptives, might indicate the dead woman had been making an effort for *someone*. But who? The manager was adamant she'd been travelling alone. And no one had called to report her missing.

By this time Gianni had started to lose interest, to goof around. He held one of the dresses to his chest – a gold lamé number – pretending to model it.

'It suits you,' Lara said gruffly, trying not to encourage him.

'Maybe *you* should try wearing one,' Gianni opined, sounding like her father.

She was tempted to dress him down, but confined herself to a 'Fuck you, Gallo' as she took the dress back from him. It was as she was returning it to the wardrobe that she noticed the suitcase on the highest shelf and realised, with a flash of irritation, that he hadn't searched it. Taking it down and unzipping it, she found an A4 manilla envelope and six more blister packs of pills in an inside pocket. Only these weren't for birth control.

She held them up for her colleague's inspection.

He whistled with surprise. 'Fentanyl!'

'Call the lab,' she ordered. 'Tell them to prioritise the tox report. I want to know if she was under the influence of this shit before she fell.'

As Gianni stepped out to place his call, Lara turned her attention to the envelope. It was sealed, and she looked around for something to open it. She settled on the handle of a bottle opener she found in the mini-bar and used it to prise up the flap as gently as possible. As the glue gave way, she was able to peer inside. Legal documents by the look of it. Some kind of insurance form? A medical questionnaire perhaps? She resealed the envelope as neatly as possible and slipped it into another evidence bag. As keen as she was for answers, it would be wise to seek legal advice before she pried further.

Signor Carlotti was doing his best to ingratiate himself as he showed the two officers to a table at the pool bar a few minutes later and offered them a drink. Coffee? A Campari? Champagne, perhaps? Gianni glanced at Lara, but she shook her head, explaining they wouldn't be staying long, they only had a few questions.

The manager briefly excused himself to deal with a guest. While Gianni grumbled in the background, Lara took the opportunity to look around. Citizens of nowhere lounged around the pool in states of undress, parading the results of plastic surgeries or Ozempic regimes. Necks and ears dripped gold, wrists sagged under chunky watches. Food and drink were ordered and discarded, barely sampled. Everywhere there was conspicuous consumption. Shannon Headley had clearly had money, Lara reflected.

Carlotti now returned and proceeded to outline the known facts about Shannon's stay in the Hotel Americano. She'd arrived three days previously, he said, on the Thursday afternoon, in a water taxi from Positano – a transfer from the hotel had been waiting on the dock at Marina Grande to meet her at 1.30pm, as arranged. On that first night she'd dined alone in her room, a Sea View Suite, but on the second she'd asked the concierge to book a taxi to take her to a restaurant on the coast for 7.30pm. Yes, of course he knew the name, Carlotti smirked, making a show of consulting his notes. Da Vinale's.

Lara wrote it down without giving any indication that the name was familiar to her. 'Do we know anything else about her movements?' she asked.

She'd breakfasted in the restaurant at the hotel on both Friday and Saturday, Carlotti said, but not this morning. There was no record of her having ordered anything from either of the bars or making use of the gym in the basement. He had no report from the staff of her in or by the swimming pool. There was CCTV in all the public spaces if they wanted to check for themselves, although he couldn't imagine that would be necessary.

'We'll be the judge of what's necessary, *Signore*,' Lara told him.

Shannon had visited the concierge's desk on two separate occasions, Carlotti continued, once on Friday afternoon, when she'd been supplied with a tourist map of the island, and the second time mid-morning on Saturday, when she'd asked about recommendations for a masseuse. Before either detective could voice a question, he produced a copy of the map from his jacket pocket and handed it to Lara, pointing out the directions it included to Villa Jovis and Tiberius's Leap.

'And the name of the masseuse?' Lara nudged him, pen poised in hand.

The manager's face fell. An assistant concierge had dealt with the enquiry and her English wasn't the best. The employee had initially misunderstood Ms Headley's request, had assumed she was asking the hotel to book her a massage, when in fact she'd already made her own arrangements but was wanting to know if the salon was a reputable one. The masseuse was not on their list of approved practitioners and the assistant had offered to make an appointment with one who was, but the offer had been declined. The name in question had, of course, been written down but the note had subsequently been discarded. The therapist's name began with an A to the best of the assistant's memory, Carlotti offered apologetically, maybe Annunziata or Assunta? But no, unfortunately, he couldn't supply a surname, or a company name, and he had no way of knowing whether the appointment had been kept.

Gianni closed his notebook and clicked his pen, signalling impatience to bring the interview to an end, but Lara was not quite ready to give up on this little peacock of a man.

'Is there anything else you can think of?' she enquired. 'Anything at all?'

It was the question he'd obviously been waiting for. Producing a piece of paper, Carlotti placed it on the table, smoothing out the fold so they could get a good look at it.

Gianni didn't have his glasses, was forced to squint. 'And who is M. Sanghera?'

'I've no idea,' the manager beamed, playing his trump card with a flourish. 'But it's the name Ms Headley's room was originally booked under.'

6

As they came down the steps to the terrace a few minutes before 4pm, Angelica in a visible state of high dudgeon and Joe still very much in the doghouse, the sight that stopped them in their tracks was more arresting than anything they'd encountered at the beach. Gennaro was stripped to the waist, sluicing away the sweat of his labours under a hand pump. Elena stood holding a bottle of shampoo and a towel. As the last of the water was pumped and then poured in a cascade over his head, the old chef slicked his hair back, twisting it into a knot and wringing it dry in a practised fashion. Elena held out the towel for him and he pretended to reach out for it but grasped her by the wrist instead, pulling her into his damp embrace.

'Gennaro!' she shrieked, bursting into hysterical laughter. 'You're soaking!'

He spun her round, covering her neck in kisses and it was then she saw Joe and Angelica, staring. 'He's an animal,' she said for their benefit, gently pushing her husband off, but smiling as she did so.

Gennaro growled jokily. He seemed entirely unabashed.

'Luca's cooked a seafood risotto,' Elena continued, attempting to straighten her hair and clothing. 'We'll eat it out here.'

Joe felt a stab of something he couldn't quite name. They still had each other, could still find moments for love and laughter in the endless grind of grief. He glanced at Angelica, who was looking equally conflicted.

'I'm not hungry,' she declared.

'Angelica!'

'I'm not.'

'Your grandparents are going to a lot of trouble to have us here.'

Angelica ignored him. 'May I be excused, Gran?'

'Of course, my darling.'

She went inside, closing the door to the restaurant with more force than required.

'Will you go after her?' Gennaro asked, coming to join them. He was towelling the water from his ears.

Joe shrugged. 'And do what?'

'Find out what's wrong,' Elena suggested. 'Talk to her.'

'She doesn't want to talk to *me*.'

His father-in-law couldn't hide his surprise. 'Your own daughter?'

'We don't exactly speak much.'

'Not even when you sit down to eat?'

Joe almost laughed. 'We never do.'

'You don't make dinner for her?'

'I don't know how to cook.'

The old chef looked stunned.

Joe felt a sudden urge to explain himself. 'Sofia . . . it made her happy . . . you know . . . to do it for us.' He trailed off, feeling a lump forming in his throat. Elena reached out to squeeze his hand. Briefly he tolerated the gesture. 'I can use the microwave,' he added, trying to lighten the mood, but Gennaro looked even more horrified, if that were possible.

'Go and wash up,' Elena pronounced, ushering Joe away. 'And then we'll eat.'

As Joe rinsed his hands in the basin of the restaurant's toilets, he experienced a mild but persistent stinging sensation and realised that his wrists and forearms must be sunburnt. It could only have happened during his jet-ski adventure at the beach, he reflected.

He'd noticed the build-up of maritime police traffic during the afternoon, and by the time a helicopter could be heard hovering somewhere to the east, he was convinced a major incident must be occurring. Making the vaguest of excuses to Angelica, he'd hired one of the jet-skis that sat idle in the shallows and set off at speed across the bay. Within minutes, he was rounding the rocky cape he'd seen from the other side, but the coast continued on for at least another kilometre in a series of shallow bays backed by high cliffs. There was no sign of activity, nowhere for the police to have made landfall.

Joe had ploughed on, rounding one spur of land and then another, passing the yawning mouths of several caves cut deep into the chalky flanks of the island. He'd almost reached the point where common sense must surely prevail, and he would have to turn back, when he saw them – a small group of boats at anchor a couple of hundred metres up ahead, surrounding a narrow shelf of rock at the foot of a truly terrifying cliff face. He'd slowed to a crawl, suddenly conscious that he was thousands of miles from his own jurisdiction, but drawn ever forward by his curiosity.

The sight that greeted him as he neared the scene was not unlike other incidents he'd seen over the years, setting aside the strange, remote beauty of the place. White-coated scene-of-crime investigators buzzed around, with plain-clothes detectives directing them, and uniformed officers standing guard.

Joe had cut his engine and let the jet-ski drift. So intent was everyone on their tasks that no one had noticed his approach, and he'd found himself nearing the cluster of police vessels, had started to make out more of the detail. He'd caught a flash of vivid red between the legs of the assembled officers and had sensed immediately a body must be lying at the foot of the cliff. He'd steered to his left, trying to get a better angle, and that was when someone had spotted him.

'*Ehi! Fuori di qui!*'

Joe had seen the female detective immediately. She was staring straight at him, waving him away. He'd no idea what she'd shouted, but he got the gist. *Get out of here!* As others had turned to look and gesture, Joe raised a hand of apology and, starting up his engine, roared away.

It was the look on her face he saw now, as he stared at his own reflection in the mirror. She was right to look outraged, he reflected, disgusted even, by his failure to observe proper boundaries, by his inappropriate snooping, by his compulsive need to *know*. Angelica's right, he thought. I'm obsessed with what I do.

Out on the terrace, Luca had joined Elena as she made preparations for their communal lunch. Joe watched with admiration as they dressed the table, attending to every detail, however trivial it seemed.

Gennaro was the last to arrive, holding two bottles of wine between the fingers of one enormous hand; the bottles had already been opened and drunk from, or perhaps the wine had been put to some purpose in the kitchen, and Gennaro eased their corks out with his teeth and proceeded to pour a measure of red and white into the glasses that were paired at each setting on the table.

'Just a little,' Joe protested; it was years since he'd drunk during the day.

The old chef ignored him. 'Will you say grace, Joe?' he asked, continuing to pour.

This was awkward. Joe was a lifelong atheist, despite Sofia's delicate teasing and prompting over the years. But equally, he was not a man inclined to give offence, to throw a person's culture or traditions back in their face. He felt himself flushing slightly, as all eyes looked to him, and he groped for something, anything to say.

'He's teasing you,' Elena intervened, taking pity on him.

Gennaro roared with laughter.

'Godless heathen,' his wife pronounced, but she was smiling again – apparently, she couldn't seem to help it when it came to Gennaro – and Luca was too.

Still chuckling to himself, the older man leaned forward to remove the lid from a large orange casserole in the centre of the table. As he lifted it, and a delicious, musky waft of aromatic steam was released into the air, there were murmurs of appreciation and appetite from those assembled. All except Joe, that is, who had retreated into his thoughts, was lost somewhere in memory.

They had met on New Year's Eve.

Joe hadn't intended to join the celebrations, had even volunteered to work crowd control, so convinced was he that the night would prove a damp squib, as the occasion usually did. It was only through a combination of dumb luck – a mix-up with the rotas – and the dogged persuasion of his friends, that he found himself at the party that evening.

The attraction had been instant and mutual. Sofia was dark, very pretty and slight – *piccola* the Italians called it – and she watched the fireworks beside him on the balcony with a childlike reverence. Joe felt an overwhelming urge to protect her, but it was quickly apparent she didn't need it. She proudly informed him she'd come to London on her own and against the wishes of her father two years previously, determined to improve her English and make it as a food stylist. She'd found work on a magazine, was hopeful of progressing to recipe books in due course, was somehow surviving, maybe even thriving, in the great metropolis, despite her sheltered upbringing on a small island off the southwest coast of Italy. She was assured and self-possessed, unapologetically direct, endlessly inquisitive, intense when she needed to be, quick to laugh at herself and him when she did not. While the party raged inside, they stayed on the balcony, wrapped up against the cold, and talked and talked. By the time her taxi arrived at 3am, he felt he knew her better than his oldest friends, who were dancing to Prince on the other side of the wall. When she asked if he was coming with her, it felt the most natural thing in the world to say yes. Her smile made his heart beat faster.

He woke in her bed the following morning, aroused and drowsy from lack of sleep and the intensity of their lovemaking in the small hours, and sensed instantly that his life was in the process of changing. He found her in the kitchen, making breakfast. There was none of the awkwardness that usually resulted from such encounters, just a lingering kiss and an obvious delight to find themselves together, alone.

'Sit,' she told him, nudging him gently away with her hip and turning her attention back to the stove. In a few minutes, while he drank her coffee and watched appreciatively, she rustled up a dish he'd never heard of.

'*Uova in purgatorio*,' she announced, placing the pan on the table.

Joe leaned forward to devour it with his eyes. It was a fiery mess of eggs, tomato, peppers and onion, topped with a coating of bubbling Parmesan. He could smell garlic and detect the catch of chilli at the back of his throat. His stomach rumbled in anticipation, and he reached for a piece of the roughly sliced bread Sofia had just then placed beside the pan, but before he could take it she tapped him lightly on the fingers with the spoon she was holding.

'Nuh-uh,' she scolded, her face suddenly serious. 'You should say grace first.'

Joe stared at her in surprise. And then Sofia giggled, a delightful peal of silvery merriment, and he found himself laughing too, with her but at himself, at the absurdity of falling so instantly, so headlong and hopelessly, in love.

'Joe!'

He emerged from his reverie to find Gennaro holding out a plate. It was heavy with an oozing risotto, exuding a bisque-like sauce and peppered with a generous sprinkling of prawns and mussels. Joe's stomach rumbled again, just like it had all those years ago.

'It smells delicious,' he said, seeking out Luca with the compliment.

The sous-chef smiled back at him. 'I hope it tastes good too.'

Joe took a forkful. It did. 'It's incredible,' he said.

This time there were smiles all round.

Later, he woke on his bed, fully dressed and disoriented. He'd been dreaming Sofia was by his side, swimming in the warm waters off the island, helping him search for something on the seabed, precisely what, he couldn't now recall. For a moment he was convinced she'd come back, and his heart leapt, before the reality of the empty room reasserted itself. He sat up, dry-mouthed and woozy, heavy with sleep. The clock by his bedside read 5.43pm. He'd have to find a way to say no to wine at lunchtime.

Joe thought he could hear the sound of crying. Getting up, he padded to the door and opened it a crack. It was Elena and she was keening softly; it sounded so naked, so at odds with the veneer of good humour she routinely presented to the world, that he almost shut the door, but his curiosity got the better of him. Stepping out onto the landing, he could hear the low rumble of Gennaro's voice, trying to soothe her, although the words were inaudible. Joe crept closer to the door of their bedroom, which was slightly ajar.

'They seem broken,' he heard Elena say, and he realised with a jolt they were speaking about him and Angelica.

'We're all broken, *tesoro*,' came Gennaro's reply.

Joe strained forward, trying to see through the gap, and managed to catch a glimpse of his in-laws sitting together on the bed, their backs to the door. Gennaro had his arm around Elena's shoulders. There was something very fragile about the way they huddled together. They suddenly looked a lot older than their sixty-odd years.

'But we have each other.' She leaned against him for comfort.

'They're here. That's something.'

'Will you try talking to him?'

'Me?'

'See if you can get him to open up.'

There was a long pause while Gennaro considered this. 'He responds better to you,' he said eventually. 'You're both English.'

Joe could only imagine the look on Elena's face.

'What would I even say to him?' Gennaro continued, his voice rising slightly.

'Think of something.'

'Food is all I know.'

'So, talk to him about that,' Elena suggested, with impeccable logic.

'But he knows *nothing*!'

'Then why don't you teach him!' She sounded equally emphatic.

It was only then, as Joe imagined Gennaro gold-fishing, grasping for a rebuttal, that Elena must have noticed the door to their bedroom was open. Crossing over to rectify this, she took a moment to glance out onto the landing, but it was empty. As she shut it, another door a few metres away closed simultaneously with an almost inaudible click.

7

It was a little before 8pm on that Sunday when Lara finally spoke to Curti.

She'd put the call through a full two hours earlier, just before six, but her boss was at his daughter's house and a late lunch was still in progress. Nothing was allowed to come between the *commissario* and his food.

Lara had sent Gianni back to Naples with the speedboat – he had a new baby and a wife who was known to grumble – and while she waited for the call back she'd spent the time looking for items of interest on Shannon's phone. There were plenty of M's in her contacts, but none of them were listed as 'Sanghera'. Almost all the apps on Shannon's home screen required Face ID to open them; the more interesting ones – Tinder, Bumble and something called Girl Cupid – would have to wait until the digital forensics team could give her access to them. Until then, she contented herself with going through the photos and getting the story she'd spent the day trying to piece together straight in her head.

When Curti had still not called back by 7.45pm, Lara accepted the offer of a beer from the old sergeant on duty, imagining that the inevitable barrage of questions from her boss might be postponed until morning. She'd just settled on the terrace of the State Police office, with its startling views out across the Gulf of Naples, even in the failing light, when the phone rang. She took a moment to collect her thoughts before she picked it up.

'Tell me what we're dealing with,' Curti instructed, without preamble or apology; he'd obviously read the text she'd sent containing Shannon's personal details and the known facts about her stay.

'I'm not a hundred per cent sure yet, sir.'

'That's what I should tell the mayor, is it?' he said irritably, launching into a tirade about his day being ruined by a succession of calls from his contacts on the Communal Council. They were worried the death of a tourist, even if accidental, might attract the wrong sort of headlines and impact bookings even this far into the season.

'Have you seen the photo, *Commissario*?' she managed to interject.

'What photo?'

'I forwarded it to your email. About an hour ago.'

There was silence on the other end of the line. Then: 'Hold on.'

She heard him put his phone to his chest and call out to someone for assistance. Lara couldn't help smiling to herself. Curti was a dinosaur when it came to technology.

While she waited, Lara picked up the print-out she'd been given of the photo and held it up to the light that was shining onto the terrace from the small open-plan office behind. In other circumstances, it might have seemed less remarkable. A young woman was posing, craning her neck to look up and across to where her right hand – Lara had recreated the pose with her own phone, and it definitely must be her *right* hand – was holding the phone with which she was taking the selfie. Her eyes were hidden behind an expensive-looking pair of sunglasses, but something about her short blonde bob with its severe fringe, the tilt of her head, and the amused pout of her lips spoke to a healthy degree of self-possession. The high angle from which it had been taken, to emphasise the proximity of the vertiginous drop behind, meant the young woman's head only occupied the bottom left-hand quadrant of the image, with the rest mostly filled by cliff edge and the sea some 330 metres below. The straps of her red dress were just visible at the bottom edge of the photo, however, and the colour of her lips matched the lipstick they'd found in her bag. A pair of sunglasses identical to the ones she was wearing were among the items recovered by a search at the location. It was definitely a photograph of Shannon Elizabeth Headley.

'What am I looking at?' Curti barked, coming back on the line.

She proceeded to run through the evidence, such as it was. Ms Headley had asked for a tourist map of the island when she'd visited the concierge's desk at the Hotel Americano sometime on Friday. Although she didn't ask for instructions for how to get there, Tiberius's Leap was clearly marked on the map and a hiking trail picked out in red.

'And that's the name of the cliff, is it?' Curti interjected.

'That's correct, sir.'

'Named after some Roman, I suppose.'

'Yes, sir.'

'He died there too?'

'No, *Commissario*. Only people he didn't much like.'

Lara explained what she'd read in the guidebook. The Villa Jovis was the favourite of the palaces the Emperor Tiberius had occupied or built on Capri in the first few decades AD. He'd enjoyed seeing his enemies thrown from the clifftop to a near-certain death on the rocks below, or finished off with clubs by the sailors waiting in boats out to sea.

'I can think of a few I'd like to throw off there myself,' Curti interjected with feeling.

Lara ignored this. According to the senior officer at the police station on Capri, a Sergeant Alfieri, there had been at least one previous death by falling at the same location within the last five years, she continued, repeating what the sergeant had told her about the row with the council over appropriate signage and the lack of sufficient safety railings.

Curti was silent. She could almost hear him calculating.

The time code on Shannon's phone suggested the selfie had been taken at 3.52pm the previous day, she ploughed on, adding 'Saturday' for clarification. Perhaps she'd taken a moment to adjust her position, and that was when she'd fallen, at the moment of trying to take a second photo. There was a name for it apparently, in the self-obsessed age in which they were living.

Death by Selfie.

The *commissario* huffed. 'And you think this is what happened?'

Lara explained it was only a working theory but the best she'd been able to come up with in the time available, based on the evidence to hand. The timings tallied with Shannon's known movements at the hotel. She'd last been seen mid-morning on Saturday. The housekeeper had cleaned her room at a little after noon on the same day and returned today, Sunday, to find her bed unslept in. They would have to wait for the autopsy and for a best approximation of her time of death, but if it broadly aligned with the time the photo on her phone was taken then it would give credence to the idea they were dealing with an unfortunate accident.

Curti must have picked up on the doubt in her voice. 'But you're not so sure?'

'We found fentanyl in a suitcase in her hotel room, *Commissario*,' Lara admitted. 'A lot of it. Enough to suggest she was a heavy user.'

Her boss digested this. 'You think it could be a factor?' he asked.

'I don't know, sir,' she answered truthfully. 'We'll need to wait for toxicology. But if we find high levels in her blood then it certainly puts a different complexion on things.'

'It might suggest she fell while under the influence of the drug?'

'Exactly, sir.'

'Or even indicate a suicidal frame of mind?'

'We shouldn't rule it out, *Commissario*.' Of course, there was a third possibility, Lara couldn't help thinking to herself.

'Anything else?' Curti asked, in a tone that implied he hoped there wouldn't be.

Lara decided to keep to herself what her instincts were telling her . . . that it could yet prove to be the case they were dealing with a murder. Curti had little patience for what he called her 'digressions', and she had no hard evidence yet to support a theory of foul play, just her nagging doubts about the victim's clothes and possessions, a feeling in her gut that the cause of Shannon Headley's death would not turn out to be as straightforward as it appeared at first sight. She restricted herself to mentioning the legal documents she'd found in Shannon's room. They could point to background factors they were currently unaware of, she told him. They couldn't rule out anything at this point.

'The British may be able to help us with those,' Curti observed.

The British?

'I've already passed on the passport details to the embassy,' her boss continued, explaining the need for liaison with the police in whichever part of the United Kingdom Shannon Headley came from. There'd be interviews with next-of-kin and associates to be conducted, paperwork to fill in, all sorts of diplomatic toing and froing. 'It's going to be a major ball-ache,' he concluded.

Curti's last words were still echoing in Lara's head as she huddled beneath her blanket in the holding cell of the island's police station a few minutes before midnight. A simple phone call to her aunt Luisa at any point during the day would have secured her a comfortable bed at the villa she rented on the island, but Lara preferred a night in the cells. That way she could avoid the usual questions about her private life.

She was exhausted, but far too wired and anxious to sleep. A liaison officer from another police force? Looking over her shoulder every step of the way? Second-guessing her decisions? Undermining the authority she'd fought so hard to establish . . . was fighting to establish still? Curti might call it 'a ball-ache', but in truth the involvement of a British officer in the investigation would be no more than a minor inconvenience for him. For her it could only fuel her doubts, remind her that whatever she did, however well she performed, *they* would always think of her as a woman doing a man's job.

I'll fucking show them, she thought, as she plumped the meagre pillow with her fist and turned over, trying to find a semblance of comfort in preparation for what she already knew would be a long and sleepless night.

8

Joe hadn't intended to eat at Da Vinale's that Sunday evening but Elena had seemed offended by his suggestion he wasn't hungry after such a late and substantial lunch. 'Nonsense,' she pronounced in her customary fashion, telling him to report to the bar any time after 9pm, when the rush would be over. The fact that Angelica had been closeted in her bedroom since late afternoon, and had not eaten at all, went unmentioned between them.

I'd hate to see it when it's busy, was Joe's first thought as he came through the door from the courtyard at a judicious thirteen minutes past the hour and looked around. Every table was occupied, both inside and out, although desserts and coffees were being served for some and the first of the diners started to drift away not long afterwards.

He was escorted to a high stool at the bar and presented with a bowl of fat green olives and a glass of something white and fizzy, which he assumed was Prosecco, but later learned was a wine called Franciacorta. He sat, expecting to be given a menu, until a waiter presented him with a plate of antipasto, and he realised the decisions about what he would eat were out of his hands. The cured beef – *bresaola*, he remembered Sofia calling it – was earthy and salty and paired with slices of a hard, nutty cheese, as well as peppery rocket leaves and a drizzle of bittersweet balsamic.

Aside from his food, it was Elena who commanded most of Joe's attention. She conducted operations with an understated virtuosity, constantly assessing the progress of the meal at each table. Discreetly, she relayed her orders, directing with a tilt of the head or a twitch of a finger, always with a smile and a nod of approval. The waiters seemed as alert to her instructions as they were to the needs of their customers. And, all the while, the diners themselves were largely oblivious, their attention given over to each other and the excellence of what was placed in front of them, gorging themselves on meat and bread, seafood and pasta, cheeses and desserts, all washed down with glasses of wine or spirits, or coffee served unapologetically hot and strong, despite the hour. They were animated, happy, totally absorbed in the experience.

Da Vinale's was built for comfort, not to impress, Joe reflected. The floor was tiled in a light stone laminate, while the wooden walls were roughly whitewashed, just like the planking and the pergola on the terrace outside. The chairs and tables were moulded from a transparent plastic the colour of cough mixture, which twinkled in the lights. The interior was decorated with seascapes and abstract arrangements of shells and driftwood, alongside the obligatory photo of Diego Maradona, the Argentinian footballer who was almost canonised in these parts. Pot plants, both large and small, were placed around the room to soften the angles, and everywhere about the terrace, but the effect was more rudimentary than refined. None of that mattered, however, because the tables were dressed impeccably and, with the lights low, and candle flames winking off the glass, the setting had charm, looked thoroughly inviting.

His plate of antipasto was replaced with a dish of pasta. Joe was distracted by it, trying to work out what he was eating . . .

some kind of diced fish, pan-fried in herbs and sprinkled with crunchy, lemony breadcrumbs. It was served without an obvious sauce, although the fish was moist and oily, and on a bed of a dense, gnocchi-like pasta. It was delicious but filling and Joe was labouring after the first couple of mouthfuls. He ploughed on, but the quantity and nature of the food defeated him, and he'd just pushed it aside, hoping it would be quietly whisked away, when Elena came to check on him.

'You didn't like it?' she asked, eyeing the leftovers.

'The portion was enormous.'

'For a man like you?'

'I don't seem to have much appetite these days,' he replied. There was no need for him to explain why.

Lips pursing ever so slightly, Elena leaned across him to take the plate and held it out to a waiter, who popped up at her side without appearing to have been summoned. 'Dessert?' she asked him, as the waiter hurried away.

'I couldn't.'

'Not even a bit of ice cream?'

'Honestly, I'm stuffed.'

Elena wasn't giving up that easily. 'Coffee then?'

'Just the bill, please.'

She had the good grace to smile. 'How about some company?' she ventured, pulling back the adjacent bar stool and preparing to sit.

'Really, Elena. I'm *fine*.'

She searched his face, clearly sceptical, but at last, with a nod of acceptance, she returned the stool to its original position and turned back to the fray.

Joe nursed the remains of the white wine that had been brought with his pasta. Without the food to occupy him, he felt more exposed, and he almost regretted rejecting her offer of company. Before he could grow too self-conscious, however, she was back at his side holding something behind her back.

'This might help pass the time.'

It was years since he'd seen what she handed him, but he recognised it straight away. *From Anchovies to Zucchini: An A–Z of Italian Cooking*.

'Remember it?' she asked unnecessarily.

Joe nodded. How could he forget? 'The first book she worked on,' he answered.

'The first she got paid for,' Elena corrected him.

Joe laid the cookbook on the bar and opened it, flicking through the pages reverentially, transported back. Before he knew it, he had come to a page near the end that was better thumbed than the rest. It was a double-page spread of the team involved in producing the photos that accompanied the recipes in the previous pages. His dead wife stared back at him, captured in a moment of time two decades before, smiling as she looked boldly down the camera's lens, her name photoshopped above her head and her title beneath her knees.

Sofia Da Vinale. Food stylist.

Elena leaned in to look. 'That was the summer after she'd met you.'

Joe felt something twist in his gut. He closed the book.

She met his eye. 'I know it's painful, Joe. But it's the memories that keep her alive.'

The book had been returned to wherever it was Sofia's mother kept it by the time Angelica appeared. Waiters were stripping tables, with Elena supervising as before.

'I'm hungry,' his daughter announced.

'The kitchen's closed,' Joe told her, trying to keep the annoyance out of his voice.

'I'll find you something,' Elena said, coming to put a grandmotherly arm around Angelica's shoulders.

'Mum used to make pastina for me,' Angelica suggested hopefully.

Joe could picture the dish in question. Tiny pasta stars cooked in stock and then combined with plenty of butter and cheese. It was comfort food.

Elena smiled indulgently at the request. 'I used to cook it for *her*,' she reassured her granddaughter, starting to usher her towards the kitchen.

The kitchen doors opened and Gennaro emerged for the first time since Joe had entered the restaurant, looking flushed and tired. Joe couldn't see the look Elena gave him as they passed, but he recalled the conversation he'd overheard on the landing. He started getting to his feet as Gennaro approached. 'I think I'll head up.'

'What for? Have a drink.'

Joe tried his best not to fold. 'It's been a long couple of days.'

'It'll help you sleep.'

Gennaro had found a bottle of grappa, was starting to fill two glasses.

Reluctantly, Joe sat back down. It was the first time he and his father-in-law had been left alone together and precisely the sort of moment he'd been vaguely dreading.

'Here,' the old chef said, placing one glass on the bar in front of Joe and raising the other. 'To family. And being together,' he added, sounding almost sincere. He downed the contents in one and smacked his lips appreciatively.

Joe eyed his grappa warily, caught Gennaro eyeing him with

a similar expression. He tossed the fiery liquid down, doing his best not to wince.

Gennaro grinned. He started to pour two more glasses. 'What's your plan?' he asked. 'For the summer.'

'Relax. Forget about work.'

'That's it?' The old chef didn't look impressed.

'Don't worry. I'll stay out of your way.'

Gennaro handed back the refilled glass. He was clearly considering something. 'Elena . . . she thinks I should teach you about food,' he blurted out.

Joe feigned surprise. 'And what do you think?'

A shadow passed across the old chef's face. 'I think I spend my whole life in a damned kitchen,' he growled. 'And I think you won't be happy if I boss you around.'

Joe sensed there was a 'but' coming.

'But I also think my wife . . . she's right about most things.'

'I'm not going to argue with that.'

'It may be good for you. For both of us. For Angelica maybe.'

Joe waited for an explanation.

'The best way to show someone you love them is by cooking them a meal.' Gennaro fixed him with a defiant look, daring him to nay-say it.

Joe's instinct was to do just that. The prospect of spending time in the kitchen with Sofia's father was unsettling. And he'd survived all right up to now without knowing how to cook. But the old chef's words about Angelica had struck a chord. Perhaps eating together more often might bring them closer. He was sure Sofia would have thought so. 'All right,' he was surprised to hear himself saying.

The old chef looked equally taken aback. 'Does that mean you want to do it?'

'If you can find the time, so can I.'

His father-in-law was grinning again as he raised his glass for a second toast.

And it was then, to Joe's relief, that his phone rang.

'I'll get to the point, shall I?' Dan Keely offered, after an exchange of pleasantries.

Joe was already anticipating the point of his superintendent's call. He recalled the flash of red at the cliff face. It had something to do with that, he was sure of it.

His boss launched into an overview. A junior official working a weekend shift on the duty desk at the British Embassy had recognised the name of the deceased when it was phoned in by the deputy head of mission, who'd been alerted by a senior contact with the State Police in Rome, Keely explained. The official had been to Cambridge with the dead woman's sister, apparently, and he knew enough about the family to realise the death might attract press attention and should be flagged.

'You know Anton Headley, I presume?' the superintendent asked.

Joe was forced to admit he didn't.

Shannon's father was a former assistant chief constable with the Met, Keely continued. He'd made a fortune in private security after retiring early and was now enjoying a third-age reinvention as a media personality, popping up all over the place to opine on matters relating to crime and law enforcement. He even had his own show on television, in which a crack group of retired police officers and security 'experts' tried to thwart various teams of celebrities as they attempted to break into a simulated bank vault and steal a valuable cash prize. Utter rubbish, of course, but good fun.

Joe sensed where this was going.

'I need you to babysit him,' Keely admitted. Headley was well-connected amongst the top brass and the deputy chief constable had driven to the family's home to break the news personally. Headley was expected to fly to Italy tomorrow, but the poor bloke was shell-shocked. Could Joe meet him off the plane, go with him to the mortuary, hold his hand through the formalities and offer support and a friendly face? And meanwhile make contact with the investigating officer, reassure himself, and Anton, that everything was being handled properly, was all being done by the book. They all knew what the Italians were like, Keely joked, momentarily forgetting Joe had been married to one. Too busy worrying about how they looked in their uniforms and arguing with each other to pay much attention to procedure, he imagined.

Joe recalled the female detective's stare.

'I know it's a lot to ask,' Keely concluded; but they couldn't justify sending an officer from London, and Joe was ideally placed, being Johnny-on-the-spot in Corfu.

'Capri,' Joe corrected him.

'Capri, of course,' the other man agreed. 'And what with, well . . . you know . . . you having lost someone yourself . . . someone so close to you.'

Joe winced at his words as he glanced across the now empty terrace to where Gennaro was still sitting at the bar. If the cooking lessons went pear-shaped, he thought, at least it would give him a ready-made excuse to stay out of the old chef's way.

9

Lara had been awake since 5am but that didn't fully account for the irritation she felt as she returned to the police station on Capri to be informed that an English detective was waiting on the terrace. She'd been anticipating the introduction, but later on, and at her own instigation. She wanted time to gather her thoughts, take a shower, eat the chocolate croissant she'd bought for her breakfast. But here he was, before eight on a Monday morning, no doubt expecting to be briefed, to be included, to be looked after.

Her walk through the deserted town at daybreak had not told her anything she didn't know but it had helped to clear her head. She'd lingered in the narrow lanes of the Tiberio district, craning over walls, peering through gates – so many of them decorated with moulded ceramic pine cones – and along wisteria-covered walkways to see the villas, their flat roofs and shutters giving little hint of the lives being lived within. Eventually the buildings had thinned out and given way to what passed for countryside on the tiny, overcrowded island. Emerging from a small stretch of woodland, she'd looked back and seen Capri laid out in front of her: its ancient orchards of lemon and orange; the buildings crowding the hillside like barnacles; the breakwater of the harbour at Marina Grande, with boats starting to putter in and out even at this hour; the looming mass of the mountain to the west, with its limestone walls, emerging from the sea like an overturned pumice stone in the bath. She'd thrilled to the sound of birdsong and inhaled the pure, fresh air like a drug, feeling invigorated, refreshed, just by being there.

Lara had wandered through the ruins of the Villa Jovis, trying to picture Shannon here in her exquisite dress and sandals. She'd ventured as close as she dared to the edge of the cliff, had felt her legs go weak as she peered over, then sat on a ledge a metre or so back from the precipice so she could contemplate what lay beyond. She took out the photo she'd brought with her and compared it to the view. There was no doubt this was where it had been taken. And it was easy to see how a fall *might* have happened.

She'd reached the central piazza on her way back and was emerging from a bakery with her breakfast in hand when Curti phoned again. He was short and to the point. As luck would have it, a senior Metropolitan Police detective was holidaying on the island. A Detective Chief Inspector Joseph Mottram. Curti would pass over his contact details as soon as they were available. He'd leave it to Lara to arrange a rendezvous and brief him.

And now here he was. In the flesh. Taking the initiative.

'Sorry to spoil your holiday, Joseph,' she said, emerging onto the terrace and offering him her hand in the way she knew the English liked.

'It's just Joe, Lara,' he responded, pronouncing her name correctly, as he turned away from the view across the bay to Vesuvius to grip her hand. 'And it can't be helped.'

Lara might not have recognised him if it hadn't been for the look of slight surprise that rearranged his handsome features. *You*, she thought. 'You were there. Yesterday.'

He raised his hands in a gesture of surrender. 'Pure coincidence.'

Lara must have looked sceptical because he was prompted to explain.

'I was at the beach. Saw all the toing and froing and . . . well, I recognised the signs. Thought I'd take a look. There happened to be a jet-ski handy.'

Lara considered this.

'I'm just hopelessly nosy,' he added. 'My daughter would tell you I'm a sad case.'

Lara kept a straight face, but inside she was smirking. Her cousin Giorgia said the same about her. 'How old is she?' she found herself asking.

'Seventeen. Going on thirty.'

That was Giorgia to a tee. Lara couldn't help smiling, and the ice was broken.

They sat on the terrace and drank coffee while Lara outlined the steps she'd taken. She'd rehearsed the story so well for Curti she had mental space to study him as she repeated it. Joe was well-built, with broad shoulders and a masculine neck she was inclined to envy. He was slender with it, however, and handsome in an understated way. With his curling black hair – greying at the temples – and his dark features, he could have passed for an Italian had it not been for the cool, greenish-blue eyes and the reserve so typical of his countrymen. He couldn't be more different from Nicky, Lara reflected, but still she felt the faint stirring of something she'd not felt since that particular relationship had ended. And with it came a flash of returning irritation at his presence. *He's not your type, Lara*, she was forced to remind herself.

It was hard for her to stay annoyed with Joe for long. He was polite and pleasant as she went over the details of the case, asking questions and nodding in the right places. He was particularly complimentary about her English, wanting to know where she'd picked it up and how she'd perfected it. Lara told him a shortened version of the truth, that she'd been introduced to the novels of Agatha Christie by her father in her teenage years to give her something to do as she kept her sick mother company. She'd been so taken with these crime novels, she admitted, in part because they were the first she'd read that featured women as detectives and murderers, not just as victims, that she'd determined to major in English at school so she could read them in the language in which they'd been written and appreciate them all the more. And decided on a career in law enforcement when the time came.

This detail seemed to tickle him, but as their conversation continued his level of engagement waned. She could tell he had stopped being fully present, that part of him had drifted off, was preoccupied with something. Whatever it was, it must weigh heavily, because the strain of carrying it was visible when he looked at her. He only seemed fully engaged once more when she mentioned the discovery of fentanyl in Shannon's suitcase.

'That stuff is lethal,' Joe observed, recalling an online training course he'd been obliged to complete following a spike in the number of deaths in London caused by illicit opioids, including street fentanyl. The drug was between fifty and eighty times more powerful than heroin, he explained to Lara, making it incredibly easy to misuse fatally. So potent was it in fact that some police officers in the United States had initially refused to handle it when making arrests. Fentanyl *was* easily absorbed through the skin, Joe insisted, but the risk of an accidental overdose through this kind of casual exposure had been disproven.

They moved on to the photo. As she laid it on the table, he leaned forward, eyes flitting from detail to detail, taking everything in. He held the selfie up to look at it more closely, and then at arm's length, tilting it this way and that to consider the angles.

'What do you think?' he asked at last.

It was definitely taken at the top of the cliff where her body was found, she told him, sticking to her script. 'I went up there this morning.'

He squinted at the photo once more.

'You don't look convinced.'

'No, no. I believe you.'

She felt her doubts about Shannon's death beginning to resurface. 'What is it?'

'Hard to say.' He thought about it. 'Was she tall?' he asked after a pause.

Lara was surprised by the question. 'I don't think so.' She attempted an estimate in her head. 'Maybe a hundred and seventy centimetres?'

'What's that in old money?' he asked. 'Five-six? Five-seven?'

Lara shrugged. She didn't have a clue.

'Long arms then?'

'Not particularly.'

He turned the photo round to show her. 'Doesn't the head look small to you?'

Lara took it back from him. *Damn it.* He was right. The proportions of the photo seemed wrong. Shannon's face *did* seem smaller than she'd expect it to look in a selfie, not outlandishly so, but enough to make it difficult to disregard now he'd pointed it out. Why hadn't she noticed? 'Maybe,' she conceded cautiously, not wanting to get too far ahead of herself. 'What are you thinking?'

'It's probably nothing,' he answered, seeming to withdraw to the place he'd previously been. Wherever that was.

Lara was showing Joe off the premises when his phone vibrated.

'What's the quickest way to get to the airport?' he asked, looking up from the screen. Shannon's father was arriving on a BA flight from London that landed just before 2pm, a text had informed him, and he was expected to meet him off the plane.

She was about to suggest she look up the ferry times for him, but she stopped herself. 'I've got a boat arriving at eleven to take me to Naples,' she offered grudgingly. 'You can come with me... take it from there.'

Joe consulted his watch. 'Does that give me enough time to return home and still make it to the harbour?'

'Where are you staying?'

'A little place on the coast.'

'A hotel?'

'It's a restaurant actually.'

'Which one?'

'Da Vinale's. Do you know it?'

That name *again*. 'I've eaten there,' she replied neutrally. 'They have rooms?'

'I'm staying with my in-laws.'

So, you're married, Lara thought. 'She may have eaten there,' she told him.

His handsome features crinkled with bemusement. 'Who?'

'The dead woman.'

She could almost see his thoughts whirring.

'When was this?'

'The night before she fell.'

He did a quick calculation of timelines. 'Friday evening?'

'She booked a taxi from her hotel to Da Vinale's. To arrive at seven-thirty.'

Joe considered this. 'Another weird coincidence?'

Lara shrugged a 'maybe'. She didn't believe in those.

10

Angelica had been lingering in the restaurant, keeping her grandmother company as she laid tables for lunch, but really she was waiting to ambush Joe on his return. She'd risen early by her standards, having come downstairs before 8am, which was almost unheard of on a non-school day at home. She was aware of the need to build bridges with her dad. Especially given what she was summoning up the courage to ask him.

The first text from Daniele had arrived the previous evening. It had developed into a flirtatious exchange, littered with gifs, memes and emojis. When she'd woken that morning, instead of turning over and going back to sleep, she'd looked at her phone and experienced a flutter of excitement as she saw the little red circle indicating a message waiting in her inbox. It was from Daniele and their conversation had begun again.

Angelica had just messaged her new friend to reassure him she'd let him know the answer to his most recent question as soon as possible, when Joe came down the steps from the street gate. She was surprised to see him dressed in a polo shirt and chinos; when her grandmother had enquired about his whereabouts, Angelica had speculated he must have gone for a run, like he did most mornings.

She felt a spasm of annoyance as he explained where he'd been, where he was going. It was the second day of their holiday and he was working. In truth, however, she was happier than she might otherwise have been. It meant her own plans had a better chance of coming to fruition. She paid scant attention to the fact someone had fallen.

Elena had already heard about the fatality and made sympathetic noises, but in truth she seemed more concerned to ensure that he didn't go off to Naples without having breakfast. She insisted he sit on the terrace while she rustled something up. Joe complied meekly enough, and Angelica retreated with her grandmother, figuring to play a part in feeding him so she could use the opportunity to state her case.

Her dad was engrossed in something on his phone – *When wasn't he?* – as she emerged a few minutes later with a cup of coffee balanced delicately on a saucer held between both hands. He didn't acknowledge her as she placed it in front of him, doing her best not to spill a drop, and she was forced to linger in the vicinity, was even contemplating clearing her throat, when he looked up, noticed she was still there.

'You're up early,' he observed, slipping his phone into his pocket.

'There's no law against it,' she replied, more spikily than intended.

'Somewhere to be?'

'I'm meeting someone.' She could see his mind working. 'That boy. From the beach,' she added, trying to sound casual. 'He's going to show me around. You know . . . all the old places. Where the stars hung out. Rita Hayworth. Audrey Hepburn.'

Her dad looked puzzled. 'I didn't know you were into all that.'

'Mum was. Remember?'

He ignored her reference. 'And how are you planning to get around?'

'I thought you might hire me a scooter,' she said, trying to sound matter-of-fact.

Joe almost choked on his coffee. 'What? No way.'

'I've got my provisional licence. That's all I need. I've checked.'

'But you don't know how to ride one.'

'Daniele says he'll teach me.'

'Is that supposed to be reassuring?'

'I'll just have to go on the back of his then,' she sighed. It was a statement not a question, but he might still have pushed back, had not Elena appeared with his breakfast. Angelica had started to beat a strategic retreat when Joe called out to her.

'Only if you wear a helmet. And promise to stay on the island.'

She could live with that. 'I promise.'

'Angelica!'

She turned back and their eyes met. '*I promise*, Dad.'

He didn't look happy about it.

But hey, I'm seventeen, she thought, heading inside before he changed his mind.

At 11am that Monday morning, about the time that Joe was stepping onto a police speedboat in the harbour at Marina Grande, Angelica could be found on the back of Daniele's black Vespa as it nosed its way along a crowded street in the heart of old Capri.

He'd first tried to take her to see the beach club at Marina Piccola, La Canzone del Mare, where Richard Burton and Elizabeth Taylor had cavorted during the filming of *Cleopatra*, and which was named after the rocks where the sirens of Greek mythology lured sailors to a watery end with their enchanting song. But the man on the gate had refused them entry, even for a look-around, had insisted they pay the €100 day rate like everyone else. The staff at the Hotel Grand were no more accommodating, despite Daniele's best efforts to charm them, and they were now on their way to the Hotel Americano, where he insisted he knew one of the concierges. If they could only force their way through the throng of summer day-trippers.

Daniele steered his scooter into a side street, but instead of navigating through the maze of narrow lanes ahead, he pulled the vehicle to the kerb, let the engine dwindle.

'This is why I hate Capri,' he said, turning to look at her.

'We might be better off walking,' she suggested, preparing to dismount.

'Let's get the ferry to the mainland,' he suggested, explaining for the first time that his mother had moved back to Naples a few years previously and that, officially at least, he still lived with her, although he spent much of his summer on the island staying with old friends and picking up casual work where he could.

Her heart sank. 'I don't think I can,' she told him, hoping he'd leave it at that.

'Why not?'

'I promised my dad we'd stay on the island,' she admitted.

If he was judging her, he didn't show it. 'He won't know we didn't,' was all he said.

You don't know my dad, Angelica thought. 'All right,' she conceded. 'Just for you.'

Daniele's grin grew broader. 'And maybe you could take this off too?' Twisting round further, he reached up to unbuckle the strap of the helmet that Angelica had insisted he provide for her, but she caught his hand as he did so. 'It's safer, I promise,' he cajoled her, meeting her eye in an effort to prove his sincerity.

'You hear better. See more. React more quickly to what's going on around you.'

Was that true? Somehow she doubted it, however much she'd like to believe him.

'And I get to look at your face,' he added gently.

Angelica felt her hand withdrawing, her objections melting away.

Daniele undid the strap and lifted the helmet from her head. '*Bellissima*,' he said, studying her face, all trace of levity gone.

Angelica felt herself flush, but it was a nice feeling. A feeling of being seen. And appreciated. For who and what she was.

With a wink, he turned and slung the helmet over one handlebar. Before Angelica had time to settle herself, he was accelerating away, and she was grabbing on for dear life.

11

Joe had been almost as glad to see the back of Angelica as she'd been to make her escape. Using much the same twisted logic as she had, he reasoned that if his daughter was happily occupied, even with someone he didn't entirely approve of, then he'd be able to go about his business feeling more or less guilt-free. And it would be easier to make discreet enquiries of Elena in her absence.

After finishing his breakfast, he found Sofia's mother in the kitchen. She and Gennaro were cuddling again, just like on the terrace the previous day, only this time there was something more tender about their embrace, a reaffirmation of bonds built through years of loving intimacy rather than a naked demonstration of the passion that still burned between them. They made no move to break apart, in spite of his arrival, and once more he felt a pang of jealousy. It was only after he'd placed his breakfast things in the sink for Aldo that they seemed to register his presence and separated; Joe saw his mother-in-law heading back into the restaurant and decided to grab his chance.

'Elena,' he called out, pushing through the swing doors to go after her.

She turned and looked at him, her face a question.

'There's a suggestion the young woman may have eaten here. On Friday night.'

'The girl who fell. *Here?*' She seemed scarcely able to process the idea.

'I'm afraid so. Is there any chance I could look at your reservations?'

'Of course,' she answered, gesturing towards the bureau that stood just inside the door to the restaurant and which served as their reception desk.

Joe half expected her to produce a ledger and to find the names scrawled in pencil, but Elena opened the compartment at the top of the desk to remove a laptop. Donning her spectacles, she tapped a few strokes on the keyboard and then turned the screen to show him a list of names and their assigned tables.

There was no mention of Shannon Headley.

'Any chance she used a credit card?' he asked, without much conviction.

Elena took a key and unlocked a drawer, producing a cash box and opening it to reveal an envelope sitting on a bed of banknotes. The envelope was unsealed, and Joe could see it was filled with receipts. 'That's about a week's worth,' she informed him, indicating he should remove it from the box.

The first receipt he turned over caught his eye. Someone called M.G. Yeats had used his Amex Card to pay a bill of almost €1,800 at just before 3pm the previous day. 'Were there a lot of them?' Joe couldn't help asking as he turned the receipt to show Elena, his curiosity aroused.

Sofia's mother examined it. 'Six, I think,' she told him, although they'd made enough noise for twice that. They'd come ashore from a yacht at anchor and ordered four of the most expensive bottles of wine on their list, she recalled. She could remember them because their purchases included a 2020 Masseto with a price tag of nearly €650, which Gennaro had insisted on stocking but Elena had almost given up hope of selling, and which their guests had left ostentatiously only two-thirds drunk when they departed.

Joe thought of the super-yacht he'd seen from the beach the previous day and the group of passengers being ferried ashore. He recalled the man in the obnoxiously loud shirt, with thinning red hair and a pale complexion, who'd been showing off to his companions. He would bet a bottle of 2020 Masseto that had been M.G. Yeats.

Elena turned away to busy herself with getting ready for lunch. Joe worked his way methodically through the contents of the envelope, but nothing else stood out, and he was about to return it, when he found what he was looking for at the bottom of the pile. A receipt for €38. Paid by a Ms S.E. Headley at 8.22pm on 4 July. Joe did a quick calculation. *Friday night.* He stared at the receipt, his mind a jumble of conflicting thoughts and emotions. He realised he'd been hoping the Italian detective had been wrong about Shannon eating at Da Vinale's. It was almost certainly irrelevant, would prove to be a tiny incidental detail in the events leading up to her death, but it was unsettling all the same. He felt his uneasiness returning, the sense he couldn't shake off that the island was not quite as idyllic as it seemed, that there were undercurrents that could wash up trouble at anyone's door. Even one as seemingly respectable as his in-laws'.

'Did you find something?'

Joe snapped out of his thoughts to find Elena looking at him. He held the receipt out to her and she came over to look.

'Doesn't seem much,' he observed. 'Compared to that other lot.'

Elena wracked her brains. 'Ah,' she exclaimed, light suddenly dawning. She turned back to the laptop and consulted the list, appeared to satisfy herself of something. 'I remember her,' she announced. 'Blonde bob. Pretty face.'

'Sounds right.'

His mother-in-law shared what she could recall. The young woman had showed up on time, but alone, for a table booked for two at 7.30pm, had ordered a glass of sparkling wine and then a bottle of Falanghina on the recommendation of her waiter, and proceeded to drink both while she waited for a companion who never appeared. 'She was definitely quite drunk by the time she left,' Elena confided in Joe.

'Was that straight after she paid the bill?' he asked.

'That's right. Eight-twenty-five,' she confirmed, checking the time on the receipt and revealing that Luca had escorted her to the taxi that turned up, although she wasn't quite sure who'd called it. The sous-chef had had a rare night off on Friday, to attend a friend's fortieth birthday party, Elena thought, but had come to Da Vinale's to retrieve something from his locker; she remembered looking at the clock as he helped the woman out onto the street, thinking he was going to be late for the party.

'So why isn't her name on your customer list?' Joe asked.

'Because it was booked by her companion who never showed up.' Elena pointed to a name on the laptop screen.

Manny.

'Do you have a number?'

No, she informed him, consulting the notes that accompanied the booking. Only an email address. But the table was reserved more than six weeks ago, she added. And it was supposed to be an anniversary dinner. 'Do you think all this might be connected to the poor girl's fall?' she asked.

Joe could only shrug. The truth was, he had no idea. But he certainly hoped not.

'Manny?'

Lara pronounced it dubiously, as if she doubted the existence of anyone of that name. They were standing quayside at the harbour as the police boat that had arrived to take them to Naples worked its way into a tight space alongside the dock; it was pretty noisy as the boat manoeuvred into position, the deep thrum of the engines mixing with the cries of the seagulls and the tour operators advertising their wares.

'If it's the same guy who booked the hotel room . . . Sanghera, I think you said . . . then it may be a shortened version of an Indian name,' Joe explained, raising his voice in compensation. 'Maybe Manish. Or Manoj.'

Lara reached into the folder she was holding. Shannon's phone was back in the evidence bag, and she donned a pair of blue latex gloves to remove it. 'I don't remember seeing a Manny in her contacts,' she told Joe, explaining that she'd disabled screen lock on the phone when she'd first gained access to it. A scroll through Shannon's contacts file confirmed it. There was no one called Manny among them.

'Mind if I take a look?' Joe asked. Lara pulled a face, and instantly he could tell what she was thinking. *This is my investigation.* 'Actually, forget I asked,' he added quickly.

'No, no. It's OK,' she said, masking her reluctance. 'Two eyes are better than one.' She reached into the pocket of her cargo pants – the same faded grey-black ones as yesterday – and removed a spare pair of latex gloves, handed them and the phone to him.

Joe gave her an appreciative nod before he started to put on the gloves.

The speedboat had now tied up and they were ushered on board before Joe had readied himself to look at the phone. The driver offered Lara his hand as she prepared to step on board, but she ignored him and jumped lightly into the vessel without assistance. Joe followed her lead with slightly less surefooted results.

While the lines were cast off and the boat manoeuvred back out, Joe flicked quickly through the contacts file on Shannon's phone. There was no Manny, just as Lara had insisted, but he was looking for another name. And there it was. He looked up to catch Lara regarding him; she was clearly wary of him, wondering what he might find, what she might have missed. 'Do you know what ICE means?' he asked, raising his voice to try and make himself heard. But it was no use. The boat had just reached open water, and the engines had sprung back into life, were running at full pitch.

'WHAT?' she shouted back.

'ICE.'

Lara shook her head and pointed to her ears. She gestured at the distant landmass they were now accelerating towards, signalling that their conversation would have to wait until they were closer to the shore.

It was only as the speedboat started to slow on their approach to the mouth of the military marina in the shadow of the Castel Nuovo, that the noise from the engines reduced sufficiently for Lara to ask Joe to repeat what he'd been saying.

'It's what we call an acronym,' he explained, retrieving the discarded latex gloves and putting them back on before picking up the phone. 'In Case of Emergency.' He opened the contacts file on Shannon's phone to show her. There it was. ICE.

She looked doubtful. 'What makes you think it's the person who booked the table?'

'My mother-in-law said it was reserved for an anniversary dinner. Which suggests a significant other. You know, like a husband, maybe?'

'I wouldn't know.'

So, you're not married, Joe thought. 'Well then, boyfriend. Or girlfriend,' he added hurriedly. 'Partner. Whatever.'

She stared at him.

He tried again. 'The person who'd get the call if something bad happened to you. It's the name my wife used to save my contact details under on her phone.'

'OK.' She finally seemed to get it.

'And look—' Joe opened the contact and turned the phone towards Lara to show her a phone number and email address . . . mannytheman1915@gmail.com.

Lara was just reaching out to take the phone back when it rang and startled them. The screen was still facing her and her eyes widened as she saw what it contained.

'It's him,' she blurted out.

Joe turned the screen so he could see the caller ID.

ICE.

Fuck.

He gestured to her. *What should I do?*

Answer it, she mimed back. 'You're English,' she added unnecessarily, signalling urgently to the driver to cut the engine.

Joe hit the answer button and put the phone on speaker. 'Hello?'

'Who's this?' It was a masculine voice on the other end of the line. Perhaps unsurprisingly, it sounded extremely wary. Joe found himself adopting his 'policeman's voice' in response. Reasonable, reassuring, authoritative. Ever so slightly formal.

'This is Detective Chief Inspector Joe Mottram.'

'Who?'

'Joe Mottram. I'm with the Metropolitan Police. Am I speaking to Mr Sanghera?'

There was silence on the other end of the line. 'That's right,' the man replied.

'We've been trying to track you down, sir.' It wasn't strictly true, Joe reflected, but it would do as an explanation for now.

'Where's Shannon?'

Joe glanced across at Lara, who raised her eyebrows in sympathy. 'Can I ask what your relationship is to Ms Headley, Mr Sanghera?'

'I'm her fiancé. Why won't you tell me where she is?' For the first time, he was starting to sound more worried than hostile.

Joe took a deep breath. 'Are you sitting down, sir? I'm afraid I've got bad news.'

It wasn't Sofia that Joe was thinking of as the mortuary assistant pulled down the zip of the body bag to reveal Shannon's face. It was his mother, Agnes. Something about the dead woman's profile reminded him of the photo he kept of her in his wallet, and he almost took it out but stopped himself. Instead, he mentally mapped Shannon's features against the image he knew so well, deciding at last that it was the severity of the fringe that had caused him to make the association.

Only a minute or so after ending his call with Manny Sanghera, Joe had received a text informing him that the plane he was supposed to be meeting would now be landing two hours late. Lara had suggested he tag along with her instead of killing time at the airport, and she would take him on afterwards to pick up Anton Headley.

As the mortuary assistant withdrew, Joe forced himself to

home in on the woman lying on the gurney. He felt his antenna rising, his inner detective reporting for duty, and it was all he could do to stop himself from pulling the zip down further to reveal more of the corpse inside. Thankfully, Lara was quick to oblige.

'Shall we test your theory?' she asked, exposing the body to the navel.

'What theory is that?'

'About her head. In the photo.'

Joe gestured non-committally. 'It was more of an observation really.'

But Lara was already working Shannon's right arm out of the body bag. She held it up by the hand, holding her own phone in her other hand so she could approximate the act of the dead woman taking a selfie. She caught Joe looking askance, and shrugged an apology, but she showed him the resulting photo nevertheless, alongside the last selfie Shannon had taken. There was no denying it, Joe thought. Shannon's head was smaller in the photo taken at Tiberius's Leap. Noticeably so. He exchanged a look with Lara, who was clearly thinking along the same lines.

'Maybe she used one of those selfie-sticks,' he suggested.

'We didn't find one at the scene.'

'It might have fallen into the sea, I suppose.'

Lara looked sceptical.

'Maybe it's just the angle it was taken from.'

'Maybe.'

They were interrupted by the arrival of the pathologist. Dr Serafina was surprisingly austere-looking, Joe observed, with grey hair swept back into the tightest of ponytails and her eyes framed by a severe pair of dark-rimmed spectacles; if it hadn't been for her white coat, which she wore over a slim-cut charcoal trouser suit, she could have passed for a mid-ranking executive in a Swiss bank. She set about giving her report in both Italian and a clipped and formal English for Joe's benefit, with what felt like an appropriate air of dispassionate efficiency.

As her words washed over him – *immediate death, massive craniocerebral trauma, fractures of the facial bones, the larynx, sternum, ribs, all four extremities, rupture of the left lung, blood in the trachea and the abdominal cavity* – Joe let his eyes roam over what remained of Shannon Headley. She was not a pretty sight. Aside from the obvious and traumatic wounds, what he could see of her body was a mass of what Dr Serafina might have labelled lacerations and contusions. Beneath the visible marks, large patches of her skin had taken on a pinkish tinge, which was odd, Joe couldn't help musing, seeing as it was usually a sign of the presence of blood, only her blood must surely now have settled in the lowest parts of her body due to the effects of gravity. He leaned in to look at the nearest patch of pink on Shannon's right upper arm, which had an outline vaguely reminiscent of Australia. The skin was raised. It looked like hives.

'Can I help you?' Dr Serafina enquired, breaking off her narrative.

'These patches of pink, Doctor. What are they?'

'We think they're unrelated.'

Everything is related, Joe thought. 'Is it a rash?' he asked.

'Some form of vasculitis, yes. Most likely.'

'An allergic reaction?' Joe persisted.

'Possibly.'

'To something she experienced before she died?'

'It would have to be pre-mortem, not post,' Dr Serafina deadpanned.

'Looks like a bad one,' Joe observed, pointing out further

patches on parts of Shannon's torso, abdomen and upper limbs. 'She had it everywhere.'

'Can we find out what caused it?' Lara asked.

Dr Serafina made no attempt to hide her displeasure. 'She didn't die of a rash.'

'All the same.' It was Lara who was now persisting.

'Is this a priority?'

'With respect, I'll decide what is and what isn't,' Lara deadpanned back.

Joe felt the urge to explain his thinking. 'It might tell us what she was exposed to in the hours before her death.'

The pathologist pursed her lips. 'We've asked to see her medical records. There may be some indication of allergies there.'

What had prompted her to ask for the medical records? Joe wanted to know.

'There's evidence of previous trauma,' Dr Serafina explained. She eased Shannon's left arm out of the body bag. A livid scar of obvious vintage ran down her forearm from above her wrist to the eye of her elbow, but it was her left hand that made Joe wince. The whole of her index finger was missing, as was the tip of her middle finger from just below where the nail would have been.

'You think it's a factor? In her fall?' Lara asked.

'It's a possibility,' the doctor acknowledged, unzipping the body bag to its fullest extent to reveal some similarly raw-looking and extensive scarring down the outside of her left thigh and in the vicinity of her knee.

'And you think her medical history may help us decide that?'

Dr Serafina allowed herself a small smile. 'I wouldn't have requested it if I didn't.'

*

They'd just left the mortuary and were making their way back to the waiting car when Joe asked to see Shannon's phone again. This time, Lara handed it over without hesitation; she'd obviously decided that as long as he was assigned to accompany her, he was welcome to make an active contribution to the investigation.

Settling into the back seat, Joe lost himself in silent contemplation of the last known image of the dead woman. He could almost feel the cogs of his brain grinding as he grappled to deconstruct what was bothering him, but try as he might, the answer remained frustratingly out of reach.

When he looked up, the car had made its way onto the seafront, was pulling up at a set of lights. The eyesore of the city's docks stretched ahead of him as far as the eye could see, a hotchpotch of cranes and containers, of passenger ferries and cargo ships, of elegant old buildings and functional new ones. Lara sat in the passenger seat, talking to the driver in a voice too low to decipher, even had Joe been able to speak Italian. He looked around, trying to calculate where they were against his mental map of the city.

It was then that he saw them.

A number of scooters had massed to his left, jockeying for position as they waited for the lights to change. To the rear of the pack, a young woman was riding pillion behind a helmetless youth, who was revving his machine as he joked with the rider on the far side of him. Something about his passenger reminded Joe of Angelica – was it the hue or length of her hair, or the tilt of her chin? – but her head was half turned away towards the sea and he might not have recognised her had the lights not changed. Engines came to life as the scooters at the front started to pull away, and the rider he was watching turned to look straight ahead, allowing Joe to register his features. It was the youth from the beach and, as his passenger also turned in the direction of travel, Joe realised with a start that it was indeed his daughter with her arms wrapped round his waist.

'Hey!' he shouted, banging on the window, but his cry was lost in the crescendo of engines all around him, and it was only Lara who turned to look at him, a question on her face. The youth and Angelica sped away through the surging traffic, happily oblivious.

12

As she watched Joe disappear into the surging tide of humanity at the airport, Lara felt relieved. From the few short hours of their acquaintance, it was obvious she could learn from him; his powers of observation were more intuitive, his angles of enquiry more creative, than anything she'd encountered amongst her colleagues. But there was also an intensity about him that was unsettling, a keenness of intellect she could detect ticking away in the background whenever she talked to him, making micro-assessments and adjustments, recalibrating. And then, of course, there was the lingering suggestion of attraction, which was as unnerving as it was unexpected. The effect of it all was to leave her feeling annoyed that she was having to deal with him.

She was still nursing this faint sense of irritation when her car reached its destination. She thanked her driver and got out, looking up to see the severe, fascist-era façade of the State Police building – La Questura di Napoli – looming over her, as forbidding and intimidating as always.

Gianni was waiting by her desk as she made her way into the office on the fifth floor. He'd texted to warn her that Manny Sanghera had turned up and was demanding to be shown Shannon's body, to speak to the investigating officer.

'Where is he?' she asked, as she made her way to her desk, which was towards the centre of the large and noisy floor, reflecting her status as one of the more junior inspectors assigned to the Central Criminal Directorate in Naples. And one of only five female officers, maybe more to the point.

Gianni pointed towards a glass-walled cubicle.

When she entered Meeting Room 2 with Gianni in tow, Manny was showing signs of a growing agitation. No sooner had she introduced herself and asked him to tell them what he knew of Shannon's actions and movements in the hours leading up to her death, than tears started to leak from his eyes and he continued to cry, on and off, both noiselessly and noisily, throughout his testimony.

They'd come to the Amalfi Coast for a holiday ahead of their wedding, Manny explained, which had been scheduled for the second week in September. Shannon had been feeling stressed, not only with the arrangements, but also because of an impending deal at work that involved a large amount of preparation and paperwork and a significant degree of legal and financial jeopardy. Manny had wanted to visit Positano since watching *Ripley* on Netflix the previous year, while Shannon was more drawn to Capri. They'd agreed to split their time between the two, four days in each location.

'Except she went to Capri alone,' Lara interjected. 'What happened?'

'We had a row.'

'When was this?'

'After breakfast. On our last morning in Positano.' They'd begun to argue, Manny admitted, pretty catastrophically. 'I stormed off,' he continued. 'Spent the morning skulking around the town, avoiding going back to the hotel.' When he finally did, a few minutes before their check-out time, he discovered that Shannon had departed without him, had booked a taxi through the concierge to take her to meet the boat they'd hired to take them to Capri.

'Why didn't you go after her?'

'I've been asking myself the same question,' Manny replied, his voice cracking with emotion. He was always the first to apologise when they were arguing, to initiate a rapprochement if it was necessary. 'I let my anger get the better of my judgement. That's something I'm going to have to live with for the rest of my life.'

Lara paused to allow a further round of sniffling and dabbing before she asked her next question. 'Do you mind telling me what caused the argument?'

Manny squirmed. 'The wedding. What else?'

'Could you be more specific?' she persisted.

'I'd rather not say.'

Gianni huffed and stirred beside her, had clearly had enough of pussy-footing around Manny's sensibilities. 'What was her state of mind when you last saw her?' he asked. 'Was she upset by the argument? Suicidal, maybe?'

Lara shot her deputy a dirty look.

Manny seemed taken aback by his implication. 'We'd argued just as badly in the past . . . but we always kissed and made up.'

'You said she was stressed,' Lara reminded him. 'The deal she was doing at work.'

'Which had just made her a millionaire,' Manny responded with a disbelieving shake of the head. 'Many times over.'

'Sounds like she had everything to live for.'

'You could say that,' Manny conceded. Shannon had spent a decade launching and building her dating app, he explained, before sealing the deal to sell it.

'A dating app?'

Shannon's fiancé took out his phone to show Lara his home screen.

Girl Cupid. That name again. 'You have that on your phone?' Lara found herself asking. 'Even though you're engaged?'

'Why not?' Manny snapped back, showing an edge for the first time. 'Shannon did.'

While Gianni called the mortuary to arrange for Manny to visit, Lara returned to her desk. Someone had been busy in her absence and a cardboard file of clippings relating to Shannon Headley had been left. It contained news reports about the impending transaction for Girl Cupid and a number of reviews of the app in magazines devoted to tech and women's interests, with the latter tending to lionise Shannon as a female entrepreneur with a unique understanding of what women were looking for when it came to sex and dating. Lara scanned the clips half-heartedly, reading about the apps' advanced GPS capabilities and the sophistication of its algorithm, but not really understanding what made it worth the money spent to acquire it. Towards the bottom of the pile she found an item that piqued her interest a little more. A lawsuit had been served in connection to the upcoming sale, launched by an Irish tech investor who was described as a university friend of Shannon's and an early partner in her business. He'd sold his shares to her when the app seemed on the verge of going under, but was now claiming to have been misled about its performance while he'd been distracted by dealing with a personal tragedy, and was demanding millions in compensation. The legal story was a sidebar in a business profile of Shannon, complete with airbrushed photo. Under the headline 'The Dating Dame', it described her as 'the founder of the latest dating app to have investors all hot and bothered'.

'"Shannon credits her success to her high sex drive,"' Lara murmured, reading from a pull-out quote that went on to explain that Shannon had been an avid user of dating apps throughout adulthood, meaning she knew 'what buttons to press'.

A thought struck Lara, and she reached into the pocket of her jacket and took out the evidence bag containing Shannon's phone. Donning gloves, she removed the phone and summoned up the home screen. There it was, the Girl Cupid app. Just as Manny said it would be. She remembered now seeing it the previous day. Instinctively, Lara reached forward with her right index finger to press on it, but there was no response. Removing her glove, she risked pressing the screen with the now unprotected tip of her finger, and this time the app responded, opening on a landing page that asked her to sign in using her passcode.

Lara sighed and put the phone down. If Shannon had remained an 'avid user' of her own dating app, it might not be straightforward to prove it.

By 5pm on that Monday, Lara's thoughts were turning towards home. It was thirty-four hours since she'd left her apartment for the early shift yesterday morning, but it felt an awful lot longer, so much had happened. Just one more duty to perform, she told herself, and then she would call it a day, would forgo her customary evening gym session in favour of a long hot shower and an hour or two on the sofa in front of that new Netflix show that Giorgia was endlessly going on about.

As she made her way down the stairs to meet Joe and Anton Headley and sign them in, she was already calculating how quickly she could cut short their meeting. If Shannon's father was planning to travel on with Joe to Capri that evening, as Curti had advised her, then she'd recommend they catch the 5.45pm ferry and postpone a proper debrief until the following morning, when she hoped to be feeling refreshed. Traffic permitting, she could be home by seven and enjoy a few hours to herself, before the whole crazy merry-go-round started again.

Joe had clearly been watching out for her arrival for, no sooner had she emerged from the doorway that led to the stairs, than he rose from the bench where he was waiting. The man sitting beside him took this as his cue and got to his feet as well. *You poor unfortunate soul,* Lara found herself thinking as she advanced across the polished floor of the foyer towards them, taking in Anton Headley's high forehead and patrician bearing, the expensive cut of his clothes and the sheen of his well-polished shoes, but also the faint aura of crumpled dissolution that now pervaded his presence – the shadow of stubble, the bags under his eyes, the stain on the belly of his shirt, the half-buttoned fly. As she went to offer him her hand, he failed to grasp hers in return and she saw that his attention had been diverted. She turned to follow his gaze across the foyer to the lifts, which had just opened. She was surprised to see Gianni walking Manny Sanghera towards the front door. *You're supposed to have left already*, she thought, only half-registering the move that Shannon's father was now making in their direction.

'YOU!' Anton bellowed, unable to contain himself.

All heads turned, including Gianni's, and a split second later, Manny himself. He was only just in time to defend himself as Anton lunged wildly in his direction, aiming a crude punch at his head but slipping and losing his footing on the marble as his intended target ducked out of the way. Anton's momentum sent him hurtling towards the floor, but he somehow managed to catch hold of Manny as he fell, and brought him crashing down on top of him. They rolled over, grappling and slapping and kicking.

With Joe's assistance, Lara managed to prise them apart and Gianni helped the younger man scramble to his feet. Bearing down on Anton with every last gram of her 57kg, Lara rolled him onto his front and levered his arms behind his back, manoeuvring him into position to handcuff him. She'd just reached for the cuffs on her belt loop, when Joe reached out a hand to stop her with a look that told her it would probably be better if she didn't. 'Then help me, please,' she responded, indicating he should take one of Anton's arms, while she kept hold of the other. Between them they hauled him to his feet and forced him face-first against the nearest wall, with Joe now lending his greater bulk to the task of subduing their prisoner, allowing Lara to release her grip. 'Stop this, Signor Headley! Or I'll be forced to arrest you,' she told him through gritted teeth, as their captive bucked and squirmed, trying to free himself.

'It's him you should be fucking arresting!' Anton snarled. His face was growing puce, and Lara briefly contemplated the possibility that he might suffer a stroke.

'That's enough!' Grasping the back of his suit, Joe heaved Anton off the wall and began to march him forcibly in the direction of the door. 'Outside! *Now!*'

'You're a madman,' Manny shouted after them.

Anton twisted to deliver a parting shot. 'And you've got blood on your hands!'

A further hour passed before Lara finally emerged into the evening heat and picked her way carefully through the crawling lanes of rush-hour traffic towards the sunny piazza where Joe and Anton were sitting on the steps of the central Post Office. All her thoughts of going home at anything resembling a normal time had long since evaporated in the face of Manny's anger and intransigence, with Shannon's fiancé insisting they charge Anton with common assault, as well as provide witness statements to support a prospective claim for slander. Lara had finally lost patience, had been forced to remind him, a little brusquely, that the woman he'd been intending to marry had fallen to her death, and Lara was better employed investigating her tragic passing than wasting time pursuing complaints against her grief-stricken father. Manny had grown sullen and uncooperative and Lara had taken a perverse pleasure in informing him they would need him to surrender his passport, at least until his movements and whereabouts over the previous days could be looked into and verified.

'You're lucky,' she said to Anton as she came to stand at the bottom of the steps. 'I think I've persuaded him not to press charges.'

'Am I supposed to be grateful?' Anton asked softly, his voice less angry now.

'He would be within his rights.'

'Then . . . thank you, I guess.'

Lara looked to Joe, trying to get a read on how best to proceed.

'Mr Headley's been telling me the background to all of this,' Joe offered neutrally.

'Do you mind sharing it with me?'

Anton sighed. He looked to Joe, who encouraged him with a gesture of his head.

'I was just telling Joe . . . I liked the guy well enough at first,' Anton ventured. He paused to wet his lips with a swig of water from a bottle. 'At least compared to some of the others.'

So it was 'Joe' now, Lara noted. 'The others?' she prompted him.

'Her other boyfriends. There have been hundreds over the years.' Anton must have seen the look Lara gave Joe because he corrected himself. 'Not hundreds, obviously, but . . . *enough*, you know. They only ever seemed to last a month or two. You just had time to learn their name. Then on to the next one.'

Shannon's father began to digress about the insecurity that had characterised his daughter's dealings in her private life compared to the confidence that had powered her rise in business. Perhaps he himself was partly to blame, he conceded, having forged a successful path in life but having left his wife during Shannon's teenage years and started again with a younger woman. He was clearly in a self-reflective mood and eager to talk but, for once, Lara couldn't find the patience to listen. She would feel more receptive to Anton Headley's *mea culpa* after a change of clothes, she told herself.

'But Manny was different?' she interjected as Anton drew breath, steering him back towards the subject in hand. 'To her usual type?'

'Well, he had a *job*, of sorts.' Anton managed a half-smile. Shannon's new man had made a reasonable impression at first, he admitted. He was polite, personable, respectful, eager to please. 'You could tell he came from a good home, if you know what I mean,' he added. 'That his parents had instilled proper *values*. Like these Asians do.'

Lara exchanged another look with Joe.

'Or at least I thought they had,' Anton continued, oblivious to how his use of that word – *Asians* – might be being interpreted.

It was Joe's turn to nudge him. 'What made you change your mind?'

'I caught him with another woman,' Anton answered bluntly.

Lara sat down, all thoughts of her sofa rapidly receding. 'Where was this?'

'In Bangalore.' He muttered the name bitterly, as if the

city itself were somehow to blame for the misfortune that had befallen his child. Manny was a middle-ranking IT manager at Shannon's company until they caught each other's eye at the work summer outing and sensibly decided not to mix business with pleasure. His work meant Manny was a regular visitor to the country of his grandparents' birth and he'd even helped Anton source a new software supplier from the city for one of his security firms. Which was ironic, considering Anton would never have been in India on a business trip otherwise, and wouldn't have encountered his prospective son-in-law dining in a restaurant with a dark-haired beauty.

'You're sure there wasn't an innocent explanation?' Joe asked him.

Lara was pursuing a similar line of thought. 'A business dinner perhaps?'

'I followed them back to his hotel room.'

Lara was about to ask Anton if he'd told Shannon, but Joe beat her to it.

'Of course I bloody told her.'

'What did she say?'

'She told me I didn't understand modern relationships.' Shannon's father suddenly seemed more pensive, gloomier.

'And you left it there?' Lara couldn't help asking.

No, he hadn't, Anton maintained, although in practice there was little he could do to try and influence her. His daughter was an adult woman of independent means, and he'd forfeited his right to intervene in matters of the heart the moment he'd initiated a messy and painful divorce from her mother. Shannon did, however, still look to him for advice when it came to business and financial matters, and he'd advised her to get Manny to sign a prenuptial agreement if she were determined to go ahead and marry him.

'And did she?' Joe enquired.

'She floated the idea with him. A year or so ago.'

'But didn't go through with it?'

'Not until the Americans came calling. With the offer for her business.'

'You mean the dating app? Girl Cupid.'

'That's right,' Anton confirmed. 'Silly name but serious money. Her earnout could be worth as much as twenty million.'

Lara let out an involuntary whistle.

'I know she had an agreement drawn up, because she used the lawyer I recommended,' Anton continued. 'She told me she was going to confront him with it on this holiday of theirs. And call the wedding off if he refused to sign it.'

If Joe hadn't been with her and Anton outside La Questura, Lara would have waited until the following morning to go through the documents she'd found in Shannon's hotel room and look for a copy of the prenup. From the moment she'd exchanged a look with him, however, on being told by Anton about Shannon's plans to confront Manny, she'd sensed him probing her for information she was withholding. As they'd made their way back across the street to make arrangements for his and Anton's transfer to Capri, she'd made a clean breast of it, and now here they were at her desk sifting through the envelope's contents while the sky darkened outside and the office emptied around her.

'It's not here,' she declared, reaching the bottom of the pile she'd assigned to herself and tossing it aside. She wiped a weary hand across her face. 'You?'

Joe shook his head, but he continued to leaf through his share of the documents.

'I don't see how it helps anyway,' Lara declared. 'Even if we could find it.'

'It might suggest a motive.'

'Except it makes no sense for him to have killed her to avoid signing it,' she parried. 'If they're not married, and Anton's right about Shannon having no will, then presumably he doesn't stand to inherit anything.'

'I wouldn't be so sure,' Joe said, extracting a piece of paper from his pile.

Lara took the document he was holding out and scanned it. It was the medical questionnaire she'd first glimpsed when examining the envelope in Shannon's hotel room.

'Where it says personal details. About halfway down. Box 3A, I think.'

As she followed his instructions, the relevant words leapt from the page.

NEXT OF KIN: MR M.A. SANGHERA.

13

As Joe pushed open the street gate a little after 11.30pm and descended to the terrace, Da Vinale's was shrouded in darkness. Elena had prepared him for this possibility when he and Angelica had first arrived; if he could remember which of the many flowerpots his mother-in-law had left the spare key under, then all would be well. As Joe cast about, however, trying to identify shapes in the shadows, a glimmer of something caught his eye and he realised that a candle was burning somewhere in the interior of the restaurant. He fumbled for the handle of the folding door and was relieved to feel it turn. Closing the door softly behind him and padding inside, he expected to find Elena waiting up for him, and was somewhat surprised to find Gennaro sitting at a table in the far corner, nursing his customary glass of grappa.

'I'm so sorry,' Joe began, as the other man registered his presence.

His father-in-law considered him. 'You missed the last ferry home?'

'There was one at nine. But we were waiting in the wrong place.'

The old chef gave a huff of amusement. 'A water taxi then?'

'It was that or a hotel.'

'Expensive business,' Gennaro observed.

'I should be able to claim it back,' Joe suggested, without much conviction.

Gennaro looked at his watch, calculating. An hour or two was unaccounted for.

'The woman's father . . . I had to get him settled at his hotel,' Joe explained, assuming that if Gennaro knew he'd been to Naples then Elena must have briefed him on the purpose of his trip. 'It took a lot longer than I expected.'

'He wanted to talk, I suppose. I know I would.'

The thought of Anton and his grief for his dead daughter reminded Joe of his own. 'Is Angelica back?'

'She came in at six. Just before the dinner service.'

Joe met Gennaro's eye. The unmentioned subject of another daughter – Sofia – seemed to hover as always between them.

'You want a drink?' the old chef asked.

'I'd better not.'

The Italian scrutinised his English son-in-law, as if trying to understand what exactly was wrong with him, but to Joe's relief he did not attempt to pour from the bottle that was standing on the table. 'What about some food then?' he suggested instead.

'I'm not hungry.'

'Have you eaten?'

As if on cue, Joe's stomach rumbled in protest, as the truth of just how empty it was hit home. 'Earlier,' he said. It was not exactly a lie.

'You can't go to bed on an empty stomach,' the old chef opined gruffly, getting up stiffly from his chair and starting to make his way in the direction of the kitchen.

Joe made one last effort to dissuade him. 'Really, Gennaro. I'm OK.'

His father-in-law waved a dismissive hand. 'It'll take five minutes.'

Sighing, and cursing his treacherous stomach, Joe had no option but to follow.

For all his talk of five minutes, Gennaro appeared in no great hurry to put food on the table. He spent at least that long knotting the strings of his apron and tying up his hair before disappearing into the storeroom, from where he could be heard muttering to himself. While he waited, Joe went over the salient points of his conversation with Anton Headley in the bar of the Hotel Americano that evening, trying to fix them in his brain.

Just as Gennaro supposed, Anton had wanted to talk. He'd insisted on buying Joe a glass of vermouth, despite the lateness of their arrival, had even guilted him into accepting a second, so great was his desperation not to be left alone. There had been reminiscences about Shannon as a child, which Joe was happy to indulge, until Anton's purpose in paying such fulsome tribute to her strength of character became clear.

'She'd never kill herself,' he said, leaning forward to confide in a low voice as a waiter carried away their empties.

Joe took a sip of his drink, waited for him to say more. His instincts were already telling him the death was no suicide . . . why not overdose quietly on the pills to hand in her room rather than put herself through the terror, pain and sheer inconvenience involved in jumping off a remote cliff? And then there were his doubts about the 'selfie'. But he didn't want to say anything at this late hour that might set Anton off again.

'I mean, she'd had her troubles, poor love,' Anton continued. 'But if you're strong to start with . . . well, then adversity . . . it only makes you stronger, right?'

Joe shrugged non-committally. He wouldn't swear to it.

'Of course, she was seeing someone about it,' Anton said. 'But for her it was more of a life-coach, counselling type of thing. For the benefit of her business, you know.'

'She was talking to a shrink?'

'Now and again.'

'How long had that been going on?'

It was Anton's turn to shrug. 'Years, I think. On and off. But then they're all at it, aren't they? Young people. Worrying about their mental health.'

'Was there anything in particular she was concerned about?' Joe asked, trying to make it sound more like a friendly enquiry than an interrogation.

Anton eyed him, suddenly wary, trying to decide what to share, and for a moment Joe thought he was going to clam up. But then the emotion, or perhaps the alcohol, got the better of him and it all came pouring out.

'She had an accident. Nearly died,' he confided, and explained how his daughter had been involved in a horrific smash on the way back from an interstate football game while at university in North Carolina in her early twenties. 'Two of the kids she was with . . . they didn't make it.' Shannon had been gravely injured. 'Broke forty bones in her body . . . almost lost a leg.' She'd suffered nerve damage down her left side that had required months of rehabilitation and had still been causing her problems, with ongoing physiotherapy and regular massages required to ease her pain and maintain her mobility, all these years later. Unsurprisingly, Shannon had become a nervous passenger. 'She didn't want to come on holiday over here,' Anton couldn't help observing. 'She knew they drive like bloody maniacs. But that little *so-and-so* . . . he insisted. Said he'd never been to Italy. Guilted her into coming.'

'I saw her scars,' Joe observed, as gently as he could.

Anton winced. 'Hard to miss.'

'Is that why she was taking fentanyl?'

'You know about that?'

'We found some among her things. Quite a lot of it, in fact.'

Shannon's father looked shaken. 'She was always careful with it.'

'I'm sure she was.'

Anton leaned forward and gripped Joe's knee with his hand, fixing him with a stare. 'She's not that type. I *swear*.'

Joe could still sense the vestiges of his grip and picture the intensity of his stare as Gennaro reappeared from the storeroom with an armful of ingredients and tumbled them haphazardly onto a work surface next to the hob. Joe took a quick inventory. '*Uova in purgatorio*?' he guessed, to the old chef's surprise.

'You know it?'

'It was the first thing Sofia ever cooked for me.'

In fact, for the first few weeks of their relationship, *uova in purgatorio* – or 'hell's eggs' as Joe was prone to call it – was the only dish Sofia cooked for him. He was working nights while studying for the exam he would need to pass to leave his uniform behind and become a detective constable, and she'd recently started a new job on the picture desk of a women's magazine. After spending most of that New Year weekend in each other's arms, it was another week before they could both make time for a second meeting and almost as long again before Joe woke in Sofia's flat once more. Sofia had made the dish again that morning and, after that, it became a ritual of their weekends together; Joe would make a joke of asking for it and Sofia would play along.

Food was not essential to their courtship in those early days. They spent most of their precious time together in Sofia's bed or out in the city, exploring or drinking in bars. Food was fuel for busy lives, an afterthought in the more delicious and nourishing process of getting to know each other. At last, however, they reached a point where the giddy round of mutual discovery began to slow and the need to surprise and impress gave way to a desire for comfort and companionship, at least on Sofia's part. The first time she'd suggested staying in so she could cook for the two of them, Joe had breezily expressed a preference for eating out. She seemed to accept this happily enough, but when she made the offer again the following Friday, and he attempted to divert her towards a takeaway, she was quick to put her foot down.

'Why don't you want me to cook for you?' she asked.

'You *do* cook for me.'

'I can make more than eggs, Joe.'

'I don't want to put you to any trouble.'

'That's bullshit. It's like you don't want to let me care for you properly.'

Lying awake in her bed in the small hours, long after this first rupture had been smoothed over, Joe reflected on her words. She was right, of course. He felt comfortable with their physical intimacy, but the thought of going beyond that, of letting her penetrate to the centre of him, was terrifying. He could tell she was capable of loving and nurturing him, but what was he capable of in return? If he allowed the blaze of their passion to die down into the warming embers of domesticity, then his lack of emotional availability would surely be laid bare. When Sofia awoke and found him sitting up beside her, contemplating the first grey filaments of dawn, Joe had confessed his fears and the whole sorry mess of Agnes's short life, and his own before meeting her, had come pouring out. Sofia had cried as she listened, in part out of sorrow for his younger self, she would later tell him, but also for the trust he'd placed in her. That afternoon, they'd shopped together in a farmers market and in the evening she'd cooked for him – homemade chicken liver pâté on crostini, rabbit stew *a la cacciatore* and a vanilla panna cotta served with syrupy, stewed nectarines. There were smoked almonds to start, red and white wines throughout, and a variety of Italian cheeses washed down with a glass of Moscato that brought the meal to a sugary, intoxicating end. It was without doubt the best food he'd ever eaten. And despite consuming so much of it, he felt lighter than he'd ever been.

The culinary floodgates had opened. There were midweek carbonaras that Sofia seemed to whip up out of nowhere when he came to her flat, starving and exhausted from a twelve-hour shift. Weekend lasagnes that took an afternoon to cook and assemble but which could be demolished in minutes at the end of the day. She liked to make him chicken Milanese, beating the breast flat with a rolling pin and coating it in flour, egg and breadcrumbs before frying it crisp and golden, serving it in a floury roll with tomatoes and red onions and a drizzle of viscous balsamic glaze. There were simpler sandwiches of prosciutto or salami paired with pecorino or Grana Padano that he took to work in a lunchbox like a schoolboy. She introduced him to the delights of fennel sausages and *bresaola*, pesto and tapenade, cannoli and *sfogliatelle*, all bought from a family-run Italian deli she'd discovered near her place of work. When he came to be weighed for his annual medical, Joe was faintly appalled to discover he'd put on a stone.

'I like you with a little more meat on you,' Sofia reassured him, slipping her arms around his waist as he stood assessing himself before her bedroom mirror.

It was necessity, not vanity, that forced him to rein in his appetites, to learn to say no again and mean it. It was one thing to allow himself to grow softer and happier in his private life, Joe reasoned, but it was not something he could contemplate in the context of his work. Having passed his exams and been accepted into CID, he was eager to prove himself, and he started volunteering for unpopular assignments and working the longest hours his rank permitted, while building his resilience in the gym. Sofia seemed to accept this pared-back version of him, his new spirit of self-denial – she had ambitions and challenges of her own, she was quick to remind him. They kept the future at arm's length, happy enough to revolve in each other's orbit. At last, however, things came to a head.

It was the night before Sofia was due to fly home for Christmas and they'd arranged to meet for dinner in the trattoria run by the owners of her favourite deli. Joe had been drinking at a departmental party and arrived late, obviously the worse for wear. To add insult to injury, he'd left the earrings he'd bought her in a bag under his desk. There were no histrionics or remonstrances. Sofia had simply informed him the time had come to choose. She was happy to support him in his work, to accommodate the more unappealing aspects of it, if she knew he was committed to her. But she wasn't prepared to let him use it as an excuse to hold back, to keep her at emotional arm's length. Joe had tried to defend himself, had resorted to the lie that he was trying to protect her and not himself, but Sofia had leaned across the table and silenced him with a kiss. She would return in a fortnight, she told him, which gave him plenty of time to make his choice.

Two weeks later, when she walked back through the arrivals gate at the airport, Joe was waiting for her. The earrings had been replaced by an engagement ring.

*

At the mention of Sofia's name, Gennaro blinked. 'Who do you think she learned it from?' he mumbled, pretending to busy himself with an inventory of the ingredients. He picked up an onion and held it out to his son-in-law. 'You think you can chop it?'

'I'll have a go.'

The old chef managed to meet his eye. 'You understand... you have to peel it first?' he teased with a slight smirk. He seemed to have recovered his equilibrium.

Gennaro removed a knife from its block and placed it on a chopping board. Joe picked up the blade and balanced the onion beside it, pausing to consider whether to slice it from top to bottom or across the middle; it was only a brief hesitation, but it was evidently a red flag for Gennaro. 'Here. Let me show you something,' he said, easing Joe aside and taking back the knife. He cut the onion in half lengthways, and nipped off the two sides of its 'nose', peeling back the brown outer layers to reveal the shiny flesh. 'Better not to cut off the end,' he advised, slicing vertical strips through the layers but keeping them attached to the root plate. Turning the onion round, he sliced horizontally across his vertical strips, leaving behind a pile of perfectly diced onion in his wake. The whole operation took less than ten seconds. 'Your turn,' he declared, handing the knife back.

Joe felt his heart sink. As he set about his ham-fisted attempt to replicate what he'd been shown, the old chef busied himself with heating oil in a pan. He peeled and sliced cloves of garlic and deseeded and chopped a red bell pepper. Joe could hear the oil beginning to sizzle as he made the last of his painstaking cuts, gripping the root of his half onion tightly to try and prevent the outer layers slipping under the knife's pressure.

'It doesn't need to be perfect.'

Joe glanced up to see Gennaro looking thoroughly amused by his efforts.

'Good work,' the old chef grunted, surveying Joe's diced onion. It was the polar opposite of his own pile: crude, irregular, flecked with flakes of skin. 'It takes practice,' Gennaro reassured him, sweeping the two piles into the pan with his hand and throwing the garlic in after them. They hit the hot oil with a satisfying sizzle and immediately started to turn translucent. Joe watched on as the edges browned, filling the kitchen with a pleasantly pungent smell. Now the chopped pepper was added to the mix and Gennaro jiggled the contents of the pan, coating everything with oil so it would cook evenly. He repeated the movement a couple of times, before turning the heat down.

'You want everything to cook through and . . . how do you say it . . . *caramelise*?' he explained, handing a spoon to Joe and indicating he should stir. 'But don't let it burn,' he added pointedly as he shook out a generous handful of what looked like chilli flakes and sprinkled them into the pan, repeating the dose with sea salt and black pepper.

As Joe did his bidding, Gennaro returned to the storeroom, emerging with a bowl of ruby-red passata and a half-full bottle of white wine. He poured the passata into the pan, letting the residue drip down, as silky and fiery-looking as molten metal.

'You put that in as well?' Joe asked, as Gennaro uncorked the wine bottle.

'Of course not,' the old chef smirked, raising it to his lips and swigging.

They stood side by side in what Joe felt to be an almost companionable silence, passing the wine and watching the sauce simmer until it began to bubble and blip.

'*Allora*. Now for the best bit,' Gennaro said. He took the

spoon from Joe and used the back of it to make four delicate but distinct indentations in the sauce, which had thickened sufficiently to hold the shape. He cracked an egg into the nearest one and then followed suit with three more, the yokes golden and unctuous, the rest slowly turning from translucent to pearlescent to brilliant white. When the eggs had stiffened, Gennaro grated Parmesan over the bubbling mess, adding a little more for good measure before transferring the pan to the grill. He let it stay there just long enough for the cheese to melt and brown before he withdrew it and set it down on the chopping board. As Joe leaned in to take a look, Gennaro broke off a chunk of bread from a loaf and handed it to him. Tearing off a second piece, he showed his son-in-law the way, using his bread to scoop a generous portion of the dish into his mouth. Joe followed his lead, leaning over the pan to reduce spillage but feeling the yolk and the sauce dripping down his chin nevertheless.

Joe chewed and swallowed, scooped again. Suddenly he was ravenous. The food was utterly delicious . . . perhaps even more so than that first time Sofia had cooked it. The tomatoes were sharp and tangy, the peppers and onions gorgeously sweet, the eggs earthy with a savoury undertone of sulphur. And the chilli suffusing the whole with a note-perfect hint of heat. He almost groaned from the pleasure of it.

'Good, no?' Gennaro enquired, smiling and breaking off more bread to dip again.

Joe could only mumble inaudibly, his cheeks too full to speak.

'Maybe we can have another lesson tomorrow.'

'Why not,' Joe heard himself say as he swallowed his mouthful. It would mean spending more time with Gennaro, but if the food tasted this good then he could bear it.

14

Having experimented with and deleted a variety of different captions, Angelica landed on the idea of using a one-word hashtag to accompany her Instagram Story.

#Capri.

After all, she reasoned to herself as she lay on her bed after a shower, the photos said it all, were suggestive enough to make her glad she had her privacy settings adjusted so that only her closest friends would see them. In the first, they were leaning together, Angelica looking straight into the lens, Daniele glancing sidelong with his cheek resting against hers. She liked the way she looked in this one . . . sleek and feline, her even white teeth peeping between parted lips, the blush of the sun on her nose and cheeks, her hair tousled, her eyes sparkling green in harmony with the sea behind. In the second, they had somehow caught themselves in the act of kissing. She could recall the feel of his hand at the base of her spine, the way his palm had traced the curve of her buttock and lingered; she felt a tingling in her groin and stretched, enjoying the sensation. But she liked the third photo best of all. It captured Daniele in an unguarded moment, after she'd confided in him about her mother's death, those painfully familiar words falling out of her mouth unplanned when he'd asked innocently after the rest of her family. He was staring out to sea, his face in profile so that it hid the slight irregularity in his features, his gaze brooding beneath the dark sweep of black hair; there was a fine angularity to the bones in his face and the jut of his Adam's apple, a sensual ripeness about his lips.

Her phone pinged with a notification, followed immediately by two more. She glanced again at her story and saw, with satisfaction, the reactions were rolling in.

Gorgeous!
Damn gurrrll!
You two are hot!!!!

She'd just responded to the first of them when a text from Daniele appeared at the top of her screen. She felt her heart skip a little, the heat rising in her cheeks.

R U free? Fancy seeing a film? His message was accompanied by a pair of eyes.

She sent him back an instant response. *On a Tuesday morning?*

His response was almost immediate. *There's a festival. In Naples.*

A link popped up in her feed and she clicked on it. Hollywood on the Tiber. A celebration of American cinema in Italy in the 1950s and 1960s.

U said ur mum liked old films.

Before Angelica could ask what film Daniele had in mind, a photo followed the link. It showed a young Audrey Hepburn holding the handlebars of a Vespa and pretending to veer comically out of control, while Gregory Peck sat behind her, his hands lightly grasping her waist, his features arranged into an expression of slight surprise. She recognised it immediately as a publicity still from *Roman Holiday*. It had been one of her mum's favourites and, in that moment, she felt herself beginning to tear up, even as she was smiling. *What time?* she managed to type back.

There's a ferry at 11.

That was an hour from now. Bringing their conversation to an abrupt close, Angelica jumped up and began to dress. In less than five minutes, she'd assembled an outfit she was halfway happy with and turned her attention to her face. She'd just applied an experimental smudge of lipstick and a trace of eyeliner, had picked up her phone to take a photo and check the effect, when the door to her bedroom opened and her dad walked in. Angelica almost dropped her phone. 'Don't you ever knock?' she barked.

Joe ignored her protest. 'Your mother couldn't abide liars,' he said, coming to stand over her. He was wearing his running kit and smelt strongly of sweat, his face red from the exertion or perhaps from the pent-up anger he was now exuding. It must have been clear to him that Angelica didn't immediately grasp what he was talking about. 'I *saw* you,' he added. 'Yesterday. After you *promised*.'

Angelica felt herself flush. 'You were spying on me!'

'I was on my way to the airport. You drove right past. You weren't wearing a helmet.'

Angelica got to her feet, the easier to stand her ground. 'Daniele says it's safer without one,' she informed him.

'Then he's an idiot.'

She felt her hackles rising. 'He's been riding since he was fifteen.'

Joe ignored her. 'I don't want you seeing him.'

'That's not up to you.'

Joe opened his mouth to respond but closed it again.

The thought of Daniele waiting for her spurred Angelica into action. Scooping up her phone and a few items of make-up, she transferred them into her bag and slung it over her shoulder.

She thought Joe might try and block her way or even physically restrain her, but he did neither. It was only once she had passed through the doorway that he reacted.

'Angelica.' He sounded unsure, even a little plaintive.

She ignored him and made her way along the corridor, hearing him leave the bedroom behind her and start to follow. As Angelica opened the front door to exit the apartment, Elena was coming the other way. She must have sensed something had occurred between them. 'What's wrong?' she asked, scanning her face for clues.

'He's being an arsehole.' Angelica didn't look back to check the effect of her words on Joe but slipped past Elena and made her escape. She could imagine her dad's look of shock and dismay, however, as she hurried on her way.

Angelica was still feeling unsettled by their encounter as she stood in the marbled foyer of a small arthouse cinema in the city's Borgo Orefici district, staring at a poster for *Roman Holiday*. He *had* been behaving like an arsehole, she told herself, but then perhaps she'd given him grounds. She knew his strictness stemmed from their mutual loss, his loving concern for her. On reflection, she couldn't help feeling guilty that she'd broken a promise to him so casually, so thoughtlessly.

'Are you thinking about your mum?' Daniele asked as he came to join her, seeing her staring at the poster and misinterpreting her troubled expression.

'Something like that,' she lied, accepting a carton of popcorn from him.

'You said she reminded you of her,' he persisted, indicating Audrey Hepburn, who was staring back at them from the poster.

Angelica considered the film star's image. There was something about her that did remind her of her mum. Not so much her looks as her mannerisms, a faint goofiness that offset her otherwise perfect beauty. It was not that Sofia had been a clown, but an outbreak of good humour was never far from the surface. She could always make Angelica smile and laugh whatever the circumstances, could defuse a moment of tension or unhappiness with a well-timed quip or a self-deprecatory comment.

God, she could do with her now.

'Maybe, just a little,' she told him.

'Is that why you like her?'

'That and the clothes.'

'Are you into fashion?'

'I used to think I wanted to work in it,' Angelica admitted, starting to make her way towards the auditorium where the film was showing.

Daniele fell in beside her. 'As a model?'

It was said so guilelessly that Angelica had to laugh. 'As a buyer. A stylist maybe.'

'But not now?'

'I don't think so.'

He held the door open for her and guided her inside, pointed her towards their seats on the second-to-last row. 'Then what else?' he asked as he helped her settle herself, holding her popcorn while she switched her phone onto silent.

It took her a moment to pick up the thread. 'I don't know,' she said. 'But definitely working for myself.'

Daniele smiled. 'Watch out, world!'

Angelica punched his upper arm playfully.

'I mean it,' he insisted. 'Just let anyone try and stop you.'

She felt herself flush. 'That's so sweet.' She leaned across to kiss him just as the lights began to dim.

It was towards the end of the afternoon that their conversation came back to her.

They were in the penultimate row once more, but this time on the passenger deck of the ferry as it ploughed across the Bay of Naples to Capri. The dingy intimacy of the cinema had been swapped for a noisy, airless cabin. Angelica was lying curled across two seats, head in Daniele's lap, enjoying the sensation of having her hair stroked, when she remembered what she'd been meaning to ask him.

'What about you?' she enquired, sitting up and looking at him.

'What about me?'

'I told you what I want to do.'

He attempted to make light of it. 'I want to sit here with you.'

Angelica couldn't help smiling. 'Do you have a job?' It was the first time in their short acquaintance it had occurred to her to ask.

'Sort of.'

'What does "sort of" mean?'

'I help a friend out at a beach club. At the weekends, mainly.'

'And what about the rest of the time?'

Daniele shrugged. 'I have other ways to make money.'

'Like what?'

'You know. Odd jobs. Seasonal stuff. This and that.'

This and that? Angelica sensed he was growing defensive, decided not to push it. 'Are you going to university?' she asked instead, changing tack.

Daniele pulled a face.

'Why not?'

'It's not for people like me.'

'Bullshit.'

He looked surprised by her vehemence. 'I can't afford it.'

'Maybe you could work more during the week. Save up. Go later.'

'Easy to say when you don't have to.'

It was said with a flash of irritation. Angelica sat up straight, putting clear water between the two of them. She stared at the passing waves, feeling her heart flutter, waiting for the moment to pass. At last she felt his hand seek out hers.

'I'm sorry. That must have sounded like I was angry with you.'

'You're right. It did.'

'I guess I'm a little . . .'

Angelica turned to look at him. 'Sensitive?'

He shrugged. 'Maybe.'

'You don't need to be,' she reassured him, but even as she said it, she wasn't entirely convinced she meant it.

15

At about the same time as the opening credits were rolling for *Roman Holiday* on that Tuesday lunchtime, Joe was staring at quite a different sort of screen as he watched a live video link of an interview that Lara was conducting in the neighbouring room.

He'd spent the morning with Anton Headley, accompanying him to the ruins of Villa Jovis, where the local sergeant was waiting to show them the spot from which Shannon was believed to have fallen. As Joe had watched Anton laying a bunch of flowers at the edge of Tiberius's Leap and confronting the cold reality of that terrifying drop, he couldn't help thinking of his row with Angelica. He imagined himself briefly in this other man's shoes, but the thought of his loss was too awful to contemplate for long.

Anton had asked to be taken to the place where Shannon's body had been found, but Joe had managed to dissuade him; he'd accompanied enough shell-shocked relatives to the sites of their loved one's passing to be confident it would not be a source of solace. Instead, he'd persuaded Anton to accompany him to the island's police station, where Lara was waiting to walk him through the investigation to date. It was only as she was summing up the forensics and explaining that they'd yet to discover evidence of third-party involvement that a hint of Anton's former belligerence returned.

'That little bastard's going to get off scot-free, is he?' he interjected.

Lara had assured him the investigation was ongoing, that she would keep an open mind to the idea of foul play and therefore, somewhat inevitably, to the possible involvement of Shannon's fiancé, particularly given their recent history. She warned Anton, however, that he should prepare himself for the likelihood that Manny Sanghera was guilty of nothing more than what he himself had called 'a catastrophic lapse in judgement'. He'd already been able to supply credit card receipts that appeared to confirm he was elsewhere throughout Shannon's time on Capri, and had willingly handed over the contact details of a third party who would vouch for him for the forty-eight hours preceding her estimated time of death. 'The most likely explanation usually turns out to be the correct one, Signor Headley,' the Italian detective concluded.

'Then you're convinced she fell?'

Lara shrugged.

Joe was unsure whether the gesture was sympathetic or non-committal. What were her instincts telling her about Shannon's death? Was she harbouring the same doubts about it being an accident as he was?

Anton looked like his bile was rising, but he kept his counsel. A short while after that he announced he needed to leave to go back to his hotel. He was due to meet a representative from the British Embassy, he explained, to discuss the arrangements for repatriating Shannon's body whenever they felt able to release her.

Joe was preparing to go with him when Lara had taken him aside.

'Actually, Joe . . . do you have a minute?'

'What is it?'

'We've got Manny coming back in for questioning in half an hour.'

Joe raised an inquisitive eyebrow.

Lara took a deep breath. 'I was thinking you might want to observe . . . you know, give us your reading on him. Let us benefit from your experience.'

Joe managed to keep a straight face. So she does have her suspicions, he thought.

And that was how he found himself sitting in the observation suite, watching an interview taking place on the other side of the wall.

Manny's body language and demeanour didn't suggest to Joe that he had much to hide. He'd waived his right to have a solicitor present and made a point of thanking Lara for her intervention the previous day, conceding that he'd been devastated by Anton's outburst, but now understood the reasons for it and was grateful she'd persuaded him not to make a formal complaint. He was quick to accept that Anton was right about the prenuptial agreement and to apologise for not being more open about the part it had played in his and Shannon's bust-up; he'd been driven by a misguided desire to protect their privacy, he explained, and anyway, he didn't really see how it was relevant to their investigation into the cause of her accident.

'Assuming it was an accident, Signor Sanghera,' Lara flashed back.

A long pause followed while they weighed each other up.

Sitting on the other side of the wall, Joe sensed Lara hadn't been meaning to imply suicide but had been positing a different theory altogether . . . the possibility of foul play. But if that was the case, she gave no indication of it. 'Can you tell me anything about the content of this prenup?' was all she said, returning to her previous line.

'Not really.'

'Shannon's father told us she'd already spoken to you about it.'

'Months ago. But only in passing.'

Joe could see Lara looking as sceptical as he was feeling.

'You didn't want to know what was in it?'

'I thought she was joking.'

'A strange thing to joke about. Leaving you without money.'

Manny shifted in his seat, said nothing.

Lara tried again. 'So, when she gave you a copy of it . . . in the middle of your holiday . . . you didn't want to read it?'

'I just saw red,' Manny responded. 'I ripped it up. Threw it in the bin.'

Lara gave this image time to settle before she asked her next question. 'Do you mind telling me where you were last Saturday? Around 4pm.'

It was expertly timed, Joe couldn't help thinking.

Manny flushed. 'I already told you. I was with a friend.'

'Ah, yes.' Lara made a show of consulting her notes. 'Laura Amendola.' She looked to Manny expectantly. 'You have friends in Positano?'

'She's more of an acquaintance.'

'Did Shannon know her?'

'No. She's a local. Someone I met.'

'Met how?'

'That's a bit . . . awkward.'

Manny was starting to sound less sure of himself.

'Try me.'

Shannon's fiancé swallowed hard. 'We hooked up through the app.'

'Girl Cupid?'

'That's right.'

'You were with another woman while your fiancée was losing her life?'

Manny at least had the decency to drop his gaze. 'I told you it was awkward.'

While Joe and Lara listened on opposite sides of the wall, incredulously in his case, stony-faced in hers, Manny proceeded to outline the nature of his and Shannon's relationship. It had been 'open' from the start. She'd insisted on it. Shannon had an unusually high libido. Often wanted to have sex multiple times a day. It was what had sparked her initial interest in dating apps.

'And what about you?' Lara interjected.

'I wasn't sure at first,' Manny replied, admitting he'd been brought up to have a more traditional attitude towards sex and relationships. He'd come to realise, however, that it was a non-negotiable for Shannon and he'd learned to be more accepting, more appreciative of some of the benefits involved.

'Such as letting you sleep with a colleague on a work trip?'

'Anton told you about that?'

Lara nodded.

Manny didn't look remotely shamefaced. If anything he allowed himself a small smirk. Shannon's father didn't get it. 'Just like my own parents, I suppose. The older generation . . . they're all so heteronormative. At the end of the day, sex is just sex.'

'And were you planning to keep it this way? After the wedding?'

His smirk disappeared. 'That was still under discussion.'

'You were discussing it? Or having an argument about it?'

Manny admitted it had been part of what they were rowing about in Positano.

'So all this is just normal to you?' Lara asked, an edge detectable in her voice for the first time. 'You and Shannon have a fight about your relationship and she goes off. But instead of following her, you go online and hook up with a complete stranger. Spend the weekend with her. And you don't think to check on your fiancée?'

It was Manny's turn to look stony-faced. 'I just assumed she'd be doing the same.'

'Having sex with someone else, you mean?'

He shrugged. 'She'd done it before. Many times.'

'And you weren't worried enough to call her? Just once? The whole time?'

He shook his head.

'Not even to let her know you wouldn't be making it to your anniversary dinner?'

For the first time since the interview had started, Manny looked close to losing his composure, as Lara outlined her theory that Shannon had turned up at Da Vinale's on the Friday evening in the hope he might be there. He had no idea she'd gone to the restaurant, he insisted, looking genuinely distraught. He was on the verge of tears as he swore he'd done nothing to encourage her. They should check his phone, he insisted. There had been no communication after their parting of the ways. He'd nothing to hide.

The heat had gone out of the interview after that. As talk turned to Manny's availability to assist the investigation in the coming days, Joe's attention began to drift, and he picked up his phone. Before he had time to consider what he was doing, he found himself checking the Find My Phone feature for Angelica's whereabouts. He located her at a cinema near the waterfront in Naples. He swiped out of the Settings menu and back to his home screen, his thumb hovering over the Instagram icon, the only social media app on which he was permitted to follow her. It was years since she'd posted anything on her main feed but the blandest pap for parental consumption, but he couldn't help checking. Sure enough, her latest post was dated a month previously.

He tossed the phone aside, feeling disgusted at himself and tuned back into the conversation in the room next door. Manny was telling Lara she was welcome to see a copy of the prenup as far as he was concerned, although his influence might be limited when it came to getting her lawyers to release it, given he was only ever intended to be a signatory and had had absolutely no involvement in drawing it up.

'She didn't email you a copy?' Lara asked, more in hope than expectation.

No, she didn't, Manny insisted, which was strange in itself now he came to think about it. 'Perhaps she wanted to give me it in person,' he mused. 'To gauge my reaction.'

'Why do you say it was strange? That she didn't email you,' Lara persisted.

'Because she normally did everything digitally. Signed everything online.'

Lara waited for him to say more.

'She had nerve damage all down her left side, broke bones, lost a finger,' Manny continued, recounting for Lara's benefit what Anton had told Joe the previous evening. 'And she was left-handed, so she had to relearn how to do everything. You know . . . eat, dress herself, clean her teeth, sign her name. Using her other hand.'

Her other hand.

Before Lara had a chance to bring the interview to an end, Joe was up and out of his seat and heading to the door. Suddenly he was sure he knew exactly what was wrong with the photo Shannon had supposedly taken of herself at Tiberius's Leap.

'I think it was taken by someone else.'

Joe was waiting for Lara by the desk that had been assigned to her in the police station in Capri as she returned from seeing Manny off the premises and dispatching a colleague to Positano in the hope of retrieving the ripped-up prenup from the bins at the hotel. He was holding out a printed copy of the selfie Shannon had taken at Tiberius's Leap shortly before she fell. Gianni must have given it to him.

She took the photo and made a show of studying it again, trying to organise her thoughts. 'You can tell that? From this?'

'Not just from this. But from what Manny said about Shannon. About having to relearn how to do pretty much everything. Using her right hand.'

Lara felt herself straining to grasp the significance that he obviously saw in this.

'Here, look again.' He took the photo back and ushered her towards the desk where he laid it down flat. She sensed his hand hovering near her shoulder as he encouraged her to lean in, and she had to fight the urge not to shrug off his phantom touch. 'What hand would you say she took it with?' he asked.

'Her right.'

'That's what I thought. Only what do you notice about her necklace?'

Lara squinted at the photo. The necklace sat just above her breastbone. It was one of the first things she'd noticed when she examined Shannon's body at the scene. It appeared to be made of white gold with Shannon's name picked out in tiny diamonds. An exquisite thing. 'Her name's back to front,' she blurted out, noticing for the first time.

'Exactly.'

'Isn't that just . . . a *trick* of the camera?'

'I don't think so.' Joe took out his phone and snapped a selfie, showed her. He pointed out the word beneath the logo on his T-shirt. It was legible. 'The camera adjusts. It shows us what we actually see, rather than a reflection of it.'

Lara stared again at the photo on the desk.

'It suggests the image has been flipped,' Joe explained. 'Horizontally.'

'Why would Shannon do that?'

'She wouldn't. But someone else might. If they'd taken the photo but wanted to make it look like Shannon had. And only realised their mistake after they'd taken it.'

The fog stubbornly refused to lift for Lara. 'What mistake?'

He sighed. 'If I'm right about the necklace . . . it means everything in the photo must have been the other way round when it was taken. You know, in real life. Which suggests, if Shannon *had* taken it, it would have to have been with her left hand. Except we both saw her left hand in the mortuary. Her index finger is missing. Plus the tip of her middle finger as well. You heard Manny . . . she'd had to relearn to do everything with her *right* hand. So there's no way she could have taken the photo with her left. Which leads us to the obvious conclusion . . . that someone else took the photo with the intention of making it look like a selfie. But realised afterwards that they should have taken it from the other side to make it look realistic. And so they rotated it one hundred and eighty degrees.'

The obvious conclusion. Was it? Lara sensed she should be feeling some of the same elation he was so obviously experiencing. After all, the idea that someone else had taken the 'selfie' would seem to support her persisting suspicions that she was dealing with a murder. In truth, however, she was still struggling to follow Joe's logic, which had left her feeling more confused than ever, less certain about what she believed had caused the death of this young woman. Suddenly she felt out of her depth. She could hear her father's voice in her head . . . *You're too soft for police work . . . stick with being a lawyer.* 'Or maybe she just put her necklace on the wrong way round,' she blurted out irritably, visited by an overwhelming urge to take this patronising Englishman down a peg or two.

Joe stiffened. He'd picked up on her tone. 'You asked for my help,' he reminded her.

'To work out whether he might be lying.'

'Well, for what it's worth . . . I don't think he was.'

'Thank you.' She tried to make herself sound grateful, not just exasperated.

Joe shrugged. As he turned away, she saw him shake his head ever so slightly.

'I'll walk you out,' she said, suddenly wanting to offer some last gesture of fellow feeling, of solidarity, before their ways parted, perhaps for good.

'No need,' he informed her, closing her down. With a faint wave of his hand, he turned on his heel and was gone.

16

As he pushed through the doors to the restaurant kitchen at a little after 4pm, Joe could tell instantly that a cooking lesson was the last thing on his father-in-law's mind. The chrome work surface in front of him was littered with invoices and receipts that had spilled from a battered box file. Gennaro was wearing the heavy bifocal glasses that usually hung unused around his neck and was squinting at a receipt he was holding, clearly bemused by it. Joe felt an overwhelming urge to retreat, but before he could do so the old chef glanced across and registered his presence, gave him a questioning look.

'You told me to come and find you for a lesson,' Joe reminded him.

'It's not a good time,' Gennaro said, gesticulating towards the mess of paper.

'Should I come back in a bit?' Joe asked tentatively.

'*Madre di Dio!* Not today!'

Joe felt himself redden. 'No need to bite my head off.'

The old chef was instantly remorseful. 'I'm sorry, Joe. But I'm drowning here.' He took off his glasses and ran a weary hand through his lank, greasy hair, looking every inch a man in desperate need of some air, as well as his customary post-service shower.

'Perhaps I could help?'

Gennaro made a noise of defeated resignation, gestured again. Help how?

'I'll leave you to it,' Joe said, considering their conversation at an end and turning away. He had just started to push the door open when the older man spoke again.

'You know . . . it took me years to come to terms with Sofia leaving.'

Joe turned back. Gennaro wasn't looking at him but was once more contemplating the chaos of paper in front of him. It was almost as if he was speaking to himself.

'And it was even more painful for me when she said she wanted to make her life in London. With you.' Only now did the old man meet his eye. 'We always talked about her coming back some day. Taking over the restaurant.'

Joe said nothing. What was there he could say?

'But now?' Gennaro picked up a handful of receipts. 'I'm happy she didn't.' He tossed them into the air like confetti, letting them fall wherever.

It was such a naked gesture of capitulation; Joe didn't quite know where to look.

He was still thinking about this conversation as he let himself into the family's apartment and closed the door with a soft click. Deep down, he'd always sensed his father-in-law's disapproval of the choice Sofia had made in favouring him over her family back in Italy. Gennaro had never voiced this sentiment explicitly, but it was obvious from his failure to come and visit them, even when Angelica had been born, although Elena had stayed for a month in their cramped flat and had been delighted to have the excuse to come back as often as possible, in the off-season, of course. Having worked in a variety of Soho restaurants throughout the 1970s he'd had enough of London to last a lifetime,

Gennaro told them bluntly when they finally brought the baby to Capri. Sofia had seemed happy enough to return home to see her parents instead, taking Angelica with her but, more often than not, leaving Joe behind; he would come out for a week in the summer, occasionally a little longer. This had been the way he'd wanted it, but now he found himself wondering if this was the way she'd secretly wanted it too. Had Sofia discussed their future with Gennaro without talking to Joe? Had she been dissatisfied with the life they'd built together, despite her reassurances that she'd no desire to return and live in Capri? This last thought unmoored him, and suddenly the notion of spending another day with his dead wife's family, let alone the rest of the summer, seemed insufferable. He felt an overwhelming urge to see Angelica, to apologise, to hug her close, to promise to do better if she'd only agree to come home immediately. He took out his phone, meaning to check on her whereabouts once more, but as he did so, he sensed he was not alone. Glancing up, he saw Elena had appeared in the doorway to the kitchen.

'She's not here,' his mother-in-law informed him, reading his thoughts.

Joe couldn't help glancing towards the door to Angelica's bedroom.

'I've checked,' Elena added.

'I suppose I'll wait for her then.'

She eyed him cautiously. 'You're not going to pick another fight, are you?'

'Not if I can help it.'

His answer seemed to satisfy her. 'Why don't you wait with me?' she suggested.

There was no polite way to express a preference for keeping his own company in his room. As he followed her into the apartment's surprisingly small kitchen, he saw that Elena had not been sitting idle. The surface of the breakfast bar was strewn with ingredients and utensils, including a food mixer of similar colour and vintage to the one he remembered his grandmother owning in his childhood.

'I'm baking a cake,' Elena explained unnecessarily.

'What's the occasion?'

'Does there need to be one?'

'I suppose not.'

She eyed him curiously. Did he even eat cake? he could sense her wondering.

'What kind of cake?' he asked, for want of anything better to say.

'See if you can tell.'

Dutifully, Joe leaned forward to look inside the bowl of the food mixer. He could smell something sweet and citrusy, but the contents were an indeterminate mess. 'Looks like wet sand,' he offered.

Elena laughed. 'It's orange zest rubbed into sugar. I'm adding butter and vanilla to it.' She proceeded to slide a quantity of softened and chopped-up butter into the mixer, followed by a generous dollop of a dark paste that she extracted from a small jar. She flicked a switch and began to mix it. 'Do you want to make yourself useful?' she asked, raising her voice to make herself heard over the grinding whirr of the machine.

'OK.'

She indicated a bag of pistachios. 'You can shell those.'

He picked the bag up and, with a little difficulty, opened it, and poured an experimental quantity of nuts into his hand. 'How many do you need?'

'All of them. It's a pistachio cake.'

With a slightly heavy heart, Joe took a seat. It was fiddly work and, initially at least, he dropped as many as he opened. Soon enough, however, he developed a better feel for the task and even felt emboldened to look up while he worked. He found his mother-in-law watching him.

She turned off the mixer. 'Have you found out what happened to this girl yet?'

'Not yet.'

'But you will.' Like her daughter before her, Elena displayed an almost childlike faith in Joe's powers of detection.

Joe was forced to tell her that was unlikely, that his involvement in the investigation was peripheral and, anyway, it could shortly be coming to an end.

'Oh no.' His mother-in-law looked crestfallen.

He tried to reassure her. 'It may well turn out to be a fall.'

Elena must have picked up on the doubt in his voice. 'You don't believe that.'

Joe had to admit he didn't. He thought about trying to explain the issue with the 'selfie' but restricted himself to telling her that elements of the death seemed staged.

'Can you prove it?'

'It's just a hunch at the moment.'

'Then you have to stay involved until you do.'

It wasn't that easy, he told her. 'It's not my jurisdiction.'

'Gennaro says the police are awful. Corrupt. Worse than that... useless.'

That wasn't his experience, Joe insisted. The female detective he'd been liaising with was impressive. Clearly very bright. And dedicated too.

Elena looked doubtful. 'Her poor father. Having to live with that terrible uncertainty.' She fixed him with a stare. 'We both know what that's like.'

It took Joe a moment to divine her meaning. 'We know what happened to Sofia, Elena,' he responded, keeping his voice neutral but feeling anything but.

'Do we?'

'She was hit by a car.'

'Yes, but we still don't know who was driving it.'

Joe couldn't hide his astonishment. 'You're saying you think it wasn't an accident?'

Elena stood her ground. 'I'm saying we don't *know*.'

'But who on earth would want to kill Sofia?'

'Gennaro and I . . . we've asked ourselves the same question.'

The silence that followed this pronouncement was deafening. Joe was so stung by her implication that the hit-and-run might have been a deliberate act, he could find no words to respond. He had never given the remotest credence to the idea – it was utter nonsense, of course – but the fact that his in-laws had considered it, not just Gennaro but Elena too, made him question all his assumptions about them. He was used to dealing with the worst of human nature, but they were restaurateurs, bringers of pleasure and joy. What had they experienced in their life together, in this seemingly idyllic place, that would guide their thinking along such sinister lines? Once again, Joe was visited by a feeling of unease, by a sense, maybe even a growing certainty, of deep, disturbing undercurrents to life on the island that were beyond his comprehension. And there was sadness too, that he'd failed in his duty to Sofia; while the identity of her killer remained unknown, there was nothing he could say to prove Elena wrong.

His mother-in-law must have guessed at these swirling, murky thoughts because she turned the food mixer on once more, preventing any further exchange between them. While Joe watched out of the corner of his eye, she broke three eggs into the bowl, then added a quantity of sieved flour, half a teaspoon of baking powder and a similar quantity of salt. Lastly, she added two scoops of something thick, white and creamy.

Joe thought he recognised this last addition and, with it, a possible way to normalise relations. 'Is that ricotta?' he asked, trying to keep his voice casual.

Elena turned the carton to show him the label. 'My secret ingredient.'

He was assailed by a memory of his dead wife doing and saying the exact same thing. 'I think Sofia used this recipe,' he told her. He busied himself with the pistachios, didn't immediately trust himself to speak further.

Elena turned the mixer off and continued mixing by hand. All Joe could hear was the scrape and clink of her spoon on the side of the bowl, the steady click of the nut shells breaking as he cracked them apart with his nail. 'It came from my Sicilian grandmother,' she said, breaking the silence at last.

Joe felt able to look up and meet her eye. 'I forget you have Italian blood.'

'My father's mother. She was Elena too.'

'Same as my nan. Eleanor. Nelly.'

A few more nuts were shelled, the cake mixture turned over a couple of times.

'Did Nelly cook?' Elena asked.

Despite himself, he couldn't help smiling. 'She loved to *feed* people.'

'She'd have had her work cut out with you.'

'You'd be surprised.'

Sofia's mother looked so doubtful he almost reached into his pocket there and then, before his customary reticence stayed his hand. He hadn't shared what he'd been about to show her with anyone but Sofia, he reminded himself. *And you wonder why they treat you like a stranger*, his inner voice chimed in. Hesitantly, he withdrew his wallet and fished inside for the photos it contained, held one out to Elena before he could change his mind. He watched her study it, face wrinkling into an instinctive smile. 'Is that you?'

Again, he heard and saw Sofia in her face and voice. 'Afraid so.'

'That's so adorable.'

He took the photo back from her and examined it in turn. It was blurred and badly framed, but the faces in it were unmistakable. His grandmother was seated on a wicker-backed chair in the garden of her home in Knaresborough. She stared back at him primly across the years, her hair perfectly set as always, her handkerchief peeping from the cuff of her cardigan, her features arranged a little self-consciously for the camera, her eyes already showing the strain of the cancer that would carry her off within eighteen months. Beside her stood his seven-year-old self, chubby arms ramrod straight, eyes mid-blink, a child's unselfconscious grin splitting his face from ear to ear. The towelling T-shirt he was wearing was at least two sizes too small and a roll of fat was visible above the waistband of his shorts. 'It's a useful reminder,' he said, as he slipped it back in his wallet.

Her eyes bored into his. 'A starving hungry little boy.'

Joe shifted uncomfortably under her scrutiny, half regretting having showed her. He indicated the pile of shelled pistachios. 'Do you need these?'

Elena relaxed her gaze. 'About half of them for the cake mix. Chop them up fine.'

He was grateful to resume his task. 'Can't you get these ready shelled?'

'It guarantees they're fresh this way.'

'Seems an awful faff.'

His mother-in-law looked ready to admonish him but before she could they were interrupted by the front door to the apartment closing. They exchanged a look, listened to the sound of footsteps making their way across the hallway. A second door opened and closed, softly. It could only be Angelica.

Elena caught Joe's eye. 'Leave her for now,' she advised. 'Let the dust settle.'

He thought about it. 'I have to say something.'

'Yes. But the longer you leave it, the more you'll both have cooled down.'

He conceded her point with a nod.

Elena rewarded him with a smile. 'Come on. I need to get this in the oven.'

Joe had just scooped up the chopped pistachios and deposited them into the mixing bowl when his phone rang. He took it out and checked the screen. It was from a number he didn't recognise, and he wasn't going to answer it, until he caught Elena looking at him encouragingly. 'Joe Mottram,' he answered, putting the phone to his ear.

'Joe, it's Lara Sarrancino.'

He said nothing, waiting for her to expand.

'From the State Police,' she reminded him, misinterpreting his silence. 'In Naples.'

'I haven't forgotten you just yet,' he joked.

She made a noise. Was it a cough or a laugh? 'Can you talk?'

'Sure.'

'The toxicology report came in.'

Again, he waited for her to continue.

'It might put your mind at ease. About the photo.'

My mind? Or yours? 'Go on,' he heard himself saying.

'I thought it would be better to discuss it in person. Maybe over a drink?'

This was unexpected. 'Tonight?'

'Only if you're not busy.'

He looked towards Elena, who was unashamedly earwigging; she'd clearly caught the gist of it and indicated he was free to do as he pleased.

'Sorry,' he found himself saying to her as he rang off. 'It should be the last time.'

Elena waved away his apology. 'Even if it does turn out to be an accident . . . it'll help you to stay busy.' His mother-in-law gestured to the littered work surface. Precisely what staying busy helped both of them with didn't need to be said.

17

While Joe read a translation of the toxicology report cover to cover, and then leafed through it slowly a second time, Lara sat and watched him. She sipped her drink and took a hit from her vape from time to time, but otherwise she was still, content to let him read in silence, determined to match his quiet intensity with some of her own.

They were sitting at one of the outermost tables at the pool bar of the Hotel Americano, with a smattering of guests for company, the low murmur of their conversations blending seamlessly with the bass harmonies of a familiar jazz classic that was playing over the speakers, and the soft hiss of the waves in the darkness. Lara had almost suggested an alternative venue for their meeting, for fear of having to put up with the manager's obsequious banalities a second time, but the negronis were particularly good here – the barman added a dash of cherry liqueur to soften the bitterness of the Campari – and, besides, she had better memories of this place than those associated with Signor Carlotti. She and Nicky had camped here for hours on the second night of their post-pandemic sojourn in Capri, drinking the same cocktail that now stood on the table between her and her companion, his so far untouched, hers drunk close to the dregs. Despite the obvious differences, there was something about the English detective that reminded her of her ex, Lara reflected as she watched him reach absentmindedly to scratch an itch on the back of his neck, his eyes never lifting from the page. Not physically, of course – they were chalk and cheese – but in his manner: his quality of stillness; the keen intelligence of his gaze; his practised reticence that forced the world to come to him; the aura of relentless control. For the first time in a long time, she felt a pang of self-pity at the thought of the love she'd so thoughtlessly let go.

Joe finally looked up from the report and caught her studying him.

She rearranged her features into an expression of casual enquiry. 'So?'

'So, what?'

There it was again. That practised reticence. 'She had four times the recommended dose of fentanyl in her system.'

He took another long moment to find the place in the report.

Lara felt herself growing irritated once again by his deliberateness. She reminded herself to take a breath. Joe tossed the report onto the table and met her eye once more.

'I'm confused,' he said simply.

'Your theory . . . about the photo . . . that it was taken by someone else . . .' She trailed off, unsatisfied with her beginning. She tapped a finger on the report that lay between them. 'Surely *this* suggests there's a more simple explanation for what happened to Shannon. Than whatever it was you were trying to put together.'

Joe pulled a face.

'The report says she overdosed.'

'Does it?'

Lara snatched up the document and turned quickly to its conclusion. 'Here. They're saying if the fall hadn't killed her, the drugs in her system would have done the same job,' she told him, folding the page back on itself to show him.

His eyes stayed on her. 'The way I read it, they can't be sure it *wasn't* the drugs that killed her. She may even have been dead before she went over the edge.'

'We found fentanyl in her suitcase!'

He gestured. So?

'She was a habitual user. Her father admitted it.'

'It doesn't necessarily follow that she took the drugs herself.'

Lara fought an urge to reach across the table and slap him. 'My boss . . . he thinks it's a suicide. She was upset by the argument with her partner. Decided to kill herself but didn't want to leave things to chance. She went to the cliff and took an overdose. Then jumped to make absolutely sure.' Lara sensed heads turning in their direction. She must have spoken more emphatically than intended.

Her companion waited for them to turn away again before he spoke. 'You and I both know there's another possibility.' He was just as measured as before.

'For God's sake,' Lara hissed, leaning in and doing her utmost to keep her voice down. 'The photo . . . it's just a *theory*.'

'I'm aware of that,' he conceded, unexpectedly giving a little ground.

'We don't have any other evidence that suggests third-party involvement.'

'That could just be because we haven't gone looking for it.'

Lara threw her hands up in disgust. She was aware she was acting in precisely the way she'd promised herself she wouldn't, but she didn't care.

'There are things that are unexplained,' he persisted. 'Other lines to pursue.'

'Go on. Like what?'

'Like the rash, for one thing.'

That was easily dealt with. 'It's unrelated to her death. They say so in the report.'

'No. The report says it's *most likely* unrelated,' he responded, picking it up and searching for the relevant section. 'Here,' he continued, turning to show it to her. 'They haven't been able to carry out a test and are waiting for her medical records from the UK to confirm known allergies.'

Lara couldn't help shaking her head.

'All right,' Joe went on, 'it's probably nothing. But what about the prenup?'

She decided it was time to play her trump card. 'It's a dead end.'

A look of uncertainty darkened his handsome features for the first time.

'Manny's alibi . . . it checks out.'

'Are you sure?'

'Gianni spoke to the woman he spent the weekend with. She's confirmed his account. And we have several eye witnesses who place them both in a restaurant in Positano on Saturday afternoon, just after 3.30pm. There's a credit card receipt. And CCTV as well. He can't have been in two places at the same time.'

Joe was silent, calculating, recalibrating. 'What about someone else then?'

'Do you have anyone in mind?'

'Someone she met through that dating app?'

The same thought had occurred to Lara. But, again, it was just supposition.

It was his turn to throw his hands up, although less theatrically than she had. 'You know what, Lara? I don't know why I'm bothering. It's your case.' He took a first sip of his drink. There was no sign he savoured it, as Lara had hoped he might. She waited for him to say something, unsure how this was going to end.

'Do you have a pen?' he asked, putting his drink down.

She felt in her pockets, found one in her gilet.

As he took it from her, he turned the report to face him and wrote something on the front page, ringed it with a flourish, slid it and the pen back towards her.

Lara turned the report to face her.

A+.

She felt her cheeks colouring, glanced up to see his reaction.

'It's what you want, isn't it? For me to mark your homework. Give you a gold star.'

'Go fuck yourself.' She pocketed the pen and picked up the report, got to her feet. The bill hadn't been paid but she didn't care. He could buy his own fucking drink.

As she turned to leave, he spoke again. 'You don't think this was a suicide any more than I do. Or a bloody accident, for that matter.'

His words stopped Lara in her tracks. She thought again of Shannon's dress and sandals. Her back-to-front necklace in the photo. Tiny details. Nagging doubts. 'It doesn't matter what I think,' she blurted out, turning back to face Joe.

'And why's that?'

'Because my boss has pretty much ordered me to close the case.'

There was silence. Joe stared, letting her words sink in. She felt a prickle of shame, an overwhelming urge to explain, to justify herself to him . . . she was newly promoted and a woman to boot, she was only where she was on Curti's sufferance, she hadn't earned the right yet to question his orders, to rock the boat. Maybe her father was right, she told herself for good measure, maybe she wasn't cut out for this kind of work. She saw Joe's lips twitch and braced for him to say something scornful, to berate her for not standing up to her superiors, but to her surprise a grin slowly lit up his face instead. 'Then *that's* what this is all about.' He gestured to the negronis, the untouched bowl of nuts.

Lara said nothing, not quite trusting herself to speak.

'You know, you could have just given me my marching orders over the phone.'

She shrugged apologetically. 'I wanted to buy you a drink. Say thank you.'

'In which case—' He turned to look for a waiter, intent on ordering another round.

In spite of everything, Lara sat back down.

They agreed not to talk about the case. For the rest of the evening, at least.

Lara was on her third glass of neat Scotch, matching Joe drink for drink, before she found the courage to ask him about the cocktail. It had sat there almost untouched throughout their row and reconciliation before a waiter finally cleared it away.

'You don't like negronis?'

'I love them.'

'You didn't drink it.'

He sighed, looked away. 'They remind me of my wife.'

Ah. So divorced, then? 'You don't want to be reminded of her?'

Joe shook his head slightly, keeping his gaze averted.

'Well, she has excellent taste in cocktails,' Lara ventured.

'*Had.*'

And with that simple correction it had all come pouring out. While Lara sat there, very still, listening intently, occasionally asking something or seeking clarification, Joe told her about Sofia. About coming across her body in the street, just a few yards from their doorstep and the safety of the home they'd shared. About his despair and how it had turned to rage on learning she'd been the victim of a hit-and-run driver, and then guilt that he, her policeman husband, had failed to protect her. And about how that guilt had been compounded over the months, as he'd been forced to sit on the sidelines while his colleagues' investigation failed to turn up a lead. There was plenty of CCTV footage of the car that had struck her, he confided in Lara, even a grainy sequence of the moments after impact, when the driver got out to see what they'd done. But the plates on the Mercedes were false – no doubt it had been stolen and was on its way to being broken down for spare parts – and the driver appeared to have a detailed knowledge of the cameras in the vicinity because the car had proved impossible to trace. There was almost nothing left at the scene to go on – a tyre track, a scattering of broken glass, a scrape of black paint on a vehicle parked nearby that the Mercedes had collided with after the impact. And other than that . . . just the usual collection of random street detritus – a lost bus pass, a playing card, a comb, a penny and a fifty-cent euro coin, plus discarded sandwich wrappers and cigarette butts and cans and bottles. And, of course, Sofia's blood.

'A playing card?' Lara couldn't help asking. It seemed an odd detail.

Joe shrugged. He'd just been reciting what he could remember from her file. For obvious reasons he hadn't been allowed to play an active part in the forensic search at the scene or in the subsequent investigation.

'I'm so sorry,' she said simply, when he'd finally run out of words.

'It's why I'm here,' Joe responded, feeling the need to say something to cover up the surge of emotion that was threatening to reveal itself. He wasn't on holiday in Capri, he explained, but for a sabbatical. It had been his daughter's idea they should come, that he should step away from the daily grind of cases he'd thrown himself into in the eleven months since Sofia's death. Here, in the place where his dead wife had been happy, they should try and find a way to reconnect.

Lara felt the last vestiges of her hostility towards him soften and evaporate. She drained her glass, felt the spirit going to her head. She was drunk, but it felt good. Liberating. 'I'm sorry I've been a bitch,' she found herself saying.

'You haven't.'

'You've been trying to help. And I've thrown it back at you.'

He waved away her self-recriminations. 'I'd be prickly as hell if you came muscling in on my patch. Flashing your badge. Sticking your nose in.'

Lara pulled a face. He'd done none of those things.

'Look, you've done me a favour,' Joe continued. 'Letting me hang out with you. Keeping me in the loop. At the very least it's got me out of the house. You know . . . kept me out of the firing line for a bit.'

'Is your daughter being difficult?'

'That's one word for it.'

'I think she has an excuse.'

'Of course she does.' He picked up his glass to drink before realising it was empty. 'And anyway . . . she'd say I was being the difficult one.'

'Is she right?'

He grimaced. 'I'm a different person at home. Here . . . at work . . . I know what I'm doing. I have training to fall back on. Experience. It keeps me calm, you know . . . sort of . . .'

She wracked her brain for the right word in English. '*Misurato* . . . um, measured?'

Joe nodded. He conceded the acuteness of her observation with a smile.

'But with Angelica?'

His smile faded. 'I'm just flailing about really. Utterly clueless. And then, of course, I get angry at myself. And at her. Start shouting. And . . . well, you know . . .'

'It makes everything worse.'

He smiled faintly in recognition of a shared experience. 'You have kids?'

Lara laughed, shook her head. 'I have a father.'

'You don't get on with him?'

'We fight like cats and dogs.'

'What about?'

'Everything. Papa . . . he *disapproves* of me.'

'In what way?'

'That I was born a girl, for one thing.' She felt a sudden urge to confide in him, to test his reaction. She didn't think he was the type to be shocked. But a waiter was passing and Joe was already turning to try and catch his attention and order a fresh round of drinks. What she'd been about to tell him would have to wait.

18

As Joe descended the steps to Da Vinale's terrace, he was aware he was far from sober. He hadn't reached an age where banisters loomed large in his consciousness but, as he proceeded downwards, step by cautious step, he instinctively gripped the handrails to either side of him. It was well past closing time and the outside lights at Da Vinale's had been turned off, meaning his way was lit by nothing more than the overspill from a streetlamp somewhere on the road above. The steps beneath his feet felt slippery with sea spray and he couldn't help imagining the consequences of a fall. Not least the look of pitying disdain on the face of Sofia's father.

He'd almost reached the bottom when he heard the sound of a door closing. He stopped and listened as footsteps came across the terrace towards him. '*Salve?*' he called out as they approached, greeting whoever it was formally, wanting them to know that he was there, that he meant no harm to them.

The outline of a man loomed in the darkness at the foot of the stairs. '*Scusi, Signore. Scusi.*' It was a smoker's voice. Deep and gravelly.

Letting go of the right handrail and flattening himself against the left, Joe sensed rather than saw the man pass. He followed his progress up the stairs, his outline growing more visible in the faint glow from above. He heard the buzz of the electronic release button and, a moment later, a click as the gate unlocked. As it opened, the neon glare of the streetlight flooded in, and the man was briefly illuminated. He turned to glance back down the stairs and Joe got a look at his face. A vicious scar ran from just below his right ear to the corner of his mouth. Joe just had time to take note of the envelope he was slipping into his pocket before he stepped out onto the street and the gate closed behind him, plunging the stairs into semi-darkness once more.

Joe became aware of his heartbeat pulsing in his temple and realised he'd tensed in anticipation of conflict. He'd started to grope his way across the semi-familiar terrain of the terrace when he heard a plate smashing somewhere inside the restaurant, followed by an angry shout. Feeling suddenly more sober, he hurried to investigate.

It was Elena and Gennaro who were arguing. As Joe pushed through the swing doors and into the restaurant kitchen, he was just in time to hear a second plate shatter.

Elena stood with her back half-turned to him. She appeared to be reaching for the uppermost of a stack of plates on the counter next to her. Gennaro was nowhere to be seen, but it was obvious she had him cornered in the recesses of the L-shaped room.

'If that man's a fishmonger, then I'm the Pope,' she shouted.

Sizing up the situation at a glance, Joe stepped forward just as his mother-in-law drew back her arm to fire again. He gripped the plate she was holding in his left hand and Elena's forearm in his right, disarming her neatly. The momentum of her failed throw swung her round to face him. She was flushed, seething. 'Stay out of this, Joe.'

He raised his hands in a gesture of appeasement, maintaining eye contact as he'd been trained. 'Just don't break any more of your lovely plates, please. You'll regret it.'

'What I do with my plates is none of your damned business.'

'OK, OK.'

She glared at him, chest heaving, nostrils flared.

Joe did his best to keep his voice calm. 'Do you want to tell me what this is about?'

'I never said he was a fishmonger,' Gennaro intervened, taking advantage of Joe's presence to emerge from the niche beside the fridge where he'd been cowering.

'Liar!'

'I said I buy fish from him,' Gennaro insisted, crouching submissively as he inched towards her. 'He just came to collect what I owe.'

Elena huffed. *You see*, her expression seemed to say, *he takes me for a fool.*

'*Per favore, tesoro*. Let's not argue.'

She refused to look at him.

'You know it makes me unhappy,' Gennaro pleaded with her.

Again, she flapped a disdainful hand in his direction, but weakly this time, and Gennaro must have taken it as a sign the fight was going out of her, for he reached out to embrace her. He'd badly misjudged her readiness to surrender, however, for the moment his hand came into contact with her, Elena lashed out, catching him on his nose. The old chef staggered back, hands going to his face. If anything, Elena looked even more shocked than he did. Joe decided it was time to intercede.

'Maybe you should go, Gennaro,' he said, stepping in between the couple. It was an instruction more than a suggestion, and the old chef must have picked up on the firmness in his tone, because with a nod of the head and a last sorrowful glance in his wife's direction, he made good his escape, checking his hands for blood as he went.

In the silence that followed, Joe looked to Elena but already she was turning away. He watched her make her way towards the far end of the kitchen, open a cupboard, and take out an upright dustpan and brush.

'Can I help?' he asked, unnerved by her lack of words.

She didn't respond. Slowly and deliberately, she started to sweep the broken fragments of plate into a pile.

He tried again. 'Elena?'

Finally, she looked at him. 'I'd like you to leave too, Joe,' was all she said.

It took Joe a little longer than expected to track down his father-in-law, who wasn't drinking a glass of grappa at the bar as anticipated. Joe had almost abandoned his search before he noticed the gate to the private jetty had been unlocked. Descending his second precarious flight of steps of the evening, he found Gennaro sitting at the end of the short wooden pier, staring out to sea, and made his way over to join him.

For a while they sat there, saying nothing, contemplating the view. The moon had risen higher, and the surface of the sea was alive with silvered motion. Across the bay, on the headland opposite, the lights of a few dwellings were visible, subdued and somehow vulnerable. Somewhere over to their left, boats were at anchor in the darkness, for the tell-tale metallic clink of wires in the rigging was audible periodically.

Joe heard the old chef shift beside him, emit a heavy sigh. He decided this was about the best cue he was going to get. 'You want to let me know what's really going on?'

'She didn't tell you?'

'I want to hear it from you.'

There was another long silence. Eventually his father-in-law spoke. 'This man . . . I have business with him. He turned up when we were closing. Asking for money.'

'I saw him on his way out. Scar on his face. Snappy dresser.'

The old chef didn't respond.

'He didn't look much like a man who sells fish for a living, Gennaro.'

Again there was no response. Joe could almost hear the cogs of Gennaro's brain whirring as he decided whether to double down on his lie. 'He doesn't,' he admitted.

'Then what *does* he do?'

'None of your damn business.'

There they were again. His nagging doubts about the island. A glimpse of its dark undercurrents. 'You're not involved in anything illegal, are you?' Joe felt he had to ask.

'*Figlio di puttana!*'

Joe wasn't ready to let him off the hook. 'But you owe him money?'

'Like I told you.'

'How much?'

'More than I had. So I took some. From the petty cash.'

'Does he normally come to the restaurant?'

'No!'

'Then why did he?'

'He said the money . . . I should have paid it last week.'

'And is that true?'

His father-in-law sighed again. 'I suppose.'

They'd reached the heart of it. 'Are you struggling financially?' Joe asked gently.

Gennaro squirmed in the darkness beside him. 'It's complicated,' he said.

19

At that same moment, Angelica was having quite a different sort of heart-to-heart.

She and Daniele were lying together under a blanket on a small semicircle of pebbled beach, less than half a mile from where her father and grandfather were sitting, and she was stoned. Not exceptionally so – the joint Daniele had shared with her hadn't been particularly potent compared with the skunk she'd made the mistake of trying at the last party she'd gone to – but stoned enough to make the night sky seem miraculous, with myriad splinters of starlight perforating the inky black heavens like a million tiny pinpricks. And enough to make the story Daniele had just told her seem particularly sad and resonant. She felt overwhelmed by her desire to show him the love he hinted had been denied to him by an absent father and a mother too preoccupied by her own ill-health to have the time or energy to care much for him. She felt his breath on her neck, and she leaned into the sensation, rubbing against him, feeling his ardour rise. When his lips found hers, she kissed him back with more fervour than she'd summoned for anything in her short life. She poured her heart and soul into the moment, into him.

She hadn't intended to see him that evening after their return from Naples. He'd invited her to go with him to the beach near the lighthouse, where he and his friends often gathered to light a fire and listen to music, to smoke weed and drink and complain about their lives. But she'd told him she'd arranged to spend time with her grandmother, which, while not exactly the truth, was not a total lie either. The shadow of their conversation about their ambitions loomed over their slightly awkward goodbye.

Angelica had emerged from her bedroom a little after 5pm to find Elena moisturising her hands and lamenting the state of them, having just finished washing up after putting her cake in the oven. Her granddaughter had offered to give her a manicure and they'd spent a happy three-quarters of an hour at the kitchen table, while Angelica cut and filed her nails and trimmed her cuticles before applying Sofia's favourite raspberry nail varnish. Elena had looked delighted as she held her hands up to examine the result.

'I hardly ever get them done.'

'You should. They look fab, Gran.'

'It never lasts long in the restaurant.'

Angelica could remember her mother saying something similar the last time they'd visited a nail bar together. 'You're just like Mum,' she told her grandmother. 'They'd be chipped or smudged within five minutes.'

'She was so impatient.'

Angelica couldn't help agreeing. 'And accident-prone.'

'Tell me about this boy, then,' Elena had suddenly suggested, taking advantage of this moment of apparent intimacy.

Instinctively, Angelica had pulled a face.

'You don't like him?'

'No, I like him. I like him *a lot*.'

'Then what's the problem?'

'I'm seventeen, Gran. It's too young to be in a relationship.'

'What's wrong with having a bit of fun?'

Nothing, Angelica declared, but she'd more important things to worry about.

'Like what?'

'Like working out what I'm going to do when I leave school.'

'You've got all the time in the world to decide that,' Elena scoffed.

Her granddaughter wasn't so sure. She was interested in studying business, she confided in Elena, but a friend of hers was already making money selling personalised plectrums and guitar tuners on Amazon, and his father had told Angelica there was no substitute for getting out there and launching something. Besides, going to university wasn't for everybody, was it? Daniele had already told her he had no plans to – which was fine, she supposed, as long as he had a good reason, an alternative plan, a goal in life that didn't depend on it.

'You only want to be with someone if they're as ambitious as you are, is that it?'

'Maybe.'

'And you want to be a businesswoman? Make a bit of money?'

Angelica had felt herself growing defensive. 'What's wrong with that?'

Nothing at all, Elena had reassured her, she was certain she could do absolutely anything she set her mind to. But what line of business was she most interested in?

It was then that Angelica had faltered. That was the problem with her life-plan, such as it was. She wasn't entirely sure. But being her own boss. Running something of her own.

'What? Like a restaurant?'

Possibly a chain of them, Angelica had suggested, not wanting to hurt her grandmother's feelings but certain her ambitions were pitched a little higher than that.

A hint of amusement had played around Elena's lips. 'Like I said, maybe concentrate on having a little fun first,' she'd told her, bringing the conversation to an end with the observation that if her granddaughter was serious about wanting to go into business then she could do worse than to spend time immersing herself in the family's restaurant. Elena would be happy to show her the ropes and go through how it all worked financially, explain all the factors and considerations involved.

Wanting to humour the old lady, Angelica had spent the first hour of the dinner service shadowing Elena and trying to feign interest. But her grandmother was distracted and Angelica had soon felt herself an encumbrance, had secretly been pleased when Elena suggested giving her a more formal introduction to the business when things were less frantic. She'd gone back to the apartment and fallen asleep listening to music, had woken, dry-mouthed, to find night had fallen and she had four missed calls from Daniele. She'd been about to message him when she heard what sounded like a small stone coming into contact with her window. She waited to be sure, long enough for the noise to come again. She got up and padded over to open it, leaned out to see Daniele standing on the street outside wearing a black and white baseball jacket and looking up at her. It was boring without her, he'd told her, wouldn't she come down, just for half an hour, they didn't have to go to the party, they could just go to the nearest beach and hang out.

And now here they were, nose to nose, lying beneath the blanket she'd brought with her. All her earlier doubts and resolutions had fallen away. She felt a powerful connection between them, as if she'd known him for much longer than a matter of days. They stayed like that for what felt like an age, kissing and touching, Angelica luxuriating in the heat their bodies communicated to one another. At last, Daniele's arm went numb, and he was forced to shift it from beneath her head. She sat up, no longer warm and revelling in sensation, but cooler now and suddenly anxious, remembering the last conversation she'd had with Joe and the pained expression she'd left imprinted on his face. She felt an urge to look at her watch but had to make a conscious effort to lift her arm and bring it to her face, the luminous colours of its dial leaving weird trails of colour in the darkness. It was well past midnight. *Shit! Where had the time gone?*

Gently, Daniele tried to pull her back down to him, but the spell had been broken. She shrugged him off and prepared to struggle to her feet. 'I need to get back.'

'Stay a bit longer.'

She ignored him and tried to rise, but as she did so she felt his hand grab her wrist.

'Daniele! Let go!'

He clung on tighter. 'Five minutes. That's all.'

'Daniele!' She tried to pull her arm away. If anything, she could feel his grip tightening, grinding the back of her hand into the stones of the beach.

'*Fai la furbetta.*'

She heard him mutter it under his breath, his voice now disembodied and impersonal, almost as if an entirely different person was suddenly lying beside her in the dark. She didn't know the word but she could guess his meaning. It wasn't the first time she'd been called a cock-tease.

In a surge of anger and paranoia, Angelica lashed out with her free arm, felt it collide with his head. He released his grip and rolled away. For a moment she thought she could hear him weeping, but as she groped for him in the darkness, she realised he was laughing instead, that he was more stoned than she'd imagined. In her relief, she began to laugh too – although a little uneasily – and the moment was forgotten.

Her plan had been to get back into the apartment the same way she'd got out, and climb through her bedroom window, which looked directly over the road. But the drop from the balcony, which had been easy enough to navigate when stone-cold sober, now proved impossible to negotiate in reverse. Daniele cupped his hands and did his best to give her a boost so she could catch hold of the balcony's edge, but the support he gave her was unsteady and her legs and arms felt unaccustomedly weak. He seemed to find the whole thing hilarious, and Angelica eventually abandoned him to find his own way back to the flat of the friend he was staying with, out of fear he would give her away. She skirted the darkened building, thinking to gain access to the compound through the street gate on the far side, but it was locked, and she'd almost resigned herself to having to press the bell and summon help, waking the whole household in the process, when she remembered the second gate at the top of the steps leading up from the private jetty. It took her some time to manoeuvre her way round to it along the foreshore, for she'd only previously accessed it by water taxi on the night of their arrival, and the rocks beneath her feet were slippery and treacherous. At last she made the safety of the solid stone steps and felt her way up along the sea wall of the terrace to the gate at the top, only to discover that it too was locked.

Angelica felt like weeping. Her only options were to feel her way back and ring the bell, which was frankly unappealing, or to attempt to climb over the wall. She spent several minutes grappling for foot- and handholds in the darkness before she finally found the strength to haul herself onto the top, and, using the blanket to cover the broken shards of glass embedded in the cement, drop her legs over. Her feet found a table that was propped against the other side and, for a moment, she thought she might finally have caught a break, but, as she let her weight descend, the table bucked alarmingly and almost tipped over, and she heard something fall to the floor with a crash. Angelica froze, waiting for the lights in the building to come on, but when they didn't, she carefully dismounted and felt about in the shadows beneath, discovering the ceramic shards of a bowl decorated with lemons. Tidying them into her all-purpose blanket, she started to pick her way across the terrace towards the door to the restaurant, where she knew a key was hidden, but as she approached she heard the door open, and someone come out.

'*Attenzione!*' she heard her grandfather growl.

'*Nonno!* It's me!'

A flashlight was turned on and shone in her face, blinding her. 'Angelica?!'

She tried to shield her eyes with her hand. 'I got locked out.'

'My God, child. I thought you were someone come to rob us.'

A light now went on in the restaurant behind him and Gennaro was clearly outlined. She could see a heavy-looking truncheon gripped in his right hand.

'I could have killed you,' he told her, sensing her alarm.

'I'm sorry, *Nonno*. I can explain.'

Gennaro glanced uneasily through the windows of the restaurant, where a bleary-eyed Elena had now appeared, dressed in her nightclothes. Joe was visible behind, looking equally bemused. 'You're going to need to explain yourself,' her grandfather advised her, ushering her inside.

Angelica braced as Joe came over, but he seemed more concerned than angry. 'Are you all right?'

It was only now Angelica became aware of the graze on her left forearm, which was dripping blood onto the floor.

'What happened?' her dad persisted.

She felt her eyes beginning to water. 'I was locked out. I had to climb over the wall.'

'But where have you been?'

'I went to the beach.'

Joe stared at her, incredulous. 'It's one in the morning.'

'I was with Daniele,' she sniffed miserably. 'We lost track of the time.'

Her dad's expression stiffened.

'Come on,' Elena said, deciding to intervene. 'We need to get you cleaned up.'

Angelica couldn't hold back her tears any longer.

When she emerged from the bathroom ten minutes later with her cut washed and bandaged by Elena, there was no sign of Joe, and Angelica's hopes rose that the inevitable confrontation between them might be postponed until the morning. As she gave her grandmother a grateful goodnight hug, however, he emerged from her bedroom. His face was pale with anger.

'What the hell is this?' he asked, holding up a small bag of weed that she instantly knew he'd found in the zip pocket on the inside of her washbag. She tried to snatch it back off him, but he was too quick and closed his hand.

Elena appeared at her shoulder. 'Let's not do this now, Joe.'

'Stay out of it, Elena. Please.'

'He's been going through my things, Gran.'

'Because you're clearly on something.'

'No, I'm not.'

'Don't lie to me. Your pupils are the size of footballs.'

'We had a couple of beers. That's all.'

Her dad held the bag up for Elena's benefit. 'So what about this?'

Angelica felt her face flush. 'I've been struggling to sleep. I thought it might help.'

'Did *he* give it to you?'

'No!'

'Then where did you get it?'

'From a friend.'

'What friend?'

'Just someone at home.'

Joe looked dumbfounded. 'You brought it through Customs?'

'Calm down. Nobody got arrested.'

'DON'T TELL ME TO CALM DOWN!'

The force of his anger was almost physical. Angelica felt her breath catch in her throat and she hiccoughed, nearly choked. She began to cry again.

Gennaro appeared in the doorway to his bedroom. 'Have you all gone mad?'

'I wish it was you that was dead,' Angelica hissed at Joe through her sobs. She saw him flinch as her words hit home, but she was in no mood to pity him. She tried to push past him, but he grabbed her arm.

'You're not going anywhere until you tell me who gave you this.'

It was Elena's turn to raise her voice. 'STOP THIS, JOE. NOW!' It had the desired effect as Joe let go of Angelica's arm. He was clearly taken aback by her vehemence.

'I could've lost my job,' he muttered, more defensive than angry.

'But you didn't,' Elena snapped back. 'And this isn't about

you.' She grabbed the bag of weed from Joe's hand and pointedly handed it back to her granddaughter. 'Go to your room,' she told Angelica. 'We'll talk about this in the morning.'

Not wanting to give Joe time to regather his wits, Angelica slipped into her room and bolted the door.

The murmur of adult voices was still audible when Angelica softly unbolted the door sometime later and stuck her head out. Light from the kitchen was flooding into the corridor. She took a few experimental steps in that direction and stopped to listen. Joe and Elena were the only ones she could hear. Gennaro must have gone back to bed.

'It's a tiny bit of marijuana,' she heard Elena say. 'Barely enough for a puff.'

'It's a gateway drug, Elena,' came her dad's response.

Her grandmother snorted derisively. 'You sound like a policeman.'

'That's because I am one.'

'Are you saying you never have?'

A chair creaked. Angelica could imagine Joe shifting in it uncomfortably. 'That's beside the point.'

'Then what is your point?'

'My point is *I'm* her parent. Not *you*.' Joe's voice had gone up a notch.

But so had Elena's. 'Then start *acting* like one.'

There was silence. Angelica pictured the glares being exchanged across the table. She almost felt a tiny pang of sympathy on her dad's behalf.

'I'm sorry if I've offended you,' Elena offered at last. 'But all this crashing about like the big "I am" . . . it's not helping you or her and it's giving me a headache. The more you shout and issue commands, the more you lecture and get angry with her . . . the less she's going to pay attention. You need to learn to listen. To really try to *understand*.'

Her dad didn't respond. Was he listening now?

'She needs the love her mother gave her,' Elena continued with obvious feeling. 'Unconditional. Non-judgemental.'

Angelica heard a chair scrape and she imagined Joe getting to his feet, ready to walk out. She retreated down the corridor and slipped into the sanctuary of her bedroom.

I wish it was you that was dead.

She heard herself saying it once more, recalled the look on his face. Of course she hadn't meant it. She just wished with all her heart that her poor mum wasn't.

20

It was apparent to Joe he'd joined Gennaro in Elena's bad books from the moment he emerged from his bedroom the following morning. Sofia's mother had the habit of leaving things out for his breakfast, but the table was bare when he entered the kitchen a little before 8am, in the grip of a hangover and unable to sleep. He heard the shower start up in the bathroom and decided to beat a retreat, unwilling to risk a resumption of the conversation from the night before. He lay low for the next hour, dozing fitfully, listening while his in-laws went about their morning routine. Normally they could be heard chirruping away companionably, but today they moved around the apartment in stony silence. One of them, almost certainly Gennaro, left to go to the restaurant a little after 8.30am, shutting the front door with an emphatic thump, but it was after nine before Joe heard the front door open and close for a second time and he felt ready to re-emerge from his bedroom, desperate now for a coffee and a paracetamol.

He spent the next half hour drinking espresso and debating what to do about breakfast and Angelica. The thought of another showdown in his current fragile state was too painful to contemplate and he decided to go for a run instead, to do what he could to speed up the process of recovery by sweating the alcohol out of his system.

Coming down the steps from the street gate three-quarters

of an hour later, his running kit soaked with perspiration, Joe was anticipating an encounter with Elena and was all the more surprised, therefore, to find Lara sitting on the terrace nursing a cup of coffee which someone in the restaurant must have made for her and smoking her vape while she waited. She rose, smiled awkwardly. 'I tried calling, but you didn't answer,' she explained. 'So I thought I'd walk down. Try to clear my head.'

Joe couldn't help glancing past her to where a print-out of Shannon's selfie lay on the table. 'Have you come to tell me all the reasons I'm wrong again?' he asked her. He grinned as he said it, but it was a forced smile.

She followed his gaze. 'The opposite. I think you're right about the photo. And about someone else being involved in Shannon's death.'

Joe found himself recalling the vehemence with which she'd told him to go fuck himself. No wonder she hadn't seemed happy about being told to close the case.

It was too late to return to Naples after they'd parted the night before, Lara explained, so she'd ended up calling her aunt and accepting her offer of a bed. The bed in question had been far more comfortable than the one in the holding cell at the police station, but still she'd barely slept, in part because of the after-effects of the Scotch, but in larger part because of her misgivings about the prospect of following Curti's orders. 'Something feels wrong, Joe,' she told him. 'Her clothes... the things in her bag... the drugs... the location... that thing you said about her hand and the photo. It all feels a bit too... I don't know... *inautentico*?'

'Yeah. Made up. *Staged*.' Joe grinned again, but this time there was no need to force it. 'So, what do you need from me?' he asked.

'Help.' It was said almost plaintively. Curti had summoned her back to the mainland, but she'd managed to persuade him to let her stay another day. She was hoping they could spend the time available going back over every aspect of the investigation, looking for something, *anything*, that might suggest the possibility of foul play and persuade her boss to let her stay on the case a little longer.

'Give me five minutes.'

Joe had just entered the restaurant on his way back to the apartment when Elena emerged from the kitchen. She greeted him with a 'There you are!' and he braced himself for fresh words of reproach, but she only wanted to remind him that Da Vinale's would be closed that evening.

Joe couldn't hide his surprise. 'On a Wednesday?'

It was the Feast of St Anne, Gennaro's mother's namesake, Elena explained, and he always took the day off in her memory. They would be going to evening mass at San Stefano's before cooking a quiet meal together in the apartment. He and Angelica would be welcome to join them, but there was no obligation. He just had to let her know.

With a promise to do just that, Joe headed off to take his shower.

The day had not been as productive as they'd hoped, Joe reflected, as he stood in the sergeant's office in the police station a little after 5pm, helping Lara to gather the scattered contents of Shannon's file. They'd spent the afternoon going back over every aspect of the investigation – the post-mortem and toxicology reports, the witness statements from Manny Sanghera and Signor Carlotti amongst others, the photos taken at the scene of Shannon's death, and of course the one retrieved from her phone, which they'd re-examined from every angle without proving to either of their satisfaction that it'd definitely been taken by someone else. Neither of them had been at their sharpest and they'd come away with nothing more than a to-do list relating to the most promising lines of enquiry. Lara would give the hurry-up to her digital forensics team to gain access to the Girl Cupid app on Shannon's phone, and she'd also contact the dead woman's colleagues in the UK to explore an alternative way to gain access to any messages she'd sent via the app while in Capri. She'd also contact Dr Serafina to ask her to re-examine the dead woman for evidence of recent sexual activity. It was nothing like enough to persuade Curti to open a murder inquiry, but it was something.

'I don't suppose you fancy a hair of the dog?' Joe found himself asking as they made their way out into the late afternoon sunshine a few minutes later. From Lara's expression it was clear she'd no idea what he was talking about. 'A drink, I mean. It's supposed to be the best thing for a hangover.'

She smiled as she grasped his meaning. 'I'm sorry, Joe. I can't.'

'No worries.'

'I'd love to, but . . . I have a family thing. I promised my aunt.'

'Another time then.' They shook hands rather awkwardly, and Joe had just started to make his way to the gate and the main road beyond, when Lara called out, 'Actually, you know what . . . why don't you come?'

He turned to look at her, feeling faintly astonished. 'Me?'

'Why not?'

'To meet your family?'

Lara shrugged. 'It's no big deal. Some kind of drinks thing. For my aunt and uncle's anniversary. They always complain I never bring anyone. You'll be doing me a favour.'

Joe hesitated. The prospect of a long and uncomfortable

evening in his own family's company stretched ahead of him. But even so.

Lara read his thoughts. 'It's not a date, Joe. We can continue talking. That's all.'

'All right,' he agreed quickly, before he could change his mind.

Lara laughed, clearly tickled by the faint absurdity of the situation and, the next thing Joe knew, he was laughing too.

It's not a date.

Lara's words were still echoing in Joe's head as he arrived at the Villa San Benedetto an hour and a half later, wearing the one smart shirt he'd packed for the summer. Lara had either been lying or misinformed when she told him the party was 'no big deal'. As Joe made his way up the drive in the company of other new arrivals, he couldn't help noticing he was the only man who wasn't wearing either a jacket or at least a tie. His self-consciousness deepened as he reached the villa itself and surveyed the scene. Eight circular tables were laid out on a broad expanse of lawn, each one crowned by a floral display and dressed in starched white linen. This was clearly not a casual 'drinks thing', but an elaborate celebratory dinner, with places laid in silver and crystal for more than sixty people. Most of those guests had arrived, and stood around chatting, while waiters circulated with trays of sparkling wine and canapés, dispensing napkins and refills. A jazz band was playing somewhere in the background and it took Joe a moment or two to locate them at the bottom of a flight of stone steps that connected the lawn to the villa, which was an older and grander yellow-brick affair than the modern concrete structure he'd somehow been expecting.

His Italian colleague was nowhere to be seen and Joe was thinking about beating a retreat and texting his excuses, when a well-preserved woman in a strikingly low-cut dress peeled away from the edge of the party and made a beeline for him. 'I was told you wouldn't be wearing a suit,' she pronounced in heavily accented English, embracing Joe unaffectedly and introducing herself as Lara's aunt, Luisa.

'I'm sorry to let the side down.'

'Don't worry,' Luisa told him, smoothing out a wrinkle on the shoulder of his shirt and unashamedly giving him the once over. 'You're the best-looking man here.' She locked her arm through his in a proprietorial fashion and steered him towards the throng, explaining that Lara was still trying to find something to wear amongst the selection of outfits that Luisa kept at the villa. 'But I'm sixty-four, Joe, and I've had three children, so I have bumps in all the wrong places,' she joked, intending to suggest Lara would have her work cut out, but really fishing for the compliment that he duly obliged her with.

She proceeded to parade him through the party, showing him off to a head-spinning array of siblings, offspring, cousins, friends, business associates and hangers-on that she and her husband, Matteo, had accumulated across the thirty years of marriage they were honouring that evening. He was introduced to all and sundry as Lara's 'English *friend*', with everything that implied, and was greeted everywhere with hugs and kisses like an old and well-loved acquaintance, although he couldn't help noticing the questioning looks that seemed to follow him as he was hustled onwards to meet the next group of smiling guests. The only person who seemed less than thrilled by Joe's presence was a sulky-faced man called Beppe, a friend of Lara's cousin Franco, who made a point of telling Joe he wasn't aware she had any *friends* since joining the police. But otherwise Luisa's insinuations were pleasantly relentless and he'd almost given up trying to explain the professional nature of their connection when Lara finally made her appearance.

He was not her date, nor even really her friend, Joe reminded himself, but that did nothing to lessen the frisson he experienced when he saw her. She was wearing a simple but elegant figure-hugging black dress and, with her chestnut hair pinned up to show off her neck and shoulders, she was unrecognisable from the pared-down, androgynous persona she adopted in daily life, apart from the simple black pumps that adorned her feet. A pair of earrings and a touch of make-up around her hauntingly dark eyes completed the transformation. Looking at her now, as she shyly showed off her outfit for her aunt's appraisal, he felt the faint stirrings of something that had lain dormant inside him for the past eleven months. She must remind me of Sofia, he told himself.

It was Matteo's turn to decide to monopolise their English guest and, to Joe's slight relief, he was whisked away from Lara before anything more than a basic greeting could pass between them. Lara's uncle had heard from his niece that Joe was a whisky drinker and he insisted on him coming to his study to sample a Laphroaig single malt he'd recently bought on a business trip to London. Matteo didn't seem to have received the memo about Joe's line of work because he proceeded to lecture him on the ceramics business, which had enriched him sufficiently to allow him to buy a fifty-year lease on the villa. He was looking to hire someone to expand his UK operations, he said, reaching for a box of cigars on his desk. Joe declined both the cigar and the job offer, explaining that he was a police officer and he didn't smoke, even when he was off-duty.

'A police officer, eh?' Matteo exclaimed, clearly amused. 'Then you're going to want to see this.' The Villa San Benedetto had been built as a holiday retreat at the turn of the last century by a Neapolitan 'gentleman', he proudly explained, ushering Joe out into the hallway without giving him a chance to object. The gentleman in question had got himself arrested for smuggling guns and tobacco, his host continued as he led Joe down a narrow flight of stairs, and the nascent Italian state had confiscated and then sold on the property, which had passed through several hands before being bought by a local family in the 1960s and lovingly restored. Matteo showed Joe into a dusty and cavernous cellar, where a secret staircase had been discovered in the course of the renovation. It had been dug beneath the villa and led all the way down through the limestone cliffs to a small cave on the coast some forty metres below. Would he like to take a tour? Lara's uncle asked, grabbing a flashlight from a shelf inside the door and using its beam to pick out a trapdoor in the floor. As well as the staircase, there was a secret antechamber that the smugglers had used to store their goods; it now housed the workings for the villa's swimming pool, he explained, but it was still worth a look. Joe demurred. Another time maybe. It sounded fascinating but he felt bad about leaving Lara alone for too long. Matteo just grinned.

As they exited the cellar, Joe heard the clatter of pots and pans and, glancing through a doorway into the adjacent kitchen, was astonished to find himself looking at a familiar face. It was Luca, and at that exact moment the sous-chef glanced up to find Joe staring at him. 'Joe!' he called out in surprise. Making his excuses to Matteo, Joe entered the kitchen and they embraced. When Joe explained why he was there, and his liaison with the Italian police, Luca reacted in mock horror. *La Pula!* If he'd known the police were involved he'd never have agreed to help out a friend on his night off from Da Vinale's. The friend in question now called Luca's attention back to a pot of delicious-smelling fish stew he'd been standing guard over.

Returning to the main lawn, Joe fell into step with a waiter ferrying a fresh tray of drinks to the party and relieved him of a bottle of sparkling wine and two glasses. He found Lara standing a little aside from the main group, talking to Beppe. There was something about their body language that immediately put Joe on alert. She was hunched, with her arms folded across her chest, her back turned slightly towards the man beside her, and her right shoulder raised as a defensive bulwark. He was leaning in *very* close to her, so close they were almost touching, pouring a stream of low chatter directly into her ear. As Joe held up the bottle to signal his presence, Lara's eyes flicked across to him and she gave him a tiny nod of acknowledgement, but as she tried to shrug off Beppe's close attentions, he grabbed her wrist and pulled her back to him.

Joe heard him hiss something. It sounded a little like *'lesbica'*, although he couldn't be sure. He was about to step in but Lara warned him off with a shake of her head. He stood, briefly undecided, before he backed away. *She can look after herself*, he thought.

Moving off a little to wait for her, he settled on a bench away from the villa, which he now saw sat on a small headland some distance above sea level, and commanded spectacular views over the coast and the Tyrrhenian Sea beyond. After looking back to check Lara was all right, he let his gaze wander. The bench was near a chain-link fence that marked the limits of the villa's grounds, and beyond it was a footpath down to the shore below. A heavy-set man was making his way along it with a wet towel slung over his shoulder, his jet-black hair gathered in a loose man-bun. Out of habit, Joe did a quick inventory of his appearance. His features were difficult to discern behind a pair of sunglasses, but he was dressed in a collared white shirt, which seemed a trifle formal for a trip to the beach. The suggestion of a tattoo across his breastbone could be seen peeping out from where the buttons of his shirt were undone.

'It's a beautiful spot, isn't it?'

He turned to see Lara approaching. There was the suggestion of something bruised in the look she gave him. 'The whole place . . . it's stunning,' he replied, not quite knowing what to say. He opted for humour. 'So much for this party being no big deal.'

Lara was blushing as she laughed. She was sorry, she told Joe, she'd been so preoccupied with the case she hadn't registered the details. 'And I've spent so many summers here,' she went on. 'I forget how grand it must seem the first time.'

'You used to come here as a child?'

'All the time.' Every year her father had shipped her off to stay with his sister Luisa in Capri for the whole of August, she explained. It had been idyllic. Spending all day at the beach. Swimming. Sailing. Sunbathing. Playing with her cousins and their friends.

'Does that include Beppe?'

The smile that had accompanied her reminiscences faded.

'Is everything all right?'

Lara looked away. Beppe was an ex-boyfriend, she admitted in a quiet voice, her first serious one in fact, who she'd met through Franco in the summer of her fifteenth year. She was young and vulnerable, still trying to work out who she was, and for a long time she thought she was in love with him. It had taken her that long to see him in his true light and to release herself from his spell, but ever since their split he had shown a streak of jealousy and possessiveness, had importuned her to restart their affair every chance he got, despite her telling him countless times she had no interest in him.

'And he thinks that gives him the right to abuse you?'

Lara fixed him in her stare. 'Don't worry. I can handle him.'

'Maybe you should tell Franco about it. Persuade your aunt not to invite him.'

Lara shook her head. 'It would break their hearts.' Her father's sister had become a second mother to her since her own had died, she explained, and her cousins were the siblings she'd never had. Marianna Sarrancino had been in and out of hospital throughout Lara's teenage years, she told Joe. Her father, Antonio, had used his wife's illness as an excuse to spend more time with the mistress to whom he already devoted the August holidays, leaving Lara as her mother's primary carer throughout her long and ultimately futile struggle with breast cancer. Isolated and in need of emotional support, Lara had developed an unhealthily dependent relationship with Beppe, with the two of them almost inseparable for much of her late teens. During a brief remission of eighteen months, Antonio had threatened to withdraw financial support if she didn't take up a deferred offer to study international law at university in Rome, and Beppe had moved there with her, but halfway through her second year the cancer was found to have spread to Marianna's lungs and lymph nodes and was pronounced terminal. Lara had moved back to Naples to nurse her through her final months of life. After revealing to her father at Marianna's funeral that she had no intention of resuming her studies and instead planned to join the State Police in Naples as a cadet, a rift had developed that persisted to this day. Beppe, with his suffocating grip on her, had been given a more gentle but no less definite brush-off. 'When you nurse someone through something like that . . . you realise how precious life is, how short,' Lara summarised. 'Too short to spend it with someone, or doing something, you don't love.'

Joe was silent. He watched out of the corner of his eye as Lara picked up the wine bottle that was sitting between them and poured a healthy measure into one of the two glasses, downing it in a single gulp. He was about to thank her for confiding in him, when the moment between them was interrupted by a piercing shriek of alarm.

They both swung around in the direction of the sound.

There was a second terrified shout and their eyes met briefly in bewilderment before they both scrambled to their feet.

'What the hell was that?' Joe blurted out.

But Lara didn't answer. She was already running back towards the house.

As the throng of guests parted at Lara's command, a young waitress was escorted past them by two colleagues; it was apparent from her tearful dismay that she'd just experienced something deeply traumatic. Lara and Joe forced their way through the crowd with even greater urgency and found themselves in a paved area between the rear of the villa and the swimming pool. A row of four portable toilets stood at one end, and beyond them was a stretch of scrubby grass leading to some equally uncultivated shrubs guarding a section of the same chain fence Joe had seen by the bench. A small group had congregated there and, as Joe made his way across in Lara's footsteps, he recognised Luisa.

'Thank God you're here,' Lara's aunt cried out, clinging shakily to her niece in shock. Lara shrugged her off as gently as she could and leaned forward to see what Luisa's companions were staring at. Joe stepped up behind her and just had time to note the depression in the top of the fence before he reached the edge and looked over.

A young woman, dressed in the same black and white garb as the waitresses, lay sprawled face-up on the rocky beach some fifty metres below, a large quantity of blood matting her golden-brown hair that fanned out in an irregular halo behind her. It took just one look at the unnatural way in which her limbs were arranged, and her staring yet sightless eyes, for Joe to tell she was dead.

It was almost midnight before Joe and Lara were able to draw breath, with the intervening hours passing in a blur. After making their way down to the beach and examining the body, Lara had put a call through to the Naples duty desk, but all her colleagues on the late shift were tied up with a drive-by shooting and it wasn't clear how soon anyone would be free to attend. By contrast, the old sergeant from the Capri station arrived with three of his constables within twenty minutes of being summoned, but it was immediately obvious to Joe that they had no real knowledge of how to secure and process a serious crime scene and that it would be up to him, in the first instance, to provide Lara with the expert assistance she needed. Witness statements had to be taken, the sooner the better. And everybody attending the event, either as a guest or employee, had to be spoken to and their details recorded before anyone could leave. While Lara, Sergeant Alfieri and one of his constables started this long and laborious process, Joe and the other two constables secured both the site from where the victim appeared to have fallen and the area on the beach where her body now lay. A photographer who'd been snapping the happy guests earlier in the evening was commandeered to document both scenes under

Joe's direction. They were only halfway through this unpleasant process when a team of paramedics arrived and everything was put on hold for half an hour, to Joe's frustration, while they confirmed the young woman's death. At last, he and his reluctant conscript were able to resume their work, until the first back-up from the mainland finally arrived around 11.45pm and they were relieved of their 'duties'.

Joe went in search of Lara and found her sitting with her aunt and uncle in Matteo's study. She'd changed back into her usual outfit of T-shirt, combat trousers and boots, had even removed the traces of make-up from her face, and he was glad of it. It was easier not to be distracted when she was in this mode.

A weeping Luisa could not stop apologising. They'd been nagging the freeholder to replace the fence for years, she said. If she'd known that staff working at the event were using that part of the grounds to take their cigarette breaks then she would have said something, would have warned them to stay back from the edge. What was supposed to be a happy day had turned into the worst of her life. It took several minutes of reassurance and cajoling before she could be persuaded to let go of Lara's hand and the two police officers were able to step out into the hallway.

Joe delivered his 'report'. The first scene-of-crime investigators had arrived but it would probably be a couple more hours before the body could be removed. Joe had done his best to preserve and document both sites with the resources available to him, but in his view the top of the cliff was already hopelessly compromised, with the rubberneckers having trampled any footprints that might have helped them work out if the victim had been alone when she went over the edge, and distinguish between a push and a fall.

'What are your instincts telling you?' Lara wanted to know.

Joe snorted softly. 'You don't believe in coincidences any more than I do.'

She nodded gravely.

He could tell they were both on the same page. 'Have you spoken to your boss?'

'A few minutes ago.' He'd been sleeping and wasn't happy to be woken, she said.

'And is he willing now to accept this is a murder investigation?'

She grimaced. 'He's arriving first thing. Wants to see everything for himself and review all the evidence before making a decision.'

'What can I do to help?'

'Go home,' Lara insisted. 'Get some sleep.' They'd be letting everyone go in the next few minutes, but it was likely to be another couple of hours before Lara herself would get to bed. It would be better if one of them was well rested and had their wits about them for the confrontation with Curti the following morning.

Joe acquiesced reluctantly, and went in search of Luca in the kitchen, thinking to ask if he wanted to share a taxi home, but the sous-chef was nowhere to be found, and when he enquired as to his whereabouts, Joe was met with shrugs and blank stares.

He returned to the main lawn, where the guests now sat at the tables, waiting sombrely for the moment of release. Joe wandered amongst them, looking for Gennaro's nephew, but there was no sign of him. He spoke to Sergeant Alfieri and consulted the list he'd compiled of the names and contact details of all the guests and staff.

But Luca Da Vinale was not among them.

21

Lara was reassured by Joe's presence on the quayside as the police boat bumped against the dock and her boss stepped ashore shortly after eight on the Thursday morning. Curti was all smiles as the introductions were made and he shook hands with Joe, thanking him in his clipped and precise English for the help he was offering 'to my department, and to Inspector Sarrancino. But we might ask you to vacation somewhere else in the future,' he joked, pointing out that the two unexplained deaths since Joe's arrival were two more than had occurred on Capri in the previous twelve months. Joe smiled grimly. The British joked about bringing the weather with them, he explained, but in his case there appeared to be a trail of death and misfortune following in his wake.

A police car was waiting to take them to the Villa San Benedetto. In the time it took them to cross the island, Lara had updated Curti on what they'd learned about the fatality. Her name was Zuzu Esposito and she'd signed up a few months back with an employment agency that supplied waiting and catering staff to private parties, had worked at least half a dozen similar events for the company before agreeing to serve drinks and wait tables at Lara's aunt and uncle's anniversary party. Zuzu was thirty years of age, according to the application form the agency had on file, and lived on the outskirts of Sorrento. Deputy Inspector

Gallo was heading there now, hoping to speak to friends or family. They had her phone number and were waiting to put a call through to her telecoms provider to gain access to her phone records. So far, that was all they had to go on.

They spent the next couple of hours walking the grounds of the villa, which had been vacated by Lara's family early that morning, and familiarising Curti with the location, as well as going over the witness statements they'd managed to gather the night before. Joe remained in the background, letting Lara do the talking, interjecting occasionally with an observation or an explanation when requested. She was grateful for his tact, as well as his foresight in having improvised crime-scene photography, for there was little else for them to go on at this stage. The ground near the fence from where Zuzu was believed to have fallen had been trampled, just as Joe said, and there was no chance of identifying a discernible footprint in the dust. And there was no CCTV installed from which to track the dead woman's movements. The witness statements were vague. The site of her fall had been hidden by the row of portable toilets and no one had seen Zuzu going over the edge. Nor had anyone heard her cry out in alarm, although it was possible a scream had gone unremarked beneath the sound of the jazz quartet. Zuzu was reported to have turned up promptly at 5pm and to have alternated between pouring and serving over the next couple of hours, with plenty of confirmed sightings of her on the main lawn prior to 8pm. She'd asked her supervisor if she could take a comfort break ahead of dinner being served and been granted permission. When there was no sign of her after fifteen minutes, a colleague, Mia, had been sent to look for her, had gone to the place they'd shared a cigarette on first arrival, and made her grisly discovery. Mia said Zuzu had seemed subdued throughout the evening, certainly preoccupied, perhaps even upset. She had hinted at troubles in her relationship, but Mia didn't really know her well enough to pry.

Lara was forced to admit to Curti that what physical evidence they had seemed to support the idea that Zuzu fell accidentally while satisfying her nicotine craving. A cigarette butt had been recovered on the beach less than a metre from where she'd been discovered and the traces of lipstick on the filter appeared to match the shade she was wearing. And then there was the perimeter fence, and the tell-tale sag in its outline. The wire was old, decades so, had lost much of its protective tautness. It was easy to imagine her leaning back against it in a moment of inattention and feeling it give way, sending her tumbling backwards over the edge.

And was there any evidence of foul play? Curti wanted to know.

'Only her phone at this stage, sir. It's missing.'

A missing phone? That was the opposite of evidence, wasn't it?

'We think someone might have taken it, *Commissario*. To prevent us finding it.'

'Maybe she didn't bring it with her.'

Lara pulled a face. A young woman going anywhere without her phone? 'More likely it's out there.' She mimicked lobbing a small object into the sea.

'You think someone pushed Shannon Headley to her death and then did the same to this young woman?' Curti persisted, his scepticism implicit in his question.

'That's what I believe, sir,' she replied firmly.

'And what about you, Detective Chief Inspector?' Curti asked, turning to Joe.

'If I was going to kill someone, then this is the MO I'd choose,' the English detective observed. 'I mean, think about it. Assuming there are no witnesses, no CCTV . . . then it's almost impossible to distinguish between a push and a fall. The injuries are going to be just as catastrophic either way and they may well mask the signs of any violence that preceded the victim going over the edge. There might be signs of a struggle up top, of course, but those are easy enough to obscure. The only thing our perpetrator has to worry about is making sure there's no digital footprint. So, they leave their own phone at home. And make sure they get rid of the victim's, just as Inspector Sarrancino's suggesting.'

Curti's mouth twitched, half-formed a moue of distaste.

Lara knew it wasn't what her boss wanted to hear. He'd been convinced Shannon Headley's death was suicide, had practically ordered her to close the case. Opening a murder inquiry involved a loss of face, would subtly alter the dynamic between them.

Joe must have sensed that his intervention was needed. 'Look, I understand your doubts. We've no real evidence of foul play in either case. But maybe that's the point.'

Curti considered this. 'One "accident" is *credible*. But two is one too many?'

'That's a neat way of putting it.'

In other words, there must be a link between Shannon Headley's death and Zuzu Esposito's, Curti continued, trying to reason it through aloud.

'Exactly. And if we can find the link, then there's our evidence.'

Curti thought about this. 'What if the man who did this . . . he's the only connection?'

It was Joe's turn to look uncertain. 'How do you mean?'

'Maybe we have . . . how would you say . . . a *madman* on our hands.'

Joe looked sceptical. 'Doesn't it all feel a bit too calculated for that?'

Lara decided it was time to step back in. 'We shouldn't rule anything out, *Commissario*. But the villa... it's a private space. We think someone must have known Zuzu was working here and deliberately come to seek her out. Someone familiar with the lay of the land. Who knew they could stage a fall here to look like another accident.'

Curti's gaze was drawn to the list of guests and staff that he held in his hand. He gestured to it. '*Allora*... one of these names?'

'Maybe, sir.'

Sensing a corner was being turned, Lara tried to shoot Joe a grateful look. But the English detective was too preoccupied to notice. He was staring dubiously at the list in Curti's hand, almost as if he doubted the name of the perpetrator was to be found there.

22

When Joe returned to Da Vinale's after his morning with Lara and Curti, Gennaro had just emerged from the kitchen and was greeting his guests on the terrace, a sure sign that the lunch service was nearly over. The old chef seemed his usual ebullient self as he made his way around the tables, with Elena at his side rolling her eyes good-naturedly and smiling at his jokes. All trace of plate-throwing fury seemed forgotten between them.

Exchanging a slight wave of acknowledgement with his mother-in-law, Joe slipped past, intending to go to the apartment for a shower and maybe a siesta. He was exhausted and mentally wrung out by the events of the previous evening. As he made his way through the interior of the restaurant, however, a waitress was exiting the kitchen and behind her he could see Luca removing his apron at the end of his shift. It occurred to Joe he should question him about his whereabouts before he forgot.

'What happened to you?' he asked, forgoing the usual niceties as he pushed through the swing doors.

Luca's instinctive smile of greeting turned into a frown.

'Last night,' Joe persisted. 'I came looking for you.'

'I got bored. With waiting.'

'A woman died, Luca.'

'I know. And I'm sorry about that.'

'Everyone else managed to grin and bear it.'

The sous-chef looked a little shame-faced. 'I feel bad for her. What else do you want me to say?'

'You could tell me why you were in such a hurry to leave.'

'That sort of thing... a death... it's for you to worry about. It's no business of mine.'

'Are you saying you didn't know her?'

'I've seen her around. But we've never spoken.'

Joe felt himself growing irritated. 'So what time did you leave?'

Luca stared at him, faintly incredulous. 'Are you questioning me?'

'I just want to know.'

'I have no idea. Eleven? Twelve maybe.'

'And which way did you go when you left?'

Luca said nothing.

'There was a policeman on the gate, Luca. With instructions not to let anyone out.'

The two men stared at one another.

'We took contact details for all the guests and everyone who was working,' Joe persisted. There was no need to add that Luca's name wasn't on the list that he'd last seen Curti holding.

A flicker of something passed across Luca's face. 'I found another way. OK?'

It was then that his conversation with Matteo about the smuggler's staircase came back to Joe. It had seemed a quaint detail at the time, and he'd barely paid attention, so disconcerted had he been by Lara's appearance. But now it seemed to take on a new significance. There was a way to access and exit the villa and its grounds undetected. He tried to recall the appearance of the stranger he'd seen walking beyond the perimeter fence. Dark hair. A man-bun. A tattoo, maybe. It was a description that covered a decent percentage of the masculine population within fifty miles of Naples.

Joe was about to question Luca further when the double doors to the kitchen swung open and Gennaro entered. It was clear from his demeanour that Luca hadn't yet informed him about the events of the previous evening. With a look towards the sous-chef that suggested now might be the time, Joe made his excuses and left.

Elena was standing by the window in the apartment's kitchen sipping from a mug held between both hands when Joe entered, freshly showered and dressed. She turned to indicate the teapot, which was standing on the table next to a cake tin, instructed him to help himself.

'It's the last bit of Englishness I'm clinging on to,' she told him, holding up her tea. 'I don't know how the Italians can stand to drink coffee all day.'

Joe poured himself a mug. Warily he took a seat. Their last meaningful conversation was painfully imprinted on his mind but, to his relief, as she came to join him at the table, a different matter was on hers.

'Luca told Gennaro what happened.'

'You mean last night? At this party?'

Elena gestured . . . *what else?* 'Why didn't you say something?'

'I was going to. At the right moment.'

Did this mean he'd have to stay involved in the investigation, his mother-in-law wanted to know.

Joe explained the situation with Lara and Curti. He wasn't sure of his own status if it turned into a murder inquiry. But he was willing to lend his expertise if requested.

Elena digested this. 'And should we be worried?'

He was momentarily nonplussed. 'For the restaurant?'

'For goodness' sake, Joe! For *Angelica*.'

The idea that his daughter might be in danger had not occurred to Joe. *Maybe I am a terrible parent*, he thought. 'I can't swear on it . . . but I don't think so.'

'You don't think you should warn her? That there might be someone out there who poses a threat to young women. Maybe to her.'

'I'm pretty sure there isn't, Elena.'

'And yet two of them are dead.'

Joe did his best to reassure her. They shouldn't get ahead of themselves. It was still possible they were dealing with two tragic accidents, unrelated and coincidental.

Elena pulled a face. He'd tried that line before, she told him. He sounded no more convinced of it now than he did then.

All right, he *did* think foul play might be involved, Joe admitted. No, more than that, he was almost certain of it. But that didn't mean they were dealing with the random acts of a maniac. 'There's going to be a connection. I know it. We've just got to find it.'

'I still think you should tell Angelica to be on her guard.'

'I will do. I promise.'

The sooner the better, she insisted. 'She's out there somewhere. With that boy.'

Joe repeated his promise. 'You've got to trust me, Elena. I know you don't think I'm much of a parent, but I wouldn't hesitate to act if I thought she was in danger.'

His mother-in-law looked mortified. 'I never said that.'

'It's OK. You were right to call me out over the way I am with her.' He took a moment to pick his words. 'I don't know how to guide her . . . how to parent her . . . without Sofia. And I get angry at myself. And then at her. Every time.'

'You're a good man, Joe. Just trust your instincts.'

He huffed with frustration. 'Believe me, I'm trying.'

There was a silence. 'I'm sorry too,' Elena said at last, looking like she meant it. 'I said some things that were . . . *harsher* than intended. I know this is hard for you. Without role models of your own to fall back on.'

Joe blinked and frowned.

'You know. The situation with your family.'

'What about my family?'

Elena flushed.

'Elena?'

She met his eye, but he could tell she knew she'd let something slip. 'We learn to parent from our parents, Joe,' she said, mustering a note of defiance.

It felt almost like she'd slapped him. 'Sofia told you?' he managed to blurt out.

'Of course.'

'Everything?'

'She thought I needed to know.'

Joe felt the old shame rising. He didn't trust himself to speak and he got up and went over to the sink to wash out his mug, for want of anything else to do. He heard Elena push back her chair and, a moment later, he sensed her presence at his side. She rubbed his upper arm with the back of her hand, trying to communicate, in that most English of ways, what she couldn't seem to find the words for.

'It's what families do. They talk.'

Still he did not risk looking at her.

'Gennaro... he always wants to know what I'm thinking,' she went on. 'What I'm feeling. Sofia was the same.'

It was true, he thought. It had been the most challenging part of learning to be intimate with her. But also the most rewarding.

'It's all so different to the way everyone is back home,' Elena continued. 'To the way I was brought up. And you too, I imagine.'

He made a noise in the back of his throat that he hoped sounded like agreement.

'It's why I fell in love with him, I suppose. And followed him here. Why I stayed.'

'She's the only person I've ever told,' he said simply, finally meeting her eye.

Elena's surprise was obvious. 'Not even Angelica?'

He shook his head. 'My mum... she made a lot of mistakes.'

'What kind of mistakes?'

'The kind that start as a bit of fun. And end up killing you.'

'Oh, Joe.' Elena's hand went to her mouth. 'Sofia told me she'd got into trouble. That she'd given you up at a young age. She didn't tell me that drugs were involved.'

'I'm trying to protect Angelica.'

'Then *talk* to her. *Tell* her. It'll help her understand.' She took his hand between hers and squeezed, her eyes searching his face for a signal of assent.

Joe nodded and squeezed back.

'Come on,' she told him, attempting to defuse the moment. 'I'm going to be offended if you don't at least *try* a bit of my cake.'

Joe let Elena usher him back to the table. The cake tin was opened and a slice was cut for him to sample. He didn't need a second invitation to sink a fork in. God, it was *good*. Light but moist. Sugary, buttery and creamy without being cloying. There were delicate citrus and vanilla high notes detectable above the bass, malty nuttiness of the pistachios that somehow managed to be both sweet and savoury at the same time. He let slip a small murmur of gratification and caught Elena smiling at him, smiled back.

'You were right about the pistachios,' he said, deploying his fork a second time.

'That's the whole point of a recipe, Joe. Every detail matters. However small.'

Joe stopped with his fork mid-air. 'Say that again.'

Elena looked bemused. 'Which bit?'

Every detail matters.

As good as it was, another mouthful of cake would have to wait. Joe put down his fork and slipped out his phone, was dialling Lara's number as he left the room.

23

'We need to get that rash on Shannon's body properly tested. It may seem insignificant, but we just don't know . . . it could be the thing that cracks the case open.'

Lara stared at the English detective, trying to work out what had lit a fire under him. He'd come barrelling into the police station a few minutes earlier, just as she was finishing a rather strained conversation with Curti, who seemed to have taken the death of Zuzu Esposito as a personal affront.

'Every detail matters, Lara,' he persisted. 'However small.'

'All right, all right. Let me get on to it.' Lara sighed. She tapped at the keyboard of the open laptop in front of her, added *Rash? Contact path lab* to her growing to-do list.

'When?'

'When I can, Joe,' she snapped. 'There are other things that need looking into first.'

'OK. Like what?'

He was like a dog with a bone, she thought. 'Like this,' she announced, finding the document she was looking for amongst her paperwork. He picked it up and examined it, and Lara felt a surge of satisfaction that he didn't appear to have spotted the lead she'd just handed him. It was a photocopy of Zuzu Esposito's ID card, which Gianni had brought back from her flat in Sorrento.

As if on cue, he looked up, his face a question. 'Don't we already know all this?'

'Look again. At her full name.'

'Azz-ur-ra.' He enunciated it syllable by syllable. 'Is that what Zuzu is short for?'

She nodded. 'It doesn't ring any bells?'

He thought about it, shook his head.

Lara took pleasure in opening her notebook and finding the page where she'd written up her interview with Signor Carlotti, manager of the Hotel Americano. She'd ringed two names on the page and now she turned the book to show Joe.

Still he looked mystified.

'The woman on the concierge desk at the hotel . . . I told you she couldn't remember the name of the masseuse that Shannon made enquiries about,' Lara explained. 'She was fairly sure that it started with an A though. Something like Annunziata or Assunta.'

'Or maybe Azzurra,' Joe added, finally twigging.

Lara couldn't help smiling.

'Feels a bit of a stretch.'

'Perhaps. But Gianni spoke to the owner of her flat. And guess how Zuzu makes her money when she's not serving drinks and waiting tables?'

The front of the beauty salon could easily have been mistaken for a domestic property, if it hadn't been for the metallic grille that covered the outsized window, and the small plastic badge stuck to the inside of the glass that spoke to some form of professional accreditation. The interior of the building conformed more closely to Lara's expectations, with a comfortably furnished reception area giving way to a nail bar fitted out with everything necessary for manicures and pedicures. To the rear there were treatment rooms for massages, as well as a couple of tanning beds in the basement, the proprietor explained. Francesca Capuso was a large woman dressed in leopard print, most likely in her late sixties, Lara guessed, although she was clearly making every effort to seem younger by taking advantage of the treatments her salon supplied.

Zuzu had been one of her 'girls', Signora Capuso confirmed, dabbing her eyes with a handkerchief. She'd been like a mother to her, the woman continued, explaining tearfully that Zuzu's own parents had died within a couple of years of her joining the salon after leaving school at sixteen. She'd been with her ever since, aside from an eight-month window when she'd handed in her notice intending to get married, only for her fiancé to lose his life during the Covid pandemic. Pietro had seemed the picture of good health, the proprietor insisted, but, as a health worker on the front line, he'd fallen critically ill in those first chaotic weeks and never recovered.

'That poor child,' she lamented. 'So much sadness in such a short life.' Zuzu had started dating again in the last year, although her other girls had implied to Signora Capuso that her new man was a womaniser and a gambler who was leeching off her and bleeding her dry. The salon owner had never met the man in question and had no way of knowing the truth of it, but Zuzu had been working noticeably longer hours in the last few months, and had seemed particularly downbeat in recent days, leading her employer to jump to the obvious conclusion, she admitted, when she heard what had happened.

Lara chose to ignore her intimation. Could Signora Capuso let them know about any clients that Zuzu might have treated in the salon the previous Saturday?

The proprietor gestured apologetically. She was looking for a buyer for the salon, she explained, and was trying to keep her costs down, which had led her, reluctantly, to move all her girls onto freelance contracts. It meant they were their own bosses and Signora Capuso just charged them a percentage of their fees for using her facilities.

'So you don't keep a record of her clients?'

Signora Capuso shook her head. Zuzu recorded the treatments she gave and the dates and times she was in the salon, because the fees she paid were calculated by the hour, but she wasn't obliged to detail the names of her clients. The proprietor waddled over to the reception desk and returned with a diary that was intended to prove her point. The page for the date in question contained an entry written in a neat hand in red biro: *Massagio profundo/impacco. Dalle 12 alle 14.*

Lara felt her heart sink. 'Is that all?'

'I'm sorry.'

She turned the book to show Joe, translated for his benefit. A deep-tissue massage and some kind of body wrap between noon and 2pm. It coincided broadly with what they knew of Shannon's movements which was something, she supposed, but not much.

Francesca was about to return the diary to where she'd found it when a thought occurred to her. Actually, there might be something else, she exclaimed, turning back and flipping to the rear of the book. 'Here,' she said, showing Lara the inside back page, where a list of names were written down.

'What am I looking at?' Lara asked, trying to make sense of it.

It was a record of products Zuzu had used, Signora Capuso explained. She was meticulous when it came to writing down and paying for things she'd utilised in the salon.

Lara squinted at the final few entries. The third last was written in the same red pen as the appointment registered on the last day Shannon Headley had been seen alive.

Trattamento in argilla per rilassare e detossificare il corpo. Una vasca. 500g. €69.99.

'What does it say?' Joe was at her shoulder now, suddenly engaged.

'Cleanse and relax body clay. One tub.'

'Expensive stuff.'

Lara was inclined to agree, although she had no way of knowing . . . her beauty regime consisted of nothing more than soap and water. She turned back to Signora Capuso. 'Can you tell us what it's used for?'

Body clay was a full body treatment that did wonders for a woman's skin, the proprietor advised. It opened pores and flushed out toxins, particularly after a massage.

Lara was about to voice her next question but Joe beat her to it.

'Ask her if we can search her bins.'

The two detectives had climbed into the dumpster at the rear of the building and were knee-deep in bags of refuse before Signora Capuso remembered to inform Lara that the bin was shared with the commercial properties on either side of her salon and that the people from the Communal Council came to empty it bi-weekly. It was possible, therefore, that whatever they were looking for had already been taken to the landfill.

'Now she tells us,' Joe said, shooting Lara a wry look as the proprietor withdrew.

'You think the body clay caused the rash on Shannon's body?'

'It must be one of the last things that was applied to her skin.'

'We don't even know it was her that was here, Joe.'

'A deep-tissue massage?' It was exactly the sort of treatment Shannon had been having regularly since her accident, he reminded her.

She conceded the point. But even assuming it *was* the dead woman who'd come to the salon, and that she'd suffered an allergic reaction to the body clay, it didn't seem to get them any closer to understanding how she'd ended up dead at the bottom of a cliff.

'If we can prove she had an allergic reaction to the body clay . . . then it confirms the connection between her and Zuzu. And, like I told your boss, if we can establish that connection, then it's a safe bet—'

'—that their deaths are related,' Lara interrupted.

'It's why we need to insist on that rash being tested.'

Lara sighed. The rash again. He was obsessed. She gestured to the bags of rubbish. 'If you think it's that important . . . maybe we'd better leave this to forensics.'

Taking a firm grip on the dumpster's metal side, Lara vaulted over it and landed nimbly on her feet on the ground. She turned back to watch Joe follow her lead but, as he swung a long leg over the side in an ungainly fashion, something must have caught his eye, because he abandoned his attempt to get out and ducked down to pick up whatever it was he'd seen. A moment later he reappeared holding a pink plastic tube, and, briefly, Lara assumed he'd found the remains of the body clay, but as Joe turned it to show her, she saw that it was something completely different.

Angelica, the label read. *Crema Emolliente.* Beneath it was a logo of a stylised figure of an angel, hands clasped together in prayer.

Lara looked to Joe for an explanation.

He dropped the tube back into the dumpster and wiped his hands on his trousers, had the decency to look sheepish. 'It's my daughter's name,' was all he said.

24

It was Curti who suggested they eat at Da Vinale's. After his phone call with his boss, the *vice questore*, he was ready to announce the launch of a murder inquiry the following morning, he told Joe and Lara. Before he did so, however, there was the small matter of dinner to attend to. What about that place on the coast he'd heard so much about? Hadn't Inspector Sarrancino said it was run by DCI Mottram's in-laws?

Their appearance at the restaurant caused a commotion, with Elena deducing that Curti was a 'somebody' in local law enforcement. They were fully booked, she grumbled *sotto voce* to her son-in-law, while insisting out loud that they wait at the bar with a complementary aperitif so she could consult her husband on whether they could accommodate them. Joe had the uneasy feeling they were about to be turned away, a feeling that was reinforced by the sight of Gennaro gesturing irritably as he emerged from the kitchen to consult the seating plan with Elena. Shortly afterwards, however, his mother-in-law returned to tell Joe they would add a table on the terrace, although it would have to be at the end furthest from the kitchen. Curti seemed happy enough and Joe felt a surge of gratitude for his in-laws for not embarrassing him. He tried to wave Gennaro over, not wanting there to be any lingering bad feeling about the imposition. At first, it seemed his father-in-law hadn't seen him and was about to return to the kitchen. 'Gennaro!' he called out, and the old chef turned in his direction.

As he and Curti were introduced, Gennaro displayed little of his customary warmth. He was civil enough, but his manner was wary, possibly even on edge, Joe couldn't help observing, and he found himself overcompensating. People travelled from every corner of the globe to eat at Gennaro Da Vinale's restaurant, he told Curti.

Curti was almost as hyperbolic in turn. He'd heard great things about the food at Da Vinale's, he told a still unsmiling Gennaro, had been meaning to visit for the longest time. Did the *maestro* have any recommendations for what they should eat?

'That depends on who's paying,' the old chef deadpanned.

The State Police would pick up the tab, Curti reassured him. It was the least they could do to thank Joe for the help he'd given them.

In that case, Gennaro told them matter-of-factly, he had an eel that had been pulled out of the sea that morning. It would be dusted with flour and seasoning, pan-fried with garlic and rosemary and served on aubergine and tomatoes.

Curti slapped his menu closed and asked Gennaro to supply them additionally with a selection of entrées as well as a decent bottle of white from somewhere in the region. 'But nothing too expensive,' he added, insisting he knew how much the restaurants marked up their prices for the tourists.

Gennaro bristled openly for the first time. 'We're just trying to make some money to live on. It's hard enough in this damned country at the best of times.'

The *commissario* raised his hands in a gesture of apology. 'It was a joke. I didn't mean to offend you.' Gennaro must be the most honest restaurateur on the island, he continued, catching

Joe's eye as he did so. 'Your son-in-law . . . he's such a good detective, there's no way you could get away with anything.' Curti was laughing as he said it and the old chef managed a slight smile in response, but as he made his excuses to return to the kitchen, it seemed to Joe his expression stiffened.

'*Allora*. To business then,' Curti suggested, helping himself from the bread basket.

Lara summarised the steps she'd be taking as senior investigative officer now the murder inquiry was confirmed. They would conduct a forensic examination of Shannon's hotel room and fingertip searches of the area around Villa Jovis and Tiberius's Leap, which had belatedly been closed to the public, as well as the various sites at the Villa San Benedetto associated with Zuzu Esposito's fall. A team would go door-to-door in Tiberio asking for footage from video doorbells or security cameras that might help them track Shannon Headley's movements more accurately. And a team back at base would review footage from the CCTV at the Hotel Americano.

Curti grunted, seemed satisfied that *something* was being done, and turned his attention to a dish of fritto misto and a platter of grilled prawns that had just arrived at the table. For a while, his sole focus was the food and the conversation lapsed, but as the plates were being cleared, he returned to the subject at hand. 'Inspector Sarrancino has told me about your *theory*,' he told Joe, fixing him with a stare. 'This thing with the photo.'

The stress on *theory* was provocative, but Joe didn't take the bait.

'Perhaps you can explain it again. For my benefit.'

Patiently, Joe talked Curti through his views on the 'selfie' and the evidence supplied by Shannon's father that implied she wouldn't have been able to take it herself.

Curti burped gently as he took his time to digest this. 'Then who do you think did?'

Ah, the difficult bit. Joe looked to Lara, who was clearly thinking the same thing.

'There's one person we're pretty sure we can rule out,' she told her boss.

'The fiancé?'

'That's right, *Commissario.*' Lara reminded her boss that their working theory was that one person was responsible for both murders. Manny Sanghera's alibi for the time of Shannon's death had now been confirmed by multiple sources and, while there was a suggestion of a motive in the prenuptial contract, it seemed certain that whoever pushed Zuzu Esposito must have had some local knowledge of the villa and its environs, which he almost certainly did not. They were working their way through the list of guests at the anniversary party, but many of them had already been able to account for their whereabouts at the time they believed Shannon Headley had died on the Saturday. They were also doing background checks on the dozen or so locals who'd worked at the event but it was just as likely that someone unknown had accessed the grounds of the villa via a back route – most likely the secret staircase, which linked the villa's cellar and the plant room for its swimming pool with the beach – and murdered her before fleeing undetected. The assumption had to be that whoever had pushed Zuzu was known to her, and that they'd also known she was working at the party. Was she targeted because she knew something about Shannon Headley's death? The description that DCI Mottram had been able to supply of a man spotted near the perimeter fence shortly after Zuzu was believed to have been pushed had been circulated to all the officers involved in the investigation, but it was only likely to be of use if a suspect was identified.

Curti wiped his hands. 'So, what leads do we have that can help us identify him?'

'We think Shannon Headley may have connected with someone on Capri via Girl Cupid,' Lara told him. Manny had testified to the open nature of their relationship and Shannon was on the record in interviews as saying she was an avid user of dating apps. She had the Girl Cupid app on her phone. Lara outlined the steps they were taking to access her messages to see if their hunch was correct, adding that Dr Serafina had yet to respond to Lara's request to re-examine the corpse for signs of sexual activity.

Curti's expression suggested this wasn't something he wanted to contemplate while he was eating. He was interested to know how dating apps worked, however, and Lara obliged him with an explanation. Was her knowledge first hand? 'I've used them once or twice,' she admitted, rolling her eyes slightly for Joe's benefit.

'To meet up with men?'

'Something like that, sir.'

Curti considered this. 'And you're certain we need these people's permission to get access to any messages that Shannon may have sent?'

'That's right. The app's got end-to-end encryption.'

'Are they going to cooperate?'

'I hope so. Given that our victim is their founder and CEO.'

Curti turned his beady eyes back on Joe. 'Is that something you can help with?'

Joe looked surprised by such a direct request over Lara's head. 'Me?'

'*Si*, Detective Chief Inspector. You.' Curti took a sip of wine.

He was going to approach the British Embassy in Rome to ask if Joe could be formally seconded to the investigation. No more consulting from the sidelines. It was time to get his hands dirty.

From the look on her face, it was clear to Joe this was the first Lara had heard of his proposal. 'It's Inspector Sarrancino's case,' he countered.

'And it will remain her case.' Curti now looked to Lara in turn. 'But it would be stupid not to take advantage of his *esperienza*. Don't you think, Inspector?'

Lara kept a straight face, nodded. 'Yes, sir. Of course.'

Joe glanced across to the far end of the terrace where Elena was supervising a table being cleared. 'I'm supposed to be on holiday. Spending time with my in-laws.'

'They'll understand. A man like you . . . he gets bored easily. Just sitting around.'

Joe made a last effort to spare Lara's blushes. 'Perhaps I can make myself available, you know . . . as and when. If Inspector Sarrancino wants to talk something through. A sort of . . . sounding board, if you like. On the other end of the phone.'

Curti shook his head decisively. He wouldn't agree to anything irregular that might be open to legal challenge and could jeopardise the investigation, he told Joe. If he was going to be involved then it had to be officially signed off, and all above board.

It was at that point that the pan-fried eel made its appearance. If Joe had been in a mood to raise further objections, he wouldn't have been able to because, from that point on, all Curti's focus was given over to the food.

There was no chance for Joe to discuss Curti's proposal with Lara and to gauge how she felt about it. They were forced to say their goodbyes in the *commissario*'s presence on the street outside Da Vinale's, with a cab waiting to take the two Italian police officers back to the marina. Lara promised to call Joe as soon as she heard anything official. It might take a day or two. He should just sit tight.

As he returned to the restaurant's terrace, Elena was waiting for him.

'Who was that?' she asked him.

Joe explained.

'He's a big fish, is he?'

'I suppose so. With the State Police.'

'He certainly ate like one.'

Joe laughed.

'Gennaro says he was treating you like you're God's anointed,' Elena continued.

'I don't know about that.'

'He thinks he's ready to make you chief of police in his place.'

'Well, he has just offered me a job.'

'About time. Someone needs to find out what happened to those two women.'

'I'll just be a consultant,' Joe clarified. 'I won't be in charge.'

'But they'll be paying you?'

'If it goes ahead.' It would need Home Office approval, Joe explained. He watched his mother-in-law calibrating what it meant.

'I didn't even know it was possible for English people to work for the Italian police,' she observed, turning back to resume her duties.

Joe had to admit inwardly that neither did he.

25

The bureaucratic wheels turned slowly.

Joe called his superintendent to inform him of Curti's request that same evening, but it was the following Monday before an approach was received from the Department of Public Security, and another two days had passed before Dan Keely rang him back. It wasn't until the Friday – a full twelve days after Shannon's body had been found – that an institutional work-around was cobbled together. Joe would be seconded until September to Interpol, in which both Britain and Italy were partners, and Interpol would accede to an Italian State Police request from Naples for assistance with the case.

With no option but to wait, Joe grew bored, just as Curti had predicted he would. His in-laws were tied up with the restaurant, and Angelica was preoccupied with the boy she'd met. At Elena's prompting, he tried to talk to her about the case, the need to be on her guard, but she saw this as an attempt to clip her wings. Daniele would look after her, she insisted.

Joe phoned Lara frequently, but she was tied up in red tape, with the lawyers at Girl Cupid insisting they needed to consult the company's incoming owners about her request to access Shannon's account, and citing data protection to justify a temporary refusal. They were keen to help, they insisted, but Shannon's connections through the app had the same right to privacy she had, and they needed to seek permission from all of them for their details and the content of their exchanges to be shared. They refused to confirm if Shannon had used the app while visiting Capri.

To add to Joe's growing sense of frustration, he also learned from Lara that Dr Serafina was absent from work following a family bereavement, although she'd omitted to put her 'out of office' on. At least it explained why Lara's emails had gone unanswered, but it also meant there was no prospect of a re-examination of Shannon's body any time soon, with her deputy refusing either to interrupt her bereavement leave or repeat an examination done by his superior without her express permission.

If Lara was annoyed about the proposed formalising of his secondment, then she did an excellent job of hiding it. Joe decided to stop worrying about whether her feelings were hurt. She should be happy for any help she could get, he reasoned to himself.

Gennaro had suggested going out in a boat a couple of times but nothing had come of it and Joe had almost forgotten about the possibility, when the old chef appeared at his bedside very early on the Wednesday of that fallow week and shook him awake.

'What is it? What's happened?' Joe asked, sitting bolt upright.

'Nothing. I thought we'd go fishing.'

As his senses reasserted themselves, Joe looked towards the window, where the grey light of dawn could be seen creeping around the edges of the blind. He glanced at the travelling alarm clock on his bedside table. 'It's five in the morning.'

'The fish don't know that.'

'Do you need some for the restaurant?'

'I buy those. This is just for fun.'

It hadn't felt much like fun as they'd lugged their tackle and a cool box to the marina and loaded it all into Luca's boat. As they motored out to sea, however, and the rising sun began to warm his bones, Joe's mood improved, and by the time Gennaro killed the outboard and let the vessel drift, he was almost starting to enjoy the experience. His father-in-law showed him how to tie his hook and then bait it with a fishy offcut. Soon enough, the lines were cast and the two men settled into a long silence, punctuated only by an occasional click of their reels. The sun rose higher. There was barely a breath of wind. The rocking motion of the boat was soothing. Joe may even have dozed off because the next thing he knew he was coming to with a start. He looked at his watch. They'd been at sea almost an hour and barely a word had passed between them. The silence that not long ago had seemed companionable was now starting to oppress him. 'Has Elena told you about this secondment?' he ventured, voicing what was front of mind. His words sounded strangely flat against the vast ocean.

Gennaro grunted his assent. He evidently didn't feel the same need to talk.

Joe left it a while before he spoke again. He'd been considering asking his father-in-law if he'd heard any gossip about the murders among his associates on the island, but now the moment presented itself, he was worried the old chef might be offended by what his question implied. 'And it doesn't bother you?' he limited himself to enquiring.

The old chef stared at him. 'Why would it?'

'Well, it's just . . . you don't seem to have a very good opinion of the local police.'

His father-in-law's face confirmed it. 'I don't trust them.'

Elena had said as much, Joe told him. And the same was obvious when he'd dined at Da Vinale's with his colleagues. 'It was like I'd brought a bad smell into the restaurant.'

Gennaro softened a little. 'I hope I didn't embarrass you.'

'Of course you didn't. But I couldn't help wondering what was behind it.'

Gennaro busied himself with his rod. 'I have a lot on my mind.'

'Money troubles?' It was out before Joe could weigh the wisdom of saying it.

His father-in-law glanced up at him sharply.

'That guy . . . who came to the restaurant.'

'Like I told you . . . the money I owe him, it was a week late.'

Gennaro's voice had gone up a notch, and Joe could sense he was getting stressed.

'You said things were *complicated*,' he reminded him as gently as he could.

The old chef sighed and ran a hand through his hair. 'They are.'

'The restaurant . . . it always seems to be booked out.'

'*Si. Si. È molto occupato.*'

'Then what's the problem?'

His father-in-law gave him what could only be described as a despairing look. 'I'm no good with money. Elena . . . she says it slips through my fingers.'

'Surely you could find ways to make more.'

'You think I haven't tried?'

'You have a name, Gennaro. A reputation. You should use it.'

Gennaro's despair was turning to exasperation. 'And write a damn cookbook?!'

'Why not?'

'You sound like Sofia.'

Joe felt himself blanch. 'Forget it,' he managed to say.

'Because I said "Sofia"?' The old chef suddenly seemed riled. 'You can't talk about something else every time I say her name.'

Joe didn't respond. He watched his fishing line twitching in the tide. Beyond it, the glassy, swirling waters stretched to the horizon in every shade of blue from cyan to cerulean. Seagulls circled above, their plaintive cries a suitably melancholy soundtrack to the thoughts and memories that still haunted him.

When Gennaro spoke again, his tone was noticeably less heated. 'It's part of grieving, Joe. Of healing. To talk about the ones we lost. With those that loved them too.'

Joe kept his head down. 'I can't.'

'Then you must learn to. It's not healthy.'

'I just can't, Gennaro.'

There was another silence. Joe felt a hand on his shoulder. He managed to look up and meet the old chef's eye. The look that greeted him was one of understanding. 'Come on,' he said. 'We should go back. The fishing gods . . . they're not smiling on us.'

As Joe gave Gennaro a grateful smile, his rod jerked and went taut in his hands.

Instantly the old chef grew animated. 'Pull, Joe!' he urged him. 'Pull!'

On a deserted semicircle of remote beach, they cleared a hollow in the stones and lit a fire, making use of the kerosene and the charcoal Gennaro had brought with him and whatever driftwood they could find. The old chef showed Joe how to prepare the fish he'd caught. It was just over a foot long, with distinctive red, yellow and silver colouring.

'A parrot fish,' his father-in-law informed him, scraping off its scales.

'It's just asking to be caught,' Joe observed. 'Looking like that.'

'To be this colourful . . . this *evidente*. It has advantages in nature.'

'What kind of advantages?'

'It helps attract females. And to lure predators away from a nest.'

'How does that work?'

'It's called . . . *una posa da distrazione.*'

Joe grasped for a translation. 'A distraction display?'

'*Sì.* You find it everywhere. Among animals.'

Joe suddenly found himself thinking of the red-haired man in the Hawaiian shirt who had posed and sung loudly as he and his companions were ferried ashore that first morning. That was surely a distraction display if ever there was one. 'And humans, I think,' he said with feeling.

Gennaro laughed gruffly as he set about slicing off the tail and fins and cutting open the belly to remove the guts. He sent Joe to rinse the fish in the sea, while he removed a small chopping board from his backpack and the various ingredients he'd brought along. When Joe returned with his cleaned and gutted catch, the old chef stuffed it with slices of lemon and handfuls of parsley and dill. He tore a length of silver foil and laid the fish on top of it, coating it lovingly with virgin olive oil, a spritz of lemon juice and a sprinkle of sea salt and cracked black pepper. The foil was wrapped loosely around the fish and it was tossed onto the edge of the fire, where it lay for the next quarter of an hour, being turned only once. While they waited for it to cook, Gennaro produced floury ciabatta rolls from his backpack. He cut them open and added slices from an enormous beef tomato and the most vividly purple onion Joe had ever seen. When he was satisfied the fish was cooked, Gennaro opened the parcel and filleted it carefully, transferring a portion of the steaming flesh to both rolls and crowning each with a last drizzle of olive oil and a sprig of dill. He handed one to Joe and raised the other in a gesture of communion, before taking an enormous bite. Joe was ravenous and he followed his father-in-law's lead. The fish was piping hot and perfectly soft, the tomato zinging with freshness, the onion spicily tart. It was the most glorious mouthful. He satisfied himself with performing a silent pantomime of appreciation for his father-in-law, who nodded his head in understanding, but seemed equally content to let the food speak for itself.

They had just doused the fire and were repacking Gennaro's rucksack when Joe felt the urge to speak again. 'You know, I *have* money, Gennaro. If you ever need it.'

'Please, Joe.' The old chef looked pained. 'Not this again.'

Sofia's life insurance had paid out, Joe persisted, with only a slight tremor as he said it, and he'd been told he was due a criminal compensation payment. With Angelica having opted out of her private day school in favour of sixth form at her local comprehensive, he had more money than he knew what to do with.

Gennaro put a hand on his arm. 'I can't.'

'Why not? We're family. We help each other.' But even as Joe said it, he couldn't help wondering if it were true. Did his father-in-law still think of *him* as family? And if he did, would that extend to passing on any intelligence about the killings if it happened to fall into his lap from his many connections on the island?

Having somewhat cleared the air with Gennaro, the fishing expedition gave Joe an idea for how he might do the same with his daughter.

He roped in reinforcements, securing agreement for the loan of Luca's boat that came with an offer from Luca himself to drive it, before he approached Angelica. There were some fantastic caves along the south coast of the island that might be good for snorkelling. Luca had agreed to take him one afternoon. Did she fancy it?

Angelica was non-committal, but he set both Elena and Luca to work on her and gradually she warmed to the idea. A date was set for the Saturday afternoon, when Daniele would be working at the beach club and she'd be at a loose end. They would set off after the lunch service was over and take a picnic with them.

The snorkelling itself was underwhelming. The emerald waters of the Grotta Verde were inviting enough but the seabed beneath was barren. They swam further out and explored a kelp forest, but there was precious little fauna, and Luca suggested they try further along the coast. They had better luck in the waters around Punta Carena, with colourful soft corals on display and an occasional grouper fish hiding amongst them, but they were all happy enough to abandon the water and take to the beach. They settled their towels on the baking rocks and let their bodies dry, luxuriating in the heat for a long time before their thoughts turned to food. Elena had done them proud, with a mouth-watering selection of antipasti in the basket she'd packed for them, as well as grapes and peaches bursting with flavour, and a bar of chocolate. There was even a bottle of wine to pass between them. Joe decided not to make an issue of Angelica drinking on this occasion.

As he'd hoped, Luca provided some much-needed ballast between the two of them. He kept them amused with his observations on their fellow beachgoers, and thrilled Angelica by recounting the more scandalous escapades of their shared Da Vinale ancestors. According to Luca, Gennaro's bloodline could be traced back through a succession of ne'er-do-wells, including pirates, sheep rustlers and even a hired killer. But at least the family had always eaten well, he concluded with a grin. Joe felt his reservations melt away about how shifty Luca's behaviour had seemed after the anniversary party. He was almost sorry when the sous-chef excused himself to go and say hello to some friends he claimed to have spotted at the far end of the beach.

His departure left father and daughter alone together, as Joe had intended, without headphones or a crime novel to fall back on. He'd practised in his head what he would say, but now the moment had arrived, the words dried up.

It was Angelica who filled the gap. 'You look relaxed.'

'I am.'

'Almost like you're enjoying yourself.'

She said it with a smile and he couldn't help smiling back. 'We should maybe try and do this kind of thing more often,' he said experimentally.

'Maybe we should.'

Joe detected a faint hint of good-humoured mockery. 'Although there's something to be said for staying busy,' he added, deciding it wouldn't do to let her get carried away.

'*Daaaad*. No lectures. Not today.'

She had inadvertently presented him with an opening. 'Actually, there's something I need to talk to you about.'

Angelica rolled her eyes. 'Is this about that weed again?'

No. That was all forgotten. And the incident with the scooter. Joe told her about the request he'd received to assist the investigation. Two young women were dead, and he felt duty-bound to help, of course, but he was also aware they'd come to Capri to get away from the all-consuming nature of his work. So, how would she feel about it?

Angelica shrugged.

He would find a way to make it up to her once it was over,

Joe insisted. He'd try harder, spend more time with her, if that's what she wanted.

'It's why we came. Supposedly.'

'You wished I was dead not long ago.'

Angelica's face crumpled. 'I just wish she *wasn't*.'

'So do I, love. So do I.'

She'd never been a 'daddy's girl'.

Sofia had insisted that Joe just needed to be patient, that his time as a parent would come. In the infant years, mother and child were too infatuated with one another to leave much room for him to insert himself between them, even more so after Sofia miscarried their second child at thirteen weeks and they were advised not to risk a further pregnancy. As Angelica blossomed into a girl and then a teenager, Sofia kept predicting she would naturally gravitate away from her mother and towards him, but it never quite seemed to happen. It was always Sofia who Angelica would turn to for support or guidance, would instinctively seek out for loving reassurance.

It was not as if Joe particularly minded. Sofia was not one of those women whose children became their sole focus on reaching motherhood. If anything, after the sting of their loss had faded, become more bearable if not quite forgotten, she was even more caring and attentive towards him, more loving and passionate in the moments when it was just the two of them again. It was them against the world now. Their little family unit.

Joe had loved his daughter profoundly from the moment he first held her, newborn and squalling, so needy and defenceless, but he couldn't pretend to understand her, had not the first idea about how to nurture her potential. Motherhood and family seemed to come so naturally to Sofia, almost as if it was embedded in her DNA. She had an easy authority when it came to making decisions that would baffle and intimidate him, had values to fall back on, an instinct for what to do or say. She had empathy in abundance, a desire to know what her child was thinking and feeling that extended to reading Angelica's teenage diary for clues to her state of mind. She was always looking ahead, anticipating bumps in the road – disappointments and rejections, spots and periods, teenage crushes and failures of friendship – so that nothing ever knocked her offspring too far off course.

Joe had done his best to support her, to be as present as his job would allow, but hovering a step back from the main action of parenting, wanting to show willing, ready to fetch and carry, provide for, ferry and retrieve, trusting to luck that everything would turn out all right, finding purpose in protecting and keeping them safe. Yet that had ultimately proved beyond him. And the one thing none of them were anticipating had happened. In leaving them, Sofia had left an unimaginable hole in both their lives, in both their hearts, which Joe didn't have the first idea how to fill.

Looking at her now, Angelica suddenly seemed incredibly young and vulnerable. 'I'd do anything to bring her back,' she said in a small voice, soft tears starting to fall.

Joe had no answer to that. He did the one thing that had always come naturally to him and opened his arms to her, hoped it would be enough. She accepted his embrace, leaned her head against his chest. They stayed like that for a long time, father and daughter together, wordlessly communicating the only way they knew how.

26

The next morning, Angelica was up early, especially so for a Sunday. She'd got into the habit of avoiding the kitchen in the family apartment for fear of bumping into her dad, but now he'd shown willing to forgive and forget, she made a point of having breakfast with him. They chatted easily enough, although inconsequentially, while she made hot chocolate and he heated up the croissants Elena had left out for them. The mood was only spoilt when Joe suggested they go to the beach and Angelica was forced to admit she'd already agreed to spend the day there with Daniele.

For most of the morning, she almost wished it was Joe who was lying on the sunbed next to her. Daniele had spent the night at his mother's flat in Naples, and she was unwell again, he complained, had kept him up half the night. Declaring that he needed to sleep, he lay comatose beside her for the next two hours, snoring softly beneath an umbrella. Angelica listened to music and read, but it was not the way she'd envisaged spending time with him. Thankfully he perked up after his sleep and agreed to go paddleboarding. They enjoyed a happy hour falling off and clambering on again, while they explored the coastline nearby. Back on the beach, they settled together on the sun lounger and Daniele pulled a beach towel over them.

Angelica was not a complete novice when it came to sex, but lying in her bikini next to a semi-naked man under the cover of a towel felt about as close as she'd been to experiencing it. At first they just kissed, while Daniele stroked her hair and neck. She tried to give herself over to the sensations that were stirred up by being so close to him, her skin in contact with his. After a while, the rhythm and the weight of his kissing gained in urgency, and she felt him growing more aroused. His hands began to wander and explore the rest of her body, and she started to feel more awkward, more self-conscious in turn. Torn by a desire not to seem prudish or naive, she let him slip a finger inside her bikini top and caress her nipple, but when he tried to pull aside the bottom part of her costume, she gripped his hand to prevent him going any further. Hoping he'd got the message, she let go but he tried to slip his hand inside her pants again. This time, pushing his hand aside more pointedly, she sat up and threw the towel off.

'It's sweltering under there,' she said, excusing herself, not looking at him directly but sensing his reaction from the sigh that escaped his lips. 'I think I'll go for a swim.'

'Now?'

'I need to cool down.' She managed to look at him. 'We both do.'

Not waiting for Daniele to reply, Angelica slipped on her beach shoes and made her way down to the water. The sea was clear and warm, and she swam out a little before she flipped over and lay on her back, floating with the current, watching a wisp of cloud form far above. After a few minutes she felt composed enough to face him and his frustrations, but as she made her way out of the ocean and up the beach, she saw the sunbed was empty. She scanned the beach, but he was nowhere to be seen.

Wrapping her sarong around her and retrieving her phone and bag, Angelica wandered up to the beach bar where they'd been interrupted by Joe on that first morning, but there was no sign of Daniele there either. She tried to text and then call him but there was no answer and the idea started to form that he was bent out of shape with her. She went to check the car park at the rear of the bar, half expecting his scooter to be gone, but it was standing exactly where they'd left it. Mystified now, she was about to go back to the beach when she heard the murmur of voices, and made her way along the rear of the bar to investigate. As she reached the end of the building, she peered down the side and immediately drew her head back. Crouching low, she leaned forward and risked another look around the corner to confirm what she'd seen.

Daniele and a man she didn't recognise had their backs to her. They were huddled together in an open doorway that gave access from the beach bar's kitchen to a small service courtyard crammed with crates of bottles. As Angelica watched, the man reached into his pocket and pulled out a couple of crumpled banknotes and handed them over. Daniele palmed the money and slipped it into one trouser pocket while he produced what looked like a small bag from the other and handed it back just as smartly. The whole transaction took no more than a couple of seconds and they said their farewells with a hand clasp. As they turned to part ways, Angelica was already scrabbling to find a hiding place amongst the vehicles. Through the grimy windows of a parked car, she watched Daniele making his way towards his scooter and lifting the lid of the lock box on its rear. He took out a can of soda but then surprised her by unscrewing the top of it in one easy motion. He transferred the banknotes into it, as well as a second bag, which Angelica could now see contained some kind of blue pills. Out of habit, he glanced over his shoulder to check no one was watching, but she ducked down as he did so. She was confident he'd no idea he was being observed.

His messages started within minutes of her leaving the car park. Angelica's instinct was to ghost Daniele, but she realised her best option was to message him if she wanted him off her back. She'd developed a headache, she replied. Too much sun perhaps? She'd come back from her swim to find him gone and decided to head home. She hoped that was all right.

She was some distance along the road when she heard the high-pitched whine of a scooter engine somewhere behind her. She ducked into the driveway of a nearby villa and crouched down, keeping her head low while it passed. She couldn't be sure it was Daniele, but it was better to be safe just in case.

As she straightened up, it only now occurred to Angelica that she was alone on the island for the first time. Joe's warning about not being left on her own, about the need for extra vigilance, came back to her and she cursed Daniele for the position he'd put her in. She felt vulnerable, maybe even a little scared, and briefly contemplated calling him and summoning him back – but the thought made her sick to her stomach. And there was no way of getting Joe involved without provoking a fresh outburst of parental disapproval. There was nothing for it but to walk. The only concession she made was to keep to the road instead of taking the short cut over the cliffs that Daniele had shown her.

By the time she got home, Daniele had called her twice and his texts were taking on a wheedling, pleading tone. He was sorry if he'd upset her. He could tell she was new to all this, and he respected that. They could go at her pace. Or not at all if she preferred. He just liked being with her. Angelica switched off the notifications on the messaging app they were using and shut it down. She didn't want to have to face this now.

Sunday lunch was still in full swing at Da Vinale's as Angelica descended the steps from the street. She was thankful that everyone was too busy to pay her much attention as she made her way across the terrace and headed towards the apartment. She went immediately to her bedroom and bolted the door. She sat on the bed, sensing the tension she'd been holding inside ease just a fraction. She felt a surge of anger replace it, whether at him or at herself she wasn't quite sure. She knew Daniele took drugs, had even taken drugs with him. Was it really so much worse that he appeared to be selling them as well?

Angelica kicked off her shoes and stretched out on the bed, but she was too on edge to try to sleep. She picked up her phone out of habit before she remembered what might be lurking there and put it down. She lay on her back, staring at the ceiling, letting her thoughts wander. The image of Daniele screwing on the lid of the fake soda can and glancing furtively around kept coming back to her.

Eventually there was a soft knock at the door. She heard someone try the handle.

'Who is it?' Angelica called out, sitting up.

That boy was at the gate, asking for her, Elena explained through the door.

'Will you say I'm sleeping.'

There was a silence while Elena considered this. 'He says he's worried about you.'

Angelica's heart sank. 'Please. Just tell him I'm tired. I'll call later.'

For a moment, Angelica thought she'd gone away, but then her grandmother spoke up again. 'Is everything all right?'

Angelica felt her eyes well with tears. Everything was definitely not all right. 'I'm fine,' she managed to say, forcing a note of brightness into her voice.

The disembodied voice came again. 'OK, my darling. I'm here if you need me.'

Daniele seemed to have got the message, for there were no more missed calls or new messages when Angelica plucked up the courage to look at her phone the following morning. Instead of feeling relieved, however, she felt confused. If he'd abandoned his attempts to contact her that easily then he wasn't that into her after all. She knew she shouldn't care, given what she'd witnessed, but she found that she did. Very much. The thought that she might not see him again made her miserable.

For the first time in a long time, she actively sought out Joe's company. She had no definite plan to tell him what had happened, but she hoped he would somehow divine she was unhappy, and they might find a way to talk around it. She located him on the terrace of the restaurant, eating an omelette and watching the highlights of the weekend's Premier League action on his laptop, and she was encouraged when he immediately paused what he was watching and closed his computer, appeared to be making an effort to give her his attention. At that moment, however, her grandmother appeared and insisted on making her breakfast. Elena suggested that she keep her company while she did so, and not knowing how to refuse without giving offence, Angelica went along with her. By the time she emerged from the restaurant kitchen some twenty minutes later, Joe was on the phone. She lurked nearby, waiting to see if he might ring off. 'That's fantastic,' she heard him say, and then: 'Have you time to give me a quick update now?' As he settled back in his chair, completely unaware of her presence, she felt what little inclination she'd had to tell him about Daniele drain away.

It was Luca who finally noticed that something was bothering her as he emerged from the sea gate, looking for a quiet spot for a mid-morning cigarette, and found her sitting on the steps that led down to the jetty. 'Is everything OK?' he asked, immediately discerning from her demeanour that it might not be.

Angelica gestured non-committally, not quite trusting herself to speak.

'Do you want to talk about it?'

'Not really.'

'OK.'

They sat in silence for a while, staring out to sea. From the corner of her eye, Angelica kept watch on her companion as he smoked. His forearms were covered with tattoos and she couldn't help staring at them. 'Do they all mean something to you?' she asked, as Luca caught her looking.

He shrugged. Some did. Some didn't. He was young and stupid when a lot of them had been done. It was a way of killing time in prison.

'You've been to prison?'

Luca nodded. 'Your grandparents . . . they didn't tell you?'

Angelica shook her head.

He stubbed his cigarette out, evidently deciding what to say. 'I served fourteen months of a two-year sentence for illegal importation and handling stolen goods,' he told her, turning his gaze on her. 'For smuggling, I think you call it in English.'

Angelica couldn't hide her shock. 'Drugs?'

'No!' He almost looked offended. 'Knock-off luxury goods. You know, fake handbags. Sunglasses. Belts. That sort of thing.' He'd been easily led as a teenager after his parents had divorced and his dad moved away, Luca admitted, had been taken advantage of by people he thought were friends. If it hadn't been for his uncle stepping in to offer him a job after his release, he didn't know where he'd be. Back inside, probably.

She considered this. 'What's prison like?'

'*Oribile.*' His face was grave. There was no hint of a smile.

'What would you say to someone you were worried might end up there?'

'Don't. Just don't.'

She felt his eyes bore into hers and looked away.

'Do I know this somebody?' he asked.

She shook her head.

'You want me to speak to them?'

'I don't think so.' Angelica got to her feet. She flashed him a grateful smile before she hurried away up the steps, leaving a concerned-looking Luca behind.

27

It felt good to be working with him again, Lara found herself thinking as she sat across from Joe on the terrace of the police station in Capri, watching him make his way through the document she'd not long handed him, methodical as always. It had stung when Curti had ambushed her with the idea of formally seconding him to the investigation, had stirred up her lingering insecurities about whether she would ever be trusted and respected by her colleagues. And yet, for much of Joe's absence, it had felt like something was missing; she'd been wading through mud on her own without him, until that very morning – coinciding happily with his return – the case had regained much-needed momentum. The digital forensics team in Naples had finally cracked Shannon Headley's phone, albeit with mixed results; frustratingly, two weeks after her death, Lara was still unable to access the apps with end-to-end encryption, including Girl Cupid, but the boffins back at base had been able to download the phone's GPS data. The document Joe was studying was a report of Shannon's movements in the thirty-six hours before her body was discovered.

The map of those movements was already imprinted on Lara's brain. Surprisingly, given her reported state of inebriation at Da Vinale's the night before, Shannon had got up early on the Saturday of her death and made her way up to the Villa Jovis and

Tiberius's Leap in some sort of vehicle, presumably a scooter or one of the island's many electric utility carts, at a little after 7am. She'd then returned to the Hotel Americano, arriving back at 8.43am. Here, she was known to have made enquiries at the concierge's desk about the massage she'd arranged, which was the last confirmed sighting they had of her alive. She'd left the hotel again at 11.13am, but instead of going straight to her massage, she'd visited the Marina Grande, where she remained for the next twenty-six minutes, according to the GPS data. Only then had she proceeded on foot to the salon where Lara and Joe had interviewed Francesca Capuso, which might be the closest they were going to get to confirmation that Zuzu Esposito had indeed treated her as a client. Her GPS signal had remained static here between 12.02pm and 2.18pm, when she and her phone started to move once more. It appeared she'd then travelled back in the direction of Tiberius's Leap, although from this point on it was hard to be certain. The phone's signal had cut off abruptly at 2.27pm, in the vicinity of a small municipal parking yard for the aforementioned utility vehicles on the edge of the Tiberio district. No further data was available until 1.18am on the Sunday when the GPS signal was again detectable, but this time from the bottom of the cliff where the phone would be recovered later that same day. It was this last detail that Lara was continuing to ponder as Joe looked up and caught her eye. She knew someone had used Shannon's phone to take the 'selfie' at 3.52pm on the day before her body was discovered, so why had no signal been picked up from it at that point? The area was remote, and it might simply be the case that the cell tower was too far away and had lost the signal. Still, the detail was bothering her.

'Why would she visit Tiberius's Leap twice in one day?' Joe asked.

'Strange, isn't it.'

'And what the hell was she doing at the harbour for twenty-six minutes?'

Lara clicked on the attachment to an email her colleague in digital forensics had sent her and turned her laptop to show him the results. He was looking at a map of Shannon's GPS movements, she told him. He should zoom in on the red circle that marked her location at Marina Grande, tell her what he saw. Joe did as instructed and she saw him raise his eyebrows.

'It looks like she was in the water.'

'And she can't have gone swimming with her phone. So maybe she was on a boat.'

Joe grinned broadly and squeezed her shoulder. 'Good work, Inspector.'

Lara felt an irrational urge to hug him, but she restricted herself to grinning too.

'Can we get a list of any vessels that were docked?'

Lara was one step ahead of him. She turned the laptop to click on another email before turning the screen back to face him.

Joe scanned it briefly. 'What about the passenger lists?'

She was still waiting for those, she was forced to admit.

His eyes flicked back to the laptop and he scrolled the list of boats, but it was obvious he felt he was wasting his time without the manifests to go with them. Lara saw that he was about to abandon the search and turn the screen back to face her when he appeared to spot something and leaned in to take a closer look.

'*Calypso*?'

A good name for a boat, she thought. 'Do you recognise it?'

Joe considered this. 'I think a fancy yacht with that name was anchored off the beach I was at on the Sunday morning.' Which was only a couple of kilometres from where Shannon's body had been found the same day, he couldn't help pointing out.

'You think it's significant?'

He shrugged. The only thing that had made the boat memorable to him was the passengers he'd seen coming ashore for a long boozy lunch at Da Vinale's.

'What was memorable about them?'

'The way they brought attention to themselves. A braying bunch of hoorays.'

Lara pulled a questioning face.

'Rich, loud, over-privileged. I just wish I could remember the guy's name.'

While Joe went away to phone his mother-in-law, Lara put a call through to the harbour-master to ask for the manifests to be sent through as soon as possible. Within five minutes an email had arrived in her inbox and she was about to click on the file attached to it, when Joe returned. 'Yeats,' he announced. 'Y-E-A-T-S.'

Yeats? It was Lara's turn to wrack her brains. She clicked to open the worksheet and quickly scrolled the list of names. And there it was.

MILES YEATS.

'*Merda!*'

'What?'

Joe crowded in to look at her screen, but already Lara was on her feet and making her way back into the police station to find Shannon Headley's case file.

He followed her inside. 'What is it? What have you spotted?'

Her heart was beating so fast she didn't trust herself to speak. Instead, she rifled through the file until she found what she was looking for. 'I know who Miles Yeats is,' she told Joe, turning to show him the copy of the magazine article that had dubbed Shannon 'The Dating Dame'. She watched Joe scanning the pages, a tingle of satisfaction growing inside. Surely it had to be significant.

'He's a friend of Shannon's from university?' he asked, looking up.

'And a former business associate. Who's suing her over the sale of Girl Cupid.'

28

Joe had almost decided not to fly with Lara to Porto Cervo, where *Calypso* was now berthed, according to the Sardinian Port Authority. He was waiting for a response from Dan Keely, who'd promised to run Miles Yeats's name through the various UK databases as soon as he returned to HQ from a meeting at the mayor's office. While he waited for a call back from London, Joe thought his time would be better spent looking into their suspect's background, first as an investor in Shannon's dating app and then as a litigant against her. Besides, he told Lara, his in-laws and his daughter were only just getting used to the idea of his formal secondment to the investigation, and he didn't want to alarm them by disappearing to who knew where for who knew how long. His Italian colleague was adamant, however, that she wanted him with her when she questioned Yeats. The trip from Naples to northern Sardinia was two hours by helicopter. She could have him back in Capri that same night if need be.

'Is that an order, Inspector?' Joe asked, but he was smiling as he said it.

He spent much of the outward flight regretting his decision. Conversation in transit was almost impossible. And he'd been obliged to turn off his phone for the duration. He used the time to re-read the report that outlined Shannon's movements on

Capri, but, other than that, the flight was exactly as he feared it would be: a frustrating waste of valuable time.

Freed from the shriek of the rotor blades, the two detectives made up for lost time in the short car journey from the heliport to the marina at Porto Cervo. Joe did his best to temper Lara's expectations. Miles Yeats's court case against Shannon Headley appeared to be the closest thing to a concrete motive for murder they'd come across. And his presence on Capri at the time of her death seemed astonishingly coincidental. It was proof he may have had an opportunity to carry out her killing. But they had no physical evidence to link him to the *means* of her murder... which was either the overdose and/or the fall, they couldn't be sure. And they had no grounds whatsoever for linking him to Zuzu Esposito's death some five days later. But Lara was not to be put off. After leaving Capri, *Calypso* had spent several days docked near Amalfi, she pointed out. It was possible it had made an unregistered stop back in Capri on the Wednesday, to coincide with the anniversary party, before sailing on to its current berth.

There was a palpable sense of anticipation in the police car, therefore, as it nosed its way through the crowds of sightseers and sailors on arrival at their destination, their driver using his siren to clear the road of pedestrians and alerting the whole marina to their presence. By the time they disembarked at the barrier, it felt like all eyes were upon them. Joe made his way along the front with Lara and an escort of two uniformed State Police officers, feeling about as conspicuous as it was possible to feel.

There was some confusion over the precise location of the boat they were looking for; two vessels with similar names – *Calypso* and *The Calypso* – were currently docked in the marina, and it took a tortuous discussion with the harbour-master before they ascertained it was the one on jetty 6 they wanted. By the time this had been clarified, they'd been at the marina for almost five minutes, and Joe was growing impatient. He pushed ahead, leaving Lara and their uniformed escort to deal with the harbour-master's questions, and quickly found the jetty where the boat was supposed to be tied up. As he set foot on it, an outboard motor roared into life nearby. His senses on high alert, Joe scanned the line of boats and quickly identified *Calypso* at the end of the jetty. A man in a baseball cap was stepping off the yacht into a speedboat at her stern. As Joe started to hurry forward, the man hastily detached the painter and sat down, apparently intent on making his escape.

'HEY,' Joe shouted, breaking into a run. 'WE JUST WANT TO TALK.'

Throttling the engine, the man started to manoeuvre the boat towards open water.

Joe didn't stop to consider what he was doing but launched himself off the end of the dock and landed feet first on the gunwale of the accelerating speedboat, tipping both him and the driver into the water. The boat righted itself but, without a hand to steer it, swerved sharply in a circle to the right. As Joe surfaced, he saw it veering back in his direction and only just had time to duck and swim downwards as it skimmed over him, the blades of the propeller scything through the water inches from his head. The boat collided with the jetty and flipped over, landing on top of Joe as he came up for air a second time, and forcing him below the surface once more. He lost his bearings and, in panic, struck out blindly in the wrong direction. As his scrambled senses reasserted themselves, however, he managed to reorientate himself and swim up towards the light.

Gasping for air, Joe took a moment to locate the capsized

boat, but there was no sign of the driver. He swam towards the spot where he thought the other man had gone under and desperately cast around. Catching sight of a dark shape in the water beneath him, he dived down and managed to grab his quarry by the collar. He kicked upwards, pulling the driver with him, and broke the surface for the last time.

He began to tow the man back towards the dock, becoming aware as he did so that Lara was standing at the end of it screaming something at him, but he was too stunned, and his ears too full of water, to understand what she was saying.

Arms reached down to haul him and the driver out.

'Are you trying to get yourself killed!' he heard Lara say as the world slammed back into place, but he was too exhausted to speak. With the last of his strength, he turned his head so he could look at the man lying capless on the dock beside him. To his relief, he recognised Miles Yeats, eyes open and breathing.

Yeats's legal representative, hastily appointed that evening, did his best to stop Joe from attending Yeats's interview the following day. Turning up at the State Police offices in the nearby town of Cannigione, a few kilometres along the Emerald Coast from the scene of the arrest, Signor Calaresu questioned why the arresting officer had a British name and accent. It took a couple of hours of wrangling before he accepted Joe's bona fides and agreed to him sitting in on the questioning.

By the time Joe followed Lara into the interview room at the tiny beachside police station, he was seething at the delay. And having spoken with Dan Keely, he was also armed with new intelligence that raised significant questions for Miles Yeats to answer.

As he took his place at the table beside Lara and waited

for her to turn on the digital recording device, Joe decided to tackle the elephant in the room. 'Sorry about that,' he ventured, pointing to the bandage on the right side of Yeats's forehead.

Yeats grimaced.

'Of course, it wouldn't have happened if you hadn't been trying to escape.'

Yeats glanced towards his brief, who shook his head, encouraging him to say nothing until he was officially under caution.

Lara duly obliged by reciting the time and the date and the suspect's name into the microphone and then reading him his rights. 'Do you know why you're here, Mr Yeats?' she asked him, kicking off the formal part of the interview.

Signor Calaresu intervened again, informing them that his client had been fully appraised of the purpose of the interview and understood their interest in speaking to him. But before he submitted to their questions, he wished to make a short statement.

Joe exchanged a look with Lara, who gestured for Yeats to go ahead.

Shannon had been one of his oldest and dearest friends, the suspect declared, looking earnestly from one police officer to the other, and whatever the difficulties they'd experienced, he was utterly distraught at her passing. On being taken into police custody, he'd been astonished to learn of her death, he insisted, eyes glistening, and he was willing to do whatever he could to assist them. But he rejected and, frankly, was outraged by the suggestion that he was responsible for killing her. Whatever their grounds for arresting him, he was confident they would prove to be mistaken. He'd nothing to hide.

'Then why were you attempting to run, Mr Yeats?' Joe couldn't help asking.

'I'm a wealthy man, Detective,' Yeats shot back. He was travelling with private security, he explained, having been advised he was under threat of robbery or kidnap while berthed in southern Italian ports. The previous day his bodyguard had gone with his fiancée, Emma, while she shopped for clothes. With the crew on a changeover day, he'd been left almost alone on *Calypso* and, in his heightened state of alert, had panicked when he'd seen Joe, an imposing figure in plain clothes, making his way along the jetty.

Joe sat back and folded his arms.

'Can you tell us what brought you to Capri on the day Shannon was killed?' Lara asked, getting their agreed line of questioning back on track.

It was a scheduled stop in their itinerary, Yeats explained. She could check with the boat's captain. He, Emma and two friends had chartered *Calypso* in Nice for a holiday to celebrate his fortieth birthday, with more friends joining them in Ostia and at various ports along the way. They had always planned to be in Marina Grande on the day in question.

'A coincidence then?'

'Exactly. A bizarre one, I'll admit. But pure chance, all the same.'

'You had no idea that Shannon was on the island?'

'None whatsoever. At least not when we arrived.'

'Then how did you find out she was?'

Social media, Yeats explained. 'She posted a photo of the view from her hotel.'

'You were still following one another? Despite the court case.'

Yeats shrugged. 'I told you. She was one of my oldest friends.'

Joe picked up the questioning. 'So, you decided to meet up?'

'Yes. It was a spur of the moment thing.'

'And how exactly did you contact her, Mr Yeats?'

The other man shifted in his seat. 'Via the app.'

'Girl Cupid?'

Yeats nodded. When they launched the app back in their twenties, they'd set up false profiles as a way of keeping tabs on the user experience. When the time had come to suggest they kiss and make-up, it had seemed a suitably symbolic way to get in touch.

'And did you? Kiss and make up?' Joe enquired, unable to keep an edge out of his voice. 'When she came to the boat?'

'I suppose we did,' Yeats responded, flushing slightly. 'I told her I was thinking of dropping the lawsuit.'

'Just like that?'

'Why not?' His milestone birthday had proved a watershed, Yeats insisted, with a bitter divorce recently finalised and Emma having accepted his proposal of marriage. He was feeling blessed and happy. And determined to try and eliminate all the major sources of stress and negativity in his life.

'How did Shannon react?'

'She said she was relieved.'

'Happy then?'

'You could say that. She certainly seemed so when we parted ways.'

Lara stepped in. 'Did you see her again? After she left the boat?'

'No.'

'You're sure about that?'

'My client has answered that question, Inspector,' Calaresu intervened.

Lara made a show of consulting the open folder in front of her. They'd already spoken to the crew of *Calypso*, she informed him. His guests had stayed on board all afternoon, but Emma had booked into the spa at one of the hotels on the island. And

Yeats? Well, his whereabouts were unaccounted for between disembarking the yacht after lunch, a little before 2pm, and returning at 6pm. What had he been doing?

'Sightseeing.'

The two detectives exchanged a look.

Yeats looked slightly abashed. 'I walked up the Phoenician Steps, if you must know. All 921 of them. I'd been told the view was fantastic.'

'Are you sure it wasn't Tiberius's Leap?' Joe couldn't help prompting.

For the first time, Yeats showed signs of losing his cool. 'I already told you . . . I had nothing to do with what happened to Shannon. The idea that I went up there with her and . . . you know . . . pushed her off a cliff . . . it's preposterous. Absurd.'

Joe decided it was time to play their trump card. 'Is that what you told the officers investigating the death of Phoebe Todd?'

The suspect had been growing animated but now he paled and clammed up.

For the benefit of Signor Calaresu, Joe outlined what Dan Keely had told him. Miles Yeats's details *were* on the Police National Computer back in the UK. He'd given a witness statement eleven years previously after a young woman had fallen to her death from a fifth-floor balcony at a party he'd been attending. Phoebe Todd had died with a cocktail of drugs in her system and Yeats had briefly come under suspicion when it emerged he'd been in a sexual relationship with the victim and had been seen taking cocaine with her an hour or so before her fall. But no one was ever charged with a crime in association with the death.

When Yeats next spoke his voice was barely above a whisper. 'I've never been to Tiberius's Leap. I don't even know where it is.'

'That seems unlikely, Mr Yeats,' Joe shot back. 'The next day you were seen at a restaurant a short way up the coast from there. Having a fine time, by the sound of it.'

It was the lawyer who answered on his client's behalf. 'It's not sufficient grounds for making an arrest, Detective. Eating near the scene of a murder.'

'But it's a known pattern of behaviour for criminals. Returning to the crime scene.'

'What exactly are you saying?'

'I'm suggesting Mr Yeats was in the vicinity to keep an eye on what he knew was happening at the foot of that cliff. And that he was putting on what you might call "a distraction display" for the world's benefit.'

It was Lara's turn to look at him. *A distraction display?*

'I think he was deliberately drawing attention to himself, in the belief that no one could possibly associate such a happy and carefree soul with the gruesome fucking discovery he knew we were about to make at the foot of that cliff.'

There was a moment of stunned silence when Joe had finished speaking; he knew he'd let his mask of impartiality slip, that he'd given away his visceral dislike of the suspect, but in that moment he didn't care.

Calaresu had just started to voice his inevitable protest when there was a knock at the door. A uniformed police constable entered and crossed silently to where Lara was sitting to hand her a note. Joe looked on as his colleague opened it and read its contents, her eyes widening slightly. She glanced up at him, communicating her surprise, before she turned back to the suspect. 'I'm afraid we need to suspend this interview, Mr Yeats.'

'Don't you think it might have been helpful to know this from the start? That the blood on her dress . . . it's not all hers.' Joe didn't bother to hide his irritation as he dragged his gaze from the latest forensic report Lara had had translated for him. They were sitting in the early afternoon sunshine on a low stone wall outside the police station, and Lara had been trying to savour her coffee and enjoy the view out over the gulf while she waited for him to finish reading. It had landed on the system while they were interviewing Yeats and she'd known he would insist on reading it cover to cover. And exactly how he'd react.

'Of course it would,' she conceded. She regretted she'd not thought to order more in-depth forensic testing of Shannon's dress as part of the autopsy. 'But remember, at the time . . . we thought we were dealing with an accident and not a murder.'

It was standard procedure in the UK, Joe grumbled. A forensic autopsy should include a complete *external* examination of the body, including clothes and accessories.

'That's what we did,' Lara insisted, holding her ground. An initial examination of her clothes had identified a large amount of blood on Shannon's dress. A sample had been tested and been found to match the victim's blood type, B negative, which was sufficiently rare to satisfy the pathology team that the blood was hers, particularly when considered in parallel to the catastrophic wounds she'd suffered from the fall. It was only once Curti had formally launched a murder investigation that a further batch of DNA testing had been ordered, of the body and clothes of both victims, and these had identified a small stain on the back of Shannon's dress that was found to belong to a different blood type, O negative. The delay was regrettable, but they could surely forgive it if the evidence ultimately helped them identify the killer.

'And you're confident it will?'

'As confident as I can be.' She hadn't had a chance to speak to Curti, she told Joe, but the team in Naples would be trying to match the DNA profile they'd extracted from the sample against the hundreds of thousands of profiles that were kept on the national database. And, of course, there was the possibility of matching the profile to the suspect they had in custody, who at this very moment was giving a blood sample and being swabbed for DNA. Lara reached down behind the wall to pick up an evidence bag containing the items that had been in Miles Yeats's possession at the time of his arrest. She took out his wallet and removed from it a small rectangle of red plastic, the size and shape of a credit card, and handed it to the English detective. It was an NHS Blood and Transplant Donor card in the name of Mr M.G. Yeats and, as she watched Joe study it, she already knew the blood type that was written there.

O negative.

Lara was anticipating the grin of recognition he was about to give her when Joe's phone pinged with an incoming text. She watched him feel in the pocket of his jeans and take it out. His face darkened into a scowl.

'What the actual fuck, Lara?'

What? 'What is it?'

He turned the screen to face her.

Come home Joe, the SMS read. *They've arrested Luca.*

29

Lara delayed her arrival at Da Vinale's that Tuesday evening, trying to arrange it so the restaurant would have emptied by the time she got there. She expected a rough reception, not so much from Joe himself, but from the old chef, Luca's uncle, if she was unlucky enough to encounter him. As a female police detective in Naples, Lara was pretty hardened when it came to personal abuse, but she didn't much fancy having a strip torn off her by Gennaro Da Vinale in front of a room full of gawping customers.

Joe hadn't been angry with her on the helicopter flight back, just icy cold. 'I don't believe you,' he'd stated bluntly as she'd tried her best to convince him she'd had no prior warning of Luca's arrest.

'I swear to God, Joe. It was Curti. He went ahead without my knowledge.'

'But you're the senior investigative officer.'

'You don't think I'm aware of that?'

Joe shook his head. 'If that's true . . . he obviously doesn't respect your authority.' From his expression, it was clear he'd decided that he didn't either.

Lara felt the confidence he'd helped instil in her draining away. 'You think I'd do that to you?'

Frankly, Joe told her, he didn't know what to think. 'But if it walks like a duck and it quacks like a duck, Lara, then it usually turns out to be a duck.' He waved an arm in the direction of Sardinia, which was disappearing rapidly behind them. 'This whole fucking jaunt . . . it has all the appearance of a crude diversionary tactic. To get me out of the way and execute the arrest warrant with a minimum of fuss or embarrassment.'

They'd spent the rest of the flight staring gloomily out of opposite windows.

If anything, it was Lara herself who was most irate when she finally came face to face with Curti back at HQ in Naples. Would he have acted in this way with any of her male colleagues? she demanded furiously, no longer caring if she angered him. He'd not just undermined her position, she went on, but caused irreparable damage to her relationship with their English colleague, who he'd insisted on co-opting onto the investigation, *once again* without prior consultation. Her boss listened impassively, letting her anger blow itself out. Had she finished? Good. Then perhaps she was ready to hear all the evidence they'd uncovered.

It was this evidence she was now coming to share with Joe, having texted while she was on the speedboat to tell him she was on her way to Capri to meet him, and then putting her phone on silent in case he tried to dissuade her. She'd lingered at the island's police station, going over the details of the arrest with Sergeant Alfieri, before deciding she couldn't delay the confrontation any longer and making her way down to the coast.

The street gate of Da Vinale's was locked when she finally reached it just after 11pm. The restaurant was silent and in darkness and she briefly contemplated the possibility that Joe had ignored her message and gone to bed. She very nearly turned tail and retraced her steps, but she knew if the rupture between them was allowed to fester then it would be harder to repair in the following days. And she was desperate for him to start believing in her again. Taking a deep breath, she pressed the buzzer. For ten or fifteen seconds there was no indication of a response, and she was about to press it once more, when she heard a door close and the sound of footsteps making their way across the terrace and then up the steps. The catch was sprung from the inside and the gate opened. It was Joe and not Gennaro. Lara breathed a small sigh of relief.

'Let's take a walk,' the English detective told her, closing the gate behind him.

She immediately divined his reasons. 'Have they taken it badly?'

It was like somebody had died, Joe told her as they made their way down to the foreshore, which, at this stage of the evening, was cold washed in silvery moonlight. One minute Gennaro was full of self-recrimination, and confessing to his son-in-law that he knew Luca had served time in prison when he'd agreed to take him on. The next he was railing against Joe for failing to protect their interests. The old chef had been all for closing the restaurant, Joe admitted as they settled themselves on a large flat rock close to the water's edge, until his wife had told him to get a grip. Elena had reassigned Aldo and two waiters to work with Gennaro in the kitchen and had roped in Angelica to help her front of house. Joe had even been enlisted to clear dirty dishes and do the washing-up, when he'd arrived back a little after 8pm. Somehow they'd got through the evening by offering a reduced menu and closing early, but in the last hour, Gennaro had continued to spiral. Luca had brought shame on them all. The restaurant was doomed. No one in their right minds would want to eat food cooked by the uncle of a murderer. Elena had finally snapped and ordered him to bed. But she was also seething, albeit more quietly, at the very public way in which the arrest had been carried out. As a courtesy to Joe, she asked, might it not have been conducted more discreetly, with Luca taken into custody when the restaurant was closed, rather than paraded across the terrace in handcuffs? He felt he owed them a full and frank breakdown of the case against their nephew, which was why he'd agreed to see her, despite his misgivings.

Lara bit her tongue. Whether Joe believed her or not, she did feel bad about the clumsy way in which the arrest had been handled. And she was determined to make it up to him in any way she could. Without jeopardising the case, of course. 'The blood on her dress . . . it's a match for Luca's,' she blurted out.

'How can you be sure?'

'His DNA . . . it's been on our system. Since his smuggling conviction six years ago.'

Joe took a moment to digest this. 'Which for some unknown reason Gennaro omitted to tell me about until this evening,' he muttered, shaking his head.

Her contact at the Public Security Department had tried to call her to share the results, Lara explained, but she was interviewing Miles Yeats at the time. Unfortunately her contact had then called Curti instead, who, on the basis of this evidence and the gravity of the crimes, had gone over her head and immediately applied to the court for an arrest warrant. He'd decided to execute it as soon as officers from the Central Criminal Directorate could be dispatched to Capri to take Luca into custody, which had ended up being at 1.45pm, while the restaurant was still packed with diners.

Joe looked like he was struggling to process it all. 'They're sure about the match?'

'A hundred per cent.'

'There's no possibility of a mix-up?'

'It's been double... triple checked.'

'And they've also checked the sample Yeats gave us?'

Lara's response was a silent nod.

'There's none of his blood on the dress?'

'Sorry, Joe. Same blood type. But it's not his.' They were planning to hold Yeats for as long as they could, to look into his whereabouts at the times the two women were killed, but the evidence against him was starting to seem circumstantial at best.

'Fuck,' he said. No other comment was needed.

Lara ploughed on, taking no pleasure in her task. 'Thanks to you, we know Shannon came to Da Vinale's on the Friday night. And your mother-in-law has already told you it was Luca who saw Shannon into the taxi.' They were working on the theory that perhaps this wasn't the chance meeting it'd first seemed. 'Maybe they went back to Shannon's hotel together. And then up to Tiberius's Leap the following day.'

Joe was silent while he considered what she'd revealed. 'He was supposed to be going to a birthday party,' he offered at last.

'An attempt to establish an alibi, maybe?'

'Has he mentioned it?'

Luca had said nothing at all, she told him, was refusing to cooperate.

'So what now?'

They'd requested his phone records and would track his movements against Shannon's GPS data, she told him, as well as looking for evidence of interaction between him and either woman. And they were planning to search his flat as soon as a forensic team was available. His DNA profile was being matched against samples found in Shannon's hotel room. And they were also intending to re-examine the victim's body for evidence of recent sexual activity, as he already knew. It was surely only a matter of time before further evidence was unearthed but, even without it, the prosecutor believed the blood on the dress might be sufficient in itself to charge him with intentional murder under Article 575 of the Criminal Code. 'I'm truly sorry, Joe,' she added, meaning it.

'And I'm sorry too,' the English detective responded, but whether for doubting her, or having to recuse himself from the investigation, he didn't say.

30

When he wandered into the kitchen of the family apartment in the uncertain light of dawn the next day and found Elena and Gennaro drinking coffee, it was immediately clear to Joe he hadn't been the only one struggling to sleep.

The old couple seemed calmer than they'd been the previous evening, more resigned perhaps to the grim reality facing them. They listened carefully as Joe outlined the evidence that had prompted the police to arrest Luca. Gennaro crossed himself and mouthed a silent invocation as Joe explained how a small quantity of what appeared to be Luca's blood had been found on Shannon Headley's dress. Could they think of how it might have got there?

His in-laws shook their heads.

Did Luca cut himself, perhaps? Joe persisted. Sometime before the Friday evening? He could vaguely remember a bandage on the sous-chef's hand that first Sunday morning after their arrival. If so, it was possible, he supposed, that some of his blood might have got onto her red dress while Luca was helping her into the waiting taxi.

Elena pulled a face. They worked with knives. They were always cutting themselves. But she couldn't recall a specific incident in the run-up to or on the day in question. 'And anyway, the girl wasn't wearing a red dress when she came to the restaurant,' she observed, cutting off this particular line of questioning.

Then they'd better hope that Luca could provide an innocent explanation, Joe observed, as otherwise the case against him seemed pretty damning. And that was before they'd taken into account his presence at the anniversary dinner, where Zuzu Esposito had died. There was something about Luca's behaviour that night that had raised his suspicions, Joe admitted to his in-laws. Their nephew had avoided registering his presence with the police and had exited the property by an unknown route, despite instructions to stay put. Given his previous conviction for smuggling, Joe couldn't help wondering whether Luca might have had a working knowledge of the secret staircase and antechambers under the Villa San Benedetto and whether he might have made use of them to escape after seeing his chance to silence Zuzu Esposito.

'Perhaps we've been wrong about him,' Elena said, turning to look at her husband. She didn't know who'd called the taxi to pick up Shannon Headley from Da Vinale's, she confessed. Perhaps it had been Luca himself. Perhaps his unexpected presence at the restaurant that Friday night, ahead of the party, hadn't been a coincidence after all.

Gennaro had been silent up to this point, but now he spoke. 'Whatever he's done, we can't abandon him,' he said.

The old chef's idea of not abandoning his nephew seemed to consist of making him a sandwich and insisting Joe take it to the police station later that morning.

When Joe was shown into the cramped open-plan office he found Lara sitting at a desk, frowning at a laptop in front of her. She looked up as he approached, and he could tell immediately she had more unwelcome news. 'You're going to want to see this,' she said, inviting him to sit. It took him a moment to work out he was looking at Luca's phone records, but their significance required no further explanation. Luca's phone had been switched off from 8.34pm on the Friday to 4.37pm on Saturday, coinciding with his first known encounter with Shannon Headley at Da Vinale's and the time she was believed to have fallen to her death at Tiberius's Leap the following day.

Lara met his knowing look with one of her own. What was there to say? Innocent people didn't turn off their phones. They had no reason to cover their tracks.

'I have a favour to ask,' Joe ventured, feeling his window of opportunity closing.

'Go on.'

He took a deep breath. 'Can I see him?'

She gave him a look.

'Please, Lara. Just five minutes.'

'It's against the rules, Joe.'

He could see her wrestling with the dilemma he'd presented her. 'I just want to check he's bearing up. Talk to him about getting a lawyer . . . you know, give him this.'

'What is it?'

Joe opened the bag to show her the sandwich.

Despite the situation, Lara smiled.

He smiled too. 'You can check it if you like.'

She was wavering and he knew it. 'Five minutes,' she agreed, holding up the same number of digits to emphasise her point. 'Not a second more.'

Whether Luca was more grateful for the sandwich or for Joe's visit it was hard to tell; he seemed preoccupied by the food as Joe outlined Gennaro and Elena's attempts to secure him a lawyer, subject to being able to raise funds at short notice. Joe felt himself growing irritated by his refusal to meet his eye, to do anything other than eat. He decided to cut to the chase. 'You want to spend the rest of your life in jail?' he asked bluntly.

The prisoner had his mouth full but gave him a look. What do you think?

Joe indicated the sandwich. 'Then you'd be better off talking to me.'

Luca dropped what remained of his food into the greaseproof paper in which it had been wrapped and made a show of wiping his fingers. 'What do you want to know?'

Joe glanced over his shoulder to check they were not being overheard. 'Do you have an alibi?' he asked, leaning in to speak in a low voice.

The other man shook his head.

'What about this birthday party?'

Luca gestured impatiently. 'I made it up. So I could get the evening off.'

'And why would you do that?'

It was clear Luca would prefer not to say.

'This is important, Luca.'

The other man relented. 'A friend . . . he needed help.'

'What kind of help?'

Gennaro's nephew rolled his eyes. 'Don't make me spell it out.'

It took a moment for Joe to understand. 'You were smuggling?'

Luca nodded. It was his turn to glance towards the door.

Joe considered what he'd been told. 'Is that why you turned your phone off?'

Luca gestured. Why else? His smuggling buddy drove a taxi, he explained in a whisper, and he'd come to Da Vinale's to pick him up at the same time Shannon Headley had been in need of a lift. Luca had taken advantage of the coincidence to help her and they'd dropped her off in the old town, at her request, before heading to the marina where Luca kept his boat. They'd driven the boat to a secluded cove on the mainland, where they'd met up with the rest of their four-man crew, and spent the next eight hours at sea rendezvousing with a cargo ship from the Philippines and receiving a consignment of fake handbags and purses, which they'd landed at a private jetty up the coast. Luca had returned to Capri after 6am and gone home to bed, forgetting to turn his phone back on. It was only when he woke after 4pm that he remembered to do so.

'Will this friend give you an alibi?'

'I won't ask.'

'You'd rather go to jail?'

'Better me than him.'

'He'll spend a lot less time inside for smuggling than you will for murder.'

Luca shrugged. 'We don't grass on each other, Joe.'

Then his hopes of getting off would rest on the reliability of the physical evidence, Joe reflected. He considered the ethics of questioning Luca about the blood found on Shannon's dress and had almost decided not to, when Gennaro's nephew raised it himself. He'd been told by his state-appointed lawyer that there was DNA evidence linking him to the dead woman. Did Joe have any idea what it might be?

'Your blood was on the dress she was found in,' Joe told him, pulling no punches.

Luca looked not so much shocked as utterly baffled. He'd cut his hand out at sea, he explained, holding it up to show Joe the traces of a deep cut across the webbing between his right thumb and forefinger. His knife had slipped as he was attempting to cut open one of the packages of handbags for inspection. But that was several hours *after* his only contact with Shannon Headley. It didn't make sense.

Joe was about to question Luca further when they were interrupted by Sergeant Alfieri. Their time was up, he stated gruffly, unlocking the door of the holding cell. Joe decided to risk a final question. 'Tell me about the dinner,' he commanded, getting to his feet and indicating to the sergeant that he was willing to comply.

'What about it?'

'Why did you disappear? After the girl was found?'

He'd been working off the books, Luca explained. He loved being a sous-chef at Da Vinale's but the pay wasn't the best and he took other jobs for cash, had even been known to drive his friend's taxi in his spare time. He didn't want to get the guy who'd hired him into trouble. It was no more sinister than that. He'd had nothing to do with what had happened to Zuzu Esposito. He swore on his uncle's life.

As Joe stepped out into the corridor, and Sergeant Alfieri locked the door behind them, he caught a last glimpse of Luca's unhappy face through the open hatch.

God knows why, but I believe you, Joe couldn't help thinking to himself.

Joe decided it was time to come clean with Lara about Luca's presence in the kitchen at her aunt and uncle's anniversary dinner. It was possible she already knew he'd been working at the Villa San Benedetto and had simply omitted to mention it when she'd given Joe a rundown of the evidence against Luca the previous evening. If she was unaware, then it was likely she'd learn the truth soon enough and would realise Joe had been holding out on her. What trust they'd built up would be shattered and Joe was keen to avoid that. He'd grown to like and respect the Italian detective, despite their fall-out over the arrest. Besides, he figured it was in Luca's best interests to not let that happen.

They were walking out of the police station when he told her. 'The first thing I want to say is . . . I don't think Luca Da Vinale is guilty of murdering anyone,' he blurted out.

Lara stopped and looked at him. 'What makes you say that?'

Joe shrugged. Experience. Intuition. He just wasn't the type.

'The evidence would suggest otherwise.'

Joe conceded that it did. But he still didn't believe it.

Perhaps he was a little too invested, Lara suggested, wasn't seeing straight.

'Perhaps,' he agreed.

Her eyes bored into his. 'So, what's the second thing you want to say?'

Joe confessed what he knew about Luca's whereabouts on the night Zuzu Esposito had died. He didn't omit anything, admitting that his own suspicions had been raised by Luca's evasive behaviour. 'I don't think he'll thank me for telling you,' he concluded, 'because it proves he's got a link to both women. But I still don't think he's guilty.'

Lara stared at him. 'Do you know why I like you, Joe?' she asked.

He shrugged.

'You have integrity.'

Joe felt himself flush.

'It's why I trust you to remain impartial, whatever your personal connections to the suspect,' Lara continued. And it was why, she reflected later when Joe had left, she was going to persuade Curti to let her keep him on the case.

31

Angelica had enjoyed waiting tables at Da Vinale's the previous evening, and she was secretly delighted when her grandmother asked if she'd mind doing so again. They were trying to find a replacement for Luca in the kitchen, Elena explained, but it was high season. They would have to muddle through for the time being.

Nobody would tell her what had happened to Gennaro's nephew. She hadn't been present to see him led away, but she'd overheard enough of the adults' conversations to understand he was in trouble with the police again. Joe refused to say what kind of trouble when she asked him. It was a misunderstanding, he insisted. Luca had gone away to help sort it out, he'd be back soon enough. Angelica was happy to accept his reassurances. She liked Luca but she had other more important things preoccupying her.

Daniele had still not messaged her. Actually, that wasn't strictly true. He'd sent her a jokey GIF of a cartoon penguin crying lonely tears. But no actual words. She knew it was deliberate, to show no sign of caring whether she contacted him or not, but to her annoyance it was working. She found herself checking her phone an unhealthy amount, hoping for something from him. It was almost a relief to be able to leave it behind when 6pm came and she headed down to the restaurant to start her shift.

Her *nonno* had a strict policy of no mobile phones during work hours in Da Vinale's.

The first couple of hours were easy. The tables that Elena had assigned to her were manageable enough, with no more than four covers on any of them and with their orders prompt and relatively straightforward. Following her grandmother's advice, she kept a constant look-out across all of them, trying to anticipate when a request was about to be made rather than waiting for someone to catch her eye.

Towards the middle of the evening, things got more hectic, with the later diners beginning to arrive and the various stragglers from the first sitting needing to be eased on their way. Angelica was briefly overwhelmed and Elena had to step in to help. But this period of transition passed, and things settled down into a similar rhythm.

Soon enough, the first empty tables began to appear on the terrace. Angelica snuck a look at the clock on the credit card reader. It was 9.08pm. The end was in sight. Her feet hurt and her calves were aching. She was looking forward to a sit down.

Her dad appeared at the bar and Elena asked Angelica to serve him. She'd just brought out a plate of antipasti for Joe when the men arrived. They were like the three bears – one big and fat, another regular-looking and a third so thin and reedy that it was hard to imagine he ate anything. All of them were dressed in dark suits and ties and were clearly enjoying making an entrance. Angelica expected Elena to send them on their way – the rule at Da Vinale's was no new bookings after 9.00pm and her grandmother was rigid in enforcing it – but to her surprise they were shown to the best of the empty tables. A short while later her *nonno* appeared to greet them and hands were shaken. Whoever these men were, they were to be treated like honoured guests.

As the tables assigned to her were vacated, Angelica found herself paying more attention to the antics of this threesome. They insisted on trying everything, loudly consulted Elena on all the choices they were asked to make. Angelica kept her distance, but her gaze kept on being drawn back to them. There was something undeniably fascinating about watching them.

By quarter past ten, Angelica was at a loose end, and she went into the kitchen to ask if there was anything else she could help with. Gennaro was plating up three portions of risotto and asked her to take them out to 'the gentlemen on table eight'. Angelica hesitated, not wanting to tread on Elena's toes, but her *nonno* was insistent. The risotto needed to be served *pronto*, while it was still piping hot. Arranging the dishes the way Elena had showed her, Angelica did as she was told.

She was greeted at the table like a long lost friend. *Bellissima.* Where had she been all evening? Angelica smiled politely and served them, withdrew without a word.

A few minutes later Elena followed her in. Angelica was washing her hands. 'You made quite an impression,' her grandmother said, dumping the dishes in the sink.

'Who are they?'

'Nobodies. Who think they're somebodies.'

Angelica saw her give Gennaro a look.

'But they tip well,' he shot back. He turned to address Angelica directly. 'Go and ask what they want for dessert, *tesoro*.'

Tip. He'd said the magic word. Without waiting for her grandmother's permission, Angelica scooped up three menus and made her way back out into the restaurant.

The terrace was now empty, aside from Joe sitting at the bar and the three men at the table. This time they all turned to watch as she approached. The fattest and baldest of the three was leering openly as she handed out the menus and asked, in her best Italian, whether they'd like anything else?

'*Questa la prendo io. Senza vestiti,*' the fat man said under his breath.

His companions guffawed with laughter and Joe turned to look. Angelica felt herself flush and hurried away to take refuge in the safety of the kitchen.

As she entered, her grandparents were huddled together, arguing in low voices, and only Aldo was otherwise present. Angelica kept her head down but her attempt to act as if nothing was the matter was thwarted when Joe hurried in behind her.

'What happened?' he asked.

She was too flustered to meet his eye. 'Nothing.'

'Did one of them say something?'

Angelica felt her resolve faltering. 'The fat one . . .' she managed to say.

'What about him?' Gennaro asked, coming to join them.

'He said he wanted to see me naked.'

There was a shocked silence before Joe shaped to head back into the restaurant.

'Dad!' she barked. 'Don't!'

Joe stopped in his tracks.

'I hear worse at school. I can handle it.' Angelica pushed past the adults and headed back through the swing doors before anyone could try and stop her, mustering a show of confidence as she went.

She took the orders at the table without any further comment being directed at her and returned to deliver them to the kitchen feeling a renewed sense that everything would be OK. When she went back out to help Elena serve them cheese and brandy, however, this confidence proved misplaced. As she leaned over to place the cheeseboard in the centre of the table, she felt a pudgy hand slide beneath her skirt and up between her legs. Angelica dropped the cheeseboard, knocking over a glass. Wine spilt out onto the white tablecloth, staining it an ominous red. Without thinking, she whipped round and slapped the man nearest to her. It was her earlier tormentor, and the grin froze on his face.

'*Stronza!*' he hissed.

Angelica knew enough Italian to recognise the word 'bitch'.

As her assailant tried to grab her wrist, Joe appeared from nowhere and grabbed the fat man by the collar, yanking him backwards and sending him and his chair crashing to the floor. In an instant, her dad was on top of him, punching with all his might.

'Hey! Hey!' The other men at the table sprang up. For the first time, Angelica got a proper look at the thin one's rat-like features and the scar that ran from one ear down to the corner of his mouth. He reached into his jacket and pulled out a gun.

'DAD!'

Her shout brought Gennaro running from the kitchen.

Joe was quick to turn, but not quick enough. The rat-man placed the barrel of the pistol against his head, and he froze. As the gun was cocked, however, Gennaro held the razor-sharp edge of a meat cleaver up to the man's throat and the assailant froze in turn.

'*Gennaro! Che cazzo?!*' It was the most regular-looking of the three diners who'd spoken and he was furious. What the fuck!

Angelica's grandfather called back an apology without removing his blade or his eyes from the gunman's throat.

'*Metti giù quel cazzo di coso!*' Angelica didn't fully understand the other man's idiom but she recognised the swear word, got the gist.

Gennaro respectfully declined to remove his cleaver with a shake of his head. He wasn't going to be first to back down.

It was Elena who stepped in to defuse the situation. 'Signor Di Biasi, please! If you could ask your friends to stay calm. I'm sure this is a misunderstanding.'

The man she'd called Di Biasi hissed an instruction to the gunman, and very slowly he removed the pistol from Joe's head and uncocked the firing hammer, before carefully sliding it back into the holster beneath his left arm. Gennaro relaxed his arm and Elena stepped forward to remove the meat cleaver from his hand.

The tension eased a little as they all stepped back from the brink. Gennaro helped Joe to his feet, while the gunman did the same for the fat man. Angelica noted with some satisfaction that his lip was cut and bleeding and his right eye was swollen shut.

'Since when did we come here to get assaulted?' Di Biasi asked, swapping to English and sliding a hand through his greased-back hair. 'To be insulted like this?'

'My son-in-law meant no disrespect,' Gennaro insisted.

Di Biasi eyed Joe warily. 'He's the husband of your dead girl?'

'That's right. He's visiting from England. With my granddaughter.' Elena beckoned Angelica forward. 'The young woman who was serving at your table.'

Di Biasi met Angelica's eye. He looked embarrassed. 'You animal, Renzi,' he muttered, turning his disgusted gaze on the fat man. 'Go and wait outside.'

Renzi had the good sense not to respond. His only comment was to spit a bloody globule onto the floor as he made his way to the steps.

'Come. Join me and Fabio. Have a drink.' Di Biasi gestured to the scar-faced man, who presumably was Fabio, to right the upturned chair. He indicated to Angelica that she should take it. When she made no move, he turned his attention to Joe. '*Amico*. Please. No hard feelings.' He held out his hand in a gesture of friendship, but her dad ignored it. He stared at Di Biasi, white with anger, almost trancelike in his focus, and, in that moment, Angelica was almost scared of him.

It was Elena who again broke the deadlock. 'Go to the kitchen, Joe,' she commanded, stepping between the two men. Her dad seemed to snap out of it. He let his eyes fall from the other man's face. They came to rest on Angelica. 'Come on,' he told her, his voice a hoarse whisper. Taking her by the arm he ushered her away.

In the time they were by themselves, they didn't talk much. Angelica was in shock and the tears came quickly. He held her, stroking her hair, letting her cry, whispering how proud he was of her for the way she'd stood her ground.

'I was scared,' she told him, lifting her head from his chest.

'I'd never let anyone hurt you, love.'

'Not for me, Dad. For *you*.'

He hugged her again, squeezing her tighter. At last she was all cried out. She wiped her eyes on her sleeve, accepted the napkin he held out to her and blew her nose.

Joe took up station by the kitchen door, watching through the glass. Elena came to check on them and he stepped aside to let her in before resuming his vigil. Her grandmother was solicitous of Angelica, taking her to the sink to wipe the mascara from her cheeks and dry her face, and then holding her hand while the waiting went on. Eventually Joe must have decided the coast was clear, for he pushed through the doors without a word. Angelica exchanged a look with Elena. There was nothing for it but to follow.

As Gennaro came down the steps after showing Di Biasi to the gate, Joe launched straight in. 'Who the hell was that?'

'His name is Rocco Di Biasi.'

'That's not what I mean, Gennaro.'

'He's a businessman. In Napoli.'

Joe snorted with derision. 'Businessman my arse.'

Elena looked indignant on her husband's behalf. 'He has a canning factory.'

'Yeah. And thugs with guns.'

The three adults glared at each other.

'The one with the scar . . . he's the one you gave money to the other night, isn't he?'

Gennaro squirmed at his insistence. 'Just stay out of my business, Joe.'

Joe snorted. 'Some *business*! He didn't even pay his bill.'

'I didn't ask him to.'

'Do you ever?'

Gennaro gave Elena a look. It seemed to Angelica that Joe had hit a nerve.

'That's a courtesy you extend to a lot of local "businessmen", is it?' Joe continued.

Gennaro's voice grew more heated. 'Leave it, Joe. Please!'

'What the hell is going on, Gennaro?'

'LEAVE IT!'

His roar of anger finally silenced Joe.

Angelica felt her eyes prickle. She hurried away before the tears could come again.

32

Damn him.

Lara's heart sank as she walked up the street from the metro a few minutes after 7.30am on Thursday, sweaty from an early gym session. The English detective was leaning against the front wall of La Questura. Why did he always seem to be everywhere before her? She needed a hot shower and a strong coffee before she would be anything close to her best self. Before she would feel anything like ready to deal with him.

He pushed off the wall as she approached, and she forced herself to sound neutral, definitely not annoyed. 'You're here early.'

'I got the 6am ferry.'

'Something must be urgent.'

'What can you tell me about Rocco Di Biasi?'

His question was so unexpected that it stopped her in her tracks. 'Di Biasi?!'

'He's some local big-shot apparently. Owns a factory, I'm told.'

She could no longer disguise her irritation. 'I know who he is, Joe. I just don't know what he has to do with you.'

Joe took his hand out of the pocket of his jeans and showed it to her. His knuckles were scabby and swollen. 'I had a close encounter with a couple of his goons last night.'

Lara looked from the hand to his face, weighing him up. He looked serious, even more so than normal. 'You better come inside,' she sighed, gesturing with her head.

She was feeling more herself by the time she walked Joe along the corridor in the basement of the building that housed the archive. She'd kept him waiting while she showered and changed, made herself ready for the day, had even lingered a little, talking aimlessly to a colleague, knowing he would be growing impatient, wanting him to feel so, sensing some of her old irritation towards him returning. *What business was Rocco Di Biasi of his?* Now she took her time to unlock the door they'd come to. She was in no hurry. She already knew what was awaiting them on the other side.

As she swung the door open and turned on the lights, she studied his face, saw his look of expectation turn to dismay. She followed his gaze into the windowless interior. It was just as she remembered it. Harsh neon strip-lights. Rows of dusty floor-to-ceiling metallic shelves. Hundreds of battered cardboard box files, many of them split or lid-less and spilling their curling and yellowing contents onto the floor.

'What is this place?'

'It's our special archive.'

A faint flicker of bemusement passed across his features.

'It's where we keep our files on historic cases relating to the Camorra. Going back nearly seventy years.'

'So our friend... he's Naples Mafia?'

'His family used to be one of the most powerful clans in the region.'

'*Used* to be?'

'They're supposed to be defunct.'

'But you don't think they are?'

Lara shrugged. 'Let's just say Rocco Di Biasi is a person of interest.'

Joe's gaze slid back to the rows of shelves. He looked thoughtful.

'You want to know about him?' She gestured expansively. 'Be my guest.' Without giving him a chance to change his mind, she placed a bottle of water on the solitary desk and exited, closing the door behind her with an emphatic clang.

She let him stew for several hours before she went back to check on him, found him just as she'd anticipated . . . simmering, ready to boil over. Serve him right, she thought, for insisting on sticking his nose into places where no one had asked him to put it. 'Did you find what you're looking for?' she asked, trying to keep a straight face.

He fixed a jaundiced eye on her. 'I was hoping you might supply a case file or two, Lara. Not a bloody history lesson.'

'But you can't investigate the Camorra without understanding its history.'

'All right, all right. Point made.'

'We've been fighting those bastards since the Risorgimento, Joe. Perhaps you'd be better off leaving Rocco Di Biasi to us.'

The English detective put his hands up in surrender.

'Now. Shall we get back to what it is we're supposed to be investigating?'

She'd been intending to suggest that Joe put in a call to Girl Cupid's lawyers to give them another hurry-up to release Shannon's messages, but before she could do so, she was ambushed by Gianni as they returned to her desk. There were hours and hours of CCTV footage from the Hotel Americano, her deputy moaned, but the colleagues who were supposed to be helping him go through it had been reassigned . . . a gang-related killing in the docks . . . and he was having to do it all himself. Lara was about to tell him to suck it up and get on with it when Joe offered to help.

'It's a long way below your pay grade,' she observed.

'I don't mind.' The purpose of the task was to find footage of Luca in Shannon Headley's company, wasn't it? But it might equally turn up footage that confirmed a connection between the victim and someone else.

'Suit yourself.' She left them to get on with it.

They were not in the video suite when she came to find them towards 6pm, having spent the afternoon in a debrief with Curti and the *vice questore*. The prosecutor was ready to proceed with charging Luca Da Vinale as soon as Lara had independent corroboration of his presence in the kitchen at Villa San Benedetto on the night Zuzu Esposito had died, and a witness statement that backed up Joe's version of events. It was a simple matter of speaking to the head chef. She was waiting for his call back.

Lara tracked the two men down to the roof terrace, where she herself was often to be found, vaping and mulling over the details of whatever case was preoccupying her. They were chatting easily about something and laughing, in that masculine workplace fashion that so grated with her. She felt a pang of possessiveness. The English detective may annoy the hell out of her, but it was her task to liaise with him, nobody else's.

'Come on,' she told Joe, cold-shouldering her deputy. 'I'm going to buy you a drink.'

The bar she took him to was not one of her usual haunts. It was in the 'wrong' part of the city, and not the kind of place that

State Police inspectors were encouraged to hang out. But she'd been there a few weeks previously for a girlfriend's birthday and had enjoyed the vibe. And anyway, she told herself, it was good to live a little dangerously.

As they descended below street level, Joe raised an eyebrow for her benefit but otherwise said nothing. The bar was already busy, and the music had been turned up. Condensation from the sweaty press was dripping off the low ceiling. Lara pushed through the throng of bodies and made her way to the bar.

She focused on getting served but once her order had been accepted – two beers, two tequilas – she glanced behind to check Joe was OK. He was staring off to the left, and she craned her neck to follow his line of sight. A huge gorilla of a man with a ruff of chest hair sticking out of his shirt was staring back at him, but now he turned his hostile gaze on her. Lara recognised him from one bust or another, she couldn't quite recall. She turned back to claim their drinks and made her way over to join Joe, maintaining eye contact with their antagonist as she went.

'Friend of yours?' Joe asked, accepting a beer and a tequila.

'A member of my fan club.' Lara felt giddy, almost reckless. She raised her shot glass in the direction of the gorilla and downed its contents in one.

The thug stared impassively back at her.

'Does he always stare like that?'

'He knows I'm police.' She took a defiant swig of her beer.

'Then why do you come?'

'Why shouldn't I?' She turned her gaze on Joe, daring him to gainsay her. 'I make them uncomfortable. By what I do. And who I am.'

'I can see that.'

Lara grinned. 'Want to really freak him out?' She indicated the shot glass she'd given him. 'Down that. We're going to dance.'

With great reluctance Joe let her drag him onto the square of empty space that served as a dance floor, but he couldn't be forced to dance. At best he swayed a little in time to the music, while studiously avoiding her eye. Several times he suggested he was going to sit down, but Lara shook her head. It was his duty to stay with her, she insisted. It would be dangerous to get separated in a place like this.

As a handful of others came to join them, she relented and sent him back to the bar to get another round. By the time he returned, the floor had filled up and, after accepting her drinks, she turned her back on him. A young couple were circling, smiling, making eye contact, showing unmistakable signs of interest. They were cool and fluid – the woman a slinky redhead, the man a dark and hungry presence at her side. Lara reeled them in, dancing with each of them in turn, grinding, gyrating, letting her inhibitions go.

And then, unexpectedly, the English detective was dancing beside her. She didn't know whether it was the tequila or the James Brown on the turntable, but suddenly he seemed more relaxed, less reticent, his long limbs flowing sinuously, his hips surprisingly flexible, his masculinity attracting admiring and flirtatious glances from dancers of both sexes. She caught his eye and laughed, delighted by this change in him, and he laughed too. They danced on for a long time, fuelled by more beers and more shots, bumping up against one another occasionally, eyes seeking one another out every now and then in the whirling, heaving throng. Lara felt that she could go on indefinitely, spinning and twisting, but at last Joe pronounced himself too drunk and exhausted to continue and she conceded a brief respite on condition he stood guard while she visited the washroom. Having relieved herself, she parked him in a booth in the corner with his back to the wall, while she went back to the bar. She returned with four shots of tequila, but no beer.

'Jesus, Lara.'

'What? Aren't you having a good time?' She sat down and leaned into him with her hip, encouraging him to scoot along.

'I am. It's just . . .'

'It's just your wife is dead.' It was out of her mouth before she could consider the wisdom of saying it. His sheen of happiness disappeared, but she was in no mood to pull her punches. 'She's gone, Joe. And I'm sorry for you. But you can't just stop living.'

'I'm trying.'

'Then try harder.' She forced one of the shots into his hand and tried to get him to drink, but he resisted, so instead she downed one of hers and slammed the glass on the table. 'And keep your nose out of my fucking cases. Unless I ask for your help.'

'You mean Rocco Di Biasi?'

'Of course, *stupido*.'

Joe acknowledged his breach of etiquette with a miserable nod of his head.

Lara couldn't resist a final dig. 'You can't put every bad man behind bars, Joe. And even if you could . . .'

There was no need for her to finish her sentence. Putting up a hand to silence her, the English detective downed both his shots of tequila, one after the other.

Lara considered depositing Joe in the drunk tank at La Questura but opted, reluctantly, to let him crash on her sofa instead. It was her fault, she decided, that he'd drunk himself into a state of incoherence and missed his last ferry home.

As she strained every sinew to help him up three flights of stairs to her flat, she regretted her decision; he was leaning heavily on her, too smashed to support himself. At last, after several minutes of struggling and shushing, they made it to her front door and she was able to lean him against the door jamb while feeling for her keys. With the door unlocked, she manoeuvred him through and they tottered together into the unlit flat. She heaved him towards the safety of the sofa in her kitchen-diner, twisting Joe's body as she did so to prevent him from face-planting into the marble tiles. The English detective landed on his back, mostly on the sofa but with one leg off it, and with Lara on top of him. They were nose to nose, so close that she could feel his breath on her cheek, could sense the exact moment that his mouth reached for hers. She felt a surge of something long suppressed, not desire exactly but a need to be held. Then she remembered who she was. And who he was. And she recoiled and pushed herself off.

'Go to sleep, you idiot,' she muttered, throwing a rug over him before retreating into the darkness towards her solitary bed.

33

Joe awoke on the Friday morning exactly where Lara had left him. He tried to lift his head but instantly wished he hadn't. The throbbing in his temples was intense, and the crick in his neck was agonising, but the physical discomfort he felt paled in comparison to his hot flush of shame as the memory of the night before came creeping back. He closed his eyes and let his head fall back against the cushions, trying to quell the rising sense of nausea.

'Coffee?'

He opened his eyes once more and turned his head, very tentatively, towards the sound of Lara's voice. She was standing behind the breakfast bar that separated the kitchen from the living room, freshly showered and dressed; her only concession to the possibility of a hangover was the pair of aviator sunglasses that covered her eyes.

Joe could only groan in response. She must have interpreted this as a signal of assent, however, because moments later he heard the buzz of the coffee machine as the water started to heat. He lay there, listening to the sounds of her preparations – a sigh of steam escaping, the rising tone as the liquid filled the cup – and letting his gaze wander around the room. Much of it was exactly as he would have predicted – a TV, a stack of fitness magazines, a pair of synthetic rubber dumbbells and a skipping rope, a scattering of photos in frames, including one of a youthful-looking Lara dressed in white and engaging in some form of martial art – but his eye was most drawn to the one thing that was not. It was a drawing of a seated female nude done in various pastel shades of chalk, with one arm attempting to cover her breasts and a hand thrown up to hide her facial features but leaving the shock of her genitals and pubic hair exposed. It was raw, intimate, personal. Joe intuited he might be looking at an image of Lara herself.

'Here.'

He started and turned his head to find her holding out a cup of coffee. She had removed her sunglasses and was regarding him with a hint of challenge in her eyes.

'And yes . . . in case you're wondering . . . it's me.'

'Right.'

'It was done by a friend.'

'OK.'

'They're a professional artist.'

Joe didn't quite know what to say, where to look. 'Lara, if I—'

She cut him off. 'Forget it, Joe. I have.'

He watched her eyes flick from his face towards the drawing.

'You're not my type,' she stated flatly, meeting his gaze with eyebrows raised.

'Good to know.'

There was really no more that needed to be said.

They did not speak again until they were in Lara's car and heading to La Questura. Joe was feeling marginally more human, although the pounding rhythm of the city's rush-hour traffic as it trundled over the ubiquitous black volcanic flagstones and the petrol fumes flooding through the open window were threatening to undo the mildly restorative effects of a hot shower and a second cup of oil-black coffee.

Lara had retreated once more behind her sunglasses and the blare of a breakfast radio show, and it was a surprise when she suddenly declared, 'I'm sorry.' It came out of nowhere and was apropos of what, he wasn't sure.

'It's me who should be apologising.'

She shook her head. 'I'm not talking about *that*.'

Joe decided staying silent might be best in the circumstances.

'I say some awful shit when I'm drunk.'

He waited for her to explain more, kept his eyes averted.

The car had pulled to a temporary halt in traffic, and he sensed her deciding how to continue. 'Like that thing about your wife,' she ventured at last. 'And what I implied.'

'And what was that?'

She risked a glance at him. 'That you're . . . *overcompensating*. Because Sofia's case remains unresolved.'

He considered this. 'You're right,' he sighed. 'I am.'

'Which is why I'd like to try and help.'

Joe finally risked a glance at her. 'Help? How?'

'Let me look at the file.'

'Sofia's?' Instinctively he shook his head.

'Why not?'

Because. 'What would be the point?'

'Your colleagues . . . they might have missed something.'

'Like what?'

'I don't know. Something that might help identify whoever it was who was driving. I'll go over it with a fresh pair of eyes. See if anything at all stands out.'

Joe tried to voice an objection, but nothing came. 'I don't know, Lara.'

'What have you got to lose?'

He shrugged. Nothing. She was right about that.

'I'll be expecting a favour in return,' she persisted.

'Oh yeah? What's that?'

She laughed. 'The rest of that CCTV footage still needs looking through.'

Lara had jokingly told Joe he was 'doing penance' as she showed him back into the video suite at HQ some time later. And that was exactly how it felt as he fast-forwarded through the hours of CCTV footage from the lobby of the Hotel Americano, freeze-framing every time someone came into view. It would have been dull and deadening work even without a hangover and it took every ounce of his willpower to stay alert, to make sure he wasn't missing anything, to avoid being distracted by the toe-curling sense of embarrassment he couldn't quite shake off, despite her reassurances.

After a couple of hours, he was heavy-lidded with fatigue and ready to quit, but the thought of Luca languishing in his cell prevented him from admitting defeat. He took a break and splashed cold water over his head and neck, and drank a good deal more. Sensing an inkling of light at the end of the dark tunnel of his hangover, he returned to his task with renewed vigour and was rewarded a few minutes later by his first sighting of Shannon Headley. The footage was unremarkable – she was crossing the lobby from the direction of the elevators – but it reinforced his belief in the value of the process, however tedious and time-consuming it might seem. Searching for a different angle, he opened a new file, and within a few minutes he'd spotted her again. This time she was leaving the hotel with her bag slung over one shoulder. A man in a logo-less baseball cap pulled low over his eyes was coming behind. Joe rewound the footage and watched it again. In the background, the man could be seen entering the lobby from the street a few minutes previously. Joe checked the time code. The footage was from just before seven on the Saturday morning. The same time that Shannon first visited Tiberius's Leap, according to the GPS from her phone. He was fairly sure the man on the video wasn't Luca. His features were obscured by the visor of his cap, but he looked too heavily built. And there was the suggestion of a ponytail that Gennaro's nephew didn't have.

With a sense he might be on to something, Joe spent the next hour trying to track the movements of Shannon and the stranger, hoping he might get a look at the man's face. There were supposed to be two security cameras covering the front of the Hotel Americano, but he soon learned neither of them was directed on the comings and goings from the hotel and were focused instead on the street outside. The closest he could get to confirming Shannon and her shadow had got into a vehicle was a brief glimpse of the rear end of a white car – possibly a convertible – driving across the top left-hand corner of one shot at 7.02am. He rewound and replayed the video several times, trying to decipher its licence plate. Was that an N or an M? Maybe a P? He couldn't be sure.

Joe was still trying to read the runes when Lara came to check on him.

'Find anything?'

Relieved to have professional matters to discuss, he showed her the footage.

'You're right,' she agreed. 'It's not Luca.'

'Do you think it's one of those soft-top taxis?' They were everywhere on Capri.

'Maybe.' If so, with even a partial numberplate it should be possible to track down whoever it was who'd given Shannon a ride on the morning of her death.

'Maybe it's the same taxi that picked Shannon and Luca up from Da Vinale's.'

'Good work. I'll have to get you drunk more often.' She squeezed his shoulder.

Joe couldn't detect any awkwardness in her demeanour as she did so.

Three hours later, they were standing outside an address near Capri port, accompanied by two constables and armed with a warrant and an enforcer. According to Lara's contact at the Communal Council, there were three taxis on Capri with licence plates ending in MP or NP, but only one was a cabriolet. It was now parked at the end of the street they were standing in. And while its owner wasn't known to the police, several members of his family were.

'No heroics, OK . . . you're just an observer,' she instructed Joe, after two rings of the doorbell had gone unanswered. She turned to her uniformed colleagues and gave them the nod to break the lock and open the door.

Joe needed no encouragement to hold back. His recovery had suffered a setback on the speedboat journey to Capri and he was still feeling sick as he watched Lara follow her colleagues up a flight of stairs and into the apartment's dingy interior. He waited for the shouts of warning before following them inside.

There was no sign of the taxi's registered owner, Dante Patalano. There were indications that the property had recently been occupied – the milk in the refrigerator was in date and the soil of a houseplant on the windowsill was still moist to the touch – but the wardrobe in the bedroom had been emptied. It was clear from a cursory examination that the apartment had been stripped of any personal effects.

He caught up with Lara in the kitchen, where she was flicking through the pages of a calendar pinned to a corkboard. 'Suspiciously empty, wouldn't you say?'

She nodded. 'Looks like someone decided to leave in a hurry.'

'Something to hide?'

Lara shrugged, not quite ready to concede that he was right. 'What now?'

'Will you let me speak to Luca again?'

The Italian detective considered his request. 'OK,' she conceded, 'but none of this proves he's innocent, Joe. They could have murdered Shannon together.'

'A simple yes or no, Luca. It's all I need. You don't even have to say his name.'

Joe's gaze was drawn back to the print-out from the security camera he'd placed between them on the bed in the holding cell. He knew, of course, it was anything but *simple* for Gennaro's nephew to do what he was asking . . . to confirm the identity of the taxi driver. There were complex codes of honour to observe. But still . . .

He decided to lay all his cards on the table. 'Look, you already told me your smuggling friend drives a taxi, and you and he gave Shannon a lift back to town from Da Vinale's on Friday night. And now we've got CCTV footage of a taxi driver coming to the hotel to pick Shannon up the morning after. And a partial read on a numberplate.' Joe tapped the photo, causing Luca to look up. 'We've a pretty good idea it was Dante Patalano. All you need to do is to look at the photo. Say whether it's him.'

Luca's gaze slid off Joe's face and briefly alighted on the print-out.

'It'll mean the police have a second suspect to go after.'

The sous-chef's only response was to shake his head very slightly.

'Why are you protecting him?'

'I'm not.'

'The taxi . . . we know it's Dante's. It's registered in his name.'

'That doesn't mean he was driving it.'

'He's scarpered, Luca. Left you in the shit. You don't owe him anything—'

Luca cut him off. 'For fuck's sake. It's not *him*.'

There was something so definite in his pronouncement it silenced Joe. He picked up the photo again, re-examined the grainy suggestion of a man's face. How could he be sure? 'You barely looked at it,' he said at last, holding it out to him.

Luca ignored the photo. Instead he held Joe's gaze. 'I don't need to see it again.'

It was Joe's turn to shake his head. 'Because of some misplaced sense of loyalty?'

'No. Because I know who it is.'

Sandro Totti *almost* looked the part, Lara reflected as she watched Gianni escort him into the interview room. His build was similar to the man in the CCTV footage, although, if Luca was right and it was him who'd picked up Shannon, then he'd had a recent haircut because it was now shaved within millimetres of his scalp. As the man she was about to interview settled himself, she glanced towards the camera mounted in the corner of the room. She knew Joe was watching in the suite next door and she couldn't help wondering if he'd made the same observations about Totti's build and hair.

With only the briefest of preambles, she placed a series of CCTV images in front of her wary-looking interviewee. They were trying to identify a taxi driver who was believed to have picked up the victim from her hotel on the morning of her death, she explained. While Sandro wasn't amongst those licensed to drive a taxi on Capri, the rumour was he sublet a vehicle from its registered owner, Dante Patalano, in return for a cut of his fares.

'Who told you that?'

It didn't matter, she informed him, glancing instinctively once more at the camera. They weren't interested in exposing his moonlighting, just in ascertaining what he might know about Shannon's movements on that particular day.

Sandro's eyes flicked from one photo to another.

Lara decided to apply a little more pressure. They had new facial recognition software powered by AI, she lied, ignoring a questioning look from Gianni as she did so. It was capable of making a facial match from the grainiest footage. He was the man the security cameras had captured in the lobby of the Hotel Americano that morning, wasn't he? There was no point denying it. The algorithm would confirm it soon enough.

Sandro shrugged insouciantly. 'Did I say it wasn't me?'

What could he tell her about Shannon Headley then?

'Nothing.'

What was he saying? That she was just another fare?

'No.'

What then?

'I wasn't there to pick her up.'

Lara snorted in disbelief. 'We have you on CCTV. Leaving the hotel with her.'

Sandro leaned forward to look again at the image of Shannon leaving the lobby, the man in the cap coming a few paces behind. He could see that's what it looked like, he conceded, but it was just unfortunate timing. They weren't leaving together.

'Then what were you doing there?'

Sandro explained that he cleaned swimming pools for a living. He'd previously enquired at the Hotel Americano about whether they might require his services, having cleaned their pool in the past, but had been told to come back and ask again when the facilities manager was present. He'd only remembered to do so when he was driving past the hotel on the morning in question. His van had broken down and, yes, Dante had kindly lent him his taxi for the day. Despite the earliness of the hour, he'd decided to stop at the hotel to show willing. But he'd quickly been sent on his way again and had been so preoccupied with his own affairs he'd failed to notice who he was leaving with.

Lara decided to cut to the chase. 'Do you use dating apps, Sandro?'

'Dating apps?'

'You know . . . Tinder, Badoo, Hinge? Girl Cupid maybe?'

Sandro was stony-faced. 'I don't need to.'

'That's not what I asked.'

'Here.' Sandro took his phone out of his pocket and unlocked it before sliding it onto the desk between them. 'See for yourself.'

But even as Gianni reached to pick it up, Lara knew he'd be wasting his time.

34

It was almost five days since Angelica had last seen Daniele and she'd been struggling to conjure what he looked like. Certainly, seeing him now, perched on his scooter behind the beach bar talking to a friend, he seemed older than she remembered, maybe a little more handsome. Observing him from the road above as he chatted and laughed, he seemed as carefree as she was miserable, and she almost abandoned the idea of a confrontation. But avoiding him, she told herself, would only compound the confusion of feelings he aroused in her. Besides, she missed him. And she was desperate to talk to someone her own age about her encounter with Rocco Di Biasi and his creepy sidekicks. Taking a deep breath, she urged herself forward.

It was his friend who noticed her approach. Daniele turned to follow his gaze a moment later. She hesitated, stopped a few yards away, her carefully rehearsed lines deserting her, her mind a blank. To her relief, Daniele turned back to his friend and made his excuses. A moment later he was on his feet and coming towards her. She walked away, far enough for them to be out of earshot, waited for him to catch up. She felt his hand brush her upper arm and turned to face him, felt a thrill of excitement as he leaned in to kiss her, yet forced herself to avoid his mouth.

His smile faded into a frown. 'Where have you been?'
'Around.'

He couldn't help rolling his eyes slightly at her evasion. 'I called you.'

'I know.'

'And messaged you.'

Angelica shrugged. 'You stopped pretty quick.'

'I don't like to play games, Angelica.'

'Neither do I.'

They stared at one another, each weighing up the depth of the other's hostility.

Daniele was the first to give ground. 'Before . . . at the beach . . .' He paused, seeking the right words. 'I went too far?'

'Maybe just too fast.'

'I'm sorry.'

To his credit, Angelica thought, he had the decency to look it.

He tried again. 'It's just . . . I like you. A lot.'

She felt the knot of anger she'd been nursing loosen inside her a little.

Daniele must have sensed it; he tried to embrace her but, again, she held herself back. 'I need to ask you something,' she managed to say.

'OK.'

She made a conscious effort to meet his eye. 'Are you dealing drugs?'

He blinked and his gaze slid away. 'No.'

'Don't lie to me, Daniele.'

He forced himself to meet her stare again. 'I'm not.'

'I saw you,' she persisted.

'When?'

'That day.' She pointed to the far end of the beach bar. 'By the kitchens.'

He took a moment, maybe to recall, maybe to calculate. 'I had some of that weed left over,' he explained cautiously. 'I gave it to a friend.'

Angelica knew what she'd seen.

Pills.

She started to walk away.

'Angelica! Wait!'

She forced herself not to look around, to carry on walking.

'OK. It's true.'

Now she stopped, waited for his approach.

He sidled up to her, glancing over his shoulder to check they were not being overheard. 'I carry things. For a friend. He lets me sell some on the side.'

'What kind of things?'

'You know . . . *things*.'

Daniele gave her a look that begged her not to make him spell it out, but Angelica was determined to know everything there was to know. 'Tell me, Daniele.'

He sighed. 'Blues, mainly. Sometimes molly, ket. Stuff like that.'

'Blues?'

'Fenty.'

'Fentanyl?'

'It's what everybody wants.'

'Isn't it dangerous?'

He laughed. 'Everything's dangerous. If you're an idiot.'

She'd set out to extract this confession, but now she had it she didn't know what to do with it. She felt her eyes prickle, kept her face averted. 'It's easy for you,' she heard him mutter. 'You have choices. Money.' He sounded bitter. But it was the first really honest thing she thought she'd heard him say to her, and instinctively she turned back to him. Daniele squirmed a little under her sad-eyed appraisal. 'I'm just trying to earn enough to give myself a future,' he blurted out.

She felt her resolve starting to waver.

He must have realised it. 'I'll stop.'

'You'd do that?'

'Of course. If it's what you want.'

This time, as he leaned in for a kiss, she didn't pull away.

35

Joe's first thought on returning to Da Vinale's that Friday evening to find the street gate locked and the restaurant beyond it suspiciously quiet was that the old chef had got his way and closed down the kitchen in Luca's absence. He was quickly disabused of this notion, however, by Elena, who almost wept with relief at the sight of him.

'Thank God you're here,' she told him, unlocking the gate and ushering him hurriedly down the steps.

'What is it? What's happened?'

'Gennaro's hurt.' And he was refusing to get help, she added, although he'd at least agreed to cancel the evening's covers at short notice. As she led him back across the empty terrace, babbling nervously, Joe thought his mother-in-law was starting to show her age for the first time since he'd known her.

The scene that greeted him as he entered the kitchen was suitably chaotic. Gennaro sat in a chair in the centre of the room, with Aldo and Angelica fussing over him. There was blood on the floor, and more of it on the grubby white apron that was straining to cover his father-in-law's belly. The pot-washer was in the process of stitching an ugly-looking gash that sat high on the right side of the old chef's forehead, while his granddaughter was dabbing at his face with a dampened wad of cotton wool. As Aldo pinched and stitched the edges of his wound, Gennaro winced and attempted to reach for a hip flask that stood on a work surface to his right, next to the open first-aid box.

'Sit still,' Elena scolded him, removing the flask from his reach.

'Are you all right?' Joe asked, coming to stand in Gennaro's line of sight.

'It looks worse than it is.'

Elena met Joe's eye. 'We'll be the judge of that.'

Joe leaned in to make his own assessment. The gash turned out to be more of an indentation, the skin lacerated and torn away from the scalp down the left side of the wound. It was clearly the result of a blunt rather than a sharp object. 'You should get that looked at,' he advised.

The old chef huffed. 'And wait hours and hours in the hospital?'

Aldo shook his head but kept his counsel.

'You could have a skull fracture,' Joe persisted. 'Maybe even a brain bleed.'

Angelica backed him up. 'See, *Nonno*. That's what I said.'

'Don't make a fuss. I feel OK.'

Elena threw her hands up in exasperation.

'What the hell happened?' Joe asked, turning to her.

'We were preparing for the dinner service . . . like always. Perfectly normal. Then someone texts him, and suddenly he says he's feeling dizzy. Needs to get some air.'

'They were waiting for him outside,' Angelica chimed in.

'Who was?'

'He doesn't know.'

'You mean he won't say,' Elena corrected her granddaughter. More angry now than worried, she seemed more like her true self to Joe. 'Aldo, finish up!' she instructed the tiny pot-washer, snapping her fingers to emphasise the command. 'You should be heading home. Angelica, you come back to the apartment with me.'

Aldo took a moment to cover his handiwork with a cotton dressing. With a raised eyebrow for Joe's benefit, he accepted his bag from Elena and did as he was told.

Elena handed Joe the hip flask with a meaningful look. 'Perhaps you can get the stubborn old fool to talk some sense,' she muttered, not waiting for either man's response before ushering Angelica towards the open door.

The two men were left alone. The old chef held out his hand for the flask, but Joe shook his head. 'Not until you tell me what's going on.'

Gennaro batted this away. 'Are you hungry?' he asked, changing the subject.

'Now?'

'I'm hungry. Let's eat.' Gennaro got to his feet and grasped the back of the chair to steady himself. With a grunt and a grimace, he removed his apron and cast it aside. Reaching across to pluck the hip flask from Joe's hands, he exited the kitchen before his son-in-law had a chance to ask where they were going.

Dark had fallen by the time they entered the piazza, which was festooned with lights and had an appealing, if faintly faded air. Gennaro headed for the tables laid out across the enclosed section of the square and, briefly, Joe imagined his father-in-law was taking him to dine among the heaving morass of tourists that thronged the island's most popular viewing spot. At the last moment, however, the old chef veered right and cut through into a smaller *piazzetta*, which was more like a confluence of roads than a space designed for meeting and eating. Here there were a scattering of food stalls, some little more than trestle tables covered in cloths, others wheeled and more elaborate, with colourful awnings and metal bases enamelled with bright patterns. His father-in-law made a beeline for the oldest and grubbiest of these and, dutifully, Joe followed.

An old man, shaven-headed and as brown as a tobacco stain, looked up as Gennaro called out a greeting and answered with a gap-toothed smile. The two men embraced and exchanged words, with Gennaro waving away his friend's obvious concern over his head wound and drawing his attention to Joe instead by gesturing in his direction. The other man turned to appraise Joe and raised a hand in greeting. Beckoning him over, he resumed his place behind his stall, signalling that he was welcome to watch.

'My grandfather . . . he had a stall like this,' Gennaro revealed, ushering Joe forward.

Joe watched as the old man took an ice-cream scoop and dug it into a pale, semi-set mixture in an aluminium cooking tray. 'What's he making?' he asked, as a series of golf-ball-sized portions of the mixture were set aside on a plate.

'Arancini. The first thing I ever cook.' His father-in-law sounded wistful.

'What are they?'

'Fried risotto balls.' Gennaro pointed to the mixture. 'You cook it. Make it cold overnight. Ready for tomorrow.'

'So, rice then?'

'Of course. The fattest grains. You fry them in butter with garlic and onions. And then in stock . . . how would you say?' He searched for the right word in English.

'Boil? Simmer?'

'*Sì*, simmer. Yes. Maybe a little milk. Then you can add what you like. Cheese, of course . . . mozzarella, maybe Parmesan or pecorino. Egg. Herb. Lemon.' He directed a comment in Italian to his friend, received an answer. 'He has *pollo* . . . chicken in his. But me . . . I put minced beef in mine. For my *nonno*. This was all he ate towards the end.'

The two of them watched as the street chef transferred his cold rice balls into a pile of flour and rolled them this way and that. He dipped each one in a shallow metal cup of whisked egg before transferring them into a bowl of breadcrumbs and coating them, snug and dry. The dozen or so balls were dropped into a wok of dark oil, which had been slumbering over a low flame but came immediately to life. The balls bobbed like tiny golden apples, the oil around them roiling and bubbling. The man herded them with a metal strainer, ducking them below the surface and flipping them, ensuring an even fry. Satisfied with his work, he fished out six, drained the excess oil off with a deft flick of one hand, and poured them into a paper cone he'd formed with the other. Gennaro took the cone and wrapped it in a paper napkin, handed it to Joe. A further exchange took place between the two old chefs over a bottle of red sauce. Laughing at something the other man had said, Gennaro picked the bottle up and, without consulting Joe, shook a dollop into his cone.

'What did you ask him?' his son-in-law wanted to know.

'If the sauce . . . it was hot.' Gennaro took a second cone of arancini as it was handed to him and liberally applied more of it.

Joe dipped a finger in the smear of red and sampled it.

'We call it *marinara*,' the old man confirmed, handing over a banknote and receiving his change. 'When we were boys, my brother and I . . . we changed the writing on the bottle –' He mimicked rewriting a label '– and gave them chilli sauce instead. They had to buy a cup of milk from us to cool their mouth down.'

Guffawing at the memory, Gennaro raised a hand of farewell to his counterpart and wandered away up the street. Joe met the street chef's smile with one of his own and shaped to follow.

They found a bench away from the throng. The cone holding his arancini had cooled in his hand, but when Joe took a first bite the mixture inside was still too hot to chew on comfortably, and he had to juggle it around his mouth and blow on it before he was able to break it down and swallow. 'Wow, they're hot,' he managed to say.

Gennaro seemed to be having no such problems. 'But good, no?'

'Amazing.' Joe blew again and took another bite to confirm it. The food really was incredible. Crunchy on the outside and gooey within. 'So much flavour. Texture.'

His father-in-law grinned. 'They pack a punch.'

It was too good an opportunity to miss. 'Speaking of punches . . .'

The old chef groaned. 'Please, Joe. Not tonight.'

Regretfully, Joe persisted. 'Was it Di Biasi's men?'

Gennaro seemed to lose his appetite. He dropped the arancina he was eating back into the cone, reached instead for the hip flask he'd slipped into his trouser pocket. He unscrewed the lid and took a swig, caught Joe eyeing him and offered the flask.

Joe shook his head. 'Well?'

'Who do you think?'

'They pistol-whipped you?' Joe mimicked the act of striking with the butt of a gun.

'Just a little tap.' The old chef was trying to put a brave face on it, but he couldn't help grimacing as he put an experimental hand up to feel around the wound.

'But why, Gennaro?'
'I think he must have asked around. About you.'
'Me?'
'My son-in-law. The *policeman*.'
'The *English* policeman.'

Gennaro shrugged. A policeman is a policeman, the gesture seemed to say. 'It's a warning,' he said, selecting a fresh arancina. 'Keep your mouth shut.'

'About what?'

The old chef slipped the fried risotto ball into his mouth to stop himself saying.

They'd finished their makeshift meal, and Joe had come to stand by the railings at the edge of the terrace offering the panoramic view that had drawn so many tourists to the piazza. He'd left Gennaro chewing the fat with an old acquaintance from the restaurant trade who claimed to have been waiting tables on Capri for the best part of sixty years. Now, as he sensed the old chef sidling up to stand beside him, he kept his counsel and contemplated the vista in front of him: the shadowy mass of Monte Solara to his left; the bright lights of Marina Grande illuminating the foreground below; the answering twinkles from the opposite coast, and the faint sheen of neon delineating the distant Neapolitan skyline, including the dark, brooding void of the volcano; the deep black-blue of the unfathomable water in between; above, the stars so high and cold.

Gennaro fidgeted beside him. 'Are you ready to go?'
'Not until you tell me.'

The old chef swore softly under his breath.
'Maybe I should just ask Elena.'
'She doesn't know.'

'I bet she has an inkling.'

'Please, Joe! Enough!'

They'd turned to face one another, were standing close enough to touch. 'Just tell me,' Joe persisted, his eyes searching the older man's face.

It was too much for Gennaro and he looked away. '*Mi sta estorcendo.*'

It took Joe a moment to guess his meaning. 'He's extorting you? In what way?'

The old chef flapped his hands hopelessly. 'I borrowed money.'

'What for?'

'Some land . . . next to the restaurant. It was for sale.'

'You were thinking of extending Da Vinale's?'

'Elena and me . . . we were going to add sixty covers. And a new kitchen.'

'Then what happened?'

Gennaro looked pained. 'The council, they told me . . . *il permesso . . . la autorizzazione* . . . it wouldn't be a problem. So, I bought the land. Spent money. Lawyers. Architects. Surveys. *Tutta quella merda.* But then . . .'

'They changed their mind?'

'Or someone changed it for them. And I'm left with this land . . . that can't be built on. Is worth *niente*. And I owe Signor Di Biasi money. A *lot* of money.'

'You couldn't pay him back?'

'I have. Every cent. But when I tried to stop the payment . . .'

The penny was starting to drop for Joe. 'He threatened you.'

'He calls them "interest" payments. He says it's in my *interest* to keep paying.'

Joe looked out over the landscape he'd been admiring just

moments before. It seemed darker now, more foreboding. 'How long's this been going on?'

'Two years.' Gennaro sighed heavily. 'If it goes on much longer . . . we're going to lose the restaurant.'

36

The Saturday morning seemed to bring a change of heart, and Angelica was glad of it. Her *nonno*, who the night before had been full of bravado, seemed less bullish in the cold light of day. Despite this, he remained opposed to seeking medical assistance and might have got his way, had his struggles not been so obvious as they sat around the breakfast table. Under questioning from a tearful Elena, Gennaro admitted he felt groggy and nauseous, far more so than might be explained by the grappa he'd drunk the night before. It was decided they should take him for an urgent consultation at the private clinic on the mainland where his stubbornly high cholesterol had previously been tested and treated.

Joe insisted on escorting them and no one had objected when Angelica asked to come along. She held Gennaro's hand throughout the consultation and kept a poker face as she listened to him explain away his wound as the consequence of a slip and a fall. The doctor advised an immediate CT scan to rule out the possibility of an underlying brain injury; Gennaro would need to stay in hospital for observation, and Elena declared her intention to stay with him, would not countenance the idea of spending the night apart. The necessary arrangements were made for Da Vinale's to remain closed for a second consecutive evening.

Coming down the steps of the clinic after saying a solemn

goodbye to her grandparents, Angelica told Joe she wouldn't be getting the ferry back to Capri, but catching the train to Naples, having promised to go to an open day at a college with Daniele. He wasn't going back either, Joe told her, but was going to the city himself for an update on the case. He seemed subdued, preoccupied even, and she found herself seeking reassurance that Gennaro was going to be OK.

It was only when they were seated in the carriage that Angelica felt the need to confess that Daniele had also invited her to a beach party by the lighthouse on the island that evening, although in the circumstances, she'd understand if Joe didn't want her to go. They'd agreed on a compromise. He'd expect her back and in bed by eleven, so she'd be ready to help provide whatever assistance her grandparents might need the following day.

'So? What do you think?'

She and Daniele were sitting outside an unremarkable sandwich bar in the back streets near the ferry terminal, having ordered Cokes and a ham and cheese toastie to share. He'd been uncharacteristically quiet since they'd left the open day a few minutes earlier, had in fact said very little for much of the previous hour as they were shown around the catering college in the company of excitable teenagers and a smattering of their parents. Had he been absorbing it all, she wondered? Or having second thoughts.

Daniele paused to let the waiter place their drinks on the table and depart before he responded. 'What do *you* think?'

Angelica felt a flash of irritation. 'I can't make the decision for you.'

'I wish you could.'

'You have to want this for yourself, Daniele.'

'I do.' He busied himself with opening and pouring his soda.

Angelica picked up hers and followed suit, waiting to be convinced.

'I guess I could just about afford it,' he continued. 'If I worked evenings. Weekends.'

'In a restaurant, maybe? Putting what you'd be learning into practice?'

It was Daniele's turn to look unconvinced.

'My *nonno* says it's a good career,' Angelica hurried on. 'If you want to travel, you'll always be able to find a job wherever you go.'

'And yet he's still in Capri.'

'But he worked in London for fifteen years. It's where he met my gran.'

The mention of that magical city seemed to do the trick. 'Perhaps I should just apply. See if they accept me. Before I make a decision.'

'It can't do any harm.'

Daniele smiled with relief and Angelica felt herself warming to him once more. 'I'll do it right away,' he said, reaching for his backpack and unzipping a pocket, feeling inside. His smile quickly faded, however, as he discovered it was empty. '*Merda*,' he swore, jumping to his feet and slinging his bag over his shoulder. 'I forgot to pick up the form.'

'I'll come with you.'

Their waiter returned with their sandwich and Daniele discouraged her attempts to rise. 'Stay. Eat it while it's hot. I'll only be a few minutes.' As Angelica sat back down, he produced a banknote from his pocket and held it out to her.

She hesitated to take it. 'It's OK. I have my own.'

'It's not what you think.'

Their eyes met and her doubts must have been clear. With a slight shake of his head, he tossed the note down on the table and turned to walk away.

Daniele's half of the toasted sandwich lay congealing as Angelica settled the bill twenty minutes later. She'd calculated he would be back by now. As she stood up to leave, she almost left the banknote lying where he'd left it, but at the last minute she picked it up and slipped it into her pocket. She didn't want it to seem like she doubted him.

It took her less than five minutes to retrace her steps to the catering college, but the secretary in the administrator's office was adamant that no one had been back to pick up an application form.

Out on the street, Angelica gave in and decided to text him.

Where was he? Why was he taking so long?

At the café, he replied almost instantly.

Angelica swore under her breath. She decided not to text back. She would only say something she regretted, she thought, slipping her phone into her bag. She'd just turned to head back in the direction she'd come when someone brushed past her in the street, close enough for her to clutch her bag to her side as her dad had taught her. She swung round to see the back of a thin man in a black suit with slicked-back hair making his way through the crowd of pedestrians. He'd disappeared before she had time to satisfy the nagging sense that she recognised him from the restaurant.

Daniele was outside the sandwich bar when she returned. The plate was empty.

'The woman at the college . . . she said you didn't go back.'

He produced the form from the main compartment of his rucksack. 'It was in the other pocket,' he told her, looking sheepish.

It was an explanation of sorts, she supposed. She had no choice but to accept it.

37

'Whippet?'

'Yeah. Whippet. W-H-I-P-P-E-T. And then 2-0-0-1-6-2.' Joe could sense Lara's amusement as she typed the password into her laptop. He felt the need to explain. 'It's a nickname. Someone called me it when I was starting. And it stuck.'

She looked him up and down, faintly bemused. 'They think you look like one?'

'Not really. It's more a reference to where I come from. Londoners . . . they think everyone from the north of England . . . we wear cloth caps and race dogs.'

Lara considered this. 'English people . . . you have a weird sense of humour,' she observed, hitting the return key with a wry smile.

As Joe watched, a series of folders appeared on screen. He'd no need to study them more closely . . . he already knew the contents of this particular file by heart. Part of him regretted accepting Lara's offer to review the evidence relating to his wife's fatal accident. But another part of him nursed a faint hope she might uncover something that, in the tumult of emotion surrounding Sofia's case, they'd all been too blind to see.

Lara's eyes flitted this way and that. 'Your colleagues were happy to let me look?'

'I went through unofficial channels. Called in a favour.'

'And what about you?'

'Knock yourself out.'

'I don't want to get your hopes up.'

'They're close to zero.' *Why put unnecessary pressure on her?* he reasoned.

'I'm going to print everything out if that's OK.'

'Just don't leave it lying around.'

She managed to tear her gaze from the screen. 'Thank you. For trusting me with it.'

He met her frank stare of appraisal with one of his own.

'Boss?'

They turned to see Gianni approaching, and the moment between them passed. Lara clicked the file closed. 'What is it?'

'I think you better see this.' He handed over a document.

Lara scanned it quickly, brow furrowing and eyes widening. She glanced up at Joe, her features rearranging themselves into a sympathetic expression.

'Something important?' he couldn't help asking.

'I think so.'

'What is it?'

'A list of Girl Cupid's registered users in Capri.'

Joe's gaze dropped to the document, but he didn't take it; from the look on her face, he had an uneasy sense he already knew one of the names it was going to contain.

Their update with Curti was much like a daily case meeting he would have held at home, Joe reflected as he watched Gianni sticking photos and documents to a whiteboard while Lara prepared to explain what each one signified to their lines of enquiry. He'd asked to be excused from the briefing, given what they'd just learned, but Lara had insisted she still wanted him to attend. She trusted him to follow the evidence trail objectively, she told him, whatever direction it happened to be pointing. Besides, Curti was expecting him, and he didn't react well to surprises.

It was after lunch and the *commissario* seemed sluggish and snappy, unhappy to be having to work on a Saturday. If it'd been up to Joe, he would've handed over the document Lara had just shown him, got the meeting over with as quickly as possible. But for whatever reason, Lara seemed anxious to ensure her boss was across everything she'd initiated and decided to leave it until last.

She started with an update on Shannon Headley's cause of death. The pathologist, Dr Serafina, had finally returned from bereavement leave and had given her permission for the rash that had been found all over the dead woman's body to be tested. As Detective Chief Inspector Mottram had suspected, she went on, giving Joe a grateful nod, the results could have a bearing on the case. Dr Serafina was of the opinion that the rash was a reaction to a specific allergen... fentanyl.

Curti's brow creased. 'You said she was a heavy user.'

She was, Lara confirmed, but she'd always taken the drug orally, according to her father. Based on the test results, they were working on the theory that Shannon might have been tricked or coerced into taking a much larger than normal dose in liquid form and through her skin. And then pushed over the cliff while she was under the influence.

Good, Curti responded gruffly, acknowledging Joe with a nod. But of course the key questions remained. Who did it? And, more importantly, could they prove it?

Lara took a deep breath. They were close to ruling out Miles Yeats as a suspect, she informed Curti, as Gianni busied himself locating the supporting evidence. He didn't have an alibi between 2pm and 6pm on the Saturday of Shannon's death, but there was no physical evidence linking him to either woman. His lawyers in London had testified to receiving an email from their client at 12.06pm that same day, instructing them to file for dismissal of his legal proceedings over the sale of Girl Cupid, which supported Yeats's account of his meeting with Shannon. More importantly, data from the vessel's GPS proved *Calypso* was at sea while the anniversary dinner was taking place at the Villa San Benedetto on the Wednesday, and there were multiple witnesses prepared to testify that Yeats was seventy nautical miles southwest of Capri at the time Zuzu Esposito was taking a fall. They had no grounds to charge him with either murder, Lara declared. Which was why they were preparing to release him, although he wouldn't yet be permitted to fly home.

Curti grunted and fidgeted, looked unimpressed.

Ignoring these signs, Lara turned her attention to Manny Sanghera. They'd received a representation from his lawyer formally requesting the return of his passport so he could travel back to the UK. Manny was willing to come back to Naples at any time to help the police with their enquiries, but he wanted to return home in the interim. He was as keen as they were to clear up the mystery of his fiancée's death, but he couldn't afford to continue paying for hotel accommodation indefinitely.

'I thought he was marrying a multi-millionaire,' Curti observed tartly.

That was precisely the point, Lara explained. He was *supposed* to be marrying Shannon, but of course the wedding would not now be taking place. Apparently his wife-to-be had controlled the couple's finances, and her bank accounts and credit cards were frozen. Without her, Manny Sanghera appeared to be a man of relatively modest means.

'What do you think, Detective Chief Inspector?' Curti asked, turning to address Joe in his formal English as Gianni handed him the lawyer's letter.

Joe played a straight bat. It was Lara's call as senior investigating officer.

'And we're sure about his alibi?'

As sure as they could be, Lara told him, outlining the steps they'd taken to verify it. There was no doubt Manny had been with company in Positano at the time Shannon Headley was believed to have fallen to her death, and that he'd been dining in the restaurant of the hotel where he was staying when Zuzu was attacked.

'Then we should agree to this?' Curti asked, holding up the letter.

'Almost certainly, sir. But maybe not just yet.' With his agreement, she'd prefer to wait until the prosecutor had made a final decision on whether to charge Luca Da Vinale with Shannon Headley's murder.

Curti sighed wearily. And how close were they to that? he demanded.

'Close. Very close,' Lara reassured him, giving Joe a knowing look. It seemed certain that Luca and Shannon had hooked up via the Girl Cupid dating app following her arrival in Capri. They were currently retesting Shannon's body for DNA evidence that she'd had sexual intercourse with him before she died. And that would be in addition, of course, to the blood they'd found on Shannon's dress, which strongly implied any encounter between her and Luca had come to a violent end.

'The blood . . . it should be enough for them,' Curti grumbled to himself.

Thanks to DCI Mottram, Lara hurried on, they could place Luca Da Vinale at the Villa San Benedetto on the following

Wednesday, at the time someone had attacked Zuzu Esposito in the same location. There were no eyewitnesses, but Luca had left the scene without giving his name to the police. He was a convicted trafficker of counterfeit goods and, in that capacity, may have had prior knowledge of the secret staircase that connected the villa's cellar and the pump room to the coast below. They were working on the theory that an exchange had taken place between Zuzu and Luca when they found themselves working together at the event, and the suspect had taken advantage of his knowledge of the location to escape undetected after killing Zuzu.

'But why kill her?' Curti asked.

Lara shrugged non-committally. They had to presume it was to prevent her from revealing what she knew about his involvement in the other woman's death.

'Never mind presumptions. How about some proof?' Curti stifled a bad-tempered yawn, glanced at his watch. Every fibre of his being communicated impatience.

Lara finally appeared to take the hint. 'I think you're going to like what we've uncovered, sir,' she retorted, clicking her fingers at Gianni to produce the list.

'What am I looking at?' Curti muttered as the document was handed to him.

'It's a list of Girl Cupid's registered users in Capri, Commissioner. It was emailed to us by the lawyers at the company just a few minutes ago.'

Curti's expression underwent a transformation. 'That's all they have?!'

Joe felt his heart sink.

'That's right, sir,' Lara confirmed. 'The app has more than twenty-three thousand users across Italy. But only two of them are registered as living on Capri.'

Curti grinned. 'Pietro Pelluso, whoever that is . . . and Luca Da Vinale.'

It was Lara who suggested they pay Pietro Pelluso a visit on the Saturday afternoon while they waited for the prosecutor to return her call. Like Curti, Joe had been inclined to think it a waste of time. The weight of evidence against Luca seemed to be reaching critical mass and he was already preoccupied with how best to break the news to the family that Gennaro's nephew was going to be charged with murder. But Lara insisted they should follow up with the second name on Girl Cupid's list. Every detail mattered, however small, she told him, quoting Joe back to himself. He had no comeback to that.

He found himself reflecting on the wisdom of those words within moments of Pietro's mother answering the door of her flat in Anacapri. No sooner had Lara flashed her warrant card and asked if Pietro was available than she burst into tears and seemed incapable of speech for several minutes afterwards. It was not until they were sitting in her kitchen and Signora Pelluso had drunk a glass of water that the reason for her distress became clear. Her beloved son, Pietro, had been dead for several years, she explained to Lara between plaintive sniffs, and every day since had been a torture.

Joe exchanged a look with Lara as she translated. According to the list, Pietro had signed up to Girl Cupid a month previously. Something here required investigating.

It took a great deal of patient explanation on Lara's part before the old woman could be made to understand the reason for their visit. The widow had little sense of what a dating app was and kept on insisting her Pietro was a good boy who'd been intending to marry his childhood sweetheart. Lara had to show her the list itself, with Pietro's name printed in black and white above that of Luca Da Vinale, before she seemed able to grasp the idea that someone must have used her dead son's credentials to sign up for an internet dating service and meet up with women. Glancing up at a picture of the Sacred Heart on her wall, she crossed herself and mouthed a silent prayer.

Did she have any idea who it might be? Lara asked as gently as possible.

The widow shook her head. The only thing she knew for certain was that her Pietro was dead. She kept his mass card by her bed, she explained, rising shakily to fetch it.

Lara tried to stop her, but the old woman was already shuffling out of the kitchen.

'What do you think?' she asked Joe, after translating what the widow had told her.

He shrugged. There could be an innocent explanation. It wasn't too hard to work out why men might want to hide their identity on a dating app. He was sure there were plenty of users who already had wives and girlfriends.

Lara rolled her eyes at him.

Joe felt himself colouring, and he rose and went to the sink, as much to escape her scrutiny as to refill his glass. He'd just turned on the tap when he saw it. A plastic tube of what looked like beauty cream standing on the windowsill. It was partially hidden behind a bottle of washing-up liquid, but the shade of pink was familiar, and he was already saying the name to himself as he picked it up to look at it.

Angelica. Crema Emolliente.

He turned the tube around to show Lara the logo of a stylised figure of an angel, hands clasped together in prayer. Like him, she recognised it instantly. It was the same as the one he'd found in the bins outside the back of the beauty salon, she confirmed.

Signora Pelluso shuffled back into the room with her son's mass card; Lara studied it briefly before handing it to Joe with a meaningful look.

The card confirmed the date of death that the widow had given Lara – 7 March 2020 – but it was the accompanying photo of her dead son that arrested Joe's attention. Pietro was pictured wearing the familiar blue scrubs of a health worker. 'I think you better ask her where she got this,' he murmured to Lara, holding up the tube of hand and body cream for the widow's inspection.

As Lara repeated the question in Italian, the widow began to cry once more.

Joe understood little of the broken stream of Italian that followed, but two words were enough for him to get the gist.

Azzurra Esposito.

38

If the face of Pietro Pelluso staring out from his mass card was familiar to Sandro Totti he was doing his best to hide it, Lara reflected as she sat across the table from him and his lawyer in the interview room of the island's police station just before 6pm on that Saturday evening, with Joe watching via video link from the room next door, and Gianni doing his best to translate for him.

Lara produced the bottle of Angelica hand and body cream and placed it on the table next to the mass card, explaining that it had been gifted to the dead man's mother by his fiancé, Azzurra Esposito, who, after Pietro's death, had continued to visit the grieving widow. Perhaps he'd heard what had happened to Azzurra, or Zuzu as she was better known to her friends?

The man across the table shrugged. 'It's a small island.'

She and a colleague had spoken to Signora Pelluso that afternoon, Lara continued, glancing at the camera for Joe's benefit, and had been informed by her that Zuzu was believed to have started a new relationship in the months before her death. A friend of the widow's had informed her that Zuzu's new man drove a taxi and was known as a rogue . . . he couldn't be said to hold a candle to her Pietro, who'd given his life to protect others. 'That's you she's referring to, isn't it, Sandro?' she added after a pause.

Sandro had been listening impassively, but now a smirk

animated his features. He cleaned swimming pools for a living, the taxi thing was a side hustle, a way to earn a little extra money. He wasn't even the only friend that Dante let moonlight in his cab. There must be hundreds of men on the island who better fitted the description given by the widow's friend – assuming, that is, she thought old women's gossip worth her attention.

It was Lara's turn to smirk. He was right, it was gossip. But what she was about to show him... that was hard evidence. She took her time, removing the CCTV still from the folder and taking a moment to refamiliarise herself with it, before placing it in front of him. The image had been discovered by her team back in Naples in a fresh batch of CCTV footage the Hotel Americano had sent over earlier in the day, she told Sandro's lawyer.

Sandro craned forward to look at it.

'That's you, isn't it?' Lara suggested, leaning forward in turn. 'Before you cut your hair.' She was showing the interviewee an image recorded by a security camera situated near the swimming pool of the Hotel Americano to cover its service entrance, she explained for the tape. The image had been recorded at 11.57pm on the Friday evening and showed him entering the grounds of the hotel in the company of a woman identified as Shannon Headley, who had fallen to her death from a cliff on the northeastern part of the island the following day. In his first interview, he'd admitted to having previously cleaned the pool at the hotel, Lara concluded, which was presumably how he knew about the service entrance. He'd clearly forgotten about or been unaware of the security camera, however, as on this occasion he'd neglected to wear his cap.

Sandro was silent. He seemed transfixed by the photo, was obviously calculating.

Lara decided to go all in. 'We've got a forensic team going

over Shannon's room in the hotel,' she told him. 'And we're retesting her body for evidence of sexual activity. We're going to find your DNA, aren't we, Sandro?'

A look passed between Sandro and his lawyer. 'She invited me up,' he admitted, after an exceptionally long pause.

'Then you're admitting you made contact with her through the Girl Cupid dating app? Using the identity of a dead man, Pietro Pelluso, to cover your own?'

'No.' She'd got it wrong, Sandro insisted, he'd never heard of Azzurra Esposito before her unfortunate demise, had never pretended to be her dead fiancé online. He'd met Shannon by chance in a bar on the Friday evening and things had progressed quickly. Yes, they'd slept together, and yes, he'd returned to her hotel on the Saturday morning to pick her up in his borrowed taxi and take her to Tiberius's Leap to enjoy the sunrise and a champagne breakfast. But after dropping her back sometime after 8.30am that was the last he saw of her. He'd nothing else to hide, he promised her.

Lara found herself recalling his arrogant manner from their first interview. He wasn't so arrogant now. 'So why did you lie to us?'

'Because I heard what had happened to her,' Sandro responded, his expression pleading with her for understanding. 'And it didn't look good for me.'

'Can you account for your movements later in the day, Sandro? Particularly in the afternoon. Around ten minutes to four.'

He smiled with relief. 'I was cleaning pools.'

'Well?'

The English detective was lurking as Lara put the phone

down. 'She confirms he was there,' she shrugged. 'Between three and five past four.'

'She saw him?'

Lara felt herself losing patience. Sandro had come to his client's front door at 3pm to get the key to the pool house, she explained carefully. And then again, just after four, to return it and to receive a cash payment.

'And this woman . . . she's sure about the timings?'

Signora Da Rosa was a hundred per cent sure, Lara assured him. She had an art class at 4pm on a Saturday and her instructor had arrived just as Sandro was saying goodbye.

Was there any way he could have driven from this woman's villa to Tiberius's Leap and back again in the course of the hour?

Lara shook her head. From one side of the island to the other? And most of it via lanes too narrow for anything other than an electric utility vehicle? It was impossible.

'Then he has an alibi for the time the selfie was taken.' Joe sounded deflated.

For the whole damned day, Lara found herself thinking as she glanced at the list of names and times that Sandro had supplied to her. 'It's even worse than that,' she said, rising and beckoning Joe to follow her over to where Gianni was working. 'Show him what you've found,' she instructed her deputy.

Gianni clicked on a file and Joe leaned in to watch the clip that popped up on his laptop. It was high-resolution footage from a video doorbell on the entrance gate of a villa in Tiberio and briefly showed Sandro Totti and Shannon Headley passing by before disappearing from view.

'When was this captured?' Joe demanded.

At 8.24am on the Saturday, Gianni confirmed in his schoolboy English. Sandro was driving one of the two-man electric vehicles that were everywhere in the main town and were the best way to navigate its narrow lanes, with Shannon sat beside him. They were travelling westward, suggesting they'd been to Tiberius's Leap and were returning to Sandro's taxi, which must have been parked some distance away.

'Which pretty much confirms what he told us,' Lara chimed in.

And yes, before he asked, Gianni continued defensively, they'd checked the footage from the doorbell for the rest of the day and there was no sign of them returning in the opposite direction during the afternoon. In fact, he'd reviewed footage from more than a dozen doorbells and security cameras in Tiberio and hadn't discovered any further footage of Shannon on the day in question.

'So we're no closer to knowing how she got back to Tiberius's Leap on the Saturday afternoon,' Lara felt obliged to point out. 'And who she may have gone with. We just know it can't have been Sandro Totti.'

'Fuck!' In his frustration, Joe kicked the desk with his foot; a wire in-tray fell to the floor, scattering its contents in all directions.

Lara exchanged a look with Gianni.

'Sorry,' Joe muttered, repeating the word more loudly for the benefit of the duty constable on the other side of the office. He dropped to his haunches and started to gather up the scattered papers. Grudgingly, Gianni dragged himself to his feet, half intending to help, but Lara signalled to him to leave her to handle it. She crouched next to Joe and started to help him sweep the contents of the fallen in-tray into a pile. She risked a glance at her English counterpart. He was staring at a document he'd just picked up, obviously transfixed.

'What is it?'

Joe turned the paper to show her.

It was a sheet of A4 on which Gianni had begun to stick the ripped-up pieces of the prenup agreement they'd retrieved from the bins at the hotel in Positano. 'It's the prenup,' Lara confirmed, explaining that the process of sticking it back together had proved unexpectedly painstaking and she'd ordered Gianni to stop once Manny was no longer their prime suspect. To underline her point, she searched amongst the scattered papers and found a plastic bag containing the remaining shreds of the agreement. There were hundreds of them.

'Look at the names,' Joe instructed her, ignoring her explanation.

Lara looked closely at the paper he was holding. About half of the first page had been pieced back together. 'This prenuptial agreement ("this Agreement")', the text read, 'made on this THIRTEENTH DAY OF JUNE between SHANNON HEADLEY and MANUELE SANGHERA...' She gave Joe a quizzical look. What was she missing?

'Doesn't "Manuele" sound local to you?'

'I suppose so. It's certainly the Italian spelling.'

'I'd assumed Manny was short for something Indian. But maybe he has dual heritage.' He turned the document to study it once more, clearly fascinated.

Lara bit her tongue, waiting for him to explain further. Nothing was forthcoming. 'I'm sorry to be stupid, Joe. But I don't get it. Why do you think this is important?'

'He said he'd never been to Italy.'

She took a moment to process this. 'When?'

'It's what he told Shannon, according to her dad. She was worried about the roads and didn't want to come. But he insisted. Said he'd never been.'

'You didn't tell me that.'

'Anton said it in passing. Over a drink. I guess it didn't seem significant.' A thought suddenly seemed to occur to Joe. 'We still have his passport, don't we?'

'We're about to hand it back.'

'Can I look?'

Lara gestured to Gianni, and he produced it from a drawer. She watched Joe open it and flick to the page containing Manny's personal details.

'"Manuele Aadesh Sanghera",' he read aloud. '"Born Ealing. October 8, 1991."'

As he turned the document to show her, Lara couldn't help shooting an accusatory glare at her deputy. Why hadn't he said anything? Gianni's response was a rueful shrug. You told me to confiscate his passport, his gesture seemed to say, not to look at it.

Joe had started to leaf through the pages. He'd almost worked his way to the end when he stopped to look more closely at something. 'He was lying,' he pronounced simply, grinning as he turned to show Lara what he'd found.

It was a passport stamp with a basic outline of a plane in the top right-hand corner, the date – 18.7.19 – picked out in red ink, and Napoli below it in black.

Lara voiced what she knew Joe was thinking. 'What else has he lied about?'

39

It was Lara who suggested she cook dinner.

As the three officers were leaving the police station a little before 8pm, Joe had asked if it was possible to get pizza delivered on the island, and his question had stopped Lara in her tracks. 'You're getting a takeaway?' she asked, faintly gobsmacked.

'Why not?'

'What about the restaurant?'

Joe had explained the situation with his in-laws.

'Then you better hide the box. Gennaro will be appalled.'

It was either order in or go hungry, Joe complained. Angelica was out at a party that evening and, despite his in-laws' efforts, he didn't think his culinary skills would stretch to cooking for himself.

'Then let me do it.'

He stopped himself from saying she didn't seem the type.

'Every Italian girl learns how to cook, Joe,' Lara told him, reading his thoughts. And anyway, he'd be doing her and Gianni a favour. By the time the two of them got back to Naples, it would be too late to eat. 'This way, we get a decent meal.'

Gianni immediately made his excuses. His wife was expecting him home.

While Lara headed for the mini-market down the road, intending to phone her aunt on the way and ask to let herself into the family's villa and sleep there, Joe returned home to shower and get things ready. He briefly entertained the thought that they should cook and eat in the apartment, but it felt too intimate, and he rejected it in favour of the restaurant. When Lara arrived laden with shopping bags, he showed her into Da Vinale's kitchen, left her there while he went to find wine.

It took longer than expected to find the key to the wine fridge and then select and open a bottle, and it was a good quarter of an hour before he pushed open the doors again to be assailed by the aroma of frying meat. 'It smells amazing,' he told her.

'It should taste amazing too.'

'What are you making?'

'*Ragu alla Campidanese.*'

'That's a bit of a mouthful.'

Lara laughed. It sounded grander than it was, she insisted. A ragu was simply the Italian name for any sauce with meat in it. And *alla Campidanese* was an indication of which part of Italy the sauce was associated with. In this case, it referred to the part of Sardinia from where her mother originated. As did the fatty fennel sausages she was using, she added, giving the cut-up pork in the pan a stir with a wooden spatula.

'Did she cook it for you?'

Lara's response was a simple nod of the head. 'And I cooked it for her . . . it was the last thing she ever asked me to make for her.'

Joe didn't know what to say. He busied himself with pouring glasses of wine, handed her one. They watched the sausage sizzle and caramelise before Lara broke the silence. 'Do you want me to talk you through it?'

'That would be great.'

Lara showed him one of the unused sausages, its interior studded with globules of pearly white lard and the green and black grit of fennel seeds and peppercorns. The pork would cook happily in its own fat, she explained, as would the other ingredients, which she listed as she gave them a stir – chopped onion, slivers of garlic, more fennel seeds and black pepper, a bay leaf, chilli flakes. She put Joe to work, instructing him to empty a can of plum tomatoes into a sieve and mash them through it into a bowl, while she set about chopping a bulb of fennel. In the time it took him to sieve the tomatoes, she'd reduced the bulb to a perfectly diced mound and added it to the mix. She let the fennel soften and go translucent before she told Joe to throw in the tomatoes, along with a generous glug of her mother's 'secret ingredient' . . . pale gold Fino sherry. The heat was turned up and soon the thick sauce was blipping away. She turned it down to simmer and handed him the spatula, instructing him to keep stirring, as she turned her attention to a large mixing bowl that stood nearby on one of the surfaces.

'What's in the bowl?' Joe wanted to know.

She tilted it to show him a ball of dough. She was making *gnocchetti*, she told him, which was half pasta, half gnocchi. She sprinkled a little flour from the packet, dumped the ball of dough onto it, and began to knead it with a practised motion.

Joe found himself picturing Sofia in the tiny kitchen of their flat, pounding away with much the same motion. He felt a familiar tremor.

Lara glanced back at him over her shoulder. 'You want to try?'

'I'll give it a go.'

She stepped aside to let him take over. He scooped up the dough and slapped it down again, scraping the residue from his fingers.

'Here – use the heel of your palm.'

As she reached forward to guide him, Joe recoiled. 'Sorry,' he blurted out. The look on Lara's face demanded an explanation. 'Sofia and me . . . we made gnocchi together.'

'Oh, Joe. You should have said.'

'Sorry,' he repeated.

'Do you want to stop?'

'No, no. It's OK.' He did his best to smile as he pinched a piece of dough and rolled it in the flour with the edge of his thumb. 'You with your mum . . . me with my wife. We're a right pair.' He showed Lara the result.

She considered it with a faint smile. 'She taught you well,' was all she said.

They ate at one of the inside tables. Neither of them spoke much as they concentrated on the food. It was as good as Lara had promised – meaty with an underlying hint of nuttiness, sweet and savoury at the same time, with a crumble of salty, tangy pecorino a perfect complement on top. Joe scraped every last morsel from his bowl.

After they'd finished washing up, Lara suggested they finish their wine on the terrace. Joe couldn't remember how to turn on the exterior lights and she told him to light a candle instead. 'Don't worry, I'm not trying to make it feel romantic,' she added, laughing at the awkward look he gave her as they settled at one of the tables. 'It reminds me of the last time I was here, that's all.'

'With Curti, you mean?'

'Not for work. For pleasure. With a friend.' She corrected herself. 'My ex.'

Joe waited for her to say more.

'Nicky adored this place.'

'The woman who did the portrait of you in your flat?'

She shot him a look. 'How did you know?'

'It was signed. Nicoletta Nocerino. I looked her up.'

Lara rolled her eyes. 'You really *are* a good detective.'

'My behaviour last night might suggest otherwise.'

She rewarded him with a faint smile.

It was a while before either spoke again. The soft murmur of the tide filled the silence. Joe rolled the wine around his glass, watching the flame through it, considering his next question. 'Are you *out* at work?' he asked eventually.

'If I was . . . maybe Nicky and I . . . we'd still be together.'

Joe made a noise intended to sound like an expression of sympathy.

'She hated that I wouldn't be open about things . . . you know, the two of us,' Lara explained. They'd rowed about it constantly, she went on, had eventually let the pressure of it break them apart. 'But it's hard enough getting people to take you seriously as a woman in the State Police in Italy,' she continued, 'let alone as an openly *gay* one.' Besides, why should that define her. It was people she was attracted to, not a specific gender. 'It just happens that in the last few years all those people have been women.'

'Do you think your colleagues suspect?'

Lara shrugged. 'I don't care. It's none of their business.' She'd dated and slept with men, she explained, including a guy who now worked in the IT department at La Questura. 'Maybe they think it's them I'm not interested in. Rather than men in general.'

'Sorry if you think I'm prying.'

She waved away his apology.

'And again . . . for last night. For being so slow on the uptake.'

'You're more perceptive than most men I know,' she reassured him.

Joe was about to say something gracious in return when his phone pinged in his pocket. As he took it out, he saw Lara checking her pockets for hers. It was a text from Angelica... a photo of her lying on her bed in the apartment. *Night Dad X*, the message read. She must have a key for the gate in the courtyard, he thought, instinctively checking the time beneath the text. 10.51pm. She'd met his curfew with nine minutes to go.

'I think I left mine in the kitchen,' Lara announced. She was rising to go and look for it when they were interrupted by a banging on the street gate.

'INSPECTOR MOTTRAM?' a male voice called out. 'BOSS?'

Joe exchanged a look with Lara as he got to his feet. 'Is that Gianni?'

This time there was no mistaking it as the voice came again. 'ARE YOU THERE?'

The hammering recommenced, and Lara disappeared up the steps. A short time later she reappeared with Gianni behind her. He was holding a digital tablet.

'I'm sorry to interrupt,' Lara's deputy said, giving Joe an apologetic look. 'I've been trying to phone you for the last hour,' he added, turning to face his superior.

She'd switched her phone to silent for the interview with the pool guy and then put it to one side while she was cooking, Lara explained. But what was so important that it couldn't wait?

'This is.' Gianni handed the tablet to Lara. The local narcotics squad were conducting a surveillance operation against Naples drug gangs and their networks of street-dealers and couriers, he explained for Joe's benefit, while Lara swiped through a succession of photos. When he'd run Sandro Totti's name and photo through the police database, as Lara had requested, his details weren't on the system and there was no record of any criminality on his part. But on his way back to Naples, he'd received an email informing him that Totti had been identified in their colleagues' surveillance photos using the latest facial recognition software.

Lara turned the tablet to show Joe. Sandro Totti had been snapped in a deserted back street conducting an exchange with a man with his back to the camera. Joe took the tablet from Lara and zoomed in so he could look more closely at what was being handed between them. It was clear that their suspect was taking possession of a small bag of blue pills. 'Do we know what he's buying?' he asked.

It was impossible to be sure from a photo, Gianni replied. But the street fentanyl sold in the city had the same colour. 'It's why they call it "blues",' he explained.

Joe exchanged a look with Lara. 'Can we identify the dealer and confirm it?'

Unfortunately they hadn't been able to trace their man, Gianni explained, but it was why he was here. 'We think you might be able to help.'

'Me?' Joe exclaimed.

Lara looked equally perplexed. 'Is this your idea of a joke?'

'No, boss. Of course not.' With an apologetic glance at Joe, Gianni took the tablet back. The dealer in question appeared in a small number of other photos taken in the last few months, he explained while he opened a second folder, including a couple shot by an undercover team near the ferry port in Naples that morning. Finding what he was looking for, he turned to show the screen to Joe once more.

It was a photo of Angelica and the boy from the beach outside a sandwich bar.

'That's my daughter,' Joe blurted out. 'And a boy she likes.'

'We know.' They'd run the photo through facial recognition

as well, he explained. 'Angelica's on the system. From when you last applied to renew her Italian passport.'

'They're drinking a Coke,' Joe pointed out. 'That doesn't prove anything.'

'No, but this might,' Gianni replied, swiping to bring up another photo. It showed a man Joe recognised as Rocco Di Biasi's scar-faced gunman from the restaurant, furtively handing what looked like a piece of paper to another man in exchange for a roll of banknotes. The second man was looking off to the left, his face partially turned, but there was no mistaking those handsome features or his distinctive black and white jacket.

It was Daniele.

As Joe opened the door to Angelica's bedroom, he sensed something was wrong. Her bed had been arranged to make it look like someone was sleeping in it, but there was something about the quality of the air, the smell and feel of the room, which denied the presence of a living, breathing being. He turned on the light and crossed to the bed to pull back the covers, but he already knew she wasn't there. The anger that had been welling inside him tilted heavily towards concern. Where was she?

'What about the photo she sent?' Lara had followed him up to the apartment and was standing in the open doorway, looking as bemused as he felt.

'Maybe she went out again. When she thought I wasn't here.'

'Is she with him?'

Joe nodded. 'They've gone to a party.'

'Do you know where?'

For a moment Joe's mind was a blank and he felt a rising sense of panic, but then he remembered the Find My Phone app and took out his phone. He quickly located the logo representing

Angelica's phone at the south-westerly tip of the island. 'It's a beach,' he said, remembering now. 'By some kind of lighthouse, I think she said.'

He turned it to show Lara, who was already dialling a number on the phone she'd retrieved from the kitchen. 'I'll get Gianni to call a car. They can be here in five minutes.'

40

Angelica had been having fun but now, suddenly, she wasn't.

She'd certainly drunk more than she intended, with bottle after bottle appearing in her hands without her really noticing how they'd got there. And she'd puffed freely on the joints that had been passed her way. But it wasn't enough to explain the intoxicating wooziness that had her in its grip, the surge of nausea she was fighting, the numbness that was reducing her legs to jelly. Only moments before, she'd been dancing, spinning and twirling in the light from the fire, free and happy. Now she felt the blood draining rapidly from her face and the bile rising in her throat, acid and toxic. The flames felt intolerable, and she stumbled away, but missed her step and tottered forward, throwing out an arm to grab hold of whatever was nearest to her. It happened to be Daniele.

'Feel sick,' she managed to mumble, doubling over to stop herself from fainting.

'Is she all right?' someone asked.

'*Ubriaco*,' someone else answered. Drunk.

Angelica dropped to her knees and retched. 'Come on. I'll take you home,' she heard Daniele say, and the next thing she knew he was lifting her to her feet. She let her head loll back against his shoulder, closed her eyes. The numbness had spread. The only part of her body she was aware of feeling was the back of her skull where it was in contact with the nub of his collarbone. It was this contact, this hint of concrete reality, which was stopping her from dissolving into nothingness.

As they staggered away into the darkness, the heat of the flames receded and the jumble of music and voices began to quieten. She felt her body being swept along, but it was almost as if she wasn't there, as if she was powerless to dictate where she was going or what might happen to her, as if all ability to decide or resist had deserted her.

'Dad,' she croaked. Her only coherent thought was that she needed him.

'He's not here, Angelica. But I am.'

The world spun and swooped on its axis, and she sensed somehow that she was on the ground, lying on her back. She tried to open her eyes, but her lids were leaden and unresponsive and the glimpse she caught of the stars in the night sky, pulsing and winking at her with terrifying intensity, made her feel even more abandoned and disoriented. Summoning the last few grains of her lucidity, she tried to push Daniele away and sit up.

'Lie still. I'm here.'

He forced her back down and rolled on top of her.

She felt her stomach lurch. The last thing she was aware of, and only vaguely, was the gritty feel of cold earth against the small of her back as her jeans slipped downwards over her hips. But whether she was taking them off or he was, Angelica couldn't tell.

41

As the police car they were riding in pulled into the car park behind the beach, Joe opened the door and jumped out. Lara immediately followed suit. 'Joe! Wait!' she called out, but already he was running towards the bonfire she could see burning on the beach ahead of them. Without waiting to give Gianni orders, she set off in pursuit.

It was very dark and the ground beneath her feet was rocky and uneven, with a covering of low scrub threatening to trip her at every step. She slowed her pace and picked her way more carefully.

As she made the relative safety of the pebbled beach and entered the corona of light thrown off by the fire, Joe was already bouncing from one knot of partygoers to another, some sitting near the flames, others further apart. *'Una ragazza inglese?'* she heard him ask. *'L'hai vista?'* People shook their heads. No one had seen an English girl at the party.

Lara produced her warrant card and showed it around. She was not there to spoil anybody's fun, she reassured the startled teenagers, they were just trying to locate a visitor to Capri who they thought might be in trouble. She was met with blank faces. From the corner of her eye, she saw Joe accost a young partygoer with her back to him, her hair the exact same shade and length as his daughter's. As she turned to face him with a startled look, Lara saw instantly that it was not Angelica.

And then suddenly two teenage girls were being ushered forward . . . they'd spent time dancing with someone who said she was from London, they admitted. They were acquainted with the boy the English girl had come with. Daniele, his name was.

'Are they still here?' Lara asked, flashing her card again.

The tallest of the two shook her head. She didn't think so. The girl had seemed pretty out of it. Almost like she'd taken something.

Taken what? Lara demanded to know.

The girl looked nervous. She wasn't into anything like that. But she thought the boy . . . Daniele . . . he was planning to take her home.

'Did they see her leave?' Joe appeared at her side, sweating and frantic.

Yes, the other girl admitted as Lara repeated the question in Italian, although not in the direction of the car park. They were heading towards the lighthouse.

Without waiting for Lara to translate, Joe ran off in the direction she was pointing.

Lara thanked the girls before she started to run after him. The pebbles quickly gave way to scrub again, but now it was taller and more hazardous. Jagged shapes loomed out of the darkness. Were they rocks or broom bushes? It was hard to tell. The light from the fire was faint here and soon it disappeared. She took off the flashlight she kept hooked to her belt and turned it on, directing the beam to make sure her feet were landing safely. Otherwise she navigated by sound, with Joe audible some way in front.

Soon the lighthouse loomed ahead of her. Its bulk, and the rocky outcrop it was standing on, cast such a deep shadow that the darkness seemed impenetrable more than a few feet in front.

She edged her way forward, on the verge of calling out to Joe and telling him this was crazy. At that moment, however, the clouds shifted and a beam of moonlight illuminated the scene. She caught sight of something pale to her left and veered towards it. Squeezing through the scratchy embrace of the bushes, she found herself in a small clearing. The pale object materialised into the naked torso of a man. He was kneeling, back turned to Lara, and leaning over a second pale object on the ground. Lara lifted her flashlight and, as she did so, the kneeling figure swung round to face her.

'Get out of here,' he shouted, holding one hand up to shield his eyes and gesturing angrily with the other. It was the boy from the photo. Daniele. And the belt and the buttons of his jeans were undone. Behind him, on the ground, she could see a naked pair of female legs. Unlike Daniele, however, they didn't appear to be moving.

'Police!' she shouted, feeling for the catch on her holster. 'Step away!'

For a split second, Daniele remained frozen in the beam of her torch before he scrabbled to his feet, shaping to escape into the dark labyrinth of scrub surrounding them. At that moment, however, Joe crashed into the clearing and tackled him to the ground. Locked together, they rolled over in the dirt, scuffling and grappling for advantage, before Joe pinned his daughter's assailant down, punching him with furious abandon.

Using all her strength, Lara managed to push Joe off and insert herself in between him and the boy. As she pinned Daniele to the ground in turn and started to handcuff him, she heard a low moan and was thankful to see her English colleague scramble across the clearing to attend to his stricken daughter.

*

By the time they returned, the car park was bathed in blue light. The squad car they'd arrived in had been joined by two more, and Sergeant Alfieri was overseeing the dousing of the bonfire and the dispersal of the partygoers. Gianni was waiting, as Lara had instructed him, to take Daniele back to the island's police station. As she handed over her prisoner into his custody, under Joe's vigilant gaze, her deputy seemed more concerned by what was going on behind.

Lara turned to see what he was looking at. Angelica was sitting with her head between her knees, retching and spewing. A policewoman was rubbing her back.

'Is she all right?' Gianni wanted to know.

'Her drink's been spiked,' Joe managed to say through gritted teeth.

Daniele attempted to correct him. 'She drank too much.'

Lara stepped in before her enraged counterpart could lash out. 'Get him out of here,' she ordered Gianni, who bundled the bloodied and frightened youth into a car.

42

Joe was woken by voices. Groggy and disoriented, he struggled to work out where he was before his gaze fell on Angelica, sleeping in the bed, and everything came flooding back. He sat up. It was Elena and Lara he could hear talking. His in-laws had returned.

It had been Lara who'd suggested she stay the night. By the time they'd got Angelica settled, he was too tired to argue. They'd agreed she would sleep in Joe's bedroom while he sat sentry in a chair in Angelica's and would wake her if needed. Unsure what exactly his daughter had experienced and how she might react, he'd been reassured to know Lara was next door. Now, however, in the cold light of a Sunday morning and with his in-laws having arrived home, her presence in their apartment, wearing a T-shirt he'd lent her to sleep in, felt more awkward. Rising stiffly from the chair in which he'd been sleeping, Joe padded across to the door and opened it softly, stepped outside.

He need not have worried. Lara's presence went entirely unremarked as Elena rushed over to embrace him, her face ashen with worry. That poor child! Was she sleeping? Could her grandmother go in and see her? Relieved to realise that Lara must have explained everything, Joe advised Elena to let Angelica rest.

Gennaro folded his son-in-law in an unaccustomed hug. He looked drawn and pale, and it occurred to Joe where they'd come from. How was everything at the hospital?

Never mind that, the old chef growled. How was Joe feeling?

'Angry.' He could have added 'relieved' and 'guilty'. 'I wish I'd followed my instincts.'

'About Daniele?' How could he have known, Elena said.

'I should have been paying more attention.'

'The boy... he was her choice to make,' she insisted.

'She's a child, Elena.'

'Only to you, Joe,' Gennaro chimed in. 'The rest of us... we see a young woman.'

'Who's lost her mother,' Elena continued, 'and needs a little joy in her life.' She took his hand and squeezed it, held on to it tightly.

Sensing that more needed to be said, Lara made her excuses and left almost as quickly as she could get dressed. She would update him as soon as they'd had a chance to interview the boy, she told Joe. And to make arrangements to follow up with Angelica.

Coffee was made and the family talked more, in low voices. Elena and Gennaro wanted Joe to tell them what had happened, and he walked them through the events of the evening step by step. The old couple listened in silence until he came to Angelica texting him the photo. Why had she messaged him rather than coming to tell him in person that she was home? Gennaro wanted to know.

It was just how young people communicated, Joe explained. At home in London, she would sometimes conduct a conversation via SMS while he was in the kitchen and she was in the living room a few feet away.

'Or maybe she wasn't here,' Elena suggested. It seemed faintly implausible, she pointed out, that Angelica had returned from the party and then taken a photo and sent it to Joe to prove she'd come home. Wasn't it more likely she'd stayed at the party but just sent him the photo at the agreed time to fool him into thinking she'd done his bidding?

'You mean she took the photo earlier?'

Why not? It was easy enough to fake.

Joe considered this. He took out his phone and found the photo, clicked on it with his finger. The location of the restaurant and apartment appeared above it in the left-hand corner of the screen and, beneath it, in much smaller type, the date and time it was taken.

26 July. 22:51.

He turned the screen to show them. 'That's the same time I received it.'

Elena tried to suppress a smile. 'Oh Joe,' she said, reaching out to take the phone. 'I didn't think you'd be so naive when it came to teenagers.' She swiped to bring the metadata up on screen and pointed to the word 'Adjust' written in blue beside the date and time. She tapped on it and a second screen popped up with two text boxes. The first read 'Original: 26 July at 18:41:23'. The box beneath it read 'Adjusted: 26 July at 22:51:18'. 'She changed the time code,' Elena explained matter-of-factly, handing back the phone to show him.

'I didn't know you could do that.'

'Neither did I. Until a certain someone showed me how.'

'And who was that?'

Elena gave him a look. Who did he think?

'Luca?'

She raised her hands to signal she didn't wish to be questioned on why her nephew might have required this knowledge. 'I told him I didn't want to know.'

Joe stared at the phone, astonished. And suddenly, everything fell into place.

'Do you still have that selfie?'

Lara and Gianni both glanced up as Joe barged his way into the office. They'd been looking together at something on a laptop and seemed surprised to see him. It was Lara who voiced what he knew they must be thinking. 'You shouldn't be here, Joe. It's a Sunday. Go home. Look after your daughter.'

He waved her objection aside. The selfie? Did she still have it?

The Italian detective sighed. 'Of course.' She signalled to her deputy to retrieve it, and Gianni opened a folder that sat beside him on his desk and handed the photo to Joe.

'Not a print-out. The photo itself. On her phone.'

Gianni looked to Lara, who gave him the nod.

The evidence bag was no sooner out of the drawer than Joe had snatched and opened it. He took the phone out using a tissue he had brought with him, and opened the photo folder, found the image he was looking for. Imitating what Elena had shown him, he called up the data screen. And there it was. In black and white.

Original: 5 July at 07:36:13. Adjusted: 5 July at 15:52:08.

The truth left him gasping. 'He edited the fucking time.'

'Who did?' Lara demanded to know.

'Sandro Totti.' Joe turned the screen to show his Italian counterparts. Their instincts had been right, he told them. Someone other than Shannon had taken the 'selfie' at Tiberius's Leap. Yet not in the afternoon, as they'd blithely assumed from the time code. Sandro had admitted going to Tiberius's Leap with Shannon for a breakfast at sunrise. He must have staged the photo during this morning trip to the landmark, but adjusted the time code to make it look like it had been taken in the afternoon.

Lara finished the thought. 'When he was cleaning Signora Da Rosa's swimming pool. And had a cast-iron alibi.' No wonder no GPS signal had been picked up from Shannon's phone when the selfie was supposedly taken at 3.52pm at Tiberius's Leap. The phone had been in Sandro's possession and turned off, nowhere near the site in question.

Something had been bothering him since his mother-in-law alerted him to the possibility of editing time codes on digital photos, Joe confessed. Shannon Headley appeared to be a complete stranger to Sandro Totti, which implied, if he was responsible for her murder, that it must be a random act. And yet all the evidence suggested a degree of meticulous and imaginative planning – the trick with the time codes, the use of fentanyl to administer an overdose through her skin, the hook-up through Girl Cupid using a dead man's ID to ensure anonymity. What was it they were missing?

Lara exchanged a look with her deputy. 'This, maybe?'

Gianni beckoned Joe over to show him what they'd been looking at. 'Your contact at the Home Office . . . the one you connected me with last night,' he explained, unable to stop himself from grinning. 'She emailed a few minutes ago.'

A reproduction of Manny Sanghera's birth certificate was visible on the laptop.

Father – Chetan Sanghera.

Mother – Maria Isabella Sanghera née Totti.

Lara was grinning too. 'We think Sandro and Manny must be cousins.'

*

Manny's room was unoccupied and there was no sign of him in any of the public spaces at his hotel, but as Joe and Lara descended the steps to return to the waiting squad car, Joe spotted him some distance away, walking in their direction, with a blue plastic grocery bag in one hand. He tugged Lara's sleeve to alert her.

'Two o'clock. Coming this way.'

Joe saw Manny slow his pace and felt sure he must have spotted them. Joe tried to act casually, casting a glance down the street in the other direction, but when he turned back to watch his approach, Manny was no longer there.

Lara had clocked it too. '*Merda.*'

They set off at a fast walk and quickly reached the spot where Manny had disappeared from view, catching sight of him some distance away down a side street. He was walking rapidly and glancing back over his shoulder as he did so. When he saw the two detectives, he dropped his bag and all pretence, and started to run.

They set off with greater urgency, Lara working hard to match Joe's loping stride, but soon they found themselves in a maze of narrow lanes and had to slow their pace. They lost sight of Manny and wasted time looking for him down a cul-de-sac before resuming the chase. Turning the next corner, they were in time to see him ducking around another some distance ahead. They increased their speed but by the time they'd reached the point where the path diverted, he'd disappeared from view again. They ran on, trusting to luck and the occasional sign that they were heading in the right direction. An old woman in a headscarf was leaning on a broom in a doorway and pointed the way. Around the next corner, they came across a young couple who'd encountered Manny coming at speed and were scrabbling to gather up scattered possessions.

They reached the edge of the built-up area. Ahead of them, on both sides of the path, was a small wood. To their left, the trees gave way to a stretch of waste ground overgrown with thick scrub, while to their right, the ground sloped upwards to a thin belt of cypress. Beyond that, the island petered out into nothingness and the sea one thousand feet below. Lara signalled to Joe to go left while she made her way to the right.

Joe followed her signal and picked his way through the trees, making no attempt to soften his footsteps or disguise his progress. On the far side of the wood, a flock of grazing pigeons scattered upwards into the sky at his approach, the rapid flap of their wings like gunshots, and a moment later Manny broke cover. Joe allowed himself to watch his hectic scurry, ever upwards, before he set off in pursuit once more.

They caught up with him in the ruins of the Villa Jovis, with Lara hanging back to block off his escape and Joe going ahead to flush him out. The sightings of him became more frequent, much closer to hand. Soon enough, Joe emerged to find Manny standing a few yards in front of him. He heard a scatter of loose stones to his right and saw Lara slide into view, catching her breath. There was nowhere left for their quarry to run.

'STAY BACK OR I'LL JUMP!' Manny shouted.

'Go ahead.' Joe gestured towards the edge. 'There'll be less paperwork.' He could almost hear the cogs of the other man's brain whirring as he risked a nervous glance over his shoulder. 'That thing they say. About passing out on the way down?' He shook his head and winced theatrically, laying it on thick for Manny, who was staring, open-mouthed.

'It's going to hurt,' said Lara, catching on and chiming in.

Manny took a slight step away from the edge and seemed to deflate a little, the last vestiges of resistance leaking out of him. It was a surprisingly simple matter for Joe to step forward and drag him back from the brink.

43

It was a relief to be the bearer of better news at Da Vinale's, Lara reflected as she accepted the cup of coffee Elena held out to her. The last but one time she'd been here, she'd been desperate to avoid a public dressing down, but that Tuesday the old chef was beaming as he made his way to greet her. He kissed her on both cheeks, insisted she take one of the *sfogliatelle* pastries he'd prepared especially. When all of this nonsense was over, Gennaro pronounced, taking his place at the table, she *must* come and dine with them, bring her husband with her if she liked, everything would be on the house.

She'd be happy just to get a table, Lara told him, advising him she couldn't accept gifts and would have to pay. She glanced at Joe to see if he'd clocked the 'h' word.

'Shall we get on with it?' was all he said.

Lara took a deep breath. Suddenly she felt nervous. When Joe had first suggested holding their latest debrief at Da Vinale's and asked if he could invite Elena and Gennaro to listen in, she'd been uncertain as to his motives. But now she thought she understood. He wanted to show himself to them in a different light, to give them an insight into the work that consumed him, that had so often taken him away from his home and his family. It was a chance to justify himself. And she wanted to do him justice.

In the day and a half since Manny Sanghera's arrest they'd

started to gain a clearer understanding of the circumstances surrounding the death of the two women, Lara declared, producing a photo from a folder and laying it on the table. They were looking at an empty tub of body clay discovered during a fingertip search of the municipal landfill site, she explained. A forensic examination had revealed it contained dangerously high traces of a potent synthetic opioid called fentanyl. Perhaps they'd heard of it?

The old couple nodded, solemn and wide-eyed.

The tub was thought to have come from the bins of the beauty salon where Zuzu Esposito worked, Lara continued. The body clay was the same brand as that used in the salon and there was evidence to suggest Zuzu had applied it to Shannon Headley's skin during the course of a body-wrap treatment on the day of her death. Shannon's corpse showed unmistakable signs of an allergic reaction to the fentanyl the clay had been infused with. Shannon was a habitual user of the drug but had no history of taking it 'transdermally' – through the skin, in other words.

Had Zuzu known what the clay contained? Elena asked.

Lara congratulated her on her question. They weren't sure, she confessed. But what didn't seem in doubt was Sandro Totti's involvement. He'd been caught on camera by a police surveillance team buying what was believed to be fentanyl from a street-dealer, Daniele Russo, who was known to Angelica. A fingerprint matching Sandro's had been recovered from the empty tub, which strongly suggested he was responsible for infusing the body clay with the drug, after dissolving it in purified water. A colleague of Zuzu's had testified to seeing a man matching Sandro's description waiting outside the beauty salon on two separate occasions to pick Zuzu up after work, implying he was the new boyfriend the widow Pelluso had been told about. And the GPS data from Sandro's phone showed him arriving at the salon at 1.38pm on the Saturday of Shannon's death, at the same time she was inside getting a body wrap from Zuzu. They were working on the theory that, having caused the body clay to be infused with a lethal quantity of fentanyl, he'd persuaded Shannon to attend the salon for the treatments with Zuzu, knowing that when the clay was applied to her skin it would cause her to overdose.

'Why choose that way to kill her?' Gennaro wanted to know.

'He knew Shannon was already a regular user of fentanyl,' Lara explained. 'And that we'd assume she'd administered the overdose herself.'

'But how did he know that she was?' Elena wanted to know. 'And how could he be sure she'd even go to the salon? Or which treatments she'd agree to?'

Joe intervened. 'We believe he planned the whole thing with Shannon's fiancé . . . Manny Sanghera. Who also happens to be Sandro's cousin.'

Lara picked up the thread. Shannon and Manny's holiday had been booked weeks in advance, giving the two men time to make arrangements. Manny must have confided in Sandro about the 'open' nature of his and Shannon's relationship, which in turn had given the cousins the idea of Manny engineering a row with Shannon in Positano over the prenuptial he already knew she wanted him to sign and then Sandro using the Girl Cupid app to hook up with her when she travelled on to Capri alone. State Police officers had recovered Sandro's laptop from his flat, as well as what looked like a burner phone, and found proof on the computer that he'd used the personal details of Zuzu's dead fiancé, Pietro Pelluso, to sign up to Girl Cupid a month before her arrival. The lawyers back in London had finally agreed to release Shannon's messages on the app, which showed her making contact with 'Pietro Pelluso' after her arrival on Capri and arranging to meet him at a bar on the Friday evening. Sandro must have been told about Shannon's accident by Manny and taken advantage of her need for regular massages to relieve her pain to lure her to the salon, having slept with her the night before.

'Imagine the scene,' she urged them. 'Shannon Headley is lying comatose in the treatment room at the salon, or maybe even dead already. Perhaps Zuzu is panicking. Or perhaps she's in on it and knows what to expect. Either way, she calls her boyfriend, Sandro, summons him to sort out the mess.'

Her audience was silent, hanging on her every word. Even Joe.

'Sandro arrives and tells Zuzu to leave, while he takes care of what needs to be done,' Lara continued. 'He washes Shannon's body and dresses her and then, using the large canvas holdall for a swimming-pool cover, he transfers her and her possessions into the boot of the taxi he's driving that day. He coolly goes about his business, storing her body in one of the pool houses of the clients he visits in the afternoon. In the small hours of the next day, under cover of darkness, he retrieves her body from the pool house and drives it up to Tiberius's Leap on an electric utility vehicle. He drops Shannon and her bag over the edge, having edited the time on the 'selfie' he'd taken on her phone at the same spot early in the morning of the previous day.

Gennaro shook his head, clearly horrified. 'Can you prove any of this?'

'Most of it.' But not all, Lara admitted. They'd uncovered security camera footage that showed Sandro transferring a heavy object in a canvas holdall into the pool house of an absent client on the Saturday before proceeding to clean his pool. There was also footage of someone returning to retrieve the holdall after dark.

Joe joined in. It was an audacious plan and almost a perfect one, he told them, with the police initially concluding that Shannon's fall had been a tragic accident and then, once the fentanyl in her system had been discovered, coming to the alternative conclusion that she'd committed suicide, just as Sandro and Manny must have hoped they would. Their mistake had been to kill Zuzu as well. He and Lara had both had their doubts about Shannon's death, but they might have remained unproven, had not this second killing convinced Curti to launch a full-blown murder inquiry.

'And you're sure Zuzu was murdered?' Elena asked.

As sure as they could be without a confession, Lara replied. Sandro had a motive . . . his desire to silence Zuzu, to guarantee she could never testify to his part in Shannon's murder. And they were hoping to prove to a judge that he'd had the opportunity and the means as well. They'd found photographs – showing Sandro with a man-bun before his haircut, and a dragon tattoo on his chest – that matched the description of the stranger Joe had seen by the perimeter fence at the Villa San Benedetto on the evening Zuzu was attacked. And Luca had testified that Sandro had once been part of the same smuggling crew as him and Dante Patalano, before falling out with one of their co-conspirators. Luca confirmed they'd used the hidden staircase to move contraband on and off the island, giving Sandro an intimate knowledge of the layout of the villa and its grounds.

Lara saw Joe exchange a look with the old couple at her mention of their nephew. Luca was cooperating, Joe told them. He was adamant Sandro's holdall had been used during the smuggling operation Luca now admitted to being part of the night before Shannon's death. After cutting himself while opening a consignment of counterfeit goods, some of Luca's blood must have found its way onto the holdall, which he claimed to have replaced in the boot of Dante Patalano's taxi on his return to Capri the following morning; Dante had told Luca the holdall would be picked up by its owner, Sandro Totti, who was borrowing Dante's taxi because his van was in the workshop. The police were working on the theory that Luca's blood must have transferred onto Shannon's dress when Sandro was using the holdall to transport her body later that day.

'And you believe him?' Elena asked, turning to Lara.

She hesitated for only the briefest moment before she nodded. They'd tested a sample of blood found on the holdall and it matched Luca's, supporting his explanation of how his blood must have got on Shannon's dress. Other than the blood, there was no physical evidence linking Luca to either Shannon or Zuzu Esposito. But Sandro Totti's DNA had been found on Shannon's body and in her hotel room. And they'd been able to lift another partial fingerprint of his from the screen of Shannon's phone.

And while Luca was a registered user of Girl Cupid from his time living in the UK, Joe added, there was no evidence he'd used the app to message Shannon Headley. His presence in the taxi that had ferried her from Da Vinale's on the Friday evening and at the Villa San Benedetto the following Wednesday were just unfortunate coincidences.

Elena's hands went to her mouth. Her relief was clear in the look she gave her husband, who could only shake his head in faint disbelief. What on earth could possess a man to kill two women in cold blood like that? he wanted to know.

The answer appeared to be simple, Lara told him. 'Money.'

The rumours about Zuzu's new boyfriend had been right. Sandro's internet search history and his bank statements painted a picture of a gambling addict. The reason his van was in the workshop was because it was old and unreliable; he'd sold a newer van for cash six months before to pay off €11,000 of debt, but his account was already a similar amount in the red again and his credit card was maxed out from payments to an online casino.

'But how did he stand to profit from the murders?' Elena enquired.

Through his cousin, Joe explained to his in-laws. Joe's colleagues at the Met had searched Manny Sanghera's flat in London the previous day and found a copy of the medical insurance questionnaire Shannon had completed in connection with the sale of Girl Cupid, naming Manny as her next of kin. He must have understood its significance, Joe speculated, just as he must have understood the significance of the prenuptial agreement she'd asked him to sign, which would have left him with nothing in the event of a separation. After first being confronted with the prenup, Manny must have realised he had a short window before their wedding in which he could reasonably make a legal claim to inherit the proceeds of the sale of Shannon's shares in Girl Cupid in the event of her death, as her fiancé and acknowledged next of kin. Once the prenup had been signed he would obviously have stood to get nothing in the likely event of the marriage ending in divorce, given the open nature of their relationship.

'Why not wait until *after* they were married to kill her?' Gennaro suggested.

Because Manny would run the risk of inheriting nothing in the absence of a will, Joe explained, with Shannon's father sure to tie him up in a legal battle using the signed prenup to indicate his daughter's intentions. Manny wasn't as desperate for money as Sandro, but his inability to pay his hotel bills in Capri proved he was a man of modest means without Shannon. Joe was convinced Manny had agreed to split any inheritance with Sandro and had persuaded his fiancée to holiday in Positano and Capri to allow the meticulously thought-out killing to go ahead. Whether Zuzu was in on it or an unwitting participant who had to be silenced when she threatened to expose them was the only thing still in doubt, as far as Joe was concerned.

Elena asked the obvious question. 'Has Manny confessed?'

No, Lara was forced to admit. And while all logic pointed to his involvement, the evidence against him was, as yet, circumstantial. Manny had been careful to ensure he'd a cast-iron alibi at the time of both murders, and it might take them some time to join all the dots, although she felt sure they'd be able to do so eventually. They'd confiscated Manny's phone and discovered he'd been using it to track Shannon's movements on Capri. And that he'd been sending WhatsApp messages to a number that wasn't in his list of contacts. They were hoping the number could be traced back to the burner phone they'd found in Sandro's flat. If they could gain access to it then she was sure they would be able to prove the conspiracy between the two cousins and secure a conviction.

There was a silence when Lara had finished speaking. Gennaro shook his head in disbelief once more. It was shocking to think what people were capable of, he ventured.

Joe sighed heavily. 'When you've been doing this as long as I have, I'm afraid nothing shocks you any more,' he told him. Greed, sexual jealousy, desperation for money. They were powerful motivators in their own right, and deadly in combination, capable of inspiring seemingly normal people to heinous, abnormal acts.

'I'm just grateful I had your son-in-law's expertise and experience to guide me through this,' Lara added, gesturing towards Joe and imitating a round of applause.

Joe put his hands up to deflect her praise. 'We haven't nailed him yet.'

Gennaro ignored this caveat, as he slapped him on the back.

A horn sounded as a car announced itself on the street outside, and they heard a door slam before the street gate opened and someone clanged hurriedly down the steps. Luca appeared with Gianni coming behind.

Gennaro got to his feet as fast as his old bones would allow and stumbled over to fold his returning nephew in his arms.

Elena was already crying openly as she went to join their huddle.

Lara exchanged a look with Joe, and he smiled back at her, looking genuinely moved. As Luca broke free to approach him, Joe briefly resorted to type as he extended a stiff hand of greeting. But the freed man ignored it and enveloped him in a bear hug. And there was nothing remotely English about that.

The text message cut short Lara's participation in the drinks that followed.

Against her better instincts she had agreed to join them for a single glass, on the proviso they wouldn't talk further about the case, which would be inappropriate, with charges yet to be laid and both her and Luca present. Elena had guaranteed it would be one glass only. The restaurant was opening again, and they had their work cut out. Besides, two young women were dead. And there were Angelica's feelings to consider, as well as the possibility Luca might still be charged with lesser offences. It was not a time for celebrations, but it was natural for them to want to show their gratitude.

Lara smiled and accepted the glass Elena pressed into her hand, but as the cork was popped and the wine was poured, she felt her phone buzz in her pocket and took it out. 'Actually,' she said, withdrawing her glass at the exact moment Gennaro was tilting the bottle, 'I'm going to have to say no after all.' Something had come up, she explained, holding up her phone. 'Joe? Do you have a minute?'

The English detective frowned. What now?

It was nothing to do with the case, she reassured the group, raising a hand of farewell and withdrawing quickly to avoid a protracted goodbye. She was relieved to see Joe put his glass down and follow her as she made her way up the metal steps to the gate.

She waited for him to join her on the street before she delivered the unwelcome news. The prosecutor had informed Curti there wasn't enough evidence to charge Daniele with an offence, either in relation to Angelica or the drug dealing.

Joe took time to process this. 'Her blood test . . . doesn't that count?' he asked at last.

The test showed she'd been drugged with a form of benzodiazepine, Lara explained, but not when, where or by whom. In the absence of eyewitnesses or any physical evidence, such as a pill packet or vial, there was no way of proving Daniele was responsible, particularly in such a loose and unregulated environment as a beach party. The prosecutor was saying that Angelica could just as easily have taken the drug herself.

'He was going to rape her, Lara.'

He said it softly, but she sensed his anger. 'I don't doubt it,' she reassured him, 'but proving *intent* is hard without evidence. We intervened before he harmed her. And thank God we did. But it makes it difficult for a prosecution to succeed. You must see that.'

The English detective mulled this over before he reluctantly nodded his acceptance. 'I suppose they're saying the same about the surveillance photos, are they?'

'I'm afraid so, Joe. You and I . . . we both know the exchange between Daniele and Sandro is almost certain to be drug-related. But in the absence of the drugs themselves the photos aren't considered to definitively prove it.'

'Will you get a warrant?' Joe persisted. 'To search his house? His bank account?'

They were trying, Lara explained, but Curti wasn't sure a judge would grant one without evidence of serious wrongdoing. The second photo – of Daniele and Rocco Di Biasi's scar-faced goon – showed an exchange of money, not drugs. Daniele was nineteen and claimed to be living at home with his mother. The courts might give him the benefit of the doubt and, if they did, they'd have no other option but to release him.

Joe looked like he'd swallowed something unpleasant. 'Fuck,' was all he said aloud, but Lara could tell he was thinking about how he was going to tell Angelica.

44

It was the following morning before Joe summoned up the courage to go and speak to his daughter. He'd toyed with postponing the conversation until a decision had been confirmed, but it was almost four days since the party and Daniele was due to be released if charges weren't going to be pressed. The thought he might try to contact Angelica prompted him to take action.

The room was in semi-darkness as he entered. Angelica kept insisting she was OK, that she wasn't going to waste emotional energy over what had happened. But her actions told a different story. She was lethargic and morose, often close to tears. She'd barely left her room, had largely stopped eating and washing. She lay in bed, behind closed curtains, either watching trash on her laptop or reading it on her phone. Elena had advised Joe to let her be. And he'd agreed. But now he was losing faith in her counsel.

As he padded softly over to her bed, he could see Angelica was dozing. He lowered himself gently onto the edge of the mattress, intending to sit there until she awoke. He didn't have long to wait. She stirred and surfaced slowly from the depths, her eyelids fluttering open, a faint smile animating her pallid face as she saw him.

'How are you feeling?'

The smile faded.

He put a palm to her forehead, feeling for a fever that he knew wasn't there.

Angelica propped herself up. 'What time is it?'

'Just after eight.'

She considered this, bleary-eyed. 'What do you want?'

Joe hesitated. 'There's something I need to tell you.'

Her gaze seemed to find focus, suddenly wary. 'That sounds a bit sus.'

He ploughed on. 'The blood test . . . the one you took . . . the results are in.'

Angelica's eyebrows flickered upwards. Yeah?

'Your drink was spiked, love. There's no doubt about it.'

A hand went to her mouth.

Joe could feel his resolution begin to waver. 'I thought you'd want to know.'

'I do. I do, Dad. It's just . . .'

He saw her eyes begin to leak soft tears. He held out his arms and she buried her face in his neck. He felt her clinging to him, her misery soaking his chest. He held on for all he was worth, silently urging her to lay it all on him. At last, she lifted her head. 'I'm sorry,' she whimpered, sniffing and wiping her cheeks with her sleeves.

'Don't be daft.'

'This is all my fault.'

'How can you say that?'

She shook her head. 'I should have told you.'

Joe felt her withdrawing from him. 'Told me about what?'

Her voice was barely above a whisper now. 'I knew.'

'You knew what, love?'

She met his worried gaze, eyes filling with tears once more. 'He was dealing drugs.'

*

As Joe crashed through the swing doors and into the kitchen, the only person present was his father-in-law, who looked up in surprise. A split second later, Luca ambled into view, carrying an armful of vegetables, and without breaking stride, Joe made a beeline for him. He grabbed him by the collar and slammed him against the nearest wall, sending zucchini, bell peppers and aubergines flying.

'Have you lost your mind?' Gennaro yelled. He barged Joe with all his strength, knocking him off balance and allowing Luca to break his grip, push him away.

'SHE TOLD YOU!' Joe yelled, taking a swing at Luca but missing as the other man rushed to take refuge behind Elena, who'd come to see what the commotion was about.

'Told him what?' his mother-in-law demanded.

Joe ignored her. 'YOU DID NOTHING!'

Luca tried to defend himself. 'She didn't say it was him!'

'She reached out to you, Luca!'

'Only because she knew there was no point trying to talk to you.'

It was a well-aimed blow and it goaded Joe to greater fury. Breaking free of Gennaro's grip, he lunged for Luca and managed to catch hold of his arm, despite Elena's efforts to prevent him. He dragged him to the floor, manoeuvring as best he could to pin him down and let his fists do the rest of his talking, while his in-laws tried to restrain him.

'STOP IT!'

Joe glanced up to see Angelica standing in the open doorway, staring horrified at the undignified mêlée he'd unleashed.

'JUST STOP IT!' she howled again, dissolving into angry tears and hurrying away.

'Angelica!'

Joe gave Luca's face a last spiteful shove as he rolled off him and scrambled to his feet, meaning to go after her, only to find Elena and Gennaro blocking his way.

'Leave her!' his mother-in-law barked at him.

Gennaro joined in. 'You should go. Come back when you've calmed down.'

Joe was out of control, but he didn't care. 'I'm going. You couldn't fucking pay me to stick around here.' With a last withering look in Luca's direction, he pushed past them and through the doors.

Joe took refuge on the jetty. He stayed staring across the water to the promontory of the next bay long after his rage had given way to embarrassment and remorse. He'd upset Angelica. Offended his in-laws. Alienated Luca. And for what? A momentary release of pent-up fury. He found himself imagining what Sofia would say.

Good job, stupido.

He realised it was the first time he'd thought of her that day and it made him even more miserable. He slipped his wallet out and opened it to take out the photo he kept of her, needing to see her face. He stared at it, stroking the small square of glossy paper with his finger. He was so intent on trying to commune with her, he didn't hear the squeak as the gate opened, or the footsteps descending the stairs. It was only as the plank on which he was sitting creaked and shifted that he glanced up to see Gennaro had joined him. His father-in-law's gaze was drawn to the photo, and Joe passed it over. Gennaro studied it, sadly but fondly, before he handed it back, meeting Joe's gaze with a quizzical look.

Joe felt the need to explain. 'I still talk to her. Ask her advice.'

'What would she say to you now?'

'Grow up. Say sorry.'

Gennaro smiled faintly, and to his surprise Joe found himself smiling too. 'You have nothing to say sorry for,' the old chef reassured him.

'I shouldn't have said that.'

'No, no. You're not wrong. I often wonder if we're doing the right thing with Luca.'

'All the same . . . I'm sorry. I know he never acts out of malice.'

His father-in-law considered this. 'He makes bad judgements.'

'Don't we all.' Joe couldn't help looking again at Sofia's photo. He felt strangely unable to put it away, almost as if she was determined to stay party to their conversation.

'Maybe. But not all of us break the law.'

Joe shrugged. 'And yet it's hard to stay mad at him.'

'Just like it will be hard for Angelica to stay angry with you.'

'She'll give it a go.'

The two men exchanged another look, another smile. The old chef indicated the photo with a tilt of his head. 'Sofia would tell you to talk to her,' he advised.

'I've tried.'

'Then try again. Make her that meal. Sit down with her. Talk.'

'I don't know if my cooking skills will stretch to that.'

'The only person who doubts that is you.'

Joe tried again to raise an objection. 'What would I even feed her?'

Gennaro threw a hand up in a characteristic gesture. 'Read a recipe book. See what's in the storeroom. Trust your *appetite*, Joe.' He squeezed his son-in-law's knee, used it to lever himself back to his feet.

Joe's gaze returned to Sofia's photo. There seemed to be the same ghost of amusement playing around the edges of those beloved features as had animated his father-in-law's a moment before. There was wisdom in the old chef's counsel, Joe decided. It was what Sofia would want him to do.

Joe was rummaging through the storeroom, ticking items off the list of ingredients for a recipe he'd found online, when Luca walked in on him. The sous-chef was already in retreat before Joe called out to him. 'Luca! Wait!'

Luca stopped and warily turned back to face him. He looked ready to run.

'I overreacted. I'm sorry.'

'No, Joe. I'm the one who's sorry.'

'You've really no need to be.'

'She needed help. I should have realised. Said something.'

'Don't be so hard on yourself.'

'But I owe you so much.'

He looked so downbeat that Joe felt sorry for him. 'Seriously, Luca. She'll be OK.'

Luca looked a little mollified. 'I'm going to make it up to you.'

An alarm bell started ringing faintly in Joe's head. 'What does that mean?'

'I have contacts. Intelligence.'

It was ringing more loudly now.

'LUCA?'

It was Gennaro's voice calling from the kitchen and Luca jumped immediately to attention. '*Si, Gennaro. Arrivo.*' With a grin for Joe's benefit, Luca turned and disappeared before he could tell him to leave well alone.

45

In the absence of Daniele, or Joe for that matter, Angelica was taking her rage out on the shirt she'd worn to the party, as if it were somehow to blame for what had happened to her, when she was interrupted by a soft knock on her bedroom door.

'Go away!'

The handle turned and the door rattled, confirming it was bolted from the inside. 'Angelica?' Elena called from the other side.

Angelica stared at the partially dismembered garment in her hands. There was still one sleeve and much of the bodice to eviscerate. And she had a *lot* more to get off her chest. But the thought of her grandmother in the corridor outside stayed her hand. Stuffing the shirt in the bottom of her wardrobe, she padded over to the door and unbolted it, to be met by such a look of anxious solicitude that it completely disarmed her. It was the same look of concern that her mother had always used. The anger she'd been nurturing evaporated, and she felt her eyes brimming once more.

Standing in front of the bathroom mirror, letting Elena wipe her cheeks with a warm flannel, Angelica sensed that this time she really had reached the point where no more tears could come. There'd been catharsis in her crying and she felt less constricted, lighter, ready to start a fresh chapter once the old one had been signed off. She stared at herself as her grandmother worked on her face. 'It's me everyone should be mad at,' she said experimentally, wanting to hear how this new, more grounded Angelica might sound.

'Nonsense,' Elena responded without looking up. 'You're not remotely to blame.'

Angelica let this sink in. 'Why's Dad so angry with Luca, Gran?'

'He feels guilty. We all do. For failing to protect you.' Elena had finished wiping Angelica's cheeks and now she met her eye. 'But that's not going to happen again.'

'What does that mean?'

'I think you should stay here,' Elena said simply, proceeding to pick up a towel and pat her granddaughter's cheeks. 'With me and your grandfather.'

She left little room for doubt in the way she said it, but Angelica was so surprised by the suggestion she felt the need to check it all the same. 'For how long?'

'For as long as you like.'

'But what about school?'

Elena busied herself with putting the towel back on the rack. 'What about it?'

'I'm supposed to go back in September.'

'We'll enrol you in something here.'

'But they won't teach in English.'

'Your Italian is good enough.'

Angelica began to raise an objection but closed her mouth again.

'You said you wanted to be your own boss, start your own thing,' her grandmother reminded her, ceasing to straighten the towels on the rack and turning her gaze on Angelica once more. 'Well, you don't need to finish school for that. You could sign up for a business course in Naples. And work here in the restaurant. Learn on the job.'

Work here?

Elena must have sensed Angelica's doubts because she continued quickly to reassure her. 'And I don't just mean waiting tables . . . although we'll pay you to do that. Procurement, pricing strategy, profit margins. Dealing with suppliers. Staff. Recruitment and HR. Marketing. Balancing the books. Filing tax returns. It's all part of it.'

Angelica felt a flicker of excitement. Perhaps that was the sound of a page turning? But of course, one substantial objection was still to be voiced. 'What about Dad?'

Elena shrugged. 'He's welcome to stay too.'

'He won't want to.'

'Then he's equally welcome not to.' Elena gently turned Angelica's head so they were both looking directly into the mirror. 'It's time he prioritised what's best for you.'

This alternative future took more shape as Angelica started to research the possibilities online after Elena left her room. There was something calling itself the Business and Technology Academy, which was affiliated to one of the universities in Naples. It offered a one-year course in business administration and marketed itself on the basis that several of the modules were internationally focused and taught in English. The website was glossy and well put together and the course promised a programme of speakers and mentors, alongside case studies of various alumni. She could imagine herself on the sunny and well-appointed campus, chatting to new friends between lectures or eating an alfresco lunch. The fees were a lot but she'd some money saved, and she calculated that she could cover the rest with what she'd expect to earn from waiting tables in the restaurant, irrespective of what Joe might contribute if he could be talked round.

There were other things to consider, of course, aside from money. The thought of bumping into Daniele if she were to stay loomed large, but hadn't her dad suggested he was likely to be facing a prison sentence? Having so recently purged herself of the shock of his betrayal, she found she was largely indifferent as to what might happen to him, but equally so to the prospect of meeting him again. She wasn't scared of crossing paths with Daniele Russo. Although perhaps, she decided, *he* should be of crossing paths with her.

A larger concern was Joe himself and how he might react. She hated the idea of hurting him and it was this fear that cast a shadow over the happy plans she'd been formulating. She even got as far as going after Elena with the intention of telling her she'd decided to travel home with him as planned. The lunch service was in full swing, with early bookings having been taken to make up for covers lost during the recent closures. Da Vinale's was so full of life and colour and sound that it gave her pause. She would miss this, she realised. The sights and smells. The loving attention to detail. The part of her heritage it spoke to. The bit of herself she was only just getting to know. More confused than ever, she retreated before anyone could question what she was doing there.

Hoping to clear her head, Angelica had a shower, the first in several days, and then spent some time tidying and airing her room, having decided not just to open the curtains but to crack the window as well. It was while she was picking up the clothes from her floor and sorting them into two piles – 'still wearable' and 'needs a wash' – that she noticed someone had slipped something under her door. It was a small plain postcard, and when she picked it up and turned it over, she saw it had something scribbled on it.

Joe Mottram requests the pleasure of your company for dinner this evening.
  Da Vinale Apartment. 8pm. RSVP.

She couldn't help smiling. It was kind of cute.

Half an hour passed. Angelica had fetched a can of soda from the fridge and was halfway through drinking it when her dad knocked at her door. He waited a beat before entering, which was long enough for her to close the laptop that lay beside her on the bed. She'd begun, very tentatively, to fill out an application form for the academy, but now she abandoned it without checking whether her work had been saved.

'It smells a bit better in here,' he announced, poking his head in.

Angelica took a swig from her soda. 'What do you want?' she asked, resting the can on the nearest flat surface, which just happened to be the back of her laptop.

'Do you have a minute?'

'Are you going to shout? Threaten to beat people up?'

Joe's face fell. 'I'm sorry I lost my temper.'

'You do that rather a lot.'

'Only when I'm worried about you.'

Angelica felt herself relent a little, but she wasn't ready to make it easy for him. 'I'm busy with something,' she told him, indicating the laptop. 'Can you make it quick?'

'Of course. I just wanted to check you got my note.'

She picked it up, showed it to him.

'And?'

Angelica found herself thinking of the half-completed form on her laptop.

'We need to talk, Angelica.'

'OK.'

Joe looked surprised by her sudden concession. 'OK? Great.'

She gestured to him that she considered their conversation to be over. He seemed to take the hint, but something caught his eye as he turned away. She followed his gaze towards the 'needs a wash' pile. 'I'm going to wash those,' she told him, feeling a prickle of embarrassment. Joe either didn't hear or chose to ignore her, because he reached for the pile and straightened up with a garment in his hand. It was black and white and strangely unfamiliar. It took her a moment to place it.

It was Daniele's jacket.

'Is this his?' her dad asked, holding it up for her inspection.

Angelica felt herself flush. Suddenly she didn't feel so indifferent after all. 'After the party . . . I was cold. That Italian policewoman. She gave me it to wear.'

Joe was silent.

'I didn't know how to . . . you know . . . give it back.'

He dad grimaced. He started to go through the pockets.

'What are you looking for?' she asked to distract herself.

'Evidence.' Of what exactly there was no need for him to say.

The last pocket he unzipped was on the sleeve. She remembered Daniele producing a joint from it on the beach all those weeks ago and she half-expected Joe to pull out another one, but when he withdrew his hand he was holding a scrap of paper. He studied it before he turned it to show her. Someone had written tomorrow's date on it.

31.07. And then three words in Italian: *Grotta. Seguaci. Martini.* Followed by the date again: 31-07.

Joe was looking at her expectantly. 'Any ideas?'

She felt a flash of indignation. 'No.'

'Something to do with his dealing maybe?'

'I told you . . . I don't know anything about that. Just what I saw.'

Joe had just turned the paper to study it again, when his phone rang and he answered it. 'Lara?' she heard him say, and then a beat later, 'OK, I'm on my way.' His gaze returned quizzically to the piece of paper as he turned to leave.

Angelica reached for her laptop. And it was then, in the act of picking up the soda can that she'd rested on top of it, she realised there was one detail of Daniele's dealing she'd omitted to share with him.

46

'What do you think?'

Joe watched a frown form on Lara's face as she took the scrap of paper he was holding out and studied it. They were standing in a dingy, windowless corridor in Daniele's mother's apartment while a team of forensic investigators explored every nook and cranny of the tiny third-floor flat. There'd been an edge of disbelief to Lara's voice when she'd called earlier to tell him the judge had surprised everyone by granting a warrant.

'The thirty-first?' She did a quick calculation. 'That's tomorrow.'

'I'm aware of that. What about the rest?'

Lara pulled a face. 'Maybe it means nothing.'

'Come on, Lara.'

'What?!'

'It must be the paper Scarface was handing to Daniele in that surveillance photo.'

She shrugged. 'It could be.'

Joe was growing exasperated. 'It relates to his next pick-up. I just know it.'

'What makes you so sure?'

Joe reminded her that the scar-faced man in the photo, who'd pulled a gun on him at Da Vinale's, had been identified as Fabio Pigozzi. Having served time for GBH *and* possession with intent to supply, Pigozzi was employed by Rocco Di Biasi as a top-level enforcer, according to her colleagues in narcotics, running the clan's network of street-dealers and couriers in the north-eastern suburbs of Naples, between the airport and Ponticelli. 'The paper tells him where to find his next consignment to sell,' Joe persisted. 'Why would Daniele be handing over so much cash in the photo if it didn't?'

'OK, but it doesn't tell *us* where.'

'Those words . . . they don't mean *anything* to you?'

She shook her head.

'Nothing local? You know . . . somewhere in Naples? A bar, maybe?'

'No, Joe. I'm sorry.'

Joe stared again at the three words as she handed the paper back, although he knew them now by heart in both Italian and English. *Grotta* – Cave. *Seguaci* – Followers. *Martini* – Martini. It was a code. 'Are you still planning to release him?' he asked.

It was highly likely, Lara informed him, if the search failed to turn up anything. 'We have ninety-six hours to charge him, put him before a judge . . . and those are nearly up.'

'But you can keep him under surveillance? If you need to?'

The Italian detective grimaced. A surveillance operation cost money and would need to be signed off by the *vice questore*. They'd need strong grounds to persuade him.

'Shit.'

'You *have* warned Angelica, haven't you?'

Joe shook his head ruefully. 'I've tried. I was going to give it another go tonight.'

Lara winced.

'Boss!'

They turned to see a white-suited Gianni beckoning from the kitchen doorway.

'We've found something.'

Exchanging a glance with Joe, Lara disappeared with Gianni into the kitchen.

Joe was about to go after them when his phone buzzed with a message from Luca. *Where R U?*

Did he have information? Joe decided it would have to wait. He thumbed back a simple message – *Naples. Back on 17.45 ferry* – before he slipped the phone away.

The scene that greeted him when he followed his colleagues into the kitchen was organised chaos; every surface was strewn with the contents of the emptied cupboards. Lara was crouching to examine something on a rectangle of plastic sheeting that had been used to cover the floor, and now she glanced up and beckoned Joe to join her, pointing his attention to a fake soda can with a screw-top lid that was lying open on its side in front of her. Half a dozen bags of blue pills were spilling out of it onto the floor.

She grinned at him. 'Your daughter was right about the can.'

'Is it fentanyl?'

They'd have to wait for the lab to confirm it, Lara conceded, but the distinctive colour of the pills made her confident it would turn out to be the case. When viewed in conjunction with the surveillance photo, it would prove to a judge's satisfaction that Sandro had acquired the drugs that killed Shannon and caused them to be administered.

Joe couldn't help grinning too. 'And it'll prove Daniele sold them to him.'

47

'I beg your fucking pardon!'

Lara flushed as she heard the words slip out of the English detective's mouth. They were sitting in Curti's office, on the other side of the desk from her boss, who had just now told them he thought they should go ahead with releasing Daniele Russo, despite the discovery of the stash of fentanyl, which was sitting in an evidence bag in front of him.

Curti's expression darkened. 'I don't like your tone.'

'And I don't like what you're suggesting,' Joe shot back, getting to his feet.

'Sit down, Detective. *Please.*'

With what looked like a supreme effort of will, Joe controlled his anger.

'Will you let me explain?'

The English detective resumed his seat next to Lara.

'*Allora.*' Curti took a moment to straighten his tie and sip from a bottle of water. It was evident to Lara he was also doing his best to control his temper. 'The boy, he's . . . *uno piccoletto* . . . a little fish,' he continued. 'You agree?'

Joe nodded. 'Small fry.'

Curti seemed tickled by the term. He picked up the evidence bag from the desk and made a show of counting the bags of pills it contained. 'With this much in his possession . . . for a first offence ... the best we can hope for is six months. And that's only if the judge's wife has been nice to him and he's in a good mood. You understand?' He was smirking as he glanced at Lara and she rewarded him with a faint smile.

'Six is better than none,' Joe observed.

'*Sì*. But it's better to catch a bigger fish, no?'

Lara glanced at her English colleague, who was listening intently now. 'What do you have in mind?' he asked.

Curti leaned back. The paper Joe had found in the pocket of the boy's jacket ... he agreed it probably referred to the date and location for the pick-up of his next consignment of drugs, but they were no closer to cracking the code and Daniele had refused to cooperate. Perhaps the smart move would be to release him under surveillance and see if they could pull off a bigger bust? If they could catch the boy in the act of picking up a new consignment to sell and link the location back to the piece of paper that Fabio Pigozzi had been photographed handing to him then they might have grounds for arresting and charging Pigozzi himself. Curti already had the *vice questore*'s sign-off for the surveillance operation. They were ready to go ahead but, in the circumstances, Curti would prefer to be doing so with Joe's blessing.

The English detective sighed heavily. 'When exactly were you thinking?'

'*Subito* ... straight away.' The boy either had to be charged or released in the next few hours, Curti explained.

Joe couldn't help rubbing a hand over his face.

Curti exchanged a look with Lara. 'You don't agree?' he asked Joe.

'No. I agree. It's the smart play. It's just ...'

Lara guessed the reasons for his reluctance. 'He hasn't told his daughter about the possibility of Daniele Russo being released.'

'I was planning to do it this evening.'

Lara's boss considered this. 'And you're worried she'll be angry?'

'Devastated, more like.'

Curti nodded his understanding. 'Then perhaps you should telephone her now.'

'It's not the kind of conversation you can have over the phone.'

The *commissario* gestured. So what now?

'Look. You should go ahead. I'll find a way to square it with her.'

'Are you sure?' Lara couldn't help asking.

The English detective nodded in response, but he looked anything but.

'And you're sure he doesn't know it's there?'

'As sure as I can be.' Lara's demeanour was less certain than her words sounded. 'That's what they told me. And I've no reason not to believe them.'

It was late on the Wednesday afternoon and they were sitting in an unmarked police van, parked on the opposite side of a wide piazza from the pizza restaurant to where Daniele had been tracked following his release. Lara was explaining how a tracker the size and weight of a €2 coin had been secreted in the heel of his boots before they were returned to him. It was the smallest and flattest one they had available.

'Maybe they have one of those gizmos . . . you know, a bug sweeper,' Joe suggested.

Her look implied she thought his anxiety was getting the better of him.

Joe was saved from having to justify himself by Gianni's

return. He slipped into the passenger seat and closed the door quietly behind him, turned to face them. The narcotics team had managed to get an undercover officer inside the restaurant, he reported, in addition to the two sitting on the inviting-looking terrace outside.

Lara picked up her walkie-talkie and pushed the side button, held it to her mouth. She spoke in Italian, but Joe knew exactly what she was asking.

Did they have eyes on Daniele?

There was a burst of static before the reply came. '*Negativo.*'

Lara turned her attention to the hand-held GPS that lay beside her on the seat. The red circle indicating Daniele's whereabouts was exactly where it had been for the thirty-seven minutes since he was seen entering the restaurant with Fabio Pigozzi.

'Do we still have all the exits covered?' Joe wanted to know.

The Italian detective nodded, but she was looking at her watch as she did so. He could tell she was thinking the same thing as he was. Something didn't smell right.

'Plan B?' he ventured.

There was no need for translation.

They'd gathered for a debrief in a narrow alley near where the van was parked, hidden from view from the restaurant; Joe watched in disbelief as one of Lara's colleagues handed Daniele's boots to her. As the conversation drew to a close and she turned back to face him, her expression told him everything he needed to know. He levered himself upright from the wall he'd been leaning against, started to walk away.

'Joe! Wait!'

He didn't trust himself to stop, continued walking.

'PLEASE! STOP!'

Joe swung round. 'I can't believe I went along with this shit!'

'What choice did I have?'

It was a fair point. And she did look suitably mortified. Joe felt his anger cooling. Very slightly. He indicated the boots she was holding. 'Where did they find them?'

'Men's toilet. First floor. Beneath the cistern.'

Joe snorted in disbelief.

Lara ploughed on, sounding more miserable by the second. 'There's a fire escape. We think he must have got away over the roofs.'

He shook his head, bit back another expletive.

'We had two sets of eyes on every door.'

'Just not on the fucking windows.'

She looked stung. 'We'll find him. I promise.'

'You'd better,' was all he said.

What was he going to tell Angelica? Joe reflected as he stood on the concrete jetty watching a ferry manoeuvre its way in reverse towards the dock. It was bad enough having to admit that Daniele was not going to be charged for what he'd done to her. Let alone that he'd given them the slip within an hour of being released.

The ferry sounded its horn, and a ripple of anticipation stirred the waiting crowd as passengers started to pick up their bags and possessions and shuffle closer to the embarkation point in the hope of ensuring a seat. Joe joined the trickle of humanity and let himself be swept along towards the quayside. He'd just joined what might loosely be termed a queue, when he felt a presence beside him and turned to see a man standing unnaturally close. He was wearing a cap with the peak pulled low and dark glasses, but there was no mistaking his profile or his figure. It was Luca.

'What are you doing here?' Joe found himself asking in a low voice.

'Looking for you.'

He remembered the earlier text message. 'Couldn't it wait until I got back?'

Luca glanced both ways before he responded. 'Capri is like the Vatican,' he muttered. 'There are eyes and ears everywhere.'

Joe almost smiled. 'Is there something you want to tell me?'

'Not here.' He started to walk away.

'Wait, Luca,' Joe called out. 'I can't miss this ferry.'

Luca stopped, looked back. 'Five minutes.'

Joe checked his watch. With a bemused shake of his head, he started to follow.

The warehouse wasn't exactly deserted, but the forklift driver working at the far end of the cavernous structure seemed sufficiently removed to satisfy Luca. They took cover behind a pallet of grain sacks just inside the doorway.

'Couldn't we have done this at the restaurant?' Joe found himself asking.

'They may have it under surveillance.'

'Who might?'

'The guys that beat up Gennaro.'

'Rocco Di Biasi's men?'

Luca's nod confirmed it. 'They know I know people. And that you're police.'

'Maybe this isn't such a good idea.'

Luca put out a hand to stop him leaving. 'I told you. I want to help.'

With a sigh, Joe relented. 'What is it you want to tell me?'

The other man leaned in. 'I asked around about Daniele. Spoke to a friend.'

'Which *friend* is this?'

'That doesn't matter.'

'It does to me, Luca.'

The sous-chef looked briefly in two minds about whether to say more. 'The guy I was with . . . you know, on the night before the first murder.'

'Dante Patalano? Your smuggling buddy?'

Luca looked faintly surprised by Joe's level of recall. He nodded silent assent.

Joe felt his antenna twitching. 'Go on.'

Luca took a beat to organise his thoughts. 'This friend . . . he tells me if you want to buy a certain kind of high then you'll come into contact with *delinquente* . . . you know, street punks. Like Daniele Russo. And it's a safe bet that in certain parts of the city they'll be working for Rocco Di Biasi, either directly or indirectly.'

Joe's sense of anticipation deflated a little. 'I already know this, Luca. The Di Biasi clan controls the black market in illegal prescription drugs in the northern part of the city.'

'All right. But do you know how he operates?'

'Through a network of couriers and dealers. Like Daniele. You said it yourself.'

'I meant how he supplies them,' Luca persisted.

Joe had to admit he didn't. 'We're still working on it.'

Luca grinned triumphantly. 'Parcel lockers.'

'Parcel lockers?'

'You know. There are hundreds of them now . . . all over the city. You can post and pick up things. All you need is a code.'

A code.

Joe took out his phone and looked at the photo he'd taken of Daniele's note before handing it over to Lara. The first sequence of numbers – 31.07 – was a date. But the second – 31-07 – was that an access code? 'I could kiss you, Luca,' he exclaimed, turning and dashing away before his startled companion had time to react.

The fifth floor of La Questura, which earlier had seemed to Joe to be humming with energy and purpose, was emptier and more subdued as he emerged from the lifts. While the majority of her colleagues had clocked off, Lara was still sitting at her desk in the middle of the office, illuminated by the roseate rays of evening sun pouring through the windows on the west side of the building. She had her head down and was so engrossed in what she was reading she didn't notice his approach. Joe had time to register the print-outs from Sofia's file spread across her desk before she looked up.

'I thought maybe you'd forgotten about that,' he suggested, unwilling to pretend he hadn't seen what she was doing, uncertain what else to say.

Lara got to her feet, sweeping the print-outs into a pile. 'Listen, Joe . . .'

He sensed a 'sorry' coming and cut her off. 'I'm not here for an apology, Lara. Or excuses. I just want to get a result.'

'Good. So do I.'

He held up his phone to show her the photo he'd taken of Daniele's note. 'The second set of digits. They're separated by a hyphen. Not a full stop.'

Lara stared at the screen.

'I think it might be an access code. Not just the date, like we thought.'

The Italian detective looked up and caught his eye. 'An access code for what?'

'A parcel locker.'

Her eyes widened slightly in recognition.

That was the good news, he told her. The bad news was there were hundreds of them in the Naples metropolitan area. He'd googled it on his way back from the port. And there was no way they could keep so many of them under simultaneous surveillance.

'You let me worry about that,' Lara told him, picking up her desk phone and starting to make a call. 'There's nothing more you can do tonight. Go home. Have dinner. Rest up.'

Dinner?

'Shit!' Joe blurted out, turning and rushing away.

48

'Shit!'

It was no more than a murmur really, but Angelica heard it from the sofa in the living room where she was lying, awaiting Joe's return. She'd registered the front door opening moments before, had listened as he made his way to the kitchen and then across to her bedroom to knock gently before opening the door. His expletive was confirmation of what she knew already. Both rooms were empty.

She'd been stretched out in the same position, leafing through *The A–Z of Italian Cooking*, when Elena had come across from the restaurant a couple of hours earlier.

'Has he called?' she wanted to know.

Angelica shook her head, not trusting herself to speak straight away.

'He's cutting it fine.'

'He always does.'

Elena wandered over to the sofa to see what Angelica was looking at, saw the cookbook open at the page with Sofia's photograph. They exchanged a sad smile.

'Have you decided what you're going to say?'

'Not yet.'

'Well, I'm in the restaurant if you need me.'

'Thanks, Gran.'

Elena paused in the doorway. 'Whatever you decide, my darling... it'll be OK.'

Lying there now, Angelica wasn't so sure. She sensed Joe moving towards the living room and braced for discovery as the light was switched on. She was hidden from view by the back of the sofa, and she lay, barely breathing, as he padded into her line of sight. He crossed over to the cabinet and took out a bottle and a glass, poured a measure. She watched, fascinated, as he downed it with a wince and wavered over pouring another, unaware he was being observed. He'd just started to tilt the bottle a second time, when Angelica decided enough was enough. 'You didn't even call,' she announced, sitting up.

'Shit!' Joe started, splashed brandy over his hand. He was sucking it dry as he turned to look at her. 'I am *so, so* sorry, love.'

'I don't want to hear it.'

'I've been ringing and texting non-stop.'

'I turned my phone off.' Angelica rose, empowered by a returning sense of indignation. 'I should be thanking you really. For helping me make up my mind.'

He looked confused. 'About what?'

'I want to stay, Dad.'

Joe said nothing, was clearly processing.

'And I don't just mean for the rest of the summer,' she added.

Her clarification seemed to kick him into gear. 'That's not going to happen.'

'I'm seventeen. You can't stop me.'

He gold-fished slightly. 'You don't have enough money to pay your way,' he said eventually.

'I'm going to get a job.'

'Your grandparents might have something to say about that.'

'It was Gran's idea. She's helping me apply to do a business course.'

He sat down, dropped his head. 'You could do that in London,' he muttered.

'But the support I need . . . the *family* I'm looking for. It's here. Not there.'

Joe glanced up. He looked distraught. 'How can you say that?'

'Because it's *true*!'

'After everything that's happened.'

'To *us*, Dad! Not just to *you*!' Now at last the tears came. She felt them hot on her cheeks. 'I need you . . . but you're never here,' she managed to add in a hoarse whisper.

'I'm here now.' He looked close to tears himself.

It was all too much for Angelica and she hurried from the room.

By the time she'd regained her composure and decided she ought to try and make some kind of amends, Joe was no longer in the living room. It was her turn to check for him in his bedroom, but he was not there either, or in the kitchen. At last she tracked him down to the balcony that looked out over the courtyard.

He was sitting with his back to her and the hubbub of conversation from the restaurant was loud enough, even at this hour, to cover the sound of her approach. As she came to stand over him, she could see he was holding a number of photos, appeared to be staring at them intently. It was only as she reached gently over his shoulder, intending to claim them from him so she could look herself, that he seemed to notice her presence. He tried to withdraw his hand, but she already had a grip on the corner of one photo and, after a brief moment, he conceded.

She studied them in turn. The first was a passport-style picture of her mother and, although she couldn't remember seeing it, the pose and the look in Sofia's eye were familiar. The other two photos were a revelation, however. The first was in black and white, and showed a plump young boy, mid-blink and grinning inanely, with an old woman seated next to him staring primly down the lens. The second was in colour, but no less faded and ancient-looking. It pictured a young woman on a tartan picnic rug staring uncertainly at an apple-cheeked baby in her lap, who gurned delightedly for the camera.

'Is that you?' Angelica asked as she took the chair opposite Joe and held up the first photograph for his inspection.

'Me and my gran. Yeah.'

She held up the second picture in turn. 'And this one too?'

He stared at it briefly before he nodded. 'With my mum.'

Angelica turned the photo round so she could drink in the details – the browns and oranges of the young woman's jumper, the spareness of her figure despite her recent pregnancy, the severe fringe and gaunt face, the hollowed-out expression in her eyes. 'You don't talk about her much,' she observed, handing the photos back.

'She wasn't really part of my life.'

'You said she died. When you were very young.'

'She'd abandoned me before that.' It was said matter-of-factly.

Angelica stared, wide-eyed but silent, waiting for him to go on.

Joe seemed lost in his thoughts. 'She was a normal kid, apparently,' he offered by way of an explanation, looking up to meet Angelica's eye. 'But her dad lost his job at the factory and . . . well, the family sort of fell apart.' He shrugged and gave her a sad smile. 'She dropped out. Got into drugs. And all the crap that goes with them. She was pregnant with me at nineteen. And pretty much absent after the birth.'

Angelica felt electrified, too shocked to move or speak.

'The last time we saw her . . . me and Nelly, my nan . . . it was my fourth birthday. She came by with a jigsaw, or so I've been told. And that was that. She turned up in Bradford six years later. On a mortuary slab.'

'Oh, Dad,' Angelica whispered. She reached out to him, but it was too much for Joe. Shrugging her off gently, he stood and wandered over to the edge of the balcony. She watched him, unwilling to speak for fear of saying the wrong thing, unable to move for fear of sending him fleeing. At last, when she judged he'd controlled his emotions, she got up and went over, took his hand. She was relieved to feel him squeeze back. She let her head rest against him and they stayed like that, breathing softly in harness, listening to the sounds from the restaurant and the sweet back-and-forth slap of the sea beyond, the breeze soft and warm in their faces. 'Why didn't you tell me?' she asked at last, sensing the moment might be passing.

There was another silence. 'I didn't want you to think I was damaged,' he answered after some time. 'Or to worry that I might have passed that damage on to you.'

She scanned his face. 'But Mum knew, right?'

'What do you think?'

They shared a look. There had been no secrets from Sofia.

'I mean, don't get me wrong, I'd tried to build up my defences,' Joe continued. 'Shuttling between care homes and foster homes after my nan died. And with all the banter and brutality coming up through the ranks, I was pretty hardened by the time she met me. Detached. Unemotional. But she bulldozed through all of that.'

'Sounds like her.'

A hint of a smile played around Joe's lips. 'She brought so much back into my life. So much love. So much hope . . . when we had you. And then I lost her . . . *we* lost her . . . and I shut down again.' He looked to her for understanding. 'It's the only way I could cope.'

'It's OK, Dad. I'm not angry. I think I've shut down too.'

He seemed calmer now, more accepting. 'Coming here . . . it's been agony . . . being reminded of her . . . almost sensing a trace of her . . . everywhere I turn, everywhere I look.'

'Maybe it was a dumb idea.'

'No, no. You were right. Mum would hate to see us barely talking. Arguing all the time when we do. Family's all that matters, she was always saying. And despite everything . . . everything that's happened . . . I've started to feel, sort of . . . you know . . .'

'Better about things?'

He nodded. 'Maybe. If that doesn't sound an odd thing to say.'

'It doesn't. So have I.'

'Maybe it's the good memories. The love and happiness she felt here.'

'Or maybe it's just the food.'

For the first time in what felt like the longest time, Joe laughed.

Delighted to have amused him, Angelica joined in.

'This was a genius idea, Dad.'

'It's your mum you should be thanking.'

They'd withdrawn to the kitchen. Joe had said he was craving something sweet and decadent. So they were making cannoli using a recipe from Sofia's cookbook.

Angelica had been set to work on the filling, whisking together ricotta and mascarpone with caster sugar, vanilla and orange zest, as her dad fished half a dozen tube-shaped pastry shells from a pan of bubbling vegetable oil to drain and dry them.

'How's that filling coming?'

She turned off the whisk. 'Do you want to taste?'

Joe dipped a finger in. 'Needs more chocolate.'

Angelica was laughing as she tipped some into the mix. 'You're out of control.'

He winked at her before picking up the tray of cannoli and transferring them to the fridge, returning with another batch, dipped in chocolate and chopped pistachios at each end, which had been cooling there. 'Let's fill these up,' he declared.

He must be drunk and she hadn't noticed, Angelica decided, watching as he filled a piping bag with pillowy dollops of the creamy mixture in her bowl. Gleefully, he proceeded to fill two cannoli in turn and hand one to her. They shared a silent countdown before taking simultaneous bites. There was a brief moment of reflection to chew and taste before Joe pronounced his verdict with his mouth half full: 'Oh. My. God.'

Angelica couldn't help giggling and Joe joined in. In seconds, they were laughing uncontrollably, coughing and choking, exhaling flecks of pastry and cream in their desperation to catch a breath. Red in the face, Joe finally managed to control his hilarity and swallow. 'God, I love the food here,' he pronounced, grinning and eyeing the other end of his cannoli with unmistakable intent.

It was a long time since Angelica had seen him look so happy and she told him.

'You too, love. You too.'

*

Angelica set her alarm for six and was out of bed the minute it sounded. In her heightened state, she'd barely slept, but she was sure Joe would be leaving early and was anxious not to miss him. She found him in the kitchen, washing up the remains of their cannoli-making. 'I said I'd take care of that,' she called out from the doorway.

He turned and saw her, broke into a smile. 'I'm almost done.'

As he turned back to rinse the last of the dishes, Angelica wandered over to join him. She picked up a tea towel and started to dry the items on the draining board, putting them away one by one. 'I think I've worked it out, by the way,' she said after a while, trying to keep her voice as neutral as possible.

Joe couldn't help glancing across at her. 'The meaning of life?'

She smiled back. 'The words. On Daniele's message.'

Suddenly he wasn't smiling any more. 'Seriously?'

'What three words.'

His brow crinkled. 'The ones that were on the page?'

'No, Dad. It's an app called what3words.' She took out her phone to show him.

49

'Could she be wrong about this?'

It was later that morning, and Lara was sitting with Joe in an unmarked van. Angelica's revelation had brought them to a petrol station on the outskirts of the city, just south of the junction on the autostrada that gave access to the airport. They were parked on the forecourt of a car showroom opposite, giving them a clear view of the parcel locker that stood against the wall of the sandwich bar occupying one side of the petrol station. In the four hours they'd been watching, only one customer had made use of the facility – a woman with false nails like daggers and a shock of pink hair who'd picked up a package a little after ten and whose car had been stopped by plain-clothed officers a block down the road. The package turned out to contain three pairs of women's jeans.

'She was right about the soda can,' Joe replied, not taking his eyes from the locker.

Lara sighed. 'All right. Then explain it to me again.'

The look Joe gave her was one of mild exasperation. The what3words app divided the surface of the world into a grid of three-metre squares, he explained, and assigned each square a unique combination of three words in English to identify it (or in any one of forty other languages, including Italian). The three words on the scrap of paper in Daniele's pocket had brought them to this exact spot. And there just happened to be a parcel locker where they'd been hoping to find one.

Lara sighed again, inwardly this time. She should be back at La Questura, she told herself, preparing for her interview with Sandro Totti. The digital forensics team had finally cracked the cousins' phones, and Manny Sanghera had cracked in turn when confronted with the messages he'd sent Sandro. He'd confessed his part in Shannon's death, but now claimed to have been driven mad with jealousy by her infidelities. He was pointing his finger at his cousin, saying he'd conceived Shannon's murder out of greed, and acted alone when killing Zuzu to silence her. Lara was looking forward to sharing this with Sandro and getting him to incriminate Manny in turn. If it weren't for Joe's obsession with this boy, she could be planning her interview strategy instead of being stuck here.

Her thoughts were interrupted as the walkie-talkie on the seat beside her crackled into life. Gianni's voice came over the airwaves, alerting them to activity on the forecourt.

'We've got another customer,' she translated for Joe's benefit, lifting her binoculars to look. A black saloon car with tinted windows had pulled to a halt with its engine running, and a hooded youth was in the process of opening one of the lockers and placing a padded envelope inside. As they watched, the youth closed the locker and keyed in a code before getting back into the vehicle. Lara pressed the speak button on her walkie-talkie, told her deputy to pull the car over, following the same routine as before.

They watched the saloon pull off the forecourt. An unmarked police car set off behind it. Two more cars were positioned at the end of the block ready to ease it to the side of the road while the package they'd deposited was retrieved and searched. Lara was about to observe that it was almost certainly nothing to get excited about when there was a squeal of tyres. A split second later the saloon came back into view. It had crossed over the central reservation and was travelling at speed in the other direction, away from the autostrada. She exchanged a look with Joe. 'Buckle up.'

Not waiting to put on her own, she started her engine and floored the accelerator, sending the van careering across the pavement and swerving onto the carriageway, narrowly ahead of a flat-bed truck, which blasted its horn. She saw the saloon brake sharply at a red light some distance ahead and dive to its left, cutting across the oncoming traffic. Beeping her horn frantically, she followed its lead.

The saloon had disappeared from view. Lara gunned the van through a succession of corners, pushing the limits of her driving skills, thankful not to encounter anything in front or coming the other way. When she dared to take her eyes off the road, she glanced briefly in the rear-view mirror to check for signs of back-up and then across at Joe. He'd barely moved a muscle. 'Right-hander approaching . . . fast,' was all he said.

She caught sight of it and swung the van into it, braking hard and swerving instantly to avoid a car skewed across the road, its front obliterated. Fifty metres ahead, the vehicle that must have struck it had hit a crash barrier.

It was the black saloon.

Lara flung her door open. 'Stay here,' she barked, drawing her gun and starting to hurry towards the crash site. As she called out a warning to whoever might be in the vehicle, she heard the door of the van slam behind her and, without turning round, she knew the English detective had disobeyed her order.

The saloon was a write-off. As Lara came alongside the

passenger door, pointing her pistol, she saw the hooded youth slumped against an airbag, unconscious.

'Lara!'

She glanced up to see Joe gesturing, and saw a man limping away across a stretch of wasteland.

'Armed police! Stay where you are!'

The fugitive swung round and raised a gun. She just had time to see his scar and recognise him as Fabio Pigozzi, before a bullet came whistling in their direction, shattering the windscreen and sending her crashing to the floor. Joe hit the ground simultaneously. 'I told you to stay in the fucking van!' she yelled, as a second shot ricocheted off the bodywork.

To her relief, she heard the sound of sirens. Back-up was on its way. She raised her head to risk a look and was in time to observe Pigozzi disappear into a thicket. Scrambling to her feet, she set off down a track choked with rubble and fly-tipped bags of rubbish and quickly came to a rusty pair of iron gates. As she went to squeeze between them, she glanced back to see Joe vaulting a fence and loping off in another direction. At least he's wearing body armour, she thought.

Lara crossed a stretch of open meadow in a crouching run and plunged after her quarry into the thicket, which thinned rapidly and gave way to a field of chest-high weeds. She saw Pigozzi break cover as he negotiated a fence on the far side, and half a minute later she'd reached it herself. The top rail was garlanded with a vivid smear of blood. The fugitive was wounded. And all the more dangerous for it.

The ground beyond rose to a small wood fifty metres away. She was deciding how to traverse it, when the walkie-talkie in her hand crackled into life. A second later there was the crack of a gunshot and a fence post exploded a matter of centimetres from her head, showering her in fragments. She threw herself flat, adrenaline coursing through her. Without thinking, she was on her feet in an instant. She loosed off a shot in the direction of the trees, giving herself cover as she hurdled the fence, and then three more while she sprinted up the incline. Diving into the treeline, she took cover behind the first tree she could find, braced for return of fire. When it didn't come, she glanced around the trunk.

The faint traces of a path wound through the trees. Forcing herself to her feet once more, she followed it as best she could without leaving herself exposed. It brought her to the edge of a small clearing. Up ahead she could see the outlines of a ruined building and started to skirt it to the right, meaning to try to get a line of sight to its rear. The undergrowth grew thicker and, as she trod a path through it, she tripped over a hidden tree root and lost her balance. Stumbling forward, she missed her footing and felt her ankle jar as she twisted sideways to avoid a stand of nettles and brambles. The ground gave way unexpectedly and she tumbled down a short slope and crashed into a fallen trunk, hitting her head. She lay there, dazed and winded, before she came to her senses and tried to get to her feet, feeling a sharp flare of pain from inside her right boot as she did so. At that moment, she heard a twig snap and looked up.

Pigozzi was standing on the edge of the small hollow. He was dishevelled now, his hair no longer slicked back but protruding wildly in all directions, his white shirt crumpled and spotted with dirt and blood. He grinned as he pointed his revolver at her.

Instinctively, she lifted her right hand, meaning to fire at him, but it was only then she realised her gun wasn't in it. This must be it then, she had time to think as she braced to accept her fate.

But at that exact moment a familiar figure loomed up behind Pigozzi and smashed a broken branch against his head.

Lara didn't know which hurt more, her ankle or her pride, as she sat on the tailgate of the police van having her foot bound by a paramedic while she recounted for Curti's benefit the events that had led to Pigozzi's arrest. They'd only been able to identify the drop-off location thanks to intelligence supplied by DCI Mottram, she informed her boss, and the suspect would have got away if it hadn't been for his intervention. In fact, without him she might not even be here to report back. As she said it, Lara shuddered slightly with an aftershock from her ordeal and couldn't help glancing across to where Joe and Gianni stood watching on, as an inspector from the narcotics division examined the contents of the package they'd retrieved from the locker. Sensing her scrutiny, Joe glanced up and met her eye. A look passed between them that spoke to everything they'd experienced together in the last few hours. She rewarded him with a faint smile. That was all he would get for now, she told herself. It would take her time to put it into words.

'*Tuo angelo custode*,' Curti observed, following her gaze and beckoning Joe over.

It was true, she thought. He had been her guardian angel every step of the way.

With a word to Gianni, Joe came to join them.

'What are our colleagues saying?' Curti wanted to know.

'They think it's fentanyl,' Joe confirmed, grasping the hand he held out to him. 'About two thousand pills. In bags of fifty. For distribution across a network of dealers.'

'And the street value?'

'A hundred thousand euros, give or take.'

Curti smiled. 'A good day's work, don't you think?'

Not bad, Joe conceded. Pigozzi would be facing a jail term of between five and eight years for a second offence of possession with intent to supply, according to one of the officers from narcotics. 'And of course we used the code from the paper we found in Daniele Russo's jacket pocket to retrieve the package from the locker,' Joe continued, looking pointedly at Lara. 'Which means we can link him to the drugs as well.'

Was the boy back in custody yet? Curti wanted to know.

Daniele had been picked up on the Naples metro an hour previously, Lara confirmed. He'd been caught on CCTV at one of the stations and identified using facial recognition.

'Your daughter . . . she'll be happy,' Curti suggested to Joe. But however gratifying it might be to see the boy punished, it was far more important to be putting one of Rocco Di Biasi's key enforcers behind bars. 'I hear we have you to thank for that, Detective Chief Inspector. And for helping us catch the killers of those two women.'

'It was a joint effort, *Commissario*. Every step of the way.'

The paramedic had finished her work, and Lara was glad for the excuse to bend over and start putting her boot back on. She kept her head down, pulling her laces tight.

'Inspector Sarrancino is a credit to you. She's a first-rate officer.'

Lara felt herself flush.

'One of the very best,' she heard her boss respond. There was a pause while she waited for him to add the expected caveat . . . *of our female officers* . . . but it never came. 'Which is why I want to bring you to Naples,' Curti went on. 'For a year. Maybe more. Put you and her together. You'll be a good team, I think.'

Lara forced herself to lift her head and look at Joe. He

was staring at Curti, open-mouthed. 'I'm not even sure that's possible,' he managed to say, finding his voice at last.

'I'm told it might be,' Curti responded, looking expectantly to Lara.

Joe turned his gaze on her with a questioning look, and Lara flushed a second time as she met his eye, wishing she had a second boot that needed lacing.

'Should I have kept my mouth shut?'

The two detectives were standing outside the front entrance of La Questura preparing to part ways. Lara had been explaining how she'd stumbled across the information about international secondments for serving British police officers on the Foreign Office's website while researching his temporary transfer via Interpol. She'd mentioned it to Curti and promptly forgotten about it. Unlike him, it would appear.

'No, no. It's flattering. You know . . . to be asked. It's just . . .'

'You're not sure. About the transfer.'

He shrugged. 'I don't know if I'm ready to move on. Leave stuff behind.'

She said nothing, waited for him to say more.

'Angelica won't be happy I'm not biting your hand off.'

'She wants to stay?'

'She's already making plans.' He raised his eyebrows, mirroring her surprise.

'And how do you feel about that?'

'I'm not sure yet. Happy, I guess.'

He didn't look it, Lara couldn't help thinking.

'For *her*,' Joe caveated. 'She knows what she wants. And I think she'll find it here.'

'You might too.'

'Maybe.'

She sensed there wasn't much conviction in that 'maybe'. Had he already made up his mind to go home? The look he gave her seemed to suggest he had; it was apologetic, almost shame-faced that he wasn't being straighter with her.

'This isn't goodbye, Lara,' he insisted. 'I'll be back. Either way.'

'You mean *ciao*,' she responded, ignoring the hand he held out and enveloping him in a tight embrace she hoped communicated everything she'd been meaning to say.

Returning to her desk on the fifth floor, the finality of Joe's departure hit home. She'd grown used to his presence over the last four weeks, to the confusing flutter of suppressed attraction he'd aroused in her that had thankfully given way to a different kind of desire . . . to be the best version of her professional self. Now she looked around the office, at the bent backs and drooping heads, and wondered where inspiration would come from. She felt deflated. Perhaps she should plead incapacity with her ankle. Take a few days off. But then it occurred to her how Joe would react to an admission of weakness, and she eased her shoulders back and straightened up.

Lara surveyed her colleagues a second time from this new mental vantage point. She could feel all her old insecurities and uncertainties falling away. She'd earned her stripes in Joe's eyes, she realised. And if *he* believed she was a first-rate officer, then she had no need to fear the judgement of any of *them*.

A fresh start required a clean slate, she decided, eyeing the mess of paperwork that had accumulated on her desk. With a sigh, she set to work to clear it up, intending to divide what she found into three piles – keep, file and discard – but almost immediately she came across a document that refused to be neatly categorised. It was a print-out from Sofia's file, and she realised with a start that she hadn't finished going through the paperwork relating to the death of Joe's wife. She'd proved unworthy of the trust she'd asked him to place in her. And now it might well be too late.

With a heavy heart, she sat down and reached for a plastic folder in her in-tray. It contained all the other documents and photographs from Sofia's file that she'd printed out but failed to interrogate. She opened it, meaning to add the contents to her 'discard' pile, and it was at that moment she saw the photograph that persuaded her there might be a chance to repay her debt to him after all.

50

Joe was the last to disembark. There was no hurry, he told himself, as he watched his fellow passengers jostling for the gangplank, impatient to resume the bustle of their daily lives. He'd nothing to do, he realised, nowhere to be. There were another two weeks of his sabbatical ahead of him, which was more than enough time for the conversations that needed to be had and the decisions that needed to be made. He'd do his best to enjoy the rest of his holiday, to relax, spend time with his daughter . . . his *family* even. To appreciate what he'd found in this place. And what he knew he'd lose by leaving.

Stepping onto the quayside in Capri and taking in that familiar view, he couldn't help thinking back to his and Angelica's arrival in the exact same spot less than a month previously. He'd come to Capri numb with despair, but how would he be leaving when the time came? It was still there . . . the heaviness in his heart. It would always be. And yet, somehow, the burden seemed more manageable now. The time they'd spent on the island had helped him and his daughter rediscover one another and a connection with Sofia's parents he'd been ready to write off. The suspicion he'd felt towards them, the jealousy they'd aroused in him, had been replaced by gratitude and love. Elena and Gennaro hadn't only taught him about food and how to parent in their daughter's absence, but also how to cope with his grief. Thanks to them he'd learn to accept it as part of who he was. To carry it. To honour Sofia and the spirit in which she'd lived. As they did.

Feeling lighter, more hopeful perhaps than he had in recent memory, Joe set off through the port, waving away the calls of the taxi drivers. He'd set his heart on walking, on enjoying the late afternoon sunshine, but he came across the sign for the funicular and changed his mind. He could recall riding on it with Sofia during one of their early visits. Angelica had been with them and the railway had enchanted her. He could picture her now, a wide-eyed wisp of a child, drinking in every detail as the weird, diagonal carriage had inched its way between the houses and the cultivated terraces where chickens strutted between lemon and orange trees laden with fruit too numerous to harvest. It was a good memory, Joe decided as he bought a ticket and waited patiently in line to take his place. He would have to learn to embrace those. Not push them away.

By the time the funicular had climbed to the central piazza, the sun was already beginning to dip below the peak of Monte Solano. On the way up, he'd contemplated stopping for a drink when he reached the top, but now he saw that the hordes were gathering and he abandoned the idea, retreating instead along the Via Roma, with its boutiques and restaurants that were readying themselves for an influx of evening custom. Dodging a steady stream of taxis and orange buses, he left the hustle of the town centre behind and soon reached the roundabout at the heart of the island, which was guarded by the tiny police station. Away to his right he could see the hazy outline of Vesuvius across the bay, no more than a greyish-purple blur in the fading light. To his left, the steps of the Via Mulo wound their way down through cypress trees and villas for half a kilometre to the south coast and Da Vinale's below. Joe had just cast a last lingering look in the vague direction of Naples and was preparing to descend, when he heard the sound of a horn beeping and glanced across to see a blue and white police car swinging right around the tiny traffic island and braking to a halt a short distance behind him. The passenger door opened, and Lara jumped out, came limping towards him.

'Thank God I found you.'

'What is it? Has something happened?'

By way of an answer, she held out the documents she was carrying in her hand.

Joe felt a stirring of unease. 'I've decided to go home, Lara.'

'I think you're going to want to see this before you do.'

He held her gaze, doing his best to ignore whatever she was offering, but his curiosity got the better of him. With a weary sigh, he took the documents. The first was a print-out of a photo. It showed a close-up of the rear of a playing card lying in a gutter at the side of a road. It was decorated with a gaudy, almost cartoonish heart, which was pierced by a dagger. And it was in flames.

He frowned and met Lara's eye once more.

'It was found in the street. Near where your wife was killed.'

Joe could vaguely remember seeing it. There had been photos of all sorts of street detritus in Sofia's file. 'So?' he asked.

'The Sacred Heart. It's a Mafia symbol.'

He almost expected her to crack a smile, but she stayed stony-faced. He glanced again at the photo, shaking his head. 'It's just a playing card, Lara. A random thing.'

'You don't believe me?' She took the second document from him and turned it to show him. It was a print-out of a document headlined 'GANG TATTOOS AND SYMBOLS'. Halfway down the page four words were highlighted: CAMORRA (NAPLES) – SACRED HEART.

Joe felt the blood draining from his face. *Surely she couldn't think . . .*

Before he could articulate his doubts, the loud retort of an explosion rent the air and the long, low rumble of its aftermath reverberated off the walls of the buildings nearby. Joe exchanged a look with Lara and turned towards the source of the sound. A plume of black smoke could be seen rising into the evening sky from somewhere to the south. He hurried to the railings, with Lara a step or two behind. The view down to the coast was blocked by trees and houses, and they strained to try and identify the exact location from which it was coming. But to Joe, at least, there was little doubt about it.

'It's the restaurant,' he told her, beginning to run in that direction.

As Joe barrelled down the last flight of steps at the foot of the Via Mulo and skidded onto the road that ran adjacent to Da Vinale's, the stench and smoke from the fire was overwhelming. Flames were leaping from the flat-roofed block that housed Da Vinale's interior seating and kitchen. A crowd of diners had fled the terrace for the street outside and were milling around uncertainly, unsure what to do, some of them filming on their phones. But Angelica, Elena and Gennaro were nowhere to be seen.

He became aware of the wail of a siren and turned to see the police car brake to a halt nearby. 'Get them back!' he yelled to Lara and her uniformed colleague as they jumped out. He waved his arms, gesturing towards the steps that led to a safer rendezvous point before he turned and ran towards the street gate and entered the restaurant. As he started down, three steps at a time, his heart leapt as he saw Angelica and Aldo coming the other way.

'Dad!' Angelica called out, throwing herself into his arms.

He hugged her more tightly than he'd ever done in his life. 'What happened?'

'Someone firebombed the restaurant.'

Firebombed? He could barely comprehend it. 'Where are your grandparents?'

'Still inside, I think.'

There was the sound of a structure collapsing nearby and a sudden flare-up of flames and sparks. 'Go!' he shouted, pushing the two of them up the stairs and seeing Lara come through the gate above as he did so.

Joe continued his descent. A hose lay abandoned on the terrace, a half-filled bucket beside it. Somebody had tried to slow the flames, but without success. The terrace was not yet consumed, but it was on its way to being so. Within five minutes at the most, Joe calculated, the whole thing might be gone.

As he ran towards the open door of the restaurant, two figures came stumbling from the interior. It was Elena and Gennaro and they were filthy, choking, gasping for air. There was an almighty bang as something behind them exploded. The last of the windows shattered in response, and the terrace was showered with glass. Elena shrieked, almost fell. Crouching low, and using his body as a shield, Joe corralled them towards the stairs, where Lara was waiting to receive them.

'Is anyone else in there?' she demanded.

Elena was too overcome to speak, but Gennaro croaked an answer: 'Luca.'

Joe turned and ran back towards the building, grabbing a napkin and dipping it in the bucket as he went. He heard Lara call out 'Don't be stupid!' before he plunged through the fire-framed doorway and all sound from outside was lost. Here there was nothing but the flames themselves, not roaring exactly, but popping and crackling. Everything that could be alight was alight. With the greatest of care, Joe picked his way forward in a crouching run and pushed open the doors to the kitchen.

The scene that greeted him was one of utter devastation. Whatever had exploded, it must surely have been in here. Gennaro's chef station, which had housed the main oven, was a twisted lump of metal, while Luca's lay drunkenly on one side. Food was scattered everywhere, feeding the flames.

'*Luca?*' Joe called out, feeling the super-heated air scalding his throat and lungs as he removed the dampened napkin from his mouth.

He was answered by what sounded like a low moan.

Joe hurried forward in his low crouch and skirted the uprooted chef's station. Luca was lying beneath it. His head and right arm were visible, as was much of his upper torso, crimson with blood from a wound hidden somewhere beneath the metal structure that was crushing him. At the sight of Joe he smiled faintly and attempted to say something, but the effort was beyond him.

'I'm going to get you out of here,' Joe told him, doing his best to ignore the thought that he must be grievously injured. Slipping his hands beneath his armpits, he attempted to pull him clear, but Luca groaned in agony, could not be shifted. Joe turned his attention to the chef station, and tried to lever it upwards, but the metal was scalding to touch. He cast about for something to wrap around his hands, and found a discarded chef's apron, but despite straining every sinew, and repeated attempts, the station refused to budge.

'I need to get help, Luca,' he told the stricken chef, reaching out to squeeze his shoulder in what was meant to be a parting gesture of reassurance.

Luca caught his wrist with his free arm, gripping hold of Joe with surprising strength. As Joe leaned in, he mumbled something. It sounded like 'My fault.'

'Ssh. Save your breath.'

The muttering continued. 'Wrong people . . . wrong questions,' he seemed to say, before he was wracked by coughing. Blood spattered his parted lips, and he passed out.

Jumping to his feet, Joe made another attempt to shift the pile of overturned metal, but the weight was simply too much and he was about to slump in defeat, when the doors to the kitchen swung open and Lara hobbled inside, wrapped in a wringing wet tablecloth to shield her from the heat. In a moment, she was at his side and using the cloth to cover them both, she joined his renewed attempt to dislodge the chef station. It resisted, but at last, with a creak and shift of momentum, it gave way and rolled over. Together they managed to slide Luca clear and drag him towards the swing doors.

The fire in the restaurant had grown more intense. Joe gasped for air as they struggled to haul Luca's unresponsive body towards the terrace. He felt his grip beginning to fail. He tried to stagger on, but the effort was too much for him and he let go, slumped to his knees, utterly spent, almost ready to give in. And it was then, with Lara screaming at him to get up, and trying to drag him back to his feet, that he saw it. Sheltering beneath a metal lampstand that stood near the door.

A playing card.

Ignoring the blows and imprecations that Lara was raining down on him, he crawled forward and picked it up.

*

Later, after the firefighters had doused the flames and he'd submitted to a spell on an oxygen tank in the back of an ambulance, it was Lara who Joe sought out first. Luca had been airlifted to the mainland and Elena and Gennaro had been persuaded to go with him, with Joe managing to convince his in-laws that he and Angelica would be fine.

He found Lara on the road outside the restaurant, talking to Sergeant Alfieri, and after receiving her nod of acknowledgement, he stepped aside to wait. At last she came to join him at the water's edge and he handed her the playing card – the Ace of Clubs – and saw the look of astonishment that crept over her face. 'Where did you find it?'

'Inside by the door.'

She turned it over to examine the other side.

A Sacred Heart.

'Any chance it's a coincidence?'

He huffed, pulled a face. 'I thought we didn't believe in those.'

She searched his face. 'I don't know what to say, Joe.'

'Then maybe don't say anything. I've got a lot of other shit to deal with before I can even start to try and get my head around this.'

A look passed between them. And then, with a nod and a slight squeeze of his arm, Lara turned back to her duties. In a moment, she'd disappeared once more into the throng of firefighters, fellow officers and lookers-on.

As Joe and Angelica were let into the apartment to retrieve a few of their possessions, he could see the interior was badly charred and that everything that could absorb water was soaked to a pulp. It would have to be gutted and refurnished and painted afresh, but at least, by some miracle of the prevailing winds and the prompt response of the fire crew, it was structurally intact.

Angelica's hands went to her mouth as she surveyed the damage. 'Oh my God,' she whispered, choking back tears. 'Poor Gran. Poor *Nonno*.'

Joe opened his arms and she accepted his embrace. 'They're strong people, love. Like Mum was. They'll come back from it. With help from the people that love them.'

She lifted her head to look at him, seeking the implication in his words. 'Does that mean you're OK with me staying?'

He nodded, not quite trusting himself to say the words, feeling her hugging him tighter. 'You can help them get back on their feet,' he managed to say at last. 'And get to know your mum's roots while you're at it. Figure out who you are. What you want to do.'

'But what about you, Dad?'

'Oh . . . I'm staying too, love. You just try and stop me.'

A huge smile brightened Angelica's tear-stained face before she buried it against his chest, hugging him even tighter than before.

And the explanation of his real reasons for staying?

Well, Joe decided, that could wait.

At last, he found himself alone on the foreshore.

Lara had gone ahead to prepare her aunt's villa to accommodate them for the night and Joe had persuaded Angelica to go with her, to shower and change her filthy clothes. He'd made up an excuse to stay a little longer – he'd promised Gennaro he would wait behind until every last ember had been extinguished, he told her – but really he wanted to have a moment to himself, to take in the enormity of what had happened, of what he'd learned.

The moon had risen and the view out to sea was an oddly tranquil one, with the tide barely raising a ripple on the silvered surface of the water. He turned back to take in the dark mass of the island that loomed behind him, reflecting, as he did so, that his instincts had been right.

It *was* a place of dark undercurrents.

He could feel them now, tugging at him, threatening to pull him under, but he was not afraid. He stood there, feeling the heat that was emanating from the blackened remains of the restaurant on his face, and sensing an echo of that same heat within at the thought of what Lara had insinuated about Sofia's fate. Mostly, though, he felt as calm as the ocean behind him. Everything was clearer now. There was only one path ahead.

He would make the island give up its secrets.

He would learn the truth.

Acknowledgements

Thanks to everyone who helped me with ideas, advice and encouragement while I was writing this book. I'd particularly like to thank Sophie Samuda for her enthusiasm and creativity in the early stages of perfecting my murders, and Walter Iuzzolino for his astute feedback and his unwavering backing, not to mention his sensitive corrections of my schoolboy Italian. I'm also hugely grateful to Stella Newing, my editor at Michael Joseph, for all her wise counsel in helping to make my story as dramatic and impactful as possible, and to Eugenie Todd for her forensic copy-edit that patiently exposed the grammatical bad habits that have become engrained over a lifetime. Most of all, I'd like to thank my wife, Jo McGrath, in both a professional capacity, for the leading part she played in shaping the original outline of the story, and personally for all the love and support she's given me in my quest to become a published author.